Champagne Float

A Novel

NISSA ALEXANDROV

ISBN: 0-9976104-0-9
ISBN-13: 978-0-9976104-0-6

DEDICATION

To *my parents, for believing in me.*
To *my husband, for supporting me.*
To *my son, for inspiring me.*
To *my friends, for their continuing supply of encouragement, entertainment, and of course, champagne.*

1

I woke up in a panic, dimly aware that I was under attack yet unable to simultaneously shake off a vicious champagne hangover and twenty pounds of high thread count Frette linens. Freeing one arm, I reached over and grabbed my phone, which was blaring "Ride of the Valkyries." Apparently my brother, Chris, had been beta testing his Ring Tone Riot software on my phone again. It looked like he'd upgraded it to include remote volume control. I'd kill the bastard.

I peered blearily at the display before picking up. "Pinkie, you are a horrible toad of a human being," I whispered into the phone, my voice cracking.

Prince Philippe von Hofstedtler, "Pinkie" to his friends, did not seem fazed by this less than enthusiastic greeting. "I know, Lora darling," he said "It's all the inbreeding. Cruel of you to mention it, though."

"Cruel of you to call at"—I squinted at my telephone—"ten thirty in the morning. Okay," I conceded, "that's not really that cruel. But it really seems much, much earlier." I fumbled around on my nightstand for a glass of water and managed to find only a glass of warm Veuve Clicquot that I must have stolen from the limousine the previous evening. I gagged slightly.

"Darling," Pinkie said, "you know I wouldn't call if it weren't an emergency."

"What's the emergency?" I asked, burrowing deeper into the

covers.

"The emergency is that I've been standing out on your doorstep for five minutes ringing the bell, and I think that crazy vegan mommy blogger who lives across the street is calling the police. Again."

I sighed loudly. "The bell is broken," I said, trying to sit up as slowly as possible. "Which you would know if you called before you came over like normal people."

"Why on earth would I want to do anything normal people do?"

I grabbed a ratty kimono off the hook and made my way to the front door, trying to slide my feet along the hardwood to minimize the impact to my brain.

As soon as I opened the door, Pinkie turned around and stuck his tongue out at Heather, the neighbor across the street. I saw her kitchen curtain twitch into place and wondered if she had called the police. It wouldn't be the first time. I had never understood why someone who was afraid of repairmen, black people, cats, and minor European royalty would choose to live in Brooklyn. And I had never figured out why the police kept responding, unless it was the muffins she always gave them. But really, they were vegan muffins. How good could they be?

"Honestly," Pinkie said. "How can you stand living so close to someone who basically does nothing but gossip and cook all day long?"

"At least she cooks," I said, collapsing at the kitchen table. "You just gossip."

"You wound me," he said. "And after I brought you this." He placed a tall cardboard cup on the table with a flourish.

"Pinkie, I take it all back," I said, reaching eagerly for the cup. "You're my best friend." I took a giant swig and almost spat it across the room.

"What the hell, Pinkie?" I spluttered, choking on the vile concoction. "I thought you were bringing me coffee! This tastes like someone French pressed an iguana."

Pinkie rolled his eyes. "There's no reason to get so dramatic. It's a green goddess smoothie. Full of antioxidants. Which you clearly need." He took in my appearance critically. "You look positively desiccated."

"Forget it," I said, getting up to get myself a cup of coffee.

"You drink it."

"As if. Make mine a double."

I had just handed Pinkie a mug of coffee when we were interrupted by a knock on the door.

"Expecting someone?"

I had a sudden flash of what I must look like. It wasn't pretty. "I hope not. I'm not really dressed for company..."

"Understatement of the year," Pinkie said. "Postal employees are under enough pressure without having to process you with a hangover. I'd better handle this." He walked over to the door and opened it. A bloodcurdling shriek rent the air. Pinkie slammed the door again and turned to me, his eyes wide in alarm.

"What the hell was that!?" I said, jumping out of my chair. "Who is it?"

"It's for you," Pinkie said, putting his hands up and backing away.

I looked at the door. "Is it safe to open?"

"Well..." Pinkie hedged, "I doubt you'll lose more than a finger."

I opened the door a crack and looked outside. Sitting on the front step was a beautiful, gilded cage. Inside the cage was an enormous bird with a bright yellow chest and a turquoise head. His multicolored wings flapped as he adjusted himself on his perch. The bird tilted his head to one side, fixing me with a beady black eye.

"Clancy loves Lora! Clancy loves Lora!" he shrieked.

"Oh my god." I ran my hand over my eyes, silently wishing away the vivid apparition on my porch.

"Clancy?" Pinkie maintained a healthy distance from the bird. "Clancy Featherstone sent you this bird? Is he *still* trying to convince you to go out with him? I thought you told him you weren't interested."

I turned to Pinkie, throwing my hands up in the air. "I *did* tell him I wasn't interested. I told him the first time he asked me out. I told him every day on the vacation he hired me to plan for him. I told him when we got back to New York. I told him when I sent the world's most evil Siamese cat back. I told him when I returned the heirloom diamond bracelet he sent me. And I told him when I had the Mercedes he delivered towed back to his house. Telling him I'm not interested is clearly not working."

"He sent a cat and a Mercedes?" Pinkie asked, bemused.

"He thinks we're soul mates."

"Wouldn't your soul mate know that you're allergic to cats and unhealthily attached to that completely dysfunctional Jag you insist on trying to nurse back to health?"

"You'd think."

"Clancy loves Lora!" the bird shrieked again.

I looked outside, hoping the delivery truck was still there. No such luck. Clancy had probably told them to dump the demonic creature and run for it. I dragged the cage inside the apartment.

Pinkie and the bird eyed each other. "What are you going to do about this thing?"

"Wrong question," I said, wrestling the cage into the corner. "The question is what are *you* going to do about this thing?"

"Me?! Why me?!"

"Because Clancy Featherstone is *your* school friend. Because *you* were the one who convinced me to plan his vacation. Because you told me he needed an event hostess...not a soul mate."

Pinkie held his hands up in defense. "He did need an event hostess. And I always thought his mother was his soul mate."

I held up a hand. "Whatever. The point is that you clearly need to get this guy under control. I've been trying to let him down gently for three months, but enough is enough. I can't live under the constant threat of being given high maintenance animals and family jewels and German cars. I've had it. You get him out of my life, or I'm filing a restraining order."

Pinkie gave me a martyred expression. "I'll deal with it," he said. "I should have known you were too much woman for Clancy. Mea culpa."

"Thank you."

"Clancy loves Lora," the bird called again, its tone plaintive.

I rubbed my temples gently, trying to soothe away my headache. "And that bird goes with you today."

Pinkie let out a gusty sigh. "Fine, but you owe me." He looked at the bird, one eyebrow raised in speculation "You know, now that I think about it, my friend Beatrice mentioned the other day that she was looking for something to bring life to that rainforest room she set up in her place in the Hamptons..."

I shook my head. Leave it to Pinkie to turn one annoying parrot into two favors other people owed him. The man was a genius.

"So," Pinkie said, turning his attention back to me. "Enough about Clancy and his attempts to buy your love. Tell me about last night. You were with Mr. Nakamoto and his band of merry salarymen, right?" He peered at me over the rim of his mug. "Looks like things went well."

"If by 'well' you mean the clients had fun, yes," I said, dragging a hand through my hair in an attempt to smooth out the snarls. "If by 'well' you mean that I had fun, you are way off the mark."

Pinkie regarded me without sympathy. "You know, you don't have to drink everything people put in front of you. In case you hadn't heard, nice girls don't swallow. Plus, isn't your job to organize fun for other people rather than indulging yourself?"

"I know," I said, fighting down a wave of nausea, "but apparently they hated to drink alone."

"You went out with a party of six, darling. They were hardly alone."

"Well then, they hated to drink without me. And these were the most anal retentive drunks on the planet, so *not swallowing*, as you so gracefully put it, wasn't an option. One of them had an app called Drink Up on his phone. You scanned the label, put in your height and weight, and it told you when you were 'happy drunk.'"

"And were you 'happy drunk'?"

I closed my eyes and took stock of the pounding in my head. "For a while, but I think the metric conversion was off, because we all ended up more toward 'sloppy drunk.' Sloppy drunk tips better than 'happy drunk,' though," I said, "So there's that."

"How many times did you have to sing 'Yesterday'?"

"You know, the idea that all Japanese business men go to karaoke bars is a terrible stereotype."

"So…three?"

"Four. Three times for 'Girls Just Wanna Have Fun.'"

"Ah. That's one of your better ones. At least they were anal retentive drunks of taste."

"Did you come over for a reason?" I asked, pressing my fingers against my eyelids. "I can't imagine you just accidentally ended up in Brooklyn. It's not exactly your home turf."

"Actually, I have a job for you."

"No Japanese again for a while," I begged.

"No, no," he reassured me.

"Thank god. Someone from a sane country."

"Like Russia, right?"

"Which part of sane don't you understand?!"

"Darling, you were the one who told me you needed me to line up more jobs for you. You can't just blithely rule out Russians and Japanese and Chinese as potential clients. It's un-American. And discriminatory. And they have all the money these days. I mean, really. And it will give me a chance to talk to Clancy and clear this whole thing up without you being here to distract him with your soul mateyness."

I stared at the ceiling for a moment, mentally tallying up my bills. My car, a vintage Jag that spent more time in the shop than on the road, was rattling again, and the only guy in town who would touch it wasn't exactly cheap. I glanced over at the parrot. I also had to admit that the thought of being in a different country than Clancy Featherstone was very appealing right now. "Fine," I grumbled. "What's the job?"

Pinkie clapped his hands. "You're going to love it. The client's name is Kyrill Antonov. He went to boarding school with Fritzie. You remember Fritzie, right?"

I cast my mind over Pinkie's endless supply of eccentric boarding school friends. "Wasn't he the guy who was always wearing purple socks? With shorts?"

Pinkie was pleased. "You *do* remember! Did you know that those socks are actually made for cardinals? It's a special license given only to this one French company. They make the pope's socks, too, which are literally divine, but they're white, which makes them very hard to work with from a fashion perspective."

Why was I not surprised that Pinkie knew where cardinals bought their socks? "Back to the job, please?" I prompted him.

"Right," Pinkie continued. "You go to Moscow. You get there, discuss the job with Kyrill over dinner, and the next day you're completely free. Check out dead Lenin, buy yourself a topless Putin commemorative plate—whatever you want. The next morning, you fly with Kyrill down to Varna, in Bulgaria. He's meeting some potential business partners from Greece on his yacht there, and he wants you to chat them up, supervise the staff, and just make sure things run smoothly.

"The trip ends in Malta, and you fly home. Four days. Ten thousand dollars for your personal expenses plus business class travel to and from. And it should be fun. Summer on a yacht with a couple of rich Greek men..." Pinkie sighed. "I wish I could go. Given the way Greeks are, I'm sure they'd have more fun with me."

"No doubt. Ten thousand dollars for my expenses seems pretty generous. What kind of expenses is he expecting me to have?"

"I told him you would have to cancel a villa you'd reserved for that week in Cannes," Pinkie said. "And of course he insisted that he compensate you for the loss, since you'd be doing him a favor."

"Of course," I said. "Someday I'd like to go visit my fictional villa in Cannes. Given how much it's supposed to be running me in rent, I can only assume it's a very nice place."

I didn't have to think about it too long. I had been stuck in New York for months now, and while Moscow wasn't exactly Paris, it was blessedly free of Clancy Featherstone, which was a big point in its favor. And the yacht sounded like it could be fun, especially if Kyrill was going to be focusing on business the entire time. Maybe they'd spend all day working and I could hang out in the pool drinking champagne and eating caviar canapés. A girl could dream.

"He does understand that I'm an event hostess and not a hooker, right?" I confirmed. "Because the last time I went out with a Russian, I spent the entire time trying to remove his hairy paw from my ass...at least until he passed out."

"'Event hostess' is a poorly understood concept in Russia," Pinkie conceded, "and Russians worth a hundred million dollars are accustomed to being quite attractive to most women, the hairiness of their paws notwithstanding. But I was quite clear that your role was to entertain the guests, supervise the staff, and make sure everyone was having a good time."

"Good," I said. "And he's not a romantic type, right?" I scowled at him. "Clancy's already making me crazy...the last thing I need is dueling stalkers."

"No worries there," Pinkie said. "You're not his type."

"What is his type?"

"Fritzie. So as long as you stay away from shorts and purple socks, you should be okay." Pinkie took another sip of coffee. "No funny business, Lora. This is a completely standard job. Kyrill wants to look like a man of sophistication and breeding while he convinces the Greeks to get in over their head on what is undoubtedly some dodgy deal. You're just there to add some class to the proceedings."

I snorted. "Ah yes...my *classy* upper crust background. If they only knew that I was just a chick from the American suburbs who spent my high school summers waiting tables at Friendly's."

"Ah, but they don't," he said, giving me a smug smile, "because I, like Pygmalion himself, have sculpted your rough suburban Play-Doh into a thing of beauty and grace." He made sculpting motions with his plump little hands.

"And into a viable source of income for you."

"One of many," he said, dismissing my comment with an airy wave "And my meager commission is really a pittance, given the color and spectacle I bring to your life."

"Is that what you're calling it these days?"

Pinkie gestured to the parrot, which was snoring softly on its perch. "Not to mention my parrot removal services. That should be worth at least 20 percent. So, are you in? I've run the usual checks. Fritzie says Kyrill is good fun, frightfully vain. Apparently, he won't let people take pictures of him because he's developing a wattle."

"What's a wattle?"

"It's that thing that hangs down under your neck. It's also the reason god invented ascots."

"Ah," I said. "And here I'd been asking myself that same question for years."

"Anyway," Pinkie continued, fingering his wattle-hiding ascot lovingly, "That's the job. Are you in?"

I sighed. "When is the flight?"

"Tomorrow morning."

"Tomorrow morning?!" I shrieked. "I can't possibly organize an event in such a short time frame. I need to plan, to go over budgets, to buy supplies, to get to know the client and guests...and anyway, don't you need a visa to go to Russia?"

Pinkie tut-tutted. "That's the best part. Kyrill's already set that all up for you. They'll do the visa for you at the airport. The boat is running with a small crew, all of whom are already there. The food and supplies are ready. All you need to do is make sure things are served on time and make witty conversation with the clients. And look dazzling, of course. Nobody likes having an ugly old hag around."

He picked up one of my hands to examine my cuticles and

dropped it as if it were covered in boils. "And on that topic, I can see that I'll need to make a few calls. Manicure, pedicure, facial…and eyebrows—my god! You're lucky birds aren't attacking those caterpillars every time you leave the building." He squinted at me as though he could see straight through the kimono. "Something tells me that a Brazilian wax is also in order."

I ignored Pinkie's loving attempts to destroy my self-esteem and tried to think around my aching head. The staff would probably need a little coaching, and maybe I'd have to do some work with the chef to go through the menus. I normally wouldn't take a job with so little prep time, but if everything had already been arranged, it should be okay. Plus, ten thousand bucks—eight thousand after I paid for Pinkie's color and spectacle—would reduce the likelihood that my mechanic would have to hold my car for ransom after he fixed it.

"Will you take my car to the mechanic while I'm gone?" I asked. "It's making that weird noise again."

"It would be my pleasure to take your money pit of a car to the mechanic. You know how much I love pushing vintage vehicles off the road and spending my afternoon getting honked at while I wait for tow trucks."

"That only happened twice," I said defensively. "I'd put the chances of it getting to the mechanic's without breaking down at upward of 80 percent. And I think if I can just get this one thing fixed, it should run fine."

"You've said that the last five…no…six times you brought it to him."

I sighed. "I live in hope."

2

Three hours and many cups of coffee later, the parrot was on his way to a life of luxury in the Hamptons, and Pinkie and I were at the salon, where I was being viciously assaulted by a tiny Thai woman improbably named Suzie Q. Pinkie had an aversion to tweezers, so he had contented himself with a so-called toning champagne facial, which seemed to involve drinking champagne with a bunch of goop on your face.

"So tell me more about the client," I said, clutching the arms of the pedicure chair as Suzie jammed what I could only assume was a sharpened bamboo splinter into the quick of my toenail.

"Well," Pinkie said, "I never met him personally, but Fritzie tells me that he's one of those 'New Russians' everyone was talking about a few years ago. Daddy was apparently in the KGB, and when the whole communism thing fell apart, he started a security firm and made a pile of cash."

"A security firm?" I asked, jerking my foot back involuntarily. "Sorry, Suzie. Like bodyguards?"

Pinkie shook his head at my naïveté. "You're thinking of an American security firm, darling," he said, taking a sip of his champagne. "You know...one that actually provides security from threats. This is a Russian security firm. They mostly provide threats to your security. Protection rackets, enforcement, that kind of thing."

"Ah...dammit!" I yelled as Suzie snipped a little deep on the cuticle.

"You be still now, or you get hurt," Suzie snapped. "This not be so painful if you take care of your feet." I rolled my eyes at Pinkie. Suzie had a degree in literature from Brown and in her normal life she spoke English with a flat Midwestern twang that brought to mind football games and pickup trucks. I had never figured out whether the Asian accent was a postmodern joke, clever marketing, or just her channeling some long-dead imperial torturer.

Pinkie removed a cucumber slice from his eyelid and peered at my foot. "Here," he said, pointing to the side of my toenail. "I think this one is getting ingrown."

Suzie nodded sharply and set to work again.

"Where was I?" Pinkie asked. "Oh yes. So Daddy was a thug, but he wanted the best for his little Kyrill, so he set him up with an import-export company. Luxury goods and furnishings. This was back in the days when Armani and Versace couldn't figure out how to get their stuff into the country without having it seized by petty bureaucrats and distributed to their fat, mustachioed wives. By the time the big guys knew whose palms to grease, Kyrill had already made a boatload of money."

"So he's retired?" I asked, my voice rising to a screech as we moved from the excavation phase of the pedicure to the excruciatingly ticklish sanding phase.

Pinkie shook his head. "Not at all. The money just allows him to follow his passion."

"Ferraris and boys in shorts?"

"Interior decoration. If you've got a budget the size of a small country, he can turn your spectacular palace into an even more spectacular palace."

"He's an interior decorator? That doesn't sound like a job for a rich guy with connections to the KGB."

"Lora, interior decorators at that level are like artists. You remember Prince Abdul?"

"The guy who owns the apartment you live in?"

"Yes. Well, Prince Abdul hired Kyrill to do his palace in Dubai. No expense spared."

"No expense spared is pretty much a given when it comes to Prince Abdul," I said. "So is Kyrill just expensive, or is he also good?"

Pinkie made a face. "Well, Geoffrey Bradfield thinks he's

disgustingly tacky, and I hear he and Kyrill practically came to blows one night at Maxim's. What does that tell you?"

"Nothing, Pinkie, because I have no idea who Geoffrey Bradfield is."

Pinkie clutched his chest. "You don't know who Geoffrey Bradfield is? The billionaire's designer? You know, 'the best way to make a home look like a million bucks is to spend two'?"

I looked at him blankly.

"My god, Lora, don't they teach anything in American public schools?"

"Enough," I said, holding up my hand. "Kyrill's an interior decorator. I get it."

"Not just. He still runs the luxury home furnishings business, too. He's best known for one-of-a-kind things, catering to the 'more is more' set, if you get my drift. You know, polar bear rugs, elephant tusks, carpets made by small children who went blind from tying so many little silk knots..."

"Are any of those things even legal?"

"It's Russia," Pinkie said, raising his glass. "Who cares? They have a proud national tradition of measuring the value of an object by the amount of suffering it takes to create it."

"In which case, this is the world's most valuable pedicure," I said. I shrieked again as Suzie *accidentally* jabbed me in retaliation.

"Jesus, Pinkie, is this really necessary? Who even looks at feet, anyway?"

"You'd be surprised," Pinkie replied, raising an eyebrow. "Stop whining. Your clients are paying for a cultured, sophisticated woman to help make their lives beautiful. You can't help someone enjoy a more beautiful life if you look like a slattern."

"I hardly think I look like a slattern."

"Not right this moment," Pinkie admitted. "But you have definite tendencies in that direction. Look. A Russian billionaire with a surly, anorexic girlfriend is just another hopped up Mafia thug. That same man with a Harvard-educated American woman of class and taste tending to his guests is a sophisticated man of the world. You are that Harvard-educated woman of class and taste."

"I don't have a degree from Harvard University," I pointed out.

"You're light on class and taste, too, but nobody has to know that. People don't check, you know. Read *The Economist*, the *New York Times*, and the *New Yorker*, and you pretty much have intelligent conversation covered. Original thoughts just make you look eccentric."

Suzie finally finished torturing me and started putting polish on my toenails. "You come back in two weeks," she told me. "Not more. And you take pumice with you. Use in shower."

I dutifully promised to use the pumice stone and to return in two weeks, neither of which I had any intention of doing. Unless Pinkie came up with photographic evidence that one of my clients had a foot fetish, I was just going to wear closed-toe shoes from here on out.

Pinkie examined my feet critically. "Suzie," he said, taking her hands, "you're a genius. I don't know what we would have done without you."

Suzie batted her eyelashes at him. "Oh, Pinkie," she said. "You beautiful even without my help." She jerked her head at me and scowled. "But this one probably get foot infection and die without me."

I secretly thought that was a chance I was willing to take if it meant never having to sit through thirty minutes of Suzie Q-induced agony ever again.

I smiled sweetly. "I'm sure you're right."

3

After the misery of the pedicure, Pinkie and I treated ourselves to a champagne brunch at Maxim's, a favorite with foodies, who appreciated the truffled soufflés, and the Botoxed set, who mainly appreciated each other. Maxim himself was working the door, and he looked positively orgasmic when Pinkie walked in, a common reaction among maître d's and restaurant owners all over the world.

"Prince Philippe!" Maxim gushed. "You're looking fabulous, as always. You must have been at Suzie Q's. I can tell, you know. You have a glow about you."

Pinkie preened slightly and allowed himself to be kissed three times on the cheeks. Maxim was originally from Switzerland, where three kisses was the norm. It was his version of the secret handshake.

"You certainly have an eye," Pinkie said. "We just came from Suzie's. I did the champagne facial, of course, and Lora had about six months of horrible dead skin scraped off her feet." I blushed as all three of us looked at my pearly toenails.

"Well, they look lovely," Maxim said, squeezing my arm supportively. I waggled my toes. They did look rather nice.

"Oh," Pinkie said, placing a pudgy hand on Maxim's arm. "I wanted to tell you that I heard from François the other day, and he said that the party he had here was absolutely fabulous. He says that your foie gras is genius and that if he had died after the duck, he would have considered his life complete."

I stifled a smile. François was a friend of Pinkie's who had been looking for a place to throw a lavish, over-the-top, hideously expensive birthday party for himself and two hundred of his closest friends. Naturally, he had gone to Pinkie for help selecting a venue. Pinkie had recommended Maxim's. And now Pinkie was ever-so-gently reminding Maxim that a favor was owed. Immediately.

Maxim, no stranger to the backscratch-based economy, was quick to jump in at his cue. "It really was a triumph," he said. "And thank you for the recommendation. I hope you'll let me treat you and Lora to our chef's finest today."

"Absolutely not!" Pinkie said. "You know how I live to bring people who love food together with artists like you. It's what I do."

I hoped Maxim didn't take Pinkie's protestations seriously. I doubted that Pinkie had more than three dollars on his elegant little person. If Maxim didn't pick up our tab, we were going to be eating at McDonald's, on me.

"I insist," Maxim said, spreading his hands. "It's the least I can do to thank you for introducing me to a connoisseur like François."

"Well, if you insist…" Pinkie conceded.

Maxim led us over to his finest table and corralled a waiter to fill our glasses with champagne, which Pinkie drank the way most people drink water. After some small talk, Maxim went off to beat a masterpiece out of his chef so that the next time one of Pinkie's big-spending friends needed a private venue, he'd be at the top of the list.

"It always amazes me how you do that," I said, regarding Pinkie with affection over my glass.

"Do what?"

"Manage to skate through life without paying for anything."

"I don't skate through life, Lora," Pinkie said with mock severity. "I provide valuable services that people are very grateful for."

"Really?" I gave him a skeptical glance. "Where are you living these days? Still Prince Abdul's flat?"

"Well, of course," Pinkie replied. "Where else would I be living?"

"And if I recall correctly, that's about five thousand square feet of Upper East Side space with park views and live-in maid service?" I confirmed.

"Don't forget the indoor swimming pool. I wouldn't want you to think I was slumming."

"Perish the thought. Where is Prince Abdul these days anyway?"

"Dubai, same as always."

"Why does he even keep that apartment when he's never there?" I asked. "You'd think he could sell it and buy, you know, an island or something."

"He's not 'never' there," Pinkie said. "He comes for Christmas shopping."

"Two weeks every year. And you never pay rent or anything. That's what I mean by skating through life."

"Pay rent?" Pinkie scoffed. "What an absurd concept. Prince Abdul is *grateful* to have me staying in his flat. You can't trust just anyone to house sit an apartment filled with Chippendales and Picassos, you know. It's not like you can put it up on Craigslist. That's what I mean by a valuable service. And who could be more trustworthy to Prince Abdul than me, a fellow member of the royal class..."

"I don't think you can count yourself as a member of the royal class when the country you're supposed to be ruling over hasn't existed for three generations," I said.

"Of course I can, my dear. It's not about the real estate. It's about the blood. Noble blood." Pinkie stretched out an arm so that I could see the veins at his wrist. "Blue, you see?"

I held up my wrist. "Also blue, and I grew up in Delaware, remember? Delaware, where when you want 'good' Italian food, you go to Olive Garden. Delaware, where the closest thing we have to an international watering hole is IHOP."

"Yes, well..." Pinkie said, crooking his little finger daintily as he sipped his champagne. "It's probably because we spend so much time together. My classiness is rubbing off on you."

There was some truth to that statement. When I met Pinkie I had been a cocktail waitress at an absurdly chic bar that catered to the rich and decorative, making a living pouring drinks that cost more than my monthly grocery bill. Now I spent a lot of time *drinking* drinks that cost more than my monthly grocery bill. As long as someone else was paying, of course. Otherwise I pretty much stuck to tap water.

"Do you remember the first time we met?" I asked. "You were air kissing that stick insect…"

"Vanessa," Pinkie said, giving a sigh of nostalgia. "And you were trying out those same old tired lines: 'Oh, I hear your country is *so beautiful.*' And you were talking to someone from Moldova. Moldova! There's nothing beautiful in Moldova."

"That line worked, I'll have you know. That guy left a 30 percent tip on a five hundred dollar bill."

"I'm sure he did. It was probably the only time he had ever heard anyone say something nice about his country. Once I realized how well you were doing with your tired old material, I knew that with my help you could be genius."

"It's a miracle I even spoke to you," I said. "After your old boarding school chum showed up…"

"Fish," Pinkie supplied.

"Looking for drugs…"

"He wasn't looking for drugs, my dear," Pinkie corrected. "He was looking to share his good fortune with me. His uncle had just died."

"How is that good fortune?"

"His filthy rich, misanthropic, childless uncle had just died," Pinkie amended, "and just the day before, poor Fish had been on the verge of selling himself on the street to pay for his scotch."

"What does a spoiled rich kid with absolutely no life skills fetch on the street these days?"

"In Fish's case, rather less than a pair of those cardinal socks Fritzie is so fond of. But the point is that it all came out fine. The uncle died, Fish inherited, and he was just coming over to buy me a drink and figure out how he could do a little more celebrating."

"With drugs."

"Well, of course with drugs," Pinkie said, exasperated. "The boy's a half-wit. That whole 'This is your brain on drugs' thing is only meaningful if you have a brain to start out with, you know. An idiot like that is going to get drugs from somewhere. At least if he comes to me I can point him toward someone who's not going to give him rat poison."

"And, of course, it means that the dealer will up the price by a hundred bucks so that he can pay your finder's fee," I noted.

"Well, making sure you don't end up snorting rat poison is

rather worth a hundred bucks, don't you think?"

"Don't you ever worry that you're going to get arrested one day?"

Pinkie raised his chin. "It's not illegal to know a criminal."

"I think it might be. Maybe you should check into that. Whatever happened to Fish, anyway?"

"More or less what you'd expect. He married some pretty, not-too-clever girl from a good family, moved to the crumbling old pile his uncle left him, and they now have three kids who are just as dim and rich as their parents. He's running for Parliament next year."

I shook my head. "You know, the fact that all your idiot friends eventually end up running governments and Fortune 500 corporations is enough to make me weep for the future."

Pinkie shrugged, unconcerned. "It's the circle of life, darling. We all have our parts to play. I play the role of bringing the wealthy and fabulous together with the boring and competent, and you play the role of event hostess."

"'Event hostess,'" I said. "Even though I've been doing it for five years now, I'm still not sure it's a real job. My mother thinks I'm a call girl, you know. Every time I talk to her, she asks me if I'm using protection."

Pinkie snickered. "Protection from what? What has it been...like six months?"

"Six months, two weeks, and three days," I said mournfully. "Not that I'm counting."

Pinkie looked at me in horror. "You have to find a man," he said. "Are you sure you don't want to give Clancy Featherstone a chance? I bet you could end this celibacy streak right now."

I pulled my phone out of my bag. "Let me show you something about your friend Clancy." I brought up my log of blocked calls. "Clancy and I got back from Cambodia what...three months ago?"

"More or less."

"And in that time, he has tried to call me—let's see—five hundred and thirty-six times." The phone buzzed. "Make that five hundred and thirty seven," I corrected. "So I don't really think I'm going to encourage him by using him for sex."

Pinkie looked at the phone. "Five hundred and thirty seven times, and you never even slept with him? My god, Lora, what did you do to the man?"

"I wish I knew. Because I definitely want to make sure I never do it again. Unless Hugh Jackman is in town."

"Okay, so Clancy's off the table," Pinkie said, holding up his hands. "But six months without sex is bordering on a medical emergency. You just need to grab someone and go for it before your uterus shrivels up." He scanned the restaurant. "What about Maxim?"

"Maxim's gay, you idiot."

"Maxim's bi," Pinkie corrected.

"Really?" I checked out Maxim, who had a sensual mouth and thick black hair that was graying at the temples. "Not bad," I admitted.

"But he does like to wear women's underwear."

I sighed. "I don't think that's going to do it for me."

Pinkie looked at me with disappointment. "You know, it's a new age. Don't be so prejudiced. That kind of thing isn't supposed to bother anyone anymore."

"It doesn't bother me in the slightest," I lied. "I just don't want my underwear to get all stretched out. I've been a little lax at the gym recently. It's already operating at the limits of its capacity."

Pinkie raised an eyebrow at me. "You know, Greek men like a little extra jiggle," he said. "Maybe you can have some fun on the job."

"I don't think so."

"Give it a try," he said, cajoling me. "Given the close and personal relationship Kyrill had with Fritzie, I doubt he's going to have the slightest interest in your nocturnal activities. If you sleep with his guest, he might even think that you're just very customer-service focused. Maybe he'll give you a bonus!"

I narrowed my eyes at him witheringly.

"Fine," Pinkie said, holding up his hands. "Don't sleep with him. But that doesn't let you out of the bikini wax I booked for this afternoon."

I made a face.

"I don't know why you don't just laser everything off like everyone else," Pinkie sighed.

"Maybe I hold out the faint hope that someday fashion will change and men will stop wanting women who look like Barbie dolls."

Pinkie chortled. "Good luck with that."

4

Pinkie was, in fact, a real prince, which is to say that his father had been a prince, and his grandfather had been a prince. Of course, none of those guys had been kings, since the area they used to rule over was now a part of Germany known for its Holsteins, wheat beer, and award-winning tractor assembly plant.

Pinkie's father had footed the bill for an education fit for a king—light on actual knowledge, but heavy on pubs, hijinks, and buggery with other members of the rich and titled. That education turned out to be the only inheritance Pinkie would ever see. Three weeks after his graduation from Oxford, Pinkie came home to find his father lying under a three-hundred-year-old oak tree, an antique pistol in one hand and a bottle of forty-year-old scotch in the other. Creditors barely waited until the body was cold before they seized everything of value, including Pinkie's ancestral home.

Short, pudgy, broke, and fabulous, Pinkie had leveraged his network of idle rich friends to put together a thriving hustle providing anything and everything, but only to the right kind of people. He still didn't have two nickels to rub together, but since he rarely paid for anything, it didn't seem to cramp his lifestyle very much.

I had only known Pinkie for a couple of months when he had offered me a job as an event hostess for some friends from Tokyo who were coming into town to see the sights and buy some professional sports teams.

"No way," I'd told him. "I've seen the movies. I'm not lying there while some member of the Yakuza eats sushi off my breasts."

"Really, Lora," Pinkie had said. "Nobody would want to eat sushi off of your breasts. Even as flat-chested as you are, it would probably fall off. And the Japanese are a very hygienic people."

"Are you saying my breasts aren't hygienic?!"

"I really hadn't put much thought into it," Pinkie had confessed. "Not my thing, you know. But anyway, it's not going to come up. I'm not asking you to be a sushi table or a hooker, for god's sake. I'm asking you to be an event hostess. It's more like being a party planner with really tiny parties. Or like being a geisha without the white face. Or like being a rich guy's wife, but without the jumbo rock and the Porsche Cayenne."

"Do people actually make money doing that?" I had asked suspiciously.

"There's more to life than money," Pinkie had sniffed. "But yes. Sometimes the clients pay a fee. Other times, when it's a friend of mine, I'll ask if they can reimburse you for the opera tickets or vacation or whatever you're cancelling to help out a friend in need."

"What if I'm not going to the opera?"

"You're never going to the opera," Pinkie had said, exasperated. "It's just a nice way for them to give you money without making it so *transactional*."

"Ah."

"Oh, and I take 20 percent, of course."

"For introducing me?"

"For making you someone they'd like to be introduced to."

Pinkie had been as good as his word. He'd corralled his web of minions to make sure I looked like a million bucks. He'd coached me on champagne and caviar and foie gras. He'd shown me thirty-five ways to tie an Hermès scarf that didn't make me look like a stewardess.

Once, in a particularly emotional moment, I had confessed to him that he was practically my Prince Charming.

He had patted me on the knee. "I love you, too, darling," he said. "But I prefer the term fairy godmother."

5

After the lunch at Maxim's, all I wanted to do was spend the day
lazing in front of the TV looking for George Clooney movies on
Netflix, but with less than twenty-four hours to get ready for the
trip, it didn't look like that was going to be possible.

I pulled out the Louis Vuitton rollerbag Pinkie had given me
from his personal collection and opened my closet door. Yachting.
That meant swimsuits. I pinched my stomach experimentally. The
lunch at Maxim's hadn't done me any favors. Obviously, I was
going to be needing cover-ups. Something in a tent, I thought.

I heard the opening bars of "Ride of the Valkyries" and grabbed
my phone out of my pocket before the volume cranked up to
deafening. I was going to have stern words with my brother about
personal boundaries when I next spoke with him. I looked at the
display. Chris. Speak of the devil.

My brother, Chris, had started out as an elfin slip of a boy with
an irrepressible sense of humor most commonly expressed in
knock-knock jokes. He had morphed into a withdrawn hulk of a
teenager with a lantern jaw and a love of computers. Today he was
a massive behemoth who hadn't left his apartment in two years,
but his sense of humor had reasserted itself with a vengeance,
powered by the kind of hacking savvy only available to
agoraphobic insomniacs with genius level IQs and a fundamental
hatred of authority. Once in a while I read about epic hacks in the

New York Times and wondered which of them he was responsible for. At least one, I knew for a fact. Less than two, I hoped fervently.

"What the hell have you done to my phone?" I asked.

"Most people start with hello."

"Most people don't get woken up by shrieking valkyries. Look, I know you don't have a lot of respect for privacy in general, but I prefer to go through life without little brother watching me."

"You know, you should actually be thanking me," Chris said.

"For invading my privacy?"

"For protecting your privacy from whoever bugged your phone," he corrected.

"Bugged my phone?! What are you talking about?"

"When I was on your phone installing Ring Tone Riot…"

"And invading my privacy," I interjected.

"Can you focus here, Lora? This is serious. When I was testing my software on your phone, I kept getting really crappy performance. I thought for a minute that it might have been an error in my program. But, of course, then I came to my senses and realized that since my programs don't have errors, it had to be something on your phone interfering with my program. I took a closer look. Something on your phone was hijacking the GPS. And not only that: emails, locations, calls, texts. Someone's been keeping track of every move you've made for the last two months."

"What?! There must be some kind of mistake."

"It's pretty hard to accidentally bug someone's phone, Lora."

I held the phone away from my ear and looked at it in horror. "Are they listening right now?"

"Of course not. You don't think I would leave someone else's tracking software on your phone? All issues of privacy aside, it was completely wrecking *my* tracking software."

I didn't argue. Suddenly having my brother monitoring me sounded less like an invasion of privacy and more like a security system. "What do I do? We have to call the police, right?"

My brother snorted. "Lora, the police can't help with this."

"Of course they can. It's against the law, isn't it?"

"Lora, it's the police. They're reasonably good at issuing traffic tickets and shooting the occasional bad guy, but they're in the Stone Age when it comes to technology. And whoever's bugging you is smart—they're not continuously broadcasting, which would be easy to trace. They're recording everything on the phone and just pinging it once in a while to download the files. As soon as they're finished, they erase the history, so the only way to find out where they're coming from is to catch them in the act.

"But you can find out who it is, right? You're supposed to be good at this stuff."

"I *am* good at this 'stuff,' as you call it. If whoever did it hits the phone again, I should be able to trace it back while the download is happening. But I don't know when that will be. So you need to think very carefully about who might be doing this. Who do you know with great tech skills and a burning need to know where you are at all times? Aside from me, of course."

I felt a creeping sensation at the idea that someone had been watching me. I thought back over my last few jobs. "Last night I was out with Mr. Nakamura and his guys," I said. "They have tech skills. But I've done jobs with them before, and they're harmless. I mean, given how rotten I felt this morning, maybe harmless isn't exactly the right word, but I don't see any of those guys wanting to go through my emails and know when I'm in the grocery store."

"I think you might be underestimating the weirdness of Japanese men," Chris said. "You should try watching anime porn some time."

"Uh, pass."

"Okay, if you don't think it's them, what about other clients? Any tech CEOs? You're not dating the head of Google, are you?"

"Unfortunately not."

"But you're usually dealing with rich guys, right?" Chris asked. "So they can hire out. Anyone who seems unusually attached to you?"

I gritted my teeth as I suddenly realized who it had to be. "Clancy Featherstone. I'm going to kill Pinkie for setting me up with that lunatic."

"Wow," my brother said. "With a name like that, I'm picturing soft, slightly pudgy, chinless, bowties and eccentric socks...how close am I?"

"Pretty close," I admitted. "But bowties and eccentric socks would show some sort of flair, and if there's one thing you can say about Clancy Featherstone, it's that he's completely lacking in flair."

"What makes you think he's unusually attached?"

"Well, the fact that he sent a parrot that had been trained to say, 'Clancy loves Lora,' to my door this morning, for starters."

"A parrot? Don't most guys start with flowers or jewelry?"

I closed my eyes. "He started with flowers. I told him I wasn't interested. Then jewelry. I sent it back. Then he sent a Siamese cat, of all things."

"He didn't realize you were allergic to cats?"

"To be honest, our entire conversation history has mostly revolved around me telling him that I'm not interested in dating him. It might be the only thing he really knows about me. Oh, and now he knows that I can't afford an extra parking space, because when he sent me a Mercedes, I sent it back, too."

"He sent you a car?!"

"I sent it back, I told you," I said defensively.

"It's not about whether you sent it back, Lora—it's the fact that he sent it in the first place. Clearly, this Clancy person is desperate to get your attention. Do you think he could be dangerous?"

I snorted. "No. He grew up with a mother who wouldn't let him tie his own shoes. He's the most passive person I've ever met. I mean, hacking my phone is creepy and absolutely unacceptable, but given how many presents I've sent back, he was probably desperate to find something that might convince me to date him. I told Pinkie this morning that he needed to get Clancy to back off. Pinkie's known him for years. I'm sure he can straighten this out."

Chris was silent for a moment. "Look," he finally said, "I don't know the guy, but I do know that someone who's willing to do something like this – to invade your privacy without your consent – is a pretty scary person."

I thought about Clancy for a minute. Yes, he was crazy, and I was absolutely furious about him hacking my phone. But could he actually be dangerous? "You know," I said, striving for a light tone, "you invade my privacy without my consent all the time. Does that make you a scary person?"

"Not to you," Chris said, "but I'm pretty sure the CIA has a different opinion. Look, your phone is clean and hopefully I'll be able to get proof that he's doing this next time he accesses it, but in the meantime, you need to be very careful. Don't confront him directly. If you want to let Pinkie handle it, fine, but if this guy continues—or gets worse—you need to call the police. And keep track of when he tries to contact you and if he sends any more gifts. They don't need to be able to track him in the virtual world if they can see that he's stalking you in the real world."

I was silent for a moment. I'd always seen Clancy as more pathetic than menacing, but maybe my brother was right. And certainly, dangerous or not, it was time for me to stop pretending that Clancy was going to give up and go away. Monitoring my phone was way over the line. He might have once been a guy in love, but somewhere over the last few weeks, he had clearly become a stalker.

"Okay," I said. "I'm going to be out of the country for a few days. If Pinkie hasn't managed to get him sorted by then, I'll call the police. I promise."

"Good," my brother said. "And Lora, until this is cleared up…"

"Yes?"

"Just be careful, okay?"

6

My neighborhood in Brooklyn was a mix of underpaid service workers, retirees, and yuppies who couldn't afford to live in Park Slope. Limousines weren't common here, so when a white stretch limo pulled up outside my door the next morning, a lot of people suddenly found reasons to be outside.

Pinkie, who always loved an audience, waited for the uniformed driver to come around and open the door for him before extending his dainty Tod's driving moccasin to climb out of the car. Dressed in camelhair pants, a tailored white shirt, and a pink ascot, he had a Louis Vuitton duffel bag slung rakishly over his shoulder and was clutching a bottle of Veuve Clicquot in one hand and a white paper bag from the bakery around the corner in the other.

I opened my door and shooed him inside.

"For the love of heaven, Pinkie," I said. "Is it really necessary to make such a spectacle of yourself?"

"What on earth are you talking about? I came in the most conservative limo I could find. They had pink Hummers, you know. That would have been making a spectacle of myself."

I raised my hands in surrender. "Fine, fine. Are you coming to the airport, too?"

Pinkie, who had a horror of both public transportation and New Jersey, looked appalled. "Not a chance, darling. I've got another car coming to take me back to civilization. I just came over

27

to make sure you had a proper breakfast before heading off to Moscow."

"Veuve is part of a proper breakfast?"

"Veuve and donuts," Pinkie corrected.

"Does Veuve even go with donuts?"

"Veuve goes with everything." Pinkie poured us each a glass and handed me a French cruller. "Eat it fast, or it will congeal."

I took a bite of cruller. "I have news about your friend Clancy Featherstone."

Pinkie sighed. "What now? Did he send a line of Rockettes to your door?"

"No. He bugged my phone."

"Impossible," Pinkie scoffed, sipping some champagne. "Clancy is a lovesick idiot, not an insane stalker."

"I thought so, too, but my brother found the software on my phone. He's been reading all of my emails and texts and keeping track of where I was. For two months, Pinkie!"

"Given the state of your love life, he must be bored to tears."

"Pinkie, you need to take this seriously. What if he's dangerous?"

Pinkie laughed. "Trust me, Lora, of all the words I would use to describe Clancy, 'dangerous' isn't one of them. Now his mother..." He shuddered.

"Look, dangerous or not, he's completely out of control," I said. "I'm giving you a chance to sort this out, but if I hear anything from him when I get back, I'm filing a restraining order."

Pinkie sighed dramatically. "Fine. I'll handle it. I'll bring a bottle of scotch, we'll drink to unrequited love, and then we'll go pick out a puppy or something."

"Before I get back from the trip."

"Before you get back from the trip," Pinkie agreed, rolling his eyes. "And speaking of the trip, I brought you a travel survival kit." Pinkie rooted around in his Louis Vuitton. "Industrial strength earplugs, eye mask, some moisturizer...oh...and some pink pills."

"Pink pills?"

"They're to relax you. You're going to be locked in a tube for ten hours with a bunch of Russians. Trust me, you'll need them."

"Pinkie, you know I don't do drugs."

"Darling," Pinkie said. "These aren't drugs. They're medicine."

"Medicine is something you get for a medical condition."

"Trust me; you'll qualify by the end of the flight."

"No pills," I said firmly.

"Whatever happened to the Delaware state motto?"

"Liberty and independence?"

"Better living through chemistry."

I shook my head. "You keep the pills. I'll take everything else."

"Don't say I didn't warn you. Are you sure you have everything you need? Did you pack swimsuits?"

"Yes, Pinkie."

"Not that one that makes your butt look like a Saran-Wrapped ham hock, right?"

I stared at him. "Which one would that be?"

"I don't remember. One of them. You didn't pack that one, did you? Although Russians are notoriously attracted to processed meat, so maybe it wouldn't be all bad…"

"Enough," I said. "I have plenty of experience with this kind of job, and I know what to pack. There's not a thing you can mention that I didn't already think of."

"Passport?"

"Dammit," I said, jumping up to head for my desk. "I hate it when you do that."

I opened the right-hand desk drawer. Pinkie peered over my shoulder. "Jesus, Lora. If we have to wait for you to find the passport in that mess, you'll have to take next week's flight."

I looked over the jumble of pencils, office supplies, manuals, and receipts. "It may look like a mess, but I know where everything is. I keep my passport inside the manual for my camera."

"Didn't you sell that camera a year ago?"

"Yes. That's why I haven't thrown the manual away. I've been meaning to give it to the guy who bought the camera, only I haven't had a chance to look up his address. I put my passport inside the manual so that I wouldn't forget about it."

Pinkie gave me a skeptical look. "I don't know whether that kind of twisted logic is a sign of genius or insanity."

"Trust me, it's genius," I assured him. I pulled out the camera manual. "And voilà!" I flipped through the pages. No passport.

"Your argument that it's genius is somewhat undermined by the fact that your passport is not there."

"It has to be here," I said. "I put it in the manual last week."

I flipped through the pages again. My passport wasn't magically appearing. I felt a prickle at the back of my neck. "Oh my god. Do you know what this means?"

"You have early onset dementia?"

"No, Pinkie. I know where I put my passport. Someone's gone through my papers." My brain made the logical jump. "Your insane friend Clancy has gone through my papers!"

"Be serious, Lora. You just forgot where you put it. It's not a big deal. I forget things all the time. Like that time I forgot that Prince Abdul's butler was on the balcony and I locked the door and went to the Hamptons for the weekend? The poor man had to sleep on the breakfast table for two days. Cold coffee and burned toast for a week after I got back, I can tell you…"

I felt a surge of irritation at Pinkie's dismissive tone. "I didn't forget," I insisted. "I put it in the manual for the camera last week. I'm telling you, Pinkie. First, Clancy bugs my phone and now he's going through my apartment. I know he's your friend, but this isn't charming or cute. It's scary."

I shivered, looking around the room. My eyes focused on the photo albums on the coffee table, aligned in a perfect stack. Had I left them like that? I couldn't remember. I shot a glance at my bedroom door. The idea of Clancy in there, his soft white hands pawing through my underwear drawer—I suddenly felt nauseated.

Pinkie shook his head. "No way. Listen, you know I wouldn't challenge Chris on anything technical, but I know Clancy. Breaking into someone's apartment is completely out of character."

"Who else would do this, Pinkie?" I realized my voice had ratcheted higher under stress. "I'm telling you. He's over the edge. All this calling, the gifts, the parrot yesterday…" I pulled my phone out of my pocket. "This ends now. I'm calling the police."

"What are you going to tell them?" Pinkie asked. "The only proof you have that someone was in here is that your passport isn't where you think you left it."

"It's not where I think I left it," I snapped. "It's where I did leave it."

"But you can't prove that," Pinkie said, pulling the phone out of my hand. "Look. You have a flight to catch. You'll be in a foreign country. I'll talk to Clancy while you're gone. If you bring the police in, people are going to hear about it. Scandal isn't good advertising for an event hostess, you know."

I bit my lip, undecided. I was furious that Clancy would violate my privacy like this, but Pinkie was right. Word would get out, and nobody would hire an event hostess without discretion.

"Fine," I said finally. "But if it's not settled by the time I get back, I'm filing a restraining order. This is completely psycho."

"I'll take care of it," Pinkie said soothingly. "Now can we please focus on finding your passport and getting you to the airport?"

I sighed and rummaged around in the drawer. My passport finally made its appearance, tucked into the manual for the refrigerator. Any doubts I had that Clancy had gone through my things evaporated. What kind of lunatic would keep their passport in the manual for their refrigerator?

"Okay," I said, taking a final mental inventory of my things. "I'm going. But Clancy..."

"I've got it."

I gave him a stern look.

"Trust me, Lora. It's handled."

"Okay." I gave him a quick peck on the cheek and grabbed my bag. "Then I've gotta run. The driver's still out there, right?"

"Of course," Pinkie said, his good humor restored. "He seems like a really nice guy. You should talk."

"Sure. Listen, the Clancy thing is the top priority, but don't forget about my car, and try not to antagonize Heather from across the street."

"I would never," Pinkie said. "I was thinking that we should make up, actually. What does one get the incredibly nosy vegan blogger in their life? Maybe I'll order her a ham."

"I mean it," I said, scowling at him.

"Fine," Pinkie said. "Have fun on the way to the airport."

"An hour in New Jersey traffic? How could I not?"

7

Pinkie's preferred limo company was owned by a friend of his in the "pink mafia" who only employed drivers with sensual mouths and rock-hard abs. The drivers wore uniforms that were cut close to show off their ridiculously perfect bodies to maximum effect. I usually tried to aim for aesthetic appreciation, but given how long it had been since my experience of a man had included anything except sending back gifts and blocking calls, I found myself harboring a few other kinds of appreciation as well.

Riding to the airport to catch my flight to Moscow, I caught sight of my driver's disconcertingly blue eyes watching me in the rearview mirror. He smiled at me. "We're running a little early, miss," he told me. "In case you wanted to stop for anything."

"Thanks. I'm fine."

"Really?" he asked, raising an eyebrow. "Not even a short stop?"

I looked at him warily. "What would I be stopping for?"

"I don't know. Maybe you're tense. Maybe you need a massage, for example. We're going to be driving right by my apartment. Maybe you'd like to come over for a coffee and a massage."

"I'm sorry, I must have missed something. Are you a licensed masseur?"

"Nope, but I'm an expert in one particular type of massage."

"I see," I said, confused. "Shiatsu? Swedish?"

"Happy ending."

"Right," I said, turning bright red. "No thank you."

The driver's voice was silky. "Come on. It'll relax you for your flight. And if it's been six months, you probably need some relaxing."

"Pinkie told you it's been six months?!"

"Umm..." the driver said, suddenly unsure of himself. "He might have let something slip..."

"Drive the car," I snapped, hitting the button to put the privacy shield up. Apparently, no man in my life had any respect for boundaries.

My cheeks burning, I opened the dossier Pinkie had prepared and tried to focus on work.

The word *dossier* implies a dry document with factual material about the client. Having been assembled by Pinkie, this was more like a teenybopper fan magazine. Despite his hideously overpriced education, Pinkie was a shameless abuser of italics, capitalization, and exclamation points, which made reading his dossiers the visual equivalent of watching MTV back when they still played music.

"KYRILL ANTONOV"

Profession: Decorator to the rich and shameless, and owner of a luxury goods business that can get you anything your heart desires. And the THINGS he sells. Gorgeous, gorgeous, gorgeous! Also in violation of SO many international laws. Seriously, did you know that you can still buy a tiger skin rug? Maybe you can get one for me. Of course, I would feel terrible if I killed the last tiger. But then again, if someone else killed the last tiger, I would still feel terrible, but I wouldn't have a tiger skin rug to comfort me. Maybe you can tell Kyrill that I have a birthday coming up and that I really love tigers and we can just let the magic work.

Speaks: English and Russian

Photo: If you can believe it, there are absolutely NO photos of Kyrill to be had. If you ask Kyrill, that's because he's afraid of kidnappers. If you ask Kyrill's friends at boarding school, it's because Kyrill is a narcissistic princess who can't stay away from the pastry table. You'll have to let me know which it is after meeting him. Right now I'm betting on narcissistic princess, but that's mostly because we narcissistic princesses have to stick together.

I shook my head. Pinkie.

Purpose of event: Kyrill will be meeting with Greek business partners to discuss the transportation of certain goods. No word as to what those goods are, but I'm guessing it's something fabulous and shady. Albino pet monkeys...no, wait...they would look just like computer programmers. That wouldn't be fabulous at all.

Other guests: The primary partner of the firm Kyrill is meeting with is Spiro Alexandropou. He's one of those terribly old school Greek shipping magnate types. Tough, tan, rich—the kind of man who swoops in and marries Jackie O. I heard he lost a bit of money in the Greek meltdown and is looking to make a deal. You've met him before (Armand Xandrou's dinner? About three months ago?). Charming older gentleman who probably looked like he wanted to stab Armand with a shellfish fork?

I cast my mind back. Yes. There had been a rather courtly old gentleman there glowering at our host. A business rival, Armand had said. We had chatted briefly about something. Boats, I thought. Given my knowledge of boats, it must have been a very short conversation.

I turned back to the dossier.

Spiro's son, Alexander, will also be there. Alexander is a complete man slut. Rips through women like tissue paper. Tragic, really, because he's terribly rich and handsome, and of course with a father like that he has simply loads to prove. You know how I love a man with something to prove.

Your mission, should you choose to accept it:

I rolled my eyes. Pinkie was a huge *Mission Impossible* fan, mostly because of Tom Cruise, who Pinkie assured me was gayer than the pope, whatever that meant.

Kyrill would like you to welcome his guests, ensure that they are comfortable, and supervise the staff.

I grumbled under my breath. I hated supervising the staff, particularly Russian staff, who tended to blend surliness and incompetence in equal measure.

According to Fritzie, Kyrill can be very demanding, but is quite charming once you get to know him. He also likes things to be done to the highest standard, which is why he needs someone equally refined to help provide the correct environment for business discussions. Fritzie said he asked about you particularly, so I guess you're officially refined…by Russian standards, at least, which is nothing to get all cocky about. Call me if you need any help. Love, Pinkie.

I smiled. Thanks to years of Pinkie's tutelage and time spent managing the lives and travels of the idle rich, I *was* pretty refined these days. But it was still nice to know he had my back.

I leaned back against the upholstery, thinking through what I had read. The dossier was a little thinner than I was used to, which I attributed to the fact that Pinkie only knew Kyrill through Fritzie. Something in it bothered me. I scanned it again. Interior decorator—that sounded innocuous enough. Maybe it was the fact that Pinkie hadn't been able to hunt down a photo.

A professional life spent living on tips had taught me that the older people got, the more you could tell about their personalities just by looking at their faces. When I met someone with laugh lines, I knew they saw the lighter side of life. When I ran across people with deep creases between their eyebrows, they usually turned out to be judgmental types. And of course, when I met someone with no lines at all, I knew that they could afford a really good dermatologist.

The fact that Kyrill had gone to the trouble of removing all photographs of himself from the Internet concerned me. I understood the impulse—I usually ended up cross-eyed with triple chins in most snapshots—but it was still worrisome. Of course, getting rid of all photographic evidence was easier said than done, even for Russian millionaires. I wondered if my brother would be able to find a photo of Kyrill. There should be some benefit to having a close relative with no respect for information security. I pulled out my phone to call Chris, managing to extricate it from my bag just as it started ringing.

My mother. I frowned. My mother called once a week, on Tuesdays at 6:00 p.m. on the dot. These calls followed a predictable pattern: She gave me a rundown on the latest doings in competitive Scrabble, she updated me on her ongoing feud with Mrs. Deckish, her cat-collecting next-door neighbor, and at the close of the call, she advised me about how important it was for a girl in my "profession" to be careful. My mother lived by her day planner. I couldn't imagine what she needed to tell me that would be important enough to trump gardening club.

"Hi, Mom," I said. "Is there a problem?"

"Does there have to be a problem for me to call you? I'm your mother, aren't I? Am I not allowed to call my only daughter?"

"Of course you are," I said, backpedaling. "It's just that I thought you had gardening club now. I was afraid something was wrong."

"Nothing's wrong," my mother said. She bit off the last word in a way that belied her steely tone. "Nothing at all."

We sat on the phone in silence for a few seconds, each waiting for the other to speak.

"So...uh...how's Scrabble going?" I asked. My mother was a regional Scrabble champion, a pastime that she pursued with the same efficiency and ruthlessness she lavished on everything from her Bronze Baby Floribunda roses to her award-winning lemon pound cake.

"I didn't call to talk about Scrabble."

"Okay," I said, completely mystified at this point. "What did you call to talk about?"

Another long silence. "I just wanted to tell you that I love you," she said, her voice cracking slightly.

Somewhere in the back of my brain, an alarm started going off. "I know that, Mom. I love you, too." I paused. "Are you sure nothing's wrong? You don't really seem yourself today."

My mother let out a noise that, had it come from anyone else, would have been a sob. But that couldn't be. My mother never cried.

"You're not...crying...are you?" I asked.

"Don't be absurd," she said, her voice suddenly brisk. "I just wanted to see if you were going to be around this week. I was thinking about driving up."

"I'm actually in a car on the way to the airport. I've got a job in Europe. Just a week." I paused again. "If something's wrong..."

"Nothing's wrong."

"I mean, even if nothing's wrong—if you just wanted to talk—I could cancel."

"I hope I taught you a better work ethic than that."

I stifled a laugh. My mother might think I was a hooker, but dammit, at least I'd be a hooker with a stellar work ethic. "You're right, Mom. Maybe when I get back we can get together. I'll drive down. We can bring Chris something with vegetables."

My mother's voice was soft when she answered. "I'd like that." She made another sob-like noise, and I clutched the phone to my ear to listen. "I don't want to keep you. Have a good trip, dear. Be safe."

"Mom?"

She had disconnected.

I stared at the phone in my hand, bewildered. Something was very wrong. I quickly dialed my brother.

"Have you talked to Mom?"

"Again, most people start with hello."

"Hello, and answer the question."

"Not since she got back from the doctor."

"She went to the doctor?!" Now I was truly concerned. It's not that my mother had never seen a doctor before—just that the last time she went, she had been completely delirious with fever and I'd had to call a sheriff's deputy to force her into the ambulance.

"She went yesterday."

"Did she say what was wrong?"

"Nope."

"Weren't you curious?" I asked. "Seeing as how our mother has never voluntarily gone to the doctor in our entire lives?"

"Nope."

"Really?"

"Maybe a little," Chris admitted.

"Enough to hack into her medical records?"

"Her doctor's office still runs on paper records," he said. "Actually, given how old Dr. Tanner is, it's probably clay tablets. In any case, yes, I did look, but there wasn't anything I could get to online. And since everyone's suddenly so concerned about their *privacy*, I decided to let it slide."

"Is there anything else you can check?"

My brother was silent for a moment. "Okay. Spill. It's not like you to encourage illegal behavior. What did Mom say to you?"

"Nothing," I said, "but I think she was crying."

My brother inhaled sharply. "Are you sure?"

"Pretty sure."

"Shit," he said. "I can't even conceive of Mom crying. Let me think for a second." Some keyboard tapping sounded in the background. "Got it. Insurance. Let me just take a look at her health insurance records. The diagnosis should be there."

More tapping, while I waited nervously.

"Oh…this is not good." Chris's voice was dire.

"What? It's cancer, isn't it?"

"Why do people always think it's cancer? There are lots of worse diseases than cancer. Bubonic plague. Ebola. Rabies."

"Our mother has rabies?!"

"No," my brother said. "But she doesn't have health insurance either. Apparently, she cancelled it."

"What do you mean 'cancelled it'?"

"She probably figured that since she never went to the doctor, she didn't need it. Why does she do any of the things she does? I'm just telling you that she's not covered."

My concern suddenly turned into active fear. "So you're telling me that our mother is probably sick with something horrible and that she has no health insurance?" I felt a tightness in my chest.

"No. *You're* telling me that you she think she's sick with something horrible, and *I'm* telling you that she has no health insurance," he said. "Although I'll grant you that the upshot is pretty much the same."

"I'm supposed to leave the country for a week," I told him. "I'm cancelling. I'll come down; we'll brace Mom. We'll make her talk to us."

My brother snorted. "Since when have we ever been able to make Mom do anything?"

"I know, but I'm telling you…something is wrong. We can't sit by and do nothing!"

"Let me ask you something," Chris said. "Do you have any money saved up?"

"No. In fact, I'm pretty sure I'm about to be a couple thousand dollars in debt. My car is on the fritz again."

"Me neither," he said. "Look. I'm not saying that something is wrong with Mom, but if it is—and she doesn't have insurance—we're going to need to come up with some money. This isn't Sweden, you know. The government doctor fairy isn't going to step in and wave a wand."

"So you think the best thing I can do is to take the job?"

"Yeah," he said. "I'll talk to Mom while you're gone. It's

probably nothing. But if it is something, maybe she'll tell me. I'm still her baby, you know. Hey…hold on a sec."

I heard some typing in the background and sighed. My brother was completely incapable of disconnecting himself from the Internet, even when our mother's life was at stake.

"Shit," Chris said.

I sat up in my seat.

"What are you looking at? Did you find out what's wrong? It's cancer, isn't it?"

"What is it with you and the cancer? No. It's not that. It's about your stalker."

"Clancy? What is it?"

"Your friend Clancy must not be as clueless as you seem to think he is."

"Trust me," I said. "He's as clueless as it is possible for a grown man to be. He probably needs his butler to zip his pants in the morning. Why? What are you looking at?"

"I got a hit on that software I put on your phone. Someone was trying to get back into your system."

"And?"

"It's the Viper."

I waited. "The Viper? That's a person?"

"Well, I actually have fifty bucks riding on it being a consortium, but what's important for you to understand is that the Viper is a very serious black hat hacker."

"English, please."

"He's the guy you call when you want to get into an uncrackable system."

"Who does he work for?"

"He works for whoever pays him."

"Well, that makes sense. Clancy's totally loaded."

"Yeah, but this is not the kind of guy who gets found by Pinkie's degenerate friends," Chris said. "He's serious. He gets hired by very shady people."

"Such as…?"

"CIA. FSB—the new incarnation of the KGB. Organized crime. Google."

"Google qualifies as shady? I love Google!"

"Google is a multibillion dollar company that knows everything about everyone," Chris said. "It is literally the incarnation of evil."

"You think Google is tapping my phone?"

"No! You told me Clancy Featherstone was tapping your phone, and I'm just telling you that if Clancy knows enough to hire someone like the Viper, he's not just some half-wit with mommy issues. He's connected to some very scary people. If Pinkie's going to tell him to back off, maybe it's not such a bad idea for you to be out of town for a few days. Just in case he decides to move his stalking from the virtual world to the real world."

I felt the back of my neck prickle. "I think he already did that."

"What do you mean he already did that?!"

"I think he broke into my apartment."

"He broke into your apartment?" My brother's voice was incredulous. "Did you call the police?"

I sighed. "I wanted to, but the only reason I know he was there was because my passport was in the wrong place. It's not exactly grounds to bring someone up on charges. And besides, Pinkie told me that if this all turned into some messy police thing, it would kill my business. Nobody wants to hire an event hostess who calls the police on her clients."

"So you're just going to let yourself be stalked by some psychopath?"

"No. I told you, Pinkie's going to handle it."

"And what if Pinkie doesn't handle it?"

"*Then* I'll call the police."

"Hmm." My brother didn't sound happy.

"But look. You're right. It makes sense to get out of town for a while. I'll make some cash, and it'll give Clancy a chance to calm down after Pinkie breaks his heart. And I'll be safe on board a yacht with a Russian oligarch."

"A Russian oligarch? That doesn't sound like most people's definition of safe."

"He's an interior decorator. Kyrill Antonov. Apparently, he's the man to see if you think that Versace is too low key."

"An interior decorator? Okay, that's slightly more reassuring." He sighed. "Have you considered getting a normal job?"

"Have you?"

"Touché. Fine. Have fun on the boat, make some money, and make sure Pinkie deals with this psycho before you get back. And if he doesn't, call the police...or I will. In the meantime, I'll see if I can figure out what's going out with Mom, and I'll keep an eye on your phone to make sure the Viper doesn't make a second attempt."

"Will do."

I snapped the phone off and stared out the window, trying not to worry. In the space of two days, Clancy had gone from an annoying lovesick dweeb to a full-blown stalker with connections to the criminal underworld. And my mother—I told myself that I was blowing this out of proportion, but I knew in my heart that something was wrong. I couldn't stop my brain from sifting through all the diagnoses I knew of to find one horrible enough to make my mother cry. Flesh-eating viruses. The black plague. Scurvy. I bit my lip and tried unsuccessfully to think of puppies.

My mother had taken on bullies to protect me when I was a chubby kid with braces. She had worked two jobs to hold our family together when my father died. She didn't judge or lecture me when she called, even though she thought I was a prostitute. I squared my shoulders. She would tell us what was wrong when she was ready, and I'd have the cash to help her.

Pinkie would convince Clancy to leave me alone and channel his disappointment into a mediocre poem or an endowment to unrequited love.

And as long as I was making a wish list, I would get seated next to Hugh Jackman on the plane to Moscow, and he would insist on buying me a penthouse apartment in Manhattan so that we could have our torrid affair in comfort.

I fixed my eyes on my perfectly manicured hands and took deep breaths. It would all be fine. Just fine.

8

The flight to Moscow was completely filled with Russians and absolutely miserable, two things that Pinkie assured me generally go hand in hand. According to Pinkie, old Russians had been poor and aggressive and filled with a completely unjustified sense of their own importance. New Russians, on the other hand, were rich and aggressive and filled with a completely unjustified sense of their own importance. Pinkie didn't find it much of an improvement.

While I generally took Pinkie's offensive sweeping generalizations about national personality traits with a grain of salt, I had to admit that the woman sitting next to me was making his case for him. She spent the entire ten-hour flight pressing the call button to demand more pillows, more blankets, more magazines, and especially more vodka.

About two hours into the flight, she cracked open her duty-free bottle and started topping herself up directly. About two hours after that, she started watching my television over my shoulder. Two hours after that, she started telling me what she thought about Americans. Turns out Pinkie wasn't the only one who could make offensive sweeping generalizations about national personality traits.

Needless to say, I wasn't in the world's best mood when we hit the airport.

Domodedovo International Airport, like all critical

infrastructure in Russia, was designed by the cousin or wife of someone who had the job of choosing who should design it, and was built by the cousin or wife of the person who got to choose who should build it. The end result of this process was a shining tribute to nepotism—an airport that brought the talents of architects, contractors, and signage experts together with one overarching purpose: to make the experience of entering Russia as miserable as possible.

There wasn't an escalator in sight, so I cursed and swore as I wrestled my rollerbag down a flight of stairs, then up another flight of stairs, then down again, then over slightly, then up one more time. It was like being trapped in an M.C. Escher print.

Coming to the main arrivals hall, I dutifully followed the signs for All Other Countries, which led me to what appeared to be a family reunion for Genghis Khan's descendants. Colorfully dressed women sporting cheap plastic bags milled around aimlessly with obviously no concept of how to form a line. Ruddy-cheeked children fought with sticks in the crowd, occasionally landing a blow on the legs of one of the unsuspecting Westerners. A particularly devious-looking man sidled by, lugging a box of something labeled Bulgarian White Cheese that was bleating piteously.

I scanned the crowd, looking for some source of order. Spotting a pair of beefy Russian women in unflattering polyester uniforms lurking near the edge of the room, I elbowed my way over to them. "Where do I go with an American passport?" I asked.

The two women shrugged in unison then returned to the conversation I had so rudely interrupted.

"Excuse me," I tried again. They ignored me. I could feel myself break out into a sweat. Clearly, American antiperspirants were not designed to cope with Russian border patrol.

"Are you American?" I heard a friendly American voice from behind me ask.

I turned to see an open-faced man about my own age with sandy brown hair and a ready smile. He was dressed in jeans and a turtleneck sweater and had a Tumi messenger bag draped over one shoulder. His eyes were startlingly green, heavily fringed with dark lashes.

"Yes," I said. "I'm trying to figure out how to get through

passport control, but this place is so disorganized and nobody speaks English."

He motioned me to follow him. "I'll let you in on a little secret," he said in a low tone. "They all speak English. Russian bureaucrats are the most passive-aggressive people in the world. They just like to see you squirm."

I followed him up another flight of stairs. "God," I said, wiping my forehead. "What is it with the stairs in this place? Aren't airports supposed to be flat?"

He smiled. "The going theory in the expat community is that the Russians purposely created a disorganized, hostile, and needlessly miserable airport experience as a way of gradually acclimating you to their disorganized, hostile, and needlessly miserable country."

"How thoughtful," I grumbled.

We schlepped our bags up yet another flight of stairs and came to a second set of passport controls marked for diplomats. He led me over to the diplomatic line. "Are you a diplomat?" I asked.

"Nope," he said. Sure enough, the man behind the desk took my passport without comment and, after scanning it and punching some information into the computer, stamped it and passed it back to me.

I waited on the other side of passport control for my rescuer. "Thanks," I said when he came through the gate. "Do you make it a point of helping all the Americans who get trapped in the airport?"

He smiled crookedly. "I try to help the ones I can," he said. "I'm pretty passive-aggressive myself."

We wandered over to the baggage carousel. "What brings you to Moscow?" he asked. "Tourism? Business?"

"A little bit of both. I'm just here for a day, really, then I'm flying out with a friend to help him with a little event he's having. I'm afraid I'm not going to have time to see much. Are you here on business?"

He nodded. "I'm actually a Russian studies professor, so I spend a lot of time here."

He fished around in his pocket for a moment, eventually producing a business card. "My name's Benjamin, by the way," he said, handing it to me.

"I'm Lora. Nice to meet you." I looked at the card before

tucking it into my pocket. "So tell me, Benjamin, as an Adjunct Professor of Russian Studies at American University, if you only had one day to see something in Moscow, where would you go?"

"Red Square," he said without hesitation.

"You're a professor of Russian studies, and you're recommending Red Square? Did you get your degree from an Internet school, by chance?"

"I know," he said, laughing. "Everybody's always looking for the inside tip. If you were staying a week, I could come up with something better, but if you're only here for a day, it's gotta be Red Square."

"Red Square it is. Any other advice you have to offer?"

He looked at me, the smile fading from his face. "Yes," he said, lowering his voice. "Don't trust anyone."

I glanced around, suddenly feeling paranoid. "Don't trust anyone? Could you be a little more specific?"

"Don't take drinks from strangers. Don't get into cars with people you don't know."

"Or I'll wake up in bed with some lowlife?"

"Or you could wake up half a world away as the permanent property of some lowlife," he said. "They've got a real issue with human trafficking here. Attractive women go missing all the time."

"And on that note," I said, "maybe I'll spend my time in Russia locked in my friend's apartment."

His serious look dissolved into a sheepish smile. "Sorry. Did I mention that I'm an academic? We're notoriously bad at small talk. Look, Moscow is a spectacular city, and it's no more dangerous than any big American city. Go to Red Square. And if you get through Red Square and you want to see something a little off the beaten path, give me a call. I'd be happy to show you around."

"Is that part of the standard service you provide to all Americans you meet in airports?"

"Absolutely."

"Well, I doubt I'll have time to see much else, but I appreciate the offer."

I stepped forward as my bag came into sight. "This one's mine."

Benjamin looked at my bag as if wondering whether he should offer to carry it. "Are you going to be okay from here? Can I drop you someplace?"

I shook my head. "I've got a car waiting," I said, hoping that was true, "but thanks all the same."

His face fell a little bit. "Okay, then. Enjoy your stay, and seriously: don't hesitate to call me if you need something while you're here."

"I won't," I said, patting my pocket. While I generally didn't make it a practice to call complete strangers I met in airports, I couldn't blame the guy for trying. I looked back over my shoulder, where Benjamin was still staring forlornly at the luggage carousel. Plus, he was kind of cute, in an adjunct-professorial kind of way.

9

Once I cleared customs, I was assailed by a crowd of taxi drivers. They were sweaty, slippery-looking men who whispered destinations and prices under their breath so as not to attract the attention of the airport police, who were studiously ignoring them despite the large signs advising that unofficial taxis were strictly forbidden. I remembered what Benjamin had told me about not trusting people. Suddenly it seemed like good advice. I clutched my bag tightly and walked through the crowd, looking around until my eyes lit on a tall, bored-looking man in uniform holding a sign with my name on it.

"I'm Lora Godwin," I said, extending a hand. He ignored the outstretched hand and grabbed my suitcase.

"Follow me."

I trailed behind him as we headed out of the airport and into the gritty, noisy parking lot. I wondered whether he worked for the Russian branch of Pinkie's standard limo service. Judging by his smoldering eyes and broad shoulders, it seemed possible. This one, however, didn't seem inclined to offer me a massage. Which was too bad, really, since the flight over had put kinks in parts of my anatomy that I hadn't known existed.

Once settled in the car, the driver dialed a number to report in. "Georgi here," he said in Russian. "Yes, she arrived. No problems." He scrutinized me carefully in the rearview mirror as I pretended to be entranced by the snarly traffic and Stalinist apartment blocks lining the six-lane road to town. "Pretty," he conceded. "Small tits. Bitchy looking. But I'd fuck her."

I smiled sweetly at him. No reason to fill him on in the fact that my few words of Russian, honed by late evenings in the company of customers behaving badly, included the words "tits," "bitch," and "fuck." It was amazing, I reflected, how many languages I could say those words in.

I looked at my watch. It was three o'clock in the morning in Delaware, which made it the perfect time to check in with Chris. My brother had chronic insomnia that he assured me was completely unrelated to his massive intake of Red Bull and Mountain Dew.

"Have you spoken to Mom?"

"Jesus, what is it with you and the phone manners?" he asked. "Hello. And yes, I talked to her."

"And?"

"And she told me that she's going to take a trip to Paris in two weeks."

I tried to process this. "Our mother is going to Paris? Has she ever left the country?"

"Nope."

"So I guess her health is okay?"

"Or she's starting down her bucket list," Chris said.

"Jesus, Chris. Why do you always jump to the worst possible conclusion?"

"I don't know. Experience?"

I sighed. "How did she sound? Was she crying?"

"No," he said. "Quite the opposite, actually. She was totally hyper. Manic, even. I hate to say it, but I think you're right. Something's going on. She's just not herself. But so far, at least, she's not willing to admit that anything's wrong. And you know Mom...there's not much we can do to make her tell us until she's good and ready."

I looked out the window at the endless march of communist apartment blocks, trying to distract myself. With their peeling paint and crumbling balconies, they looked diseased, which just brought me back to whatever was wrong with my mother. "I know. Can we talk about something more cheerful? Is there anything new on the whole stalking thing?"

"Your definition of 'something more cheerful' clearly needs

work. But yes. I put a tracker on your friend Clancy's phone, so now I'm stalking your stalker."

"And?"

"And you're right, the man is phenomenally dull. And completely neurotic. He literally has his therapist on speed dial. Yesterday his dinner reservation got lost, and he called to ask what he was supposed to do."

"That sounds like the Clancy I know," I said. "What did the therapist say?"

"The therapist told him to take deep breaths and to walk across the street to the Thai place. You know, he probably paid, like, two hundred bucks for that advice."

"Money well spent," I said. "Anything else going on with you?"

"Can't complain. Lone Star just signed up with a home delivery service, so I've been living on nothing but cow for the last week."

"Sounds awesome," I said unconvincingly. "Hey…you didn't by chance decide to look up Kyrill, did you?"

"No. I was busy with a little thing called 'trying to make sure my sister's stalker isn't following her to a country that doesn't extradite.' And besides, I thought Pinkie already checked Kyrill."

"He did."

"So?"

"I guess I'm just feeling paranoid."

"Given what's been happening, that's pretty reasonable," Chris admitted. "Lemme take a look." I heard some clicking. "Wow," he said. "I'm looking at Kyrill's business page. Did you know that you can gold plate a polar bear?"

"I did not."

"Don't you think that would negate the whole point of a polar bear? I mean, under the gold, it could be any color bear. Who would know?"

"I guess *you* would know."

"Right." More clicking. "Okay, I can tell you right now that this guy isn't totally legit."

I felt a surge of panic. "Why?"

"Because there's no way that a Russian with a legit 'luxury home goods' business can afford a"—couple more clicks—"forty-meter yacht called *Boy Toy*. Classy. At least you won't have to worry about being molested."

I perked up. "Forty meters? Nice. And for your information,

luxury home goods can be very lucrative."

"Especially when they're packed with heroin," Chris said. "The boat is nice, though. And some pricey custom work too, looks like. Wine cellar, one hundred twenty-five thousand bucks. Hmm. How much wine do you need on a boat, anyway?"

"Well, he's Russian. So probably a lot." I frowned. "What are you looking at?"

"Nothing publicly available," he assured me.

"Oh, well that's a relief. What does he look like?"

More clicking. "Huh. No photos. How is that even possible?" The keyboard noises picked up in intensity.

"Pinkie says he has a wattle and won't let his photo be taken," I volunteered.

An edge crept into my brother's voice. "Yeah, well, these days keeping photos of yourself off the Internet isn't that easy to do."

"It doesn't matter," I told him. "I'll see him in a few minutes anyway. I was just curious."

"It does matter, Lora. This guy looks reasonably legit online—I mean, for a Russian—but how do you know you're meeting the same guy?"

"Because he got my number from a friend of Pinkie's who knew him intimately—and I mean that in the biblical sense. Because we're going on his yacht, and with a name like *Boy Toy*, I'm pretty sure I won't get on the wrong one by mistake." I dug out the folder Pinkie had given me. "Check this address," I said, reading off the address Pinkie had given me. "Is that Kyrill's address?"

Chris typed for a couple of seconds. "Yep. And man, you wouldn't believe what he paid for it. Makes New York look cheap." He sighed. "Look, I get it. The guy checks out. The photo thing still bothers me, though. I would have said before today that it was impossible for any rich person to keep personal photos off the Internet."

"Have you ever just considered the possibility that you might be wrong?"

"Obviously not," he said. "That would fly in the face of an entire lifetime of experience."

"Fine. Keep looking for the photo if it makes you happy, but focus on Clancy and Mom. I think you have enough to keep you occupied, right?"

"Yes, but I should warn you that figuring out what's up with

Mom is probably going to be way tougher than cracking into Clancy's phone. She never uses a computer. She doesn't even text."

"Try talking to her."

"Not really my strong suit," he sighed, "but I'll do my best."

10

After about an hour of stop-and-go traffic, we finally pulled up to Kyrill's city center digs. A fifteen-minute walk from Red Square, the location alone made it clear that Kyrill was one of Moscow's elite. The imposing Stalinist architecture, prominently emblazoned with carved hammers, sickles, and stars, reinforced the message, in case you were slow. A beefy security guard opened the door for me and led me over to the reception desk, where armed men took my passport and photo and made me sign a ledger.

As I waited for them to finish filling out paperwork, I looked around. If Kyrill was really from the "more is more" school of decoration, he was living in the right place. Everything here was crystal or marble or gold leaf.

I watched as a golden elevator door slid open, revealing a sleek woman in a red dress with high cheekbones, icy blue eyes, and bouncing waves of black hair that shone blue under the chandelier. Despite silver stilettos that must have been five inches tall, she moved smoothly across the lobby, prowling like a jungle cat. As she passed, she flipped her hair over her shoulder and gave me a superior half smile. Even the women in the building were shiny. Except for me, of course. After my flight from hell, I was feeling anything but.

The guards finished copying my passport, taking my photo, and giving me suspicious looks, and finally one of them led me to the elevator. He used a key to unlock the pad, and pressed the button for the top floor.

Upstairs, the security guard ushered me into a foyer that was obviously intended to display the owner's wealth and taste. The only furniture I had ever purchased had come with sets of wrenches and instructions in Swedish, but even I could tell that I was looking at serious money. Murano glass chandelier. Antique Chinese altar table. Baccarat vase. The view, however, was what really grabbed my attention. Overlooking the Moscow River with a panorama of the Kremlin's spires in the background, it was breathtaking. In a city with more billionaires than any other on earth, the cash required to outbid the competition was staggering to contemplate. Luxury goods indeed, I thought.

The housekeeper, a solid woman with a closed, unfriendly face, shuttled off to another part of the apartment to alert Kyrill to my arrival. I heard a door shut. Then another door, farther on. Then a third, which sounded as though it were a block or two over. I waited patiently. Maybe the reason rich people were so thin was because they had to do so much walking just to get around their apartments.

I was expecting Kyrill to look like Pinkie's usual school chums—chubby, eccentric, and sexually ambiguous—so when the actual Kyrill finally managed to make his way back from the wilds of his penthouse, my mouth dropped open in shock. Kyrill looked like no interior decorator I had ever seen, and given my profession, I had seen plenty.

Despite the gorgeously tailored suit, this guy looked like he broke knees for a living. He was over six feet tall and broad across the shoulders, with a well-trimmed black beard and wavy black hair kept longer than would be fashionable in the states. I closed my mouth with a snap and looked into his eyes, which were black and penetrating.

"You must be Lora," he rumbled, a slight Slavic accent coloring his English. "I'm Kyrill."

I forced myself to stop staring and plastered my best professional smile on my face. "Yes. It's a pleasure to meet you," I said, stepping forward.

Kyrill took my hand in his massive paw and squeezed it gently, as though it would break if he shook it properly. "Welcome to Moscow," he said. "I trust you had no trouble getting here."

"Not at all," I lied. "Smooth as silk."

"Good." He took in my appearance critically. I had managed to refresh my makeup in the car, but there wasn't too much I could do about twelve hours next to the seatmate from hell. Kyrill apparently agreed with my assessment.

"I am sure you will want to freshen up after your journey," he said. He gestured to the housekeeper, who had silently materialized behind me. "Nina will show you to your room. We will leave for dinner in three hours, and we can discuss the trip then. Please be on time." He nodded sharply and left the entry through the door he had come in by.

Okay, I thought. Not so big on the small talk. Fritzie had said he was quite charming when you got to know him. Apparently, I had yet to get to know him. But truth be told, after the flight over I was happy not to have to make stilted small talk with some socially challenged gazillionaire. All I wanted to do was chug a gallon of water and lie down on a surface that didn't have a seatbelt.

I followed Nina through a dizzying range of corridors, ending up in a beautifully appointed guest room with blue silk curtains and a sleigh bed that looked like something out of a fairy tale castle. An ornate carved golden mirror leaned against the wall. I had to admit that Kyrill's taste in décor, at least, was flawless. I guess that was to be expected in a man who nominally made his living selling good taste to the wealthy and tacky.

Latching the door behind me, I quickly stripped off my clothes, knocked back a bottle of water Nina had thoughtfully provided, smeared La Mer cream over my face with reckless disregard for cost, and passed out.

11

The alarm went off what seemed like five minutes after I had fallen asleep, and it was all I could do not to moan. I was the world's worst traveler. My mouth tasted of sand. My skin, I confirmed in the mirror, had developed a peculiar crepe-paperiness that I was sure I would see permanently in a decade. I had weird gumminess at the corners of my mouth and breath that could kill small animals. I opened another bottle of water and set to work laying out the tools of my trade.

In the ten years or so since I had left Delaware, my beauty routine had gone considerably upmarket. Cover Girl mascara and cherry ChapStick had been replaced by a who's who of the kinds of brands given out at Oscar parties. I pulled out the staples: Epidermal Growth Factor from Iceland. La Prairie eye bag reducer. Chanel eyeliner and eye shadow. Dior lipstick. Sisley foundation. Shiseido mascara. Bronzer. Blusher. Gel for the roots of my hair. Texturizer for the body of the hair. Oil for the ends of my hair, which had become brush-like on the flight over. Creed perfume. Cuticle oil. Hand cream. Spray oil. Deodorant. If I'd had to pay for all these potions out of pocket, I would have been the most dewy-skinned homeless person in town. Fortunately, Pinkie always seemed to be getting samples, testers, goodie bags, and other freebies that kept me maximally maintained for minimum cash.

I looked in the mirror critically. Pinkie told me that my eyes were my best feature, and I tended to agree. Depending on what color I wore, they could be gray, blue, green, or teal. I went through a bottle of mascara every two weeks. Eyelashes could never be too long in my book.

The rest of my face was, I thought, more problematic. Mouth was a little too full. Face was a little too round. Nose was ridiculously small. While the overall result wasn't exactly displeasing, I would have preferred a little more aristocratic elegance and a little less Japanese manga character.

My worst feature was definitely my hair. Baby fine, shiny, and soft, it fought all attempts to make it do anything except lie there, limp and stick straight. Even Pinkie had finally admitted it was hopeless. "Just put it in a French twist and leave it," he'd advised me.

I finished with my face and jabbed in a few pins to hold up my hair, then looked through my suitcase for something appropriate to wear for dinner with the world's most macho interior decorator. I came up with a charcoal silk shift trimmed with thin strips of python. The charcoal silk, I decided, said, "Elegant." The python trim and matching pumps were a low-key nod to the Russian aesthetic, which tended toward what Americans would term "trashy."

Standing in front of the full-length mirror, I checked out all of the angles. I came from a long line of women who started out plump and ended up patrolling the nacho aisle on Jazzy scooters. I hadn't quite figured out a diet I could stick to, but I made up for it by constantly being on some variation of one.

In preparation for this job, I had kicked off an intermittent fasting diet. This meant I could eat whatever I wanted on the trip then repent by spending a couple of days on green tea and boiled eggs when I got home. Of course, by the time the fasting part rolled around, I'd probably have to switch to low carb because living on boiled eggs and green tea sounded absolutely disgusting.

I sat down on the edge of the bed and checked my phone. No messages.

I dialed my mother. No answer. I waited until the voicemail picked up. "Mom," I said, "Chris sounded like he was coming down with something, and I'm a little worried. Can you swing by to check on him? Maybe you can bring him some chicken soup."

I switched off the phone. Even if my mother didn't tell Chris what was wrong with her, at least he'd be forced to eat something with more nutritional value than Red Bull and steak. I pushed down a lingering pang of concern and took a deep breath before leaving the room.

Kyrill was standing with his back to the room when I entered, looking out the window with a gleaming crystal glass of scotch in one hand. He turned when he heard me come in and scanned me dispassionately. I waited for the traditional "You look nice," which is pretty much what any civilized man says to a woman wearing lipstick and heels. Apparently, Kyrill had not gotten the civilized man memo.

He tossed back his drink and set it on a table, leaving Nina to silently scurry over to clear it before it could leave a ring. "Let's go," he said.

I smiled in what I hoped was a friendly manner and followed him into the private lift and to the front of the building. Five BMW 7 series were idling on the street, each with a dark-suited, thick-necked man attending it.

"Which one is ours?" I asked.

"All of them," he grunted, climbing into the rear of the middle car. I jumped in behind him, barely managing to get the door closed before the convoy pulled out into the street, cutting off several people who slammed on their brakes but refrained from honking their horns or otherwise expressing their fury. I guessed that in Moscow, honking your horn at five expensive cars driven by body doubles for the Incredible Hulk was a good way to shorten your lifespan significantly. Since the average lifespan for men in Moscow was already only slightly longer than that of a fruit fly, I could appreciate their caution.

I wrestled with my seatbelt as the cars moved swiftly through the city, using headlights and sheer intimidation to muscle lesser vehicles out of the way. Finally snapping it into place, I gave a small sigh of relief.

Kyrill waited until the cars were well underway then turned to me and unfastened my seatbelt. *Oh god*, I thought. *Pinkie, you scrofulous bastard, I'm about to be molested.* "My driver is very safe," he told me. "You don't need to wear a seatbelt."

"Of course." I gave him a stiff smile and tightened my grip on the door handle. At this point, we were weaving in and out of traffic with abandon. *Air bags*, I thought. *Air bags will probably save me when we crash.*

"We should talk about this trip," Kyrill said bluntly. "I will be helping to arrange the transport of certain…items from Bulgaria to Russia. The shipping company that has asked for my assistance is based in Greece. This kind of business is very sensitive, so we need to have trust between us before we help their merchandise"—he said, holding up a finger—"come into our country." He made an O with his other hand and demonstrated the placement of their merchandise into his country, repeatedly, in a gesture that brought back vivid memories of smutty little Jimmy Brunhammer's explanation of sex in third grade.

"I understand," I said, trying to avoid looking at his thrusting fingers.

"Security for these discussions is the most important thing. When we are talking about business, we must not be disturbed."

"I understand," I said. I didn't really. How top secret could coffee tables and armoires be?

"Interior decoration is a very competitive business," Kyrill said, perhaps picking up on my skepticism.

"Of course," I said, glad I had boned up on the competition. "You wouldn't want Geoffrey Bradfield to get wind of you were doing, right?"

He looked at me blankly.

"You know, Geoffrey Bradfield?" Nothing. "The billionaire's decorator?"

Kyrill froze for a moment then shook his head decisively. "Exactly. This is exactly the kind of person we must guard against. 'The billionaire's decorator' Geoffrey Bradworth."

I paused. Maybe I had gotten the name wrong. "Right," I said. "So what do you need from me?"

He nodded approvingly at my attitude. "I need you to make sure our guests are having a good time. I will be discussing business with Spiro, the head of the company. You will be responsible for keeping his son and his accountant entertained and relaxed. I think for a woman of your skills this will be very easy.

"You will also need to make sure that meals are properly done, that drinks are served…that kind of thing," Kyrill continued. "There will be staff to see to this, of course, but you will need to help them with timing and presentation. They are sailors, not waiters, and they are not accustomed to this kind of work."

"How many staff members will there be?"

"Because this business is very confidential, we will not have too many people on the boat. Just the captain, the chef, and Sergei."

I nodded, trying to hide my surprise. I was no expert, but I was pretty sure a forty-meter yacht would normally be running with at least twice that staff. "Sergei is the engineer?" I prompted.

"Sergei is…" he looked up as he searched for the word. "The lackey?"

"Lackey?" I repeated in some confusion. "Someone who just does whatever you tell them to do?"

"Exactly," Kyrill said, smiling. "A lackey. He does engineering, helps the captain, cleans up."

"Is there anything you need to tell me about the staff?" I asked, keeping my tone studiedly neutral. "Any concerns that I should be aware of?"

"No concerns," he reassured me. "They are good men. Loyal. But I do not spend much time on this boat, and like all sailors, they are lazy. Probably the furniture will need to be dusted. Maybe the chef needs some help to put together the menu and to get supplies. You will need to make sure we have enough alcohol. This is very important," he advised. "These Greeks are men who love luxury. They must be comfortable so that we can focus on our…business."

I nodded, privately wondering if his way of pausing every time he said "business" was an indicator of criminality or just a mannerism picked up from a James Bond supervillain. Either way, it was creeping me out.

"Can you tell me more about the guests?"

Kyrill grunted. "I am expecting three people. Spiro Alexandropou is the head of Chiros Shipping. I think you have met him, no?"

"At Armand's dinner a few months ago," I said. "How did you hear about that?"

Kyrill looked evasive. "Friends of friends," he said. "Anyway, he is the man I will be working with. We may spend a great deal of time in the salon, going over the business details. It's very important that we not be interrupted."

I nodded.

"He will also bring his son, Alexander, and his accountant, Howard."

"Do you know anything about Alexander and Howard?"

"They both work in senior positions in the business," he said. "That is all that I know. Oh, and Howard is American also, so you will have something in common."

"I presume that you will be introducing me as a friend?" The big difference between being an event planner and being an event hostess was that I was rarely represented as an employee. The rich were awfully keen to make sure they didn't speak to employees for one moment longer than necessary. Friends, of course, were a different story.

Kyrill bared his teeth at me in what I figured I was supposed to take as a friendly smile. "Not just a friend—an old friend," he said. "We know the same people, do we not? Fritzie was a classmate of your friend Pinkie? I'm sure we have been at many parties together. Perhaps we even met at one of them and just don't remember."

"It's possible," I said doubtfully. I really had been to a lot of parties since I had known Pinkie. I thought I would have remembered someone like Kyrill, though. He didn't look like your typical globe-trotting socialite. It was easier to picture him downing vodka with the Russian equivalent of the Hells Angels than swapping witty banter with the beautiful and useless.

Kyrill nodded briskly. "Good," he said. "I am not a man who enjoys talking. I was raised to be a man of action, not to sit around chattering like an old woman. But Greeks..." He shrugged his shoulders. "They love to talk. They are always talking and talking and talking. Fine, that's what they like; you talk to them. I want to see what kind of men they are. They will talk. I will listen."

I nodded. "Is there anyone else I need to aware of? Girls, perhaps?"

"No girls," he grunted. "This is serious business. This is why I looked for someone like you." He waved his hand vaguely, searching for the word. "Old."

Oof. That hurt. Thirty is not old unless you're eighteen or a pedophile, I thought, but I smiled tersely and let it slide.

"Should I assume that drinking will be an important part of this meeting?"

Kyrill's stern face cracked in an improbably impish smile. "I never trust a man who will not drink with me," he said. He cocked an eyebrow at me. "Or a woman, for that matter."

"In vino veritas," I agreed.

He stared at me flatly, all traces of momentary charm erased. "I don't speak Spanish," he said, turning back to the window.

12

Dinner was typical of high-end Russian restaurants, which meant a lot of mayonnaise, a lot of rare steak, a lot of vodka, and a bill that would have been a payment on a Porsche. I had a revulsion for mayonnaise that bordered on a phobia thanks to a rather unpleasant mayonnaise-in-the-Tennessee-summertime experience as a child, so I managed to control my genetically programmed tendency to snarf everything in sight.

Kyrill and I ate for a while in silence. Or rather, he plowed through two steaks, and I pushed my peas around in their mayonnaise sauce to make it look like I was eating. When he looked like he was starting to slow down, I made another attempt at conversation. "Russia is such a fascinating country," I said.

"Fascinating how?" he asked, taking another huge bite of bloody steak.

I scrambled for an answer. Usually when you told people that their country was fascinating, they were all too happy to pick up from there. Left to my own devices, I was a little adrift. Fascinatingly unable to create a functional airport? Fascinatingly willing to put up with a breathtaking level of incompetence? Fascinatingly wedded to a Cold War script that had been out of date for the last twenty-five years?

"Such a rich history," I finally managed. "I'm always moved when I read about the past in this country. So much tragedy. The

Russian people must be very strong."

"Hmmph." Kyrill snorted. "The Russian people are very weak. For hundreds of years now, they allow themselves to be oppressed. The boyars. The tsars. The Communist Party. And now the oligarchs. They will never stand up for themselves. And they believe that this makes them special…better. The idea that suffering brings you closer to god is the invention of rich people to keep poor people in their place." He took a particularly vicious swig of vodka.

"Rather an interesting perspective for a man in your position," I said.

He looked at me questioningly, and I waved a hand around the restaurant. The steak house was filled with Russia's nouveau riche, who were dripping with gaudy gems and blithely oblivious to the waiters scurrying from the bar to the kitchen and back with grim efficiency. "Not exactly a place that caters to the oppressed masses."

Kyrill flushed slightly. "Ah," he said. "Yes, I'm probably not the best one to talk about this."

"Not at all. Caring about the downtrodden is the new AIDS."

"It is a sexually transmitted disease?" he asked in confusion.

"No," I laughed. "It's the charity cause that everyone wants to be associated with. Just wait. This time next year, all of these people will be holding benefits for the poor of Russia. You're just ahead of the curve. What's the big charity here now?"

He looked a little uncomfortable. "Russians are not really so big on charity," he said. "I have heard about some people giving money to the dogs."

"The dogs?" I pictured a schnauzer holding a little tin cup in his teeth. "What dogs would those be?"

Kyrill warmed to his topic. "The subway dogs. Actually," he said, "Moscow subway dogs are very famous. Lots of studies have been done on them."

"They live in the subway?"

"They commute on the subway. Food is better in the city, but many people here hate dogs. Sleeping in the suburbs is safer. So the dogs sleep in the suburbs, and in the mornings they take the Metro into the city to find food. At night, back home." He smiled. "Russian dogs are very smart."

"Smarter than American dogs?"

"Oh yes," Kyrill said seriously.

"Why do you think that is?"

"Very simple. If American dogs are not smart, no big deal. Someone will feed them and take care of them. If Russian dogs are not smart, they starve to death."

"Rather tough on the stupid dogs, don't you think?"

"This is Russia," he said, shrugging. "It's tough on everyone."

"Well, at least your job lets you travel," I said. "I hear Prince Abdul's palace is lovely."

"Prince Abdul?"

I looked at his blank expression and felt a surge of alarm. Maybe I had been wrong about Geoffrey Bradfield's name, but I sure as hell wasn't wrong about Prince Abdul.

"I understand you decorated his palace in Dubai," I prompted, suspicion creeping into my tone.

"Ah." He blinked. "Yes." There was an awkward silence, and I tried to keep my face still. Pinkie had never been wrong about a client before, but something was wrong with this whole setup. Why didn't Kyrill know anything about his competition or clients? What was going on here?

Kyrill cleared his throat, clearly uncomfortable. "I prefer not to talk about clients. Confidentiality, you know."

"Of course. My apologies. Would you excuse me for a moment? Ladies room." I smiled winningly and picked up my bag.

Kyrill stood up and watched me, eyes narrowed, as I went to the ladies room.

As soon as I was in the bathroom, I shot the bolt on the door and scrabbled in my purse for my phone.

"Pinkie!"

"Lora? Aren't you supposed to be in Moscow?"

"I am in Moscow," I whispered. "But something's not right here."

"Well, it's Moscow, isn't it? 'Not right' is pretty much par for the course."

"It's not that. I mean that Kyrill, who you told me was arch enemies with Geoffrey Bradfield, didn't recognize the name at all and then called him Geoffrey Bradworth."

"Lora…"

"And Prince Abdul? I swear he had no idea who that is. And he decorated his palace, right? I mean, how do you explain that?"

"Lora, I know you've been under some pressure recently," Pinkie soothed.

"'Some pressure'!?" I hissed. "Clancy tapped my phone and broke into my apartment! Parrots are showing up on my doorstep! My mother is probably dying! And now I'm about to get on a boat with someone who is clearly not who he claims to be! And you think I'm under 'some pressure'!?"

"Your mother is probably dying?"

"I...yes...I can't discuss that now," I said. "Let's focus on Kyrill, or whatever this man's real name is."

"Look, Lora. You're being paranoid. Which is understandable. But Kyrill called Fritzie about you. Trust me, Fritzie wouldn't be fooled by an imposter. You're in Kyrill's apartment, right?"

"Right," I said. "But how do you explain the fact that he didn't know Geoffrey Bradfield?"

"Of course he knows Geoffrey Bradfield, Lora, but he probably didn't expect you to know who he was. Or maybe he didn't want to acknowledge him as being competition. These artistic types can be very touchy."

"He called him Geoffrey Bradworth," I insisted.

"Maybe it was a slip of the tongue. Maybe it's some kind of pet name. It doesn't mean anything."

"And Prince Abdul?"

"Well of course he's not going to talk about clients with you. The designer-client relationship is very personal. Would you want your designer blabbing about your love of IKEA and inability to coordinate your rugs and throw pillows?"

I set my chin stubbornly and remained silent.

"Look, Lora. What do you think is going on here? You think the real Kyrill called Fritzie, arranged to hire you, then gave his house and his yacht to some other person for the sole purpose of tricking you? Think about that for a second. It makes absolutely no sense."

I thought about it, juggling the pieces in my mind, looking for a combination that worked. I hated to admit it, but Pinkie was right.

"Fine," I said finally. "I agree that it doesn't make sense, but I'm still getting a bad vibe from this guy."

"It's the Russian thing," Pinkie reassured me. "They're naturally menacing."

I pictured Kyrill. "You have no idea. Look...I have to get back

65

to the table. You're sure that this guy is legit, right?"

"I'm sure," Pinkie said. "I mean, as legit as Russians get, anyway. You have to make allowances, you know."

I sighed, still not convinced. "And you're clearing up the Clancy thing?"

"It's on my to do list for tomorrow," he promised me. "It'll all be taken care of before you get back."

"Okay, Pinkie. Look…I'm sorry for doubting you on the whole Kyrill thing. It's probably just the combination of Clancy and jet lag that's got me on edge."

"Don't worry about it, darling. Just try to relax. You know I'm only a phone call away from you, and literally everyone who matters in the world is only a phone call away from me."

I let out a laugh. "Modest as always. I'll talk to you later."

"Ciao, bella."

I put the phone in my bag and looked in the mirror, forcing myself to flatten out the lines of worry that were etching my forehead. Pinkie was right. This whole Clancy thing had made me completely paranoid. I took a few deep breaths, forced a bright smile onto my face, and returned to the table.

Kyrill had finished his food and was tapping his fingers on the side of his plate impatiently.

As soon as I had seated myself, he started talking. "Listen. I will be getting up early tomorrow morning. I still have some things to take care of before we leave for Bulgaria. I won't be back until late, so you will be on your own all day. I will leave a driver and a car at your disposal. Just tell Nina what you'd like her to fix. She makes an excellent borscht."

"That sounds…wonderful.…" I said, groping around for a word that would fully encompass my hatred of borscht. "But if it's okay with you, I'll just go out on my own. It's safe, right?"

Kyrill shrugged. "Safe is perhaps not the best word for Moscow, but if you stick to the tourist places, you are fine." He pulled a business card out of his wallet and scribbled a number on the back of it. "If you change your mind and want someone to pick you up, call this number. Yuri will come to get you."

I tucked the card into my wallet. "Perfect," I said with genuine enthusiasm.

Kyrill looked at the carnage of peas and mayonnaise on my plate. "Are you finished?"

"Uh...yes." I gave him a bright smile.

"Watching your weight," Kyrill said approvingly. "At your age, this is probably a good idea."

My smile vanished. Clearly, this was going to be a long trip.

13

I got up the next morning to find that Kyrill had already left for the day. Nina laid out a breakfast of salmon, pickled onions, and smoked trout. I looked at it unenthusiastically. Something about going through the rest of the day smelling like burned fish didn't appeal to me. "I'm not really hungry," I said. She shrugged, making it clear that she really didn't care what I did.

"Will Kyrill be around later?"

"Kyrill out late," she said. "You want I cook dinner? Borscht? Fish?"

"That will not be necessary," I said, mentally shuddering. "I was planning on looking around downtown for a bit, seeing the sights. I'll stop at a restaurant."

I rushed through my coffee and headed back to my room, where I grabbed my bag and telephone. I pondered taking one of Kyrill's drivers, but after yesterday's hour in gridlock, decided that I was probably better off walking. Heading out of the building, I pointed myself toward the spires of the Kremlin and set off.

About two minutes into the trip, I was already questioning my decision. The paving stones were uneven, and every side street was clogged with cars that had been pulled up onto the sidewalk to skirt parking regulations. The Russians climbed, antlike, around the cars and potholes, seemingly accustomed to the obstacle course. Most of the women were wearing platform heels so high that I would have struggled to get out the door in them. I found myself unwillingly impressed.

The streets I was walking through had clearly once been beautiful, but neglect and exuberant use of stick-on advertising materials had not been kind to them. I was also puzzled to see that all of the fences and many of the buildings appeared to be gradually descending into a lumpy shapelessness. That mystery was explained when I passed by a team of men painting what had once been a wonderfully ornate cast iron fence. The fence was covered in mud from the spring, and the men, most of whom had cigarettes handing out of their mouths despite the cloud of flammable fumes they were working in, stoically painted over everything, relying on the sticky, shiny paint to cover the mud as well as the iron. Moscow paint jobs were apparently the urban equivalent of tree rings.

I had brought a Fodor's guide with me, determined to get maximum touristing in on my day off. After all, I didn't know when I'd be in Moscow again. Given the flight over, never seemed like it might be my first choice.

Red Square, Fodor's informed me, had originally been a marketplace, had become famous as the scene of those endless goose-stepping Cold War parades that left American schoolchildren cowering under their desks, and currently had the highest percentage of umbrella-toting tour guides in the country. The most famous building in the square was undoubtedly Saint Basil's, a Technicolor fantasy of domes and spires that looked like something Walt Disney would have put together after dropping acid. The book advised starting with Lenin's tomb, however, since lines in the summer months could take hours to get through.

At this hour, the line was relatively short, and after a brief wait I was ushered into the dark red bunker where Lenin's body had lain in state for decades. After the warm sun, it was cold in the tomb, and I crossed my arms over my chest.

A guard hissed at me in Russian. "What?" I asked.

He repeated himself. Apparently, whatever he was saying wasn't covered by my late night lessons in profanity, because I didn't get it. "I don't speak Russian."

He reached out and grabbed my arms, arranging them back down at my sides, tin solider style, grunting as he turned his attention to the person behind me, who had apparently snapped his chewing gum too loudly. Enforced reverence was apparently the order of the day.

Suitably chastened, we filed silently around the viewing room, which was dominated by a glass tomb with a tiny, sallow man inside. The design of the room allowed you to get quite close to the body, and I, like the rest of the tourists, peered intently at the corpse. I wondered what other people were thinking. Was it *There but for the grace of god?* Maybe *All hail our great national hero?* Or maybe the same, slightly less poetic thing that I was thinking, which was *How do they keep him from stinking?*

After we had completed our creepy little circuit, we exited the tomb and were shuttled down the outside of the building, where there were busts of some of Russia's famous leaders. Some of the older women carried flowers with them, which they laid on the ground under the busts of their favorites. An adorable little babushka approached the bust of Stalin, which was littered with red flowers. She brushed away a tear and laid a red carnation down, crossing herself and muttering a prayer.

I sat down on the wall outside and pulled out the Fodor's. Apparently, the body of Lenin was maintained through weekly patdowns with bleach and monthly paraffin dippings. That explained the rather waxy skin pallor. After so many paraffin dippings, the guy was probably more candle than corpse.

Fodor's also had a section on Stalin, which noted that he was considered by some to be the greatest mass murderer in history due to a famine that he had created in the Ukraine. He had been a great one for purging, apparently. He had overseen the purge of Russia's intellectuals, then had purged the purgers, and had repeated this in cycles until he died in his bed of natural causes.

I looked back toward the little babushka who had laid the flower by his bust. She didn't look like someone sympathetic to mass murder. Unless flowers in Russia were the equivalent of spitting in the US, I was confused.

Wandering over to Saint Basil's, I bought a ticket for entry. Given the soaring domes and wild patterns, I expected something truly magnificent inside. In this, I was to be disappointed. The church was weirdly cramped on the inside and looked like it needed a good dusting. According to Fodor's, the church was dedicated to Saint Basil, who was apparently best known for shoplifting and going around naked except for a bunch of chains. I guessed that if mass murder made you a national hero, it was only fitting that thievery and sexual deviance would make you a saint. I was getting the hang of Russia already.

In fact, I decided, I had already learned so much about Russia that I could take a break from the churches and museums and get a coffee. I headed for GUM, the gilded age agricultural exchange that had been turned into one of the world's most exclusive shopping malls. In contrast to the relative dilapidation of the cultural monuments, GUM was booming. Gazelle-like young women wearing Pucci and Etro prints swarmed across the floor trailing fat old men with purses.

I climbed up the stairways until I found a café that afforded a good view over three levels of the mall, where I collapsed gratefully into a chair. The tour of dead and naked men had apparently piqued my appetite. I called over the waitress to order a large water and a salad.

"I'd like a glass of champagne and a strawberry sundae," I told her. She scuttled off to get my order, and I was left pondering my mouth's ongoing campaign to land me in plus sizes when I heard a voice call my name.

"Lora!"

I looked around in surprise, wondering who I could possibly know in Moscow, and looked straight into a pair of dazzlingly green eyes. Benjamin, my savior from the airport, was coming up the stairs behind me smiling broadly. "What are the chances?" he asked.

"That in a city of ten million people we'd run into each other again?"

"More like twenty million people," he said. "Do you mind if I join you?"

"Please." I waved at the chair across from me. "I was just having breakfast," I said, as the waitress returned with my order.

"An ice cream sundae and a glass of champagne?"

"Translation error," I lied, tucking into my sundae with relish. "I was totally trying for tea and eggs. Russian's such a tricky language. But how lucky for me that you showed up here! I am completely in the market for a little professional expertise from a professor of Russian studies."

"Adjunct professor," he said ruefully. "Hopefully professor someday. But happy to help, in any case. Have you been out

71

sightseeing?"

"Just started, actually," I said. "I saw dead Lenin and Saint Basil's, and I was just wondering where to go next."

Benjamin tapped a finger on his jaw thoughtfully. "Well," he said, "If you're really interested in seeing icons and churches, you could spend the rest of the day here. The icons in particular are wonderful. Lots of them have great historical importance."

I tipped my head. "That's incredibly tempting. Do we have any options that don't involve icons and churches?"

"Well, if you're in the market for nesting dolls or Soviet-era junk, there's always the flea market. It's definitely interesting, but the prices are outrageous. Apparently, years of Americans spending wildly at the sight of a hammer and sickle has spoiled them."

"Any place where a normal Russian might be seen?" I asked. "I took a look at the prices here, and unless Russia pays a lot more than New York, I assume this isn't where most people are spending their time."

Benjamin gave me a speculative look. "If you're okay with taking the Metro, I know a place. And if you haven't taken the Metro yet, you really should. It's a tourist destination in and of itself. If you don't mind me crashing your day of Russian fun, I'd be happy to take you."

"I'm sure my day of Russian fun will be even more fun if I'm not left to plan my own itinerary," I said. "You don't have work or anything?"

"Oh, tons of it," he said smiling boyishly, "but nothing that I can't blow off for another day. Just let me make a few calls."

14

I had been on the Metro in Washington, DC, and of course like most New Yorkers, I spent was more time on the subway than I would have liked. But the Moscow metro was something completely different.

"The Moscow Metro," Benjamin said as we descended into the Ploschad Revolyutsii station, "was supposed to be a cultural statement as much as a transportation network. The government at the time was headed by Stalin, and he wanted to prove to the rest of the world that a socialist country, where people were working together for the common good, could build something truly remarkable.

"Every station on the Moscow line is unique," he continued. "They're designed to showcase revolutionary ideals, Soviet achievements, local handicrafts, and of course revolutionary leaders."

"Lots of pictures of Lenin?" I guessed.

"Stalin too. For all their socialist ideas, the planners didn't forget who was paying the bills."

"Let me ask you something about Stalin," I said. "I thought Stalin was like the Hitler of Russia. Why are people still putting flowers on his grave? I mean, I'm pretty sure you'd have to look far and wide to find a picture of Hitler in Germany these days, and the little babushka I saw crying over the bust of Stalin had way less tattoos than the average neo-Nazi."

Benjamin shook his head. "It's complicated. A lot of older people in Russia remember the days under Stalin as a time when they were strong and respected in the world. Stalin didn't just build the Metro, he built a lot of what you see in Moscow today. The current government has also done a lot to rehabilitate him. And even everyday Russians have a long tradition of being able to overlook brutality at home if they think it's making them look strong to the rest of the world. They're not exactly big on electing nice guys, even if the elections were fair."

"Which they're not, right?"

"Right," he said. "So, here we are in the Metro. This station was opened at the end of the thirties and is famous for its bronze sculptures. They're supposed to represent the new figures of the revolution."

I looked around. The hall was massive, separated from the trains by low red marble arches. Tucked into the arches were life-sized bronze statues of people. "Wow," I said, trailing my hands over a discus thrower. "This is wild. How many of them are there?"

"There were originally eighty," he said. "There might be fewer now—they put in a new entrance a few years after it was opened. I'd have to look it up."

I flashed him a look. "And you call yourself a professor of Russian studies," I said. "I should report you to the university."

Benjamin led me over on a tour of the statues. "Let me see if I can redeem myself," he said. "Here we've got a member of the Red Guard. This one's a soldier. This guy over here is a peasant. You can't spit without hitting a peasant in revolution-era art. It's like kittens on the Internet."

"What's this one?"

"Ah. That one is a female parachutist. There's a gunner girl over there as well. Russian women are very tough, you know."

"I know," I said. "I've seen the shoes they wear."

He laughed. "I've seen women here in six-inch platform heels. Running. On ice. I'm sure there's some original academic research to be found somewhere in there."

I wandered around, looking at the statues. "Is it my imagination, or does everyone look really squashed?"

"Good eye," Benjamin said. "Back when the station was being

designed, the guy doing the statues and the guy doing the station had a bit of a falling out. The arches ended up being a lot more cramped than the sculptor wanted. There's a saying in Russia that the statues are perfect representations of the people under the Soviet system—always on their knees."

He led me over to a statue of a young man with a dog. "It's good luck to touch the dog's nose," he said. I thought of my mother. While I wasn't usually superstitious, I was willing to take help from wherever I could get it. I gave the dog's nose a dutiful rub and immediately wished I had a wet wipe. Who knew that hope could be so sticky and germ-ridden?

"There's also a foot you're supposed to touch if you're having problems with a love affair."

"We can skip that one," I said. "I'd need to have a love affair to have problems with a love affair, and things have been a little slow in that area recently."

"For some reason, I find that hard to believe."

I laughed. "Who knew professors of Russian history—adjunct professors"—I corrected myself—"could be so charming?"

He smiled. "It's the adjunct part. Once we get tenure, we become crusty old misanthropes. Are you ready to go?"

"Absolutely. Where are we going, by the way?"

"To the weirdest place in Moscow," he said. "VDNH."

15

The rattling of the battered looking Metro car made it difficult to speak, so we sat in silence as the train barreled through the stations, switching lines at one point to head out of town. As the train filled up, young men started standing up to give their seats to the elderly, women, and children.

"These guys should go to London," I shouted at Benjamin over the din of the train. "I had a girlfriend who practically gave birth on the Tube. She said nobody stood up until her water broke."

"I know," Benjamin said. "I've never figured out why the Metro is so much different than every other place in Russia. It's like everyone declares a temporary truce while they're on the train."

"How far are we going?" I yelled.

"Just a couple more stops. This is going to take us a bit outside of the center, but I think it's the best place to see the past and present of Russia really come together."

I sat by him in silence, happy not to have to make any decisions. I really was the world's worst tourist. I had no idea how I would have spent my time in Moscow if we hadn't met this morning, but searching WebMD for terrifying and incurable diseases that my mother might have would have been a safe bet. I felt a rush of gratitude toward Benjamin for the distraction.

When we finally got off the train and made our way back up to the surface, I could see that we were in a leafy suburban area. We followed along in the general direction of the rest of the populace and as we came around the corner, I caught sight of massive stone gates topped by what appeared to be giant bronze peasants.

"Peasants again," I said. "Now I know we're getting close to something interesting. Let me take a picture of you." I pulled out my phone.

"No chance," Benjamin said. "I'm not as photogenic as you are." He neatly whisked the telephone from my hand and aimed it in my direction. "Jeez," he said, "you look deliriously happy. Try to look more depressed, or nobody will believe you really took these pictures in Russia."

I pulled the corners of my mouth down into a scowl. "Perfect," he said, snapping a few shots. "Now look toward the horizon, and raise your fist at the capitalist oppressor."

I dissolved in laughter as he shot a couple more before handing the phone back.

"So what is this place?" I asked, slipping it into my pocket.

"VDNH," Benjamin explained, "was set up in the 1930s to showcase the cultures of the various Russian republics. Every republic got a pavilion, and there were also pavilions devoted to things like atomic energy and radioelectronics and stuff like that."

"Because who doesn't love a good pavilion on radioelectronics?" I asked.

"Exactly. There's a massive fountain in the middle of the thing that is simply choked with golden statues. It looks like something out of Versailles. And the pavilions themselves are just a crazy mash-up of styles. Domes, pillars, log cabins, you name it."

"What does VDNH stand for, anyway?"

"Do you speak Russian?" Benjamin asked.

"A little. Is it about drinking or having sex?"

"Nope."

"Then my Russian probably won't help," I admitted.

"It loosely translates to something like Exhibition of Achievements of the People's Economy."

I blinked. "That is the most communist-sounding thing I ever heard."

"I'm pretty sure this will be the most communist-looking thing you've ever seen," he replied.

We walked through the gates and into the main square where chubby little kids were driving electric four-by-fours with reckless abandon, creating a miniature version of the traffic chaos typical to Moscow streets. A rollerblade rental place on our right was doing brisk business. Ice cream vendors and hot dog vendors were set up next to each other to appeal to the children exiting their tiny gold Land Rovers.

"It's like a carnival," I said, snapping a couple more photos.

"There's an actual amusement park over there," he replied, pointing toward a gaggle of rides that appeared to be held together with rope and duct tape.

I peered over the other direction. "Is that a model of a space shuttle?"

"Not a model," he said. "A real space shuttle. At least so they claim...I've looked it over pretty carefully, and it does seem to have quite a bit of plywood on it."

"Given what I've heard about Russian construction," I said, "that seems like it might be proof that it's the real thing."

"Probably," Benjamin laughed. He gestured at a billboard plastered with liquidation deals ranging from mobile phones to fur coats. "This is also a great place to get your Christmas shopping done."

"Speaking of which," I said, "I wanted to pick up a gift for a friend."

"Like nesting dolls?"

I considered Pinkie's preferences. "Do you have something more in the line of a topless Putin riding a tiger?" I asked.

"Action figure or commemorative plate?"

"Ooh," I said. "Tough call. But I'm going to have to go with action figure."

Benjamin led the way over to a pavilion that had been converted into a low-rent mini-mall, where we passed by booths selling everything from no-name electronics like SANY to what I assumed was radioactive honey from the Ukraine.

We stopped outside a small booth with a tasteful collection of needlepoint. The fresh-faced young man behind the counter broke into a smile upon seeing Benjamin. "Benjamin! How's it going?" he asked in English.

"Can't complain, Ivo," Benjamin said, shaking his hand. He gestured to me. "My friend here is interested in your needlework. Do you have something in a partial nude with a tiger?"

Ivo grinned. "Nothing says 'Russia' like needlework," he told me, winking. He pulled a box out from under the counter, revealing dozens of G.I. Joe-sized action figures. He rifled through them quickly. Putin attached to a giant bird. Putin fishing. Putin flexing. Putin on a horse. Putin in a French maid costume.

"No tiger," he said. "Maybe topless and wrestling a bear?" Benjamin looked at me questioningly.

"Bear is good," I said.

"Polar or grizzly?"

"Grizzly, I think," I said, thinking of my brother. "Oh, and a Putin in a French maid costume for my friend Pinkie."

"Great eye," Ivo said. "It's one of our most popular models." He wrapped them both up and accepted my money. "Just for the record, you probably don't want to unwrap them until you're out of the country."

"Are they going to put me in jail for Putin action figures?"

"Oh no," Ivo said cheerfully. "They don't put pretty American tourists in jail for that kind of thing. They put dodgy Russian embroidery-sellers in jail for that kind of thing."

"Got it," I said. "I'll keep them wrapped. Your secret is safe with me."

I made a mental note to hide French maid Putin in a box of feminine hygiene products for the trip back. In my experience, that was the safest place to keep anything you didn't want men to look at.

Benjamin and I said goodbye to Ivo and went outside, strolling past felt yurts, an exhibition on sheep cheese, and a potbellied Spider-Man sprawled on a bench, smoking a cigarette and pointedly ignoring the small children dancing around him gleefully. Benjamin looked at me and raised an eyebrow. "What do you think?" he asked. "Better than Red Square?"

"Way better," I agreed.

Benjamin looked smug. "I know. It's like the USSR's greatest hits. Rockets, empire, pomp, and circumstance."

"And bargain prices on fox stoles," I said, gesturing to a sign with a deranged-looking fox wearing a fox stole. I quickly snapped a shot of the sign with Benjamin in front of it before he could object. "One to remember you by," I said. "So why do you come here? The French maid Putins or the fox stoles?"

"Neither," Benjamin said, steering us into an open-air restaurant that smelled of lamb and hookah pipe smoke. "I come here for this place. They have the best kabobs in town."

We collapsed onto giant cushions and I let Benjamin order for both of us. "Georgian food," he explained. "It's spectacular. I can't believe it hasn't taken the world by storm. Probably because people get it confused with food from the Georgia in America, which I think is mostly about fried chicken, right?"

"If you're implying that fried chicken hasn't taken the world by storm, I don't know what rock you've been hiding under."

The ice cream I had eaten for breakfast hadn't exactly done wonders for my blood sugar, and I tore into the food with abandon. I thought I had been exposed to literally every world cuisine, but even I couldn't recognize some of the dishes they came out with. "Walnuts," Benjamin explained succinctly. "They're in everything."

Once we had run out of steam on the walnuts, we chatted comfortably about nothing for a while. "So you live in New York, you're here to help a friend with an event...what do you do for a living?" Benjamin asked, settling back into his cushion and leveling his gorgeous eyes at me.

I sighed. "It's a little tricky to explain."

"Fetish porn?"

"What? No!"

"Arms dealer?"

"Wrong again," I said.

"Lobbyist?"

"No chance. Are those always your top three guesses?"

Benjamin smiled. "Only when people tell me that what they do is tricky to explain. I can see how those might be tricky to explain."

"No, it's not like that," I said. "I'm a hostess."

He raised his eyebrows. "Like the lady who seats you at Denny's?"

"No. Well, maybe. I help social events run smoothly. Like say you were really rich and you were having some business acquaintances over to your country house and you wanted to make sure that they were having a good time."

"I'd hire you?" he asked. "And what would you do, exactly?"

"Well, first, for an event like that you wouldn't hire me; you'd invite me. And you'd pick up my ticket. And you'd throw in some cash for expenses since I'd be helping you out."

"Very generous of me."

"You bet. And then I'd do a little research into your guests. I'd have your staff bring them their favorite drinks. I'd hang out with them and tell them funny stories about hobbies that we had in common. I'd hang on their every word and just generally make them feel like the most fascinating people in the room."

"I take it my guests are male?"

"Mostly," I admitted. "But not always. I do occasionally end up keeping old ladies company. Or unofficially chaperoning some of the wilder young members of the family. I once had to literally pry the sixteen-year-old niece of a charming old Italian gentleman out of the arms of the stable boy. She was not happy. It was like something straight off the cover of a cheesy romance novel."

"Sounds like fun."

"Sometimes," I agreed. "But those jobs are just a few times a year. Mostly I take businessmen out on the town, show them the sights, organize special dinners for them at restaurants...like a tour guide. Bread and butter hostess work, with some light event planning thrown in."

"You get to hit the strip clubs often?"

"All the time," I said, laughing. "The girls love me because I always tell the guys to overtip."

"I'm going to go back and have some stern words with my high-school guidance counselor," he said. "That's the most awesome job I've ever heard of. Can you actually make a living doing that?"

I tilted a hand ambiguously. "It's not a steady paycheck, obviously. But between the fees and the tips and the gifts, I do okay. Enough to quit waitressing, anyway." I took another bite of a delicious brown paste that I assumed was more walnuts. "How about you? Can you make a living as an adjunct professor of Russian studies?"

"Just barely," he said. "But enough to pick up lunch."

"That sounds like enough to me."

16

After lunch we walked around a bit more before heading back into town. "If you've only got a bit of time left, you really should see the Church of Christ the Savior," Benjamin said.

"Really? Some old church?" I asked. "My religious upbringing pretty much stopped at the Easter Bunny."

"It's not really a religious place," he said. "They only built it a few years ago, and it's the biggest, tackiest, most horrible building you can imagine."

"Wow...you make it sound so tempting."

"It's all about the new Russia," he said. "Government in bed with the church, petrodollars on display, designed to impress, and completely without a soul."

"They should hire you to write their tourist brochures."

He grinned. "I know."

"Okay," I said. "You had me at 'completely without a soul.' Let's see it."

The church itself dominated the skyline, which was hard to do in a city like Moscow where everything was designed to dominate the cityscape. Made out of white marble and topped by a massive golden dome, it was surrounded by a paved court completely devoid of people.

"It's supposed to be an exact copy of the church that was here before," Benjamin said.

"What happened to that one?"

"The communists tore it down to build a swimming pool. Most of the locals would rather have the pool today, truth be told."

We toured the church, wandering slowly through the marble halls. It was a ghastly pastiche of crystal and marble and ironwork and surly guards. Pinkie would have loved it. "The original cathedral took more than fifty years to build," he said. "This one took around six."

"How many more years do you figure it will last before chunks start falling off?"

"Oh…at least two or three."

I pulled out my phone and snapped a photo of a peeling column that looked like it would be one of the first to go.

"Gospozhitsa!" a voice snapped out.

"Here we go," Benjamin sighed.

"What did I do?"

"You're technically not allowed to take pictures here," Benjamin said in a low voice. "They don't usually care, but apparently you were lucky enough to find the only church museum guard in town who still believes that cameras have the power to steal souls."

"I thought this church didn't have a soul," I whispered.

"Actually, he's probably more afraid that your photos will steal the revenue from the official souvenir book," Benjamin whispered back.

The guard approached us, a scowl on his face. "Telephone."

"He wants my phone?" I asked, concerned. "I need this phone."

Benjamin spoke to him briefly. "He won't keep it," he said. "He just wants to delete the picture of the cathedral."

I sighed in surrender and gave him my phone. He deleted the photo and handed it back, shaking his finger at me as he subjected me to a torrent of what sounded like highly irritated Russian.

"Do you need me to translate?"

"Don't take photos of our stuff?" I hazarded.

"See…you're picking up the language already," Benjamin said, taking my elbow to guide me away from the glaring guard.

We left the building, and I looked at my watch. "Jeez," I said. "This day has just vanished. I've gotta find something to eat, and then I need to get back. I'm catching a flight to Varna in the morning, and I need to be able to hit the ground running."

I looked at Benjamin. "This has really been a great day," I said, placing a hand on his shoulder. "Let me treat you to dinner."

"Absolutely not," he said. "But I will let you accompany me to dinner. I know just the place."

The place he picked out looked like a Cracker Barrel and was tucked under a freeway overpass. The sign, which I could not read, was surmounted by a picture of a bug-eyed man with a crazy look and a topknot.

"Taras Bulba," he told me. "From a story about a Cossack."

"War hero?" I guessed.

"He kills his younger son for treason and winds up nailed to a tree and set on fire, so yes," Benjamin said, "I guess he's like the Ukrainian version of a war hero."

"Do Russian stories ever have happy endings?"

"Well, they took a depressing story about a Ukrainian nationalist and turned it into a fairly decent chain of cheap restaurants," Benjamin said thoughtfully. "Some might call that a happy ending."

We slid into a booth and ordered. I wasn't hungry, but I had enjoyed the day and wanted to prolong it, even though I knew I should be getting back to Kyrill's place and getting some rest in preparation for tomorrow.

"Look, Benjamin," I said, after we had finished, "I really have to go, but I had a great time today. Maybe when we're back in the States we could meet up sometime. I know a really great hostess who can show you around."

He smiled. "I would like that."

"But right now I'm going to call my friend and have him send a driver," I said. "I think it's probably faster than taking the Metro."

Benjamin looked at his watch. "At this hour, you're probably right." I dialed the number Kyrill had given me and handed Benjamin the phone to explain where we were. After a few seconds of rapid-fire Russian, he hung up. "He said he'll be here in fifteen minutes. Why don't we take a walk around while we're waiting?"

We wandered out into the street. The sun had just set, and the energy of the city had changed. What in the daylight had looked shabby took on an exotic feeling of glamour and danger.

"Moscow doesn't really come alive until night," Benjamin said. "Most of these people work long hours just to have enough to get by. Living here is hard. Everything is so needlessly bureaucratic that just getting through basic daily functions is enough to sap your will to live."

"Like a perpetual trip to the DMV?"

"Exactly. A friend of mine here once got a package at the airport that took him a week to pick up. First, he sent his driver, then he had to come himself, then he waited in the line to prove his identity, then the line to pay for the duties, then the line for customs…"

"That does sound like hell."

"Well, the whole thing could have been avoided if he'd just slipped the first guy a hundred bucks."

"I freak out when I have to tip the bellboy," I said. "Figuring out how much to bribe an airport official would literally be the death of me."

I looked around. We had wandered off the main path and were walking through a block with some dilapidated buildings. I glanced behind me. Near the restaurant, the sidewalks had been full of people, but suddenly the streets were empty. "Are you sure this neighborhood is safe?"

Benjamin shrugged. "Most of Moscow is pretty safe, although you do run into the occasional bad element. But not to worry…we're just a couple of blocks away from the restaurant. We should head back."

I felt a prickle starting on the back of my neck and glanced behind us again. A large, dark shadow peeled itself away from one of the buildings to follow us. I tried to convince myself that it was just a local out to pick up some pickled fish for breakfast. There was no reason to assume the worst, right?

I looked back over my shoulder again. Whoever it was had drawn closer to us. The shadow passed beneath a street light, and I caught a view of arms covered with swastikas. "Benjamin," I whispered in alarm, "there's someone following us."

Benjamin glanced casually back over his shoulder and tensed. He turned around to face the man, pushing me behind him. "Can I help you?" he asked in English.

The man came to a stop in front of Benjamin, weaving slightly. His head was shaven, and a strong smell of alcohol came off of him, not only from his breath but seemingly from his pores. He took a step forward and regarded us through narrowed eyes, then let out a torrent of Russian directed at Benjamin.

Benjamin looked remarkably calm. He said something back, his tone low and relaxed.

I looked at the man. He smiled. Thank heavens, I thought. Probably just asking for directions or something. Still smiling, the man reached into the back of his pants and came up with a wickedly sharp hunting knife.

"What's going on?" I asked urgently.

Benjamin responded without taking his eyes off of the man. "He's drunk. He wants our wallets and jewelry."

My eyes were fixed on the knife. "Why don't we just give him our wallets and jewelry? I can live without a wallet and jewelry. I'm less sure that I can live without, say, my liver. Or my heart. Or any of my organs, actually, except possibly my appendix." I realized I was babbling and snapped my mouth shut.

"Well, that would generally be the right move," Benjamin said, "except that in this case I very much doubt he'll stop with wallets and jewelry. He seems to have taken a shine to you."

I looked up sharply. The man leered at me, showing a mouthful of chipped, stained teeth. My stomach lurched alarmingly, and I took a step back. A quick glance around showed me that the street was completely deserted. I scanned the towers of the decrepit apartment blocks, but in a neighborhood like this residents probably didn't spend much time staring out the windows, and if they did I knew they wouldn't get involved. Nobody was coming to our rescue. We were on our own. I looked again at the man, who was breathing heavily as he stared at me, one hand working obscenely in his pocket.

"Benjamin," I whispered, hoping the man didn't speak English. "We need to make a run for it. He can't catch both of us. Whoever makes it through can go for help." Maybe the man was too drunk to run. Maybe we would both make it out. I tried not to think about what would happen if he caught me. How long did it take to rape and kill someone? I pushed the thought down.

"Benjamin!" I hissed.

"We're not running."

"Benjamin, he's going to kill us." Clearly, Benjamin was in a state of shock. "We need to make a run for it, *now*."

"Lora, can you please be quiet?" Benjamin asked. "I really need to concentrate here."

I looked at Benjamin, who was five inches shorter than the man in front of him, unarmed, and wearing, of all things, a cardigan sweater with elbow patches. "What are you concentrating on?" I asked. "We need to run! Now!" I grabbed his arm to try to pull him into motion.

Benjamin shook off my hand and took a step toward the giant, his face breaking into a smile. Holy shit, I thought. This is how it ends. Raped and killed by a psychotic Russian drunk because some adjunct professor of Russian studies had been reading too many Captain America comics.

The man looked slightly bemused by this unexpected reaction, but he was clearly not concerned. I really couldn't blame him. Benjamin didn't look like much to be concerned about.

Benjamin grinned and said something in Russian. I caught the words "fuck" and "your mother." I felt my adrenaline ratchet up another notch. Benjamin was obviously insane. My mind was screaming at me to make a run for it, but I couldn't seem to make my feet work. I stood there, paralyzed, watching.

The giant roared in rage and lunged toward Benjamin, swiping at him with the hunting knife. I shrieked and jumped back.

Benjamin dropped his upper body to the ground under the knife and lashed out with a high kick. The knife flew out of the man's hand and went skittering across the street.

Bellowing in fury, the man threw himself at Benjamin, aiming to get him in a bear hug where he could crush him to pulp. I shrieked. "Watch out!"

Benjamin neatly sidestepped the lunge and tripped the thug while delivering a sharp chop to the back of his neck, using the big man's momentum to bring him crashing to the ground. Pivoting neatly in his Hush Puppies, Benjamin landed a vicious kick to the guy's kidneys then put his foot on the mugger's thick neck. The man was gasping and struggling to breathe, his eyes bulging. The whole thing had happened so quickly and cleanly that my jaw didn't drop open in shock until the very end.

Leaning over, Benjamin spoke briefly to the man. The man shook his head wildly then looked over at me and said something in Russian.

"Our friend here would like to tell you that he's sorry," Benjamin said.

I snapped my jaw shut with an audible click. "No problem," I said, my voice wavering. "Just a little misunderstanding." I leaned against the wall, as out of breath as if I'd just sprinted a mile.

Benjamin took his foot off the man's neck and took a step backward. "Go," he said.

Without a word, the giant lurched to his feet, still gasping, and stumbled off into the alley.

"What just happened?" I asked. I was trembling all over. I took a step back from Benjamin, wanting an explanation for what I had just seen.

"I'm sorry," Benjamin said, reaching out to take my elbow. "I should have stuck to the main roads. I was just enjoying your company so much, and I kind of lost track of where we were." He scanned the buildings. "We should probably go quickly. I wouldn't want to be here if he decides to come back with a gun."

I pushed aside my reservations and allowed myself to be led back the way we had come. "You mean you're not bulletproof?" I asked shakily. I meant for it to come off lightly, but the tremor in my voice gave me away.

Benjamin didn't appear to notice. "Afraid not," he replied cheerfully.

I picked up my pace, and we quickly made our way back to the main street. Once we seemed to be in a safe neighborhood, I turned to Benjamin and stopped him with my hand on his arm. "Do you want to tell me what happened back there?"

Benjamin shook his head. "That guy was drunk. Drunk guys have terrible reflexes."

"That guy was armed with a knife and twice your size, and you crushed him." My heartbeat felt like it was slowly returning to normal, and I resisted the urge to check my pulse. "I wasn't aware that being an adjunct professor required ninja training."

Benjamin laughed. "Well actually, when it comes to budget discussions, ninja skills are very handy," he said. "You wouldn't believe how sociopathic the English department can get. But no, the ninja skills are courtesy of my mother."

"Your mother was a ninja?"

"No, my mother was a helicopter mom, and I was the runt of the neighborhood. I had karate and judo from age five."

"Oh," I said, blinking at him.

"Yep," he said, "I could kill you with just this finger." He held out his pinky finger for inspection.

"Terrifying," I said, only partially joking. I took a deep, calming breath. "But seriously, thank you. I don't know what would have happened if I had been alone."

Benjamin's face darkened. "If you'd been alone, you wouldn't have been there. The fault was mine. I should have been more careful. I don't usually worry too much about what neighborhood I'm in."

"Yeah," I said, glancing back over my shoulder to scan for would-be murderers. "I can see why that wouldn't necessarily be a great concern for you."

We rounded the corner and found ourselves back at the restaurant, its bug-eyed mascot looking comfortingly tacky after the experience of the evening. One of Kyrill's interchangeable goons was waiting impassively by the car. He looked like someone who would just as soon shoot you as look at you. At that moment, I could have kissed him.

As soon as Benjamin caught sight of the man, he went rigid. "Yuri," he said neutrally.

I looked at Benjamin in surprise. "You know each other?"

"Yes, we do," Benjamin said. His eyes were locked on Yuri in a way that was far from friendly. I hoped I wasn't about to see another demonstration of Benjamin's ninja skills.

"Yuri works for Kyrill," I said, stepping in front of Benjamin. "He's my ride. No need to kill him. You don't even have to maim him. How do you know each other, anyway?"

Yuri looked impassively at Benjamin. "Yuri and I are old friends," Benjamin said. "Would you mind giving us a moment? It's been so long since we've had a chance to catch up. Unfortunately, he doesn't speak English."

"No problem," I said. I snuck a look at Yuri. He emphatically did not look like an old friend. More like a murderous thug.

Benjamin reached out his hand and drew Yuri close, a flat smile fixed on his face. He spoke quickly, and I strained to hear. Given the expression on both of their faces, I figured a Russian vocabulary that revolved around profanity might actually serve me well.

I didn't catch the words, but whatever Benjamin said didn't have the desired result. Yuri responded forcefully, shaking his head. He jerked his chin at Benjamin, which I was pretty sure was international for "fuck off."

Benjamin leaned forward over their still-clasped hands, his green eyes glittering. His face suddenly looked cold and menacing. Another low torrent of Russian, and then he leaned back, smiling tightly. He thumped Yuri once on the shoulder in a way that would have been friendly, had it not been hard enough to leave a bruise.

"Yuri and I used to spend a lot of time together," he said. "But it's been a while. Perhaps we'll be seeing more of each other in the future."

I looked at Benjamin closely. I hadn't quite figured out whether Kyrill was legit, but it didn't take a brain surgeon to realize that Yuri was just what he looked like—hired muscle. I couldn't imagine the circumstances under which an adjunct professor of Russian studies was spending "a lot of time" with someone whose job description included the words "shoot to kill."

I felt a thread of suspicion worm its way into my brain. "Really," I said, my voice cool. "How do you know each other? Exactly?"

Benjamin's eyes narrowed slightly at my tone. The friendly adjunct professor I had spent the day with vanished for just a moment, and I took an involuntary step back.

"We go to the same gym," he said. "Martial arts." He gave me a boyish smile that didn't quite reach his eyes.

"I see," I said. If Benjamin were training with guys like Yuri, I could understand his confidence with the mugger. Something told me that practicing judo in a Russian school filled with Mafia and bodyguards probably prepared you a little better for a real fight than your average suburban mini-mall tae kwon do school. Perhaps Benjamin really was just an adjunct professor who could kill someone with his pinkie finger—but I couldn't shake the feeling that there was more to it.

Benjamin looked at me steadily. "Lora, I know this evening didn't end up in the perfect place, but I wanted to tell you how much I enjoyed spending time with you today." He took my hand and held it awkwardly.

"I enjoyed our time together as well," I said carefully. "I really appreciate you taking time out to show me around today. I don't know what I would have done without you."

"Well, you probably would have at least managed to steer clear of drunken muggers," Benjamin noted, sighing ruefully. "But what I wanted to say was that I hope that when you get back to the

States, you'll give me a call. Let me make it up to you."

"There's nothing to make up," I said. I left it at that, not even clear in my own mind whether I would call him when I got back.

"Can we offer you a ride somewhere?" I asked. Despite my suspicions about Benjamin, Yuri was armed, and I knew Benjamin wasn't bulletproof.

"My hotel's right around here," he said, gesturing vaguely. "I'll walk." He looked at me intently, a slightly wistful smile on his face. "Goodbye, Lora," he said. "I hope I'll see you again. Until then, be safe. And remember what I told you in the airport." He glanced at Yuri meaningfully.

I got into the car and sat back as we drove through the empty streets of Moscow. The day had been fun, and I definitely found Benjamin intriguing, but the evening had left me with a vague feeling of unease that I tried unsuccessfully to ignore as our car wound its way through the gritty night.

I thought back to what Benjamin had told me in the airport. "Don't trust anybody." At this point, I wasn't even sure I trusted Benjamin. But tomorrow he'd be behind me, and I'd be alone with Kyrill and his guests. Somehow that didn't make me feel any better.

17

I was asleep when Kyrill got in that evening, but at eight o'clock the next day I found him in the dining room tucking into a plate of palachinki and jam. Despite his fresh-pressed suit, he looked tired, as if he hadn't gotten much sleep the night before. Relieved that it wasn't fish for breakfast again, I attacked a plate of pancakes with relish. A good night's sleep had eased my mind, and I was ready to get to work.

Kyrill watched me eat, his face impassive. "Did you manage to find your way around Moscow alone yesterday?"

"Luckily, it didn't come to that," I said. "I ran into someone I met at the airport at GUM, and he showed me around."

Kyrill grunted noncommittally. "Did you enjoy the city?"

"Well, except for the part where I almost got raped and killed, yes."

Kyrill looked up from his pancakes. "You almost got killed?"

"And raped," I reminded him. "We were just walking around, waiting for Yuri, when this gigantic guy came out of the alley with a knife and mugged us."

Kyrill's face darkened. "Mugged you?! What happened?"

"Benjamin—the guy from the airport—kicked him and threw him on the ground, and the guy ran away." I pictured the scene in my mind. It still seemed unreal. "Benjamin really doesn't look very tough. It was like watching Mickey Mouse kick someone's ass.

Look, I've got a photo of him looking particularly not-ass-kicking."
I pulled out my phone and scrolled through the shots from
yesterday. The one of Benjamin was missing. "Dammit!" I said.
"That guard at the church must have deleted the picture of
Benjamin, too. Maybe he's planning on a tour book featuring
adjunct professors and disturbing fur coat ads."

Kyrill looked at me grimly. "You should not have been out
alone. From now on you must take a bodyguard everywhere."

"I wasn't alone," I pointed out. "I was with Benjamin. He
knows Yuri, apparently."

Kyrill's eyebrows shot up, and he snatched his cell phone off
the table. He punched some keys, glaring at me. "Yuri," he
snapped. I sat there silently as Kyrill barked out questions at Yuri
over the phone. As he listened to the responses, his eyebrows
lowered. Finally, he ended the call and turned to me.

"This 'Benjamin' that you were talking to is a very dangerous
man."

"That's what I was just telling you. And thank heaven, right? Or
I'd be lying dead in a gutter somewhere."

Kyrill shook his head. "No. Not just dangerous to muggers.
Dangerous to us. Do you think it is a coincidence that this man just
ran into you at GUM?"

"I, uh…" Suddenly I had to admit that it did seem far-fetched.
"I mean, he told me I should see Red Square, so it probably wasn't
a total coincidence," I hedged.

"Did he ask you about our business?"

I tried to think back. "I don't think so. He seemed pretty
surprised when Yuri came to pick me up."

"You understand my concern," Kyrill said. "This man—this
very dangerous man—shows up and attaches himself to you right
before our trip. Right before we begin top secret negotiations."

"I really don't think he's a threat to your interior decoration
business."

Kyrill scowled at me. "I don't think you are in a position to
judge who is a threat to my business. And why else would he be
talking to you? Is there some reason someone would be following
you?"

I swallowed, my mouth suddenly dry. My hand crept down to
my pocket, where my phone was. A thought suddenly came to me,
unbidden. Chris had said that if Clancy knew someone like the

Viper, he was in with some pretty serious people. What if Clancy had hired Benjamin to watch me?

I played back the time with Benjamin in my mind. The casual meeting at the airport. *Accidentally* running into me in a city of twenty million people. The fact that Benjamin could take down a guy like the mugger showed that he was more than just a weedy academic on the make. What if he was a private investigator hired by Clancy to keep tabs on me? The more I thought about, the more sense it made.

My face must have betrayed my thoughts because Kyrill's gaze suddenly became suspicious.

"*Is* there some reason someone would be following you?" he asked again.

I snapped to my senses, realizing that disclosing a deranged stalker with connections to the criminal underworld was probably not the best selling proposition for a hostess who was supposed to be managing very confidential business. Plus, if my suspicions were correct, the safest place for me to be was on Kyrill's boat, where none of Clancy's hired thugs could reach me. What could I tell Kyrill that would set his mind at ease?

"There's no reason anyone would be following me," I said. That much, at least was completely true. "But I do think Benjamin came to Red Square hoping he'd run into me."

"Because he is interested in our business."

"Because he was hoping to find some romance," I said.

Kyrill looked unconvinced.

"Haven't you ever found someone attractive and tried to turn up where you thought they might be?"

"No."

I shrugged. "Well, believe it or not, it happens a lot. Benjamin is no threat."

Kyrill looked at me, considering. "You may be right, Lora, but I will tell you that a man who wants to find some romance can still be a very dangerous man."

I thought of Clancy. "I'm not arguing the point. But trust me—I'm a great judge of character, and Benjamin's a good guy." I smiled winningly, hoping that my confident lie was enough to put this topic to rest.

Kyrill's mouth tweaked. "Really? If you're such a good judge of character, am I a good guy?" He looked at me challengingly.

I regarded him steadily as I chewed my pancake. "I'm going to put you firmly in the gray category."

"Gray? Like *Fifty Shades of Grey*?" Kyrill asked, obviously confused.

"Lord, no," I said, blushing. Had everyone in the world read that book? "Like not black for bad guy, not white for good guy, just gray for normal guy."

Kyrill snorted. "Take a bodyguard when you are out in Bulgaria," he said. "I'm not so trusting of your character-judging abilities as you are. And if you see this Benjamin again, promise to tell me immediately."

"I promise," I said. On that point, at least, we were agreed.

He wolfed another few bites of pancakes and looked at his Breitling. "We've got to go. The plane is waiting."

Kyrill and I headed out to the airport, where a small jet was waiting to take us to Varna, Bulgaria. I didn't know much about Varna except that it featured heavily in British package beach tours and had been the place from which Vlad the Impaler had left for England in Bram Stoker's *Dracula*. I was having difficulties reconciling those two in my mind. A pub filled with Goths? A castle filled with sunburned Brits?

As it turned out, there weren't any castles unless you counted moldering communist concrete blocks as castles. There were, however, loads of sunburned Englishmen wandering the streets. By the time we cleared the airport and made it downtown, it was 11 a.m., and the streets were already crammed with tubby, peeling Liverpudlians staggering around gawking at lithe young women playing volleyball topless on the beach.

I peered out the window as we drove through the streets. It looked like Varna had once been pretty, with graceful pastel art deco buildings lining broad streets, but lack of maintenance and the overzealous architectural attention of communist planners had left it as a collection of rotting, turn-of-the-century buildings rubbing shoulders with equally pockmarked concrete blocks. Parts of the buildings were swathed in nets designed to catch the plaster and concrete from decaying balconies and ornaments before they fell and crushed the pedestrians below. The combination of apathy and safety-consciousness was intriguing.

A few blocks away from the beach, the main pedestrian thoroughfare was lined with high-end shops and filled with mangy wild dogs that menaced the elderly and peed territorially on ice cream and cotton candy carts. Dangerously brittle-looking women in four-inch heels puffed away at toothpick-thin cigarettes as they tottered gamely through potholes and piles of dog shit, clinging to the arms of fat old men who paid their companions less attention than they did their cell phones.

We were booked into the Balkan Palace, which was the nicest hotel Varna had to offer. That, as it turned out, was not saying too much, and I wondered how a man who lived in the lap of luxury could tolerate a hotel that managed to be simultaneously unfinished and falling apart. I snuck a covert glance at him as we passed by the impressively mildewed fountains on the way into the hotel. He didn't appear to notice.

We entered the lobby, which reeked of carpet glue. Dizzy from the fumes, I collapsed into a vinyl chair and tried to minimize my breathing. When it became clear that Kyrill was the man paying for the entire top floor of the hotel, a frenzy of scraping and groveling ensued. I waited for fifteen minutes as the staff energetically typed on their keyboards and moved papers from stack to stack. I wondered what they were doing since they didn't actually appear to be making progress on checking us in.

Looking at my watch, I grimaced. I wasn't sad that we were here only for one night, but it meant that I didn't have much time to get the boat checked out, and what little time I did have looked like it was going to be spent watching the hotel staff try to learn how to use their check-in system.

"Excuse me, Kyrill," I said, tapping him on the elbow. "I'd like to get to the boat as soon as I can, in case there's anything I need to do." He nodded, shrugging. "Fine. Take Andrei." He jabbed his finger at the smallest thug in his collection.

"And if there is anything I need to buy, how shall I pay for it?" I prodded him sweetly.

He shuffled around in his pockets and pulled out a black American Express card. "Use this."

I raised my eyebrows. "Should I be working within a budget?"

"I don't care. Just make sure everything is perfect."

"Well, that certainly simplifies things," I said, snatching the card before he could change his mind.

I grabbed Andrei, and we jumped into a waiting Mercedes sedan. "Take us to the yacht, please," I told the driver. I settled back into the upholstery and looked across at my mini-thug. He stared back at me. I tried a smile. No response.

"Tell me, Andrei," I said. "Have you been with Kyrill long?"

He looked at me flatly through Ray-Bans. "No."

"How long?"

"Not long."

I waited for a moment for him to expand on this answer, and when it became clear that he was intent on personifying the strong, silent type, I mentally wrote off the concept of small talk and turned my attention to the rusting and crumbling buildings lining the road. Kyrill had said the purpose of the trip was to discuss the transport of goods from Bulgaria. It was hard to imagine what a luxury goods importer would be importing from this country. Moldy stucco? Incompetent repairmen? Feral dogs?

The mind boggled.

18

~~~

We pulled up to the pier. The boat, a Princess forty-meter yacht, looked spectacular from the shore, and I felt my spirits lift for the first time since leaving New York. The boat would be fine. The crew would be competent. I'd be paid ten thousand dollars to sit around drinking champagne with the rich and handsome heir to a shipping fortune.

"Hello!" I called out, approaching the boat. "I'm Lora Godwin. Kyrill sent me here to make sure the boat is ready. Hello?"

I got no response, so I walked onto the deck, my mute Russian shadow trailing behind me. I looked around in silence, my fantasy trip quickly crumbling into dust. While the furnishings had been chosen with the kind of care and over-the-top taste lavished on Kyrill's apartment, the similarity stopped there. Empty liquor bottles littered the flat surfaces, including the floor. Pizza boxes were stacked in the corners. Cigarette butts floated forlornly in plastic cups of stale beer. It looked like a fraternity house on Sunday morning.

"Hey!" A gap-toothed young man in a striped shirt had appeared at the door to what I assumed was the galley. "What you are doing on this boat?!"

"Ah, good," I said, striving for a professional tone, "My name is Lora Godwin. Kyrill has asked me to make sure the yacht is ready to receive his guests in the morning. And you are…"

"Sergei," he said, ducking his head and extending a none-too-clean hand.

I took it gingerly in mine. "Sergei," I repeated, giving it a shake.

I took another glance around. There was bird poop on the hardwood, sand in the rugs, and it smelled like...I sniffed the air experimentally. "Does someone have a cat on this boat?" I asked.

"Not cat," Sergei said. "Ferret."

As if it had been summoned, a black animal went streaking across my line of vision before pausing on the opposite side of the room to study me intently.

"Is that Kyrill's ferret?" I asked, unsure of my authority.

"It is captain's ferret," Sergei corrected.

"And where is the captain now?"

"He is sleeping."

The ferret, its beady eyes locked on me, raised one leg and peed defiantly on the carpet.

I took a deep breath. It seemed that menu planning was going to be the least of my concerns. "I suggest you get him," I said, breathing deeply through my mouth.

Sergei looked at me apologetically. "He will not be happy," he said. "Little bit vodka last night."

I took a menacing step toward him. "Get the goddamned captain up here now before I fire every person on this ship. And get that fucking ferret off of this boat immediately. I want every person and animal on this ship to be up here within three minutes."

Whether it was shock at my use of profanity, a quick glance at Andrei's silent and unsmiling presence behind me, or more likely, the crazy look in my eyes, Sergei scuttled off to round up the inhabitants of the boat.

The six men that assembled in the salon ten minutes later were a sorry-looking lot indeed. The stench of body odor and cigarettes clung to them, and from their bloodshot eyes and shambling gaits it appeared that many of them had spent more of the previous night under the table than at it.

The captain, an unshaven, potbellied man with fuzzy teeth and a particularly suspicious-looking mole under one eye, decided to go on offense.

"What is meaning of this?" he blustered. "I take orders from Mr. Antonov. Who in hell are you? You can't come on this boat and start ordering people around."

"My name is Lora Godwin, and I am the person Kyrill hired to make sure this boat was up to the standards he requires for his business trip tomorrow," I said. "Who are you?"

He drew himself up to his full height. "I am Captain Vladimir Sergeyevich," he said. "And Mr. Antonov did not tell me that I should take orders from you."

Thanks for making this easy, Kyrill, I thought. "Well, if you'd like, we can call Kyrill right now," I said, stressing his name to make it clear that we were on a first-name basis. I held up my phone. "I'm sure he would love to hear how his captain and crew refused to prepare the boat for the business meeting that he hired me to organize."

The captain looked as if he wanted to argue. He gnawed on the inside of his cheek indecisively. Finally, he dropped his gaze. "Of course, we are happy to do as Mr. Antonov requires," he said. "What is problem?"

"The problem," I said, "is that three important clients are going to be on this boat tomorrow morning. The problem is that the boat stinks. The problem is that there is a fucking ferret running around here. And I'm sure the problem is also that whatever you've laid on in the way of provisions is woefully substandard.

"But let's start by getting acquainted," I said. "Would you care to explain to me who these people are? I am expecting one captain, which apparently is you, one 'lackey,' Sergei—" Sergei ducked his head nervously. "Which one of these men is the chef?"

"Uh...none of them," the captain said. "Chef left two weeks ago."

I sucked in air. "Did you think to tell anyone?"

"It is no problem," the captain said. "Sergei here is excellent cook." Sergei smiled, embarrassed.

"Do you have any training as a chef?" I asked Sergei.

"It is nothing. I just put the food on tray and heat it...just follow instructions and is fine!" Sergei said cheerfully.

"What kind of food are we talking about?" I asked, feeling a panic attack coming on.

"You know...fish fingers, French fries..."

"Tater tots," one of the unidentified men chimed in helpfully.

"I see," I said. "Tater tots. And who might the rest of these gentlemen be?"

There was a pause as the men looked guiltily at each other and then at the floor. "Friends?" the captain tried experimentally.

"Friends," I repeated. "You've been treating Kyrill's boat as a crash pad for your buddies?"

The captain, realizing that discretion was the better part of valor here, remained silent.

"Hmm," I said. "Normally, I'm sure that would be a firing offense, but in this case I think you're in luck because you and Sergei need to make sure this boat is immaculate within six hours, and given its current state, I think you're going to need a few 'friends' to help you."

"Why six hours?" the captain objected. "We have until tomorrow morning, no?"

"Because I have to leave in six hours, and I would be stone cold stupid to trust you to do anything on your own. You can start at the top of the boat. Scrub the decks. Clean the walls. Dust the furniture. I will have a carpet steamer here within an hour, and somebody better know how to read Bulgarian instructions because I sure as hell don't."

The captain lowered his eyebrows and looked at me for a moment. I stared right back at him, which gave me an excellent opportunity to watch as two young ladies with long black hair extensions and short neon skirts crept off of the boat behind him.

"Two more of your 'friends' just left," I said. "I suggest that if you have any more friends on this boat, you either get them to help out or get out. Am I understood?"

"Yes," the captain muttered. He turned to his buddies. "You heard 'lady,'" he said, stressing the word "lady" as though it were the foulest insult in the book. "Get to work."

I took a deep breath and stopped to consider the situation. I was on a filthy boat with an incompetent crew. I had no chef. I had a freezer full of fish sticks. And I had six hours to fix it. Given the likelihood that Kyrill was into something dodgy, I figured there was a small yet not infinitesimal risk that I could be actually drowned for incompetence if I couldn't manage to pull this together. Maybe the best thing to do was to flee the scene of the crime. Surely I could hide out in one of Pinkie's friend's houses until all this blew over, right?

"If you'll excuse me for a moment," I said to the bodyguard, smiling mechanically. I walked into the salon, closed the door, and pulled out my phone.

"Pinkie!" I yelled into the phone. "What the hell have you gotten me into?!"

"Again?" asked Pinkie. "Fritzie told me he was gay...I didn't think it would be a..."

"He's not trying to sleep with me, you ass," I said. "This boat is a mess. The chef is missing. They have nothing but tater tots in the freezer. There is a ferret running around here peeing on everything. And the trip is tomorrow morning. I thought this guy was supposed to be renowned for his taste...this crew looks like it rolled straight out of a Third World prison."

Pinkie sighed. "Russians...they're so delightfully savage. Did he give you any money to get things ready?"

"Yes," I said. "I've got his credit card. It's a black AmEx, and he told me to spend whatever I had to."

"Oh," Pinkie said, considerably more cheerfully. "Then why are you calling me? The card comes with concierge service. Just call them, and tell them what you need. They'll take care of it."

"Really?"

"Of course," he said. "How do you not know this?"

"How would I know that?" I asked. "I'm not exactly in the income bracket for a black AmEx, you half-wit."

"That's your own fault," Pinkie sniffed. "If you'd just give Clancy Featherstone a chance, you'd probably have three black AmExes, and you could give one to me so that I could show you how to use it properly."

"If I had to spend time with Clancy Featherstone," I said tetchily, "I'd need black AmEx concierge service to find me a hit man to kill him."

"That might even work," Pinkie said. "They're really very good."

"For both of our sakes let's hope so," I said, hanging up.

19

Feeling considerably bolstered, I returned to the deck where the men were milling about doing nothing but muttering and shooting me evil looks.

"Clean the deck," I said. "You." I pointed to the most innocuous-looking man, who still looked like he ate nails for breakfast.

"Me?" he asked. "Why me?"

I held up my phone like a talisman. "Because Kyrill told me to do what I have to do to get this boat into shape. Because if you don't do what I tell you, I will tell him, and he will fire you, or— seeing as how you weren't supposed to be on this boat in the first place— have you arrested for trespassing. And that's assuming that he even bothers to report you to the police. Most Russians of Kyrill's type probably prefer to deal with this kind of problem"—I paused menacingly—"in-house. Are we clear?" I held my breath. I wasn't sure how Kyrill would take me calling him up to rat out his staff, and I really didn't want to find out.

"Fine." he said, taking the mop with ill grace.

After that, things went a lot more smoothly.

Aside from a full boat cleaning including rug shampooing, windows, beeswax polish, and extensive use of Febreze, the list of things that had to be done included the eviction of two additional prostitutes and the aforementioned ferret from the crew's quarters, replacement of two throw pillows with mysterious crusty stains on them, and wholesale removal of the bed linens, which were a cotton/poly blend with cheap floral, puppy dog, and in a particularly mysterious choice, Lightning McQueen patterns on them.

"Where in god's name did these sheets come from?" I asked the captain.

The captain looked at the floor. "We had to buy new ones. Other ones got…dirty," he said.

"Did you not think to wash them?"

He pursed his lips. "Very dirty," he amended.

I looked at him hard for a moment. "Fine," I said. I really didn't want any more detail than that.

With the cleaning under control, I went down to the galley to check on the supplies. The liquor cabinet had apparently been refurbished by the same people who had done the buying for the sheets. The champagne was a local product that smelled like diabetic cat urine. The whiskey was improbably labeled John Walking. And there were three bottles of shocking red liquor called Draculina that came labeled with a naked, bow-legged female vampire cunningly twisted in such a way as to expose butt, breasts, and fangs. Pornography and alcohol in one portable package. Who said Eastern Europeans weren't inventive?

"Classy," I said to the captain, tossing him a bottle. "Get it off the boat."

The captain stroked the label fondly. "I will take care of it."

"Not *to your quarters* off the boat," I said darkly. "Off. The. Boat. You and Sergei will not be drinking on this trip."

The captain's jaw hung open. "That has never been rule on this boat," he said firmly.

"It is a rule on this boat until this trip is over and I am no longer employed by Kyrill to manage it," I said, iron in my voice. "It's three days. The second we hit Malta and our guests have departed, you can be as drunk as you want. Go out. Get wasted. Pick up hookers. Mainline heroin for all I care. But starting now, and for the next three days you are to be sober, courteous, and respectful. Am I clear?"

He narrowed his eyes at me as if imagining my gory death.

"Yes?" I prompted.

"Clear," he muttered.

"Something's missing," I said. "Wine. Where do you keep the wine? This boat is supposed to have a wine cellar, right?"

"Is downstairs. Next to cabins."

We headed downstairs to the wine cellar. I was keen to see what a $125,000 wine cellar designed by a Russian oligarch would look like. *Thirty bucks says there's at least two...no...four drunken cherubs,* I bet myself.

I opened the door to see a small space filled with climate controlled metal racks. I looked at the ceiling. No cherubs. The floor was a similarly uninteresting linoleum tile. I didn't know how much these big wine units went for, but unless I was very off on my calculations, Kyrill had been royally ripped off. I peered into a few of the units to check on the contents, sure they would have been replaced with bargain-basement plonk from the local megamart.

I was pleasantly surprised to see that in this case, at least, the crew seemed to have restrained themselves. I recognized enough of the bottles to be impressed. Lots of nice Bordeaux, some good wines from South Africa and California. I went to open the cabinet for the whites.

Captain Vlad inhaled sharply and jumped forward, smacking my hand off the case. "Not to open cases."

"Relax," I said. "I'm not going to touch anything. I just want to see what we've got here."

"Mr. Antonov is very clear, any crew member who opens cases is immediately terminated."

"Terminated like fired?"

"Terminated," Captain Vlad repeated, his voice dropping to a menacing hiss.

"Ah," I said, dropping my hand from the door. "Well, given the condition of everything else I've seen today, I'm sure that was a wise precaution. I'll talk to him about it when he arrives. I wouldn't want to be 'terminated.' Anyway, I'm happy to see that there's at least one thing I don't need to do today, because at last count, I've got two hours to locate five sets of high thread count linens, twenty bottles of Krug, four kinds of whiskey, vodka, tequila, ouzo, rum, and all of the fixings—and a chef."

"You cannot do all of that," the captain said spitefully. "It is impossible."

I pulled out the black AmEx card. "Concierge service," I said, waving it like a magic wand. "Watch and learn."

Two hours and fifty thousand dollars later, the larder had been restocked, a chef had been hired and choppered in, and the boat was, I thought, in good shape. The faint smell of potpourri from Grasse in France scented the air in the salon, the beds had been remade with Egyptian cotton sheets, and fresh flowers adorned the main rooms.

The men that assembled again (this time on the deck, where they could do a limited amount of damage) were sweaty, filthy, and completely exhausted. "Excellent work, gentlemen. Now anyone who's not Sergei, Captain Vladimir, or Jacques," I said, nodding toward the recent culinary school graduate AmEx had managed to hunt up, "can get the hell off this boat."

Muttering under their breath, the men filed off the boat, leaving me with the three crew members.

"Captain Vladimir. Sergei," I said. "I have arranged for hair appointments, manicures, and massages for both of you at the Balkan Palace. Your uniforms have been sent out for cleaning and pressing and will be back in your closets in the morning. I advise you to get a good night's sleep because tomorrow at 10 a.m., I will be back on this boat with guests in tow, ready to cast off for our trip."

"Jacques," I said, turning to the chef, "We've been through the menu, and I think you have everything you need. Double check it, and if anything is missing, make sure you get it before we leave."

Jacques nodded.

"For the next three days, there will be NO drinking, NO drugs, NO whores, and NO animals OF ANY KIND on this boat," I commanded. "Everyone is expected to take daily showers and wash your hands every time you touch anything dirty.

"The touching of any part of your anatomy currently covered by your clothes counts as 'anything dirty,'" I clarified. Sergei grinned and elbowed the captain, who did not look amused. "I am now going to go back to the hotel to meet and entertain our guests," I said. "If you need to say anything to me, I suggest you say it now."

I gave the captain a narrow stare until he dropped his eyes. "Excellent," I said. "I will see you all bright and early in the morning."

I glanced at my watch. Allowing ten minutes to get back to the hotel, I would have approximately fifteen minutes to get ready to be the charming international hostess Pinkie billed me as. I sniffed my arm experimentally. I smelled like hookers and ferrets.

Flopping into the back of the Mercedes, I pulled up the *New York Times* on my phone, looking for topics of interest that I could chat about with our guests. Given how tired I was, something all-absorbing in the news would be very helpful. Something like *British royal family all dies of food poisoning; succession in doubt.* That would certainly suck up at least an hour of the evening. I scanned the front page. Apparently, absolutely nothing had happened today anywhere in the world. Spectacular. I sighed and closed my eyes.

Andrei, who had trailed me all day, watching as I browbeat the crew, bounced out the prostitutes, conspired with the concierge at AmEx, and reviewed the menus with the chef, took off his glasses, revealing a remarkably boyish face.

"It is hard, your job."

"Thank you for noticing," I sighed.

20

As soon as the car pulled up in front of the hotel, I tore past the bellhop and into my room. Hopping on one foot toward the shower as I fought heroically against the spandex in my jodhpur-style pants, I managed a look at my watch. Thirteen minutes. "Dammit!" I panted.

I danced around in a circle under the shower, silently blessing the wax job that allowed me to skip the razor. One minute for hair and scrubbing, another minute for fingernails, and I was out. The hairdryer, as it turned out, had all the strength of a baby hamster blowing out birthday candles. I smoothed some wet look gel over my hair, twisted it into an upsweep, and savagely jabbed pins into it until it felt secure.

Quickly applying evening makeup, I grabbed an ivory cotton sateen sheath dress and a pair of tan crocodile sandals. Chucking the essentials into a matching clutch, I glanced at my watch. Two minutes left. I turned in front of the mirror, checking for hanging strings, panty lines, spots, and lipstick on my teeth. Flinging myself out the door, I stabbed the elevator button and took a deep breath.

When I reached the lobby, I saw that Kyrill had been joined by four men. The oldest, who I vaguely recognized from the dinner at Armand's place, was dressed simply in a white linen shirt and slacks. He was deeply tanned with sparkling blue eyes and a full head of white hair, and I saw a couple of the older ladies in the hotel giving him the once over approvingly.

"Ah, there she is," Kyrill said. "This is Lora Godwin. I've asked her to join us on the trip. Lora, this is Spiro Alexandropou. He will be our guest."

I cocked my head slightly to the side as I looked at him. "I do believe we've met," I said, smiling. "Armand's dinner a few months ago? I think we spoke briefly about one of your boats, didn't we?"

Spiro smiled broadly. "Of course, you are right!" he said. "What a memory you must have to keep track of even us poor old men."

I laughed. "I somehow doubt you're overlooked too often," I teased.

"Well," he said, "more often than you, I imagine. You were wearing a red dress. Very elegant."

"Impressive."

"Yes," he said, winking, "it was. What good luck that you're coming on this trip! How do you know Kyrill?"

"Oh, I know everyone," I said, waving a hand airily. "Kyrill's an old friend. We met through the school chum of a friend of mine. You know what a small world it is. When he asked me if I'd like to come along and help keep things running, I jumped at the chance to get away from the dreadful heat in New York."

Spiro shuddered theatrically. "I hate New York," he confessed. "Whenever we have business there, I send my son. Which reminds me—Lora, this is my son, Alexander."

Alexander stepped forward and took my hand. In his midthirties, he was fit and tanned with a square chin and the same brilliant blue eyes as his father. Where his father exuded a slightly naughty Old World charm, Alexander came across as flat-out sex on a stick—and he was clearly very much aware of it. "Pleased to meet you," I said, smiling professionally.

"I assure you, the pleasure is all mine." He quickly swept his eyes over my figure. "Really," he said. "Suddenly I have hopes that this trip will be much more interesting than I had expected."

"I'm sure your business discussions will be fascinating," I said, ignoring the innuendo. I turned to the next man.

"And this," continued Spiro, "is Howard, who works with us in our shipping business."

Howard was a soft, earnest-looking young man who was about five shades lighter than his companions. While Spiro looked as though he spent all of his time standing on a boat somewhere, intimidating longshoremen, Howard looked like he spent a lot of time with spreadsheets. "Nice to meet you," he said.

"You're American?"

"Yes," Howard said, clearing his throat nervously. "I've been living in Greece for several years now, working, but I was born and raised in the United States."

"Whereabouts?"

"Philadelphia."

"Ah," I said. "Pat's or Geno's?"

"Geno's Whiz wit," he said, looking suitably impressed. "You?"

"Prov for me. I overdosed on Cheese Whiz in summer camp one year."

Kyrill looked at us both as though we had gone completely mad.

"Philadelphia cheese steak sandwiches," I explained. "I grew up in Delaware. Howard and I are practically neighbors."

I turned to the last man, who was hanging back behind the others, watching silently. He was tall and bulging with muscle underneath his black button-down shirt and pants. The inky tendrils of a tribal tattoo crept up slightly over his collar. His hair was cut short, military style. His face was set in a polite smile, but his almost colorless eyes held no warmth.

"And this is Dieter, our head of security," Spiro finished.

I looked into Dieter's flat eyes and mustered a smile. "Will you be joining us on the yacht?" I was expecting only three, and I had no idea what I was going to do if Kyrill suddenly sprang another guest on me. Maybe he could sleep on a deck chair.

"He will not," Kyrill said, cutting in. "This is a meeting between future partners. Yuri and Dieter will rejoin us in Malta."

I extended my hand to Dieter, trying not to let my relief show. "Well, it's lovely to meet you anyway, even if it's just for this evening." He took my hand and squeezed hard, causing me to let out an involuntary gasp. I yanked my hand back.

"A pleasure to meet you as well," he said. He looked me in the eyes and licked his lips, his tongue darting out in a way that was almost reptilian. I took a step back and glanced over at the other men. Only Howard seemed to have realized what had just happened. His lips thinned, and he casually moved closer to me, forcing Dieter to take a step back behind the rest of the group.

"Wonderful!" Kyrill said, oblivious. "Now that we all have met, let's go eat. And more importantly, let's go drink. I have booked a table at the restaurant here. It's right this way."

"Dieter, I'll give you a call when we're finished," Spiro said, dismissing him. Dieter nodded and flicked a glance in my direction before turning on his heel and walking away.

"Germans. Terribly humorless," Spiro whispered, taking my arm. "But very detail oriented. I would never trust my security to a fellow Greek."

I nodded. Apparently, Spiro wasn't really up on the differences between humorless and sadistic. But since I wasn't going to see Dieter again, I didn't feel the need to enlighten him. We followed Kyrill down the corridor. "Tell me," Spiro said, breaking into my thoughts, "have you gotten much of a chance to see Varna?"

"Not really," I said. "We just got here this morning. I just saw it as we were driving through. It looks like it was once quite lovely." *As long as you don't mind feral dogs and getting killed by falling masonry*, I added silently.

"Maybe a long time ago," Alexander chimed in from behind us, "but now it's just lots of hideous apartment buildings crumbling into ruins and drunk Brits on cheap holiday packages broiling themselves and behaving badly."

"Hey," Howard objected. "Bulgaria has lots of really nice places."

"I wouldn't bet money on that," Alexander said, "but in any case, this doesn't happen to be one of them. Howard spent a few years in Bulgaria working for the Peace Corps," Alexander explained. "He knows more about this country than most of the Bulgarians. And he's more interested in spending time here than they are as well…most of the Bulgarians with any get-up-and-go got up and went as soon as they had the chance."

"Don't listen to him," Howard said. "He just prefers to spend his time in boring countries where nothing ever changes. If you want to see how real people live, this is a great place to be."

Having experienced plenty of how real people lived up close and personal, I had to side with Alexander on this one. "Well," I said diplomatically, "next time I'm here, I'll be sure to give you a call. Today I was pretty much occupied making sure the yacht was all ready for our trip tomorrow."

"Smart woman," Spiro said approvingly. "Why stay here on

land when you can be out on the boat relaxing? What a perfect way to spend the day—alone on the yacht, a glass in your hand, enjoying the breeze, the ocean all around you... There's nothing better in this world."

"Absolutely," I said, casting my mind back to the hooker evictions of the morning. "Nothing as relaxing as time spent on a boat."

"So tell us, Lora," Alexander said, "what is it that you do, exactly?" He raised an eyebrow at me, as if to tell me that he had his suspicions about my profession.

I waved my hand as if to brush off the very notion of paid employment. "Oh, a little of this, a little of that," I said. "Consulting, mostly. But when Kyrill asked me to join him for this trip, I couldn't say no. Work is always there, isn't it? But you don't always have an invitation to go sailing. And for someone like me, who really loves the sea, a trip like this is an opportunity not to be missed. *Adraxe ti méra*, right?" Pinkie had taught me that one over eyebrow maintenance, and I was happy to get it in early so that I could forget it again.

"Seize the day," Spiro translated. "A woman who loves the sea and speaks Greek! Kyrill," he said, "if your expertise in business is as keen as your expertise in women, I believe that this is going to work out very well."

Kyrill smiled smugly. "Let's hope so."

I turned my attention back to Alexander. "And what is it that *you* do?"

Alexander shot a glance at this father. "Account management."

"I see," I said. "And what does that encompass, exactly?"

"Alexander, he has the job that I hate," Spiro said. "He has to meet with the clients, take them out, show them a good time. These things are not for men like me. I need to be doing real work." He extended a calloused paw for my inspection. "I started out on the docks, saved up and bought my own boat, and today we are one of the greatest shipping companies in the world. But I am still a simple sailor at heart. I go down to the docks every day. I can't stay away," he beamed.

From the corner of my eye I could see Alexander's eyelid twitch.

"But of course, account management is also very critical," I said, trying to smooth things over.

"Of course!" Spiro said with enthusiasm. "It's just not work for real men."

A rage-filled choking noise, quickly stifled, came from Alexander's general direction. Given Alexander's ever-so-subtle implication that I was a prostitute, I was tempted to explore this topic in more depth, but since my job was to make sure the trip ran smoothly, I sacrificed my personal desires and switched the topic to the weather.

21

Dinner was a rousing success, for which about half of the credit was mine and about half belonged to two bottles of rakia, Bulgaria's local firewater. Bulgarians, having a tragic history in which they were conquered and occupied by literally everyone with a horse and a sword, had apparently fought back by moving their hard liquor to the salad course, where it hit hard and fast. While this dietary change didn't manage to save them from the invaders, it did have the advantage of making them care a good deal less. As far as I could tell, that complete lack of interest in what happened around them had served them well to this day.

Two hours into our salad course, I was feeling no pain and trying to protect my glass from the enthusiastic ministrations of Spiro, who had seized the bottle of rakia from the waitress and was brandishing it cajolingly at me whenever I took a sip of water. "We have all day tomorrow to rest on the boat," he said enticingly. "Have another."

The image of what was probably waiting for me on the boat stiffened my resolve, and I managed to keep myself relatively sober until the salads had finally been cleared and we had switched to wine.

Once the serious eating had commenced, Spiro and Kyrill began talking earnestly, leaving me with Alexander and Howard. Howard was showing his dish, cow's tongue in butter, a level of focus one generally associated with calculus equations. "You should try it," he said, offering me a sliver of meat covered in bumps and glistening with fat. "It's one of Bulgaria's signature dishes."

"No thanks," I said, shuddering internally. "I had tongue for lunch."

I turned my attention to Alexander. "Have you worked with Kyrill before?"

Alexander shook his head. "We've just started to get into the Russian market in a big way," he said. "It's very frustrating. There is huge demand there. Lots of money. Very sophisticated clientele. And rich Russians want what they want, and they're willing to pay for it, whatever it takes. But it is a very tough environment. The government sets up the rules so that you will always be in violation. That way they always have power over you."

"What do you mean?"

"Well," he said. "Say you are moving to Russia. The rules about what you must declare are very strict. Anything over fifty years old must be declared. Any original art. Anything made of natural materials like bone or stone or fur. You cannot bring any food or alcohol or pornography."

"What?!" I said in mock outrage, "I'd have to sell my furs and pornography?"

Alexander shook his head. "You'd have to sell your pornography and declare your furs," he corrected.

"Still."

"The point is that in a normal household, something is going to break the rules. A piece of furniture you got at a flea market may be more than fifty years old. You can't prove that it's not and they can't prove that it is, but if they say that it is, you're in violation of the law. Your rock collection might be tagged as natural specimens that you didn't declare. A drawing that your nephew did could be taken as original art."

"That's the craziest thing I've ever heard of."

"Actually, it's brilliant," Alexander said. "They will always be able to find something that you have done wrong, and once they've found it, they can charge you a fine or threaten you with prison or blackmail you."

"But they don't usually do that, do they?" I asked. "I mean, I've known people who have moved to Russia, and they haven't been harassed at the border."

"For most people it's not a problem," Alexander said, "and that's why nobody really pays attention to the law. If you're not someone they want to cause problems for, they won't bother you. But if you're a political dissident or just happen to annoy the border guard that day, they can make your life a complete hell."

"I think the IRS works on the same principle," Howard said around a mouthful of buttered tongue.

"So if following the law doesn't keep you safe, how do you do business?"

"Well, you know you're always going to be in violation of the law," Alexander said. "The trick is knowing which violations are serious and which are not. The little violations are usually a small fine. Just the cost of doing business. The big violations are prison time. Nobody wants to spend time in a Russian prison. But the government is only one of the obstacles. The Mafia is by far the more serious one."

"I guess you need to avoid the Mafia," I said, sipping my wine.

"Unfortunately, that is not possible," Alexander said matter-of-factly. "If you are making money in Russia, you are paying the Mafia. But you need to know who to pay. And you need to negotiate terms. You need a local partner who knows how business gets done in Russia."

"And you want Kyrill to be your Mafia wrangler?"

Alexander shrugged. "We will see. That's what this trip is all about. My father and Kyrill will talk about the business. They will decide which are the little violations and which are the big violations. We will all get to know each other. In a business like ours, you need to make sure that your partner is someone you can trust. Reputable. Discreet."

"I wasn't aware that the luxury home furnishings business required such discretion," I said.

"Oh, you'd be surprised what people keep in their houses," Alexander replied. "It takes all tastes, right?" He looked at me, eyebrow raised, as if challenging me to ask more questions.

"I'm sure it does," I said, refusing to rise to the bait. Chris's speculation that Kyrill was a heroin dealer was looking increasingly likely. I wondered whether heroin smuggling fell into the big violation or the little violation pot. Big, I would think, but then again it was Russia. Either way, it was the kind of business transaction I wanted to know as little about as possible.

Thinking about Chris reminded me that hadn't checked my phone since I had called Pinkie. Given the way the evening was going, I thought I'd better check in before we hit the after dinner drinks. "Would you excuse me for a moment?" I asked. The men stood up, and I picked up my bag and headed for the restroom, which was almost hidden down a dark corridor behind the bar. I locked myself in the stall and pulled out my phone. Nothing from my brother. Nothing from Pinkie.

I ground my teeth and reflected that my ability to deal with dodgy Russians and Greeks would be greatly improved by knowing that my mother was fine and Pinkie had convinced Clancy to stay away from me. I sent text messages to everyone, demanding updates, and dropped the phone back into my bag.

I washed my hands, checked my teeth, and started back down the corridor to the restaurant when I suddenly found my way blocked by a large man in black. "Excuse me," I started to say, but the words died on my lips as I realized it was Dieter, Spiro's head of security.

I looked into his colorless eyes, forcing a polite smile. I had spent a lot of time second-guessing my instincts in the past few days, but with Dieter I had no doubts. The man was dangerous.

"Dieter," I said. "I was just heading back to the table. If you'll excuse me…" I moved to right, intending to slip by him. He put an arm out to stop me, and before I could step away, he moved forward, pinning me against the wall.

"Don't run off so fast," he said. He locked a hand around my wrist, keeping me from doing just that. "I wanted to talk to you."

"About the trip I'm taking with your employer?" I asked, trying to ignore the fingers digging in around my wrist. I stressed the word "employer," hoping it would bring him to his senses.

Dieter's tongue darted out to lick his lips as he looked at me. "About something more personal. You see, I'm thinking that when this dinner is over, we should spend a little time together before you go."

"I'm afraid I really don't have time to spend," I said, striving to keep my tone level. "I have to prepare for the trip. We have an early start tomorrow."

He took another step forward, close enough that I could feel his breath on my face. His hips brushed against my stomach, and I realized that he had an erection.

"I think you can make time," he said. "I promise it'll be worth your while."

"I'm not interested in making time," I said, moving as far away from him as his grip on my wrist would allow. "And you're hurting me."

He pressed himself against me and leaned in to whisper in my ear, his breath hot against my neck. "I know." He squeezed my wrist harder, smiling as I choked back a gasp of pain. I glanced down the hallway, back toward the restrooms, hoping that one of Kyrill's security guys had picked that moment to pee. Nobody. We were completely alone.

I pushed down my rising panic and mustered a steely glare, knowing that exposing weakness would only egg him on. "If you don't let go of me this instant, I'll scream so loudly that the whole restaurant will hear it, and then you'll get to explain to Kyrill why you were trying to assault his friend."

He paused, and his eyes flicked to the bathroom door. I could almost see him weighing his chances of getting me into that room. I knew if he managed to get me behind that door, it was all over. Could I scream loud enough to be heard over the din of a thousand drunken Bulgarians? I took a deep breath and prepared to find out.

He glanced to the side, back toward the lobby, and suddenly dropped my wrist. He took a step back. "Apologies," he said. "You can't blame a man for trying." He smiled tightly.

I pushed past him and walked out of the corridor, not trusting myself to speak, tears of rage and relief blurring my eyes. As I walked out of the hallway, I saw what had caused Dieter to stop—a man was standing stock still in the lobby, looking straight at us. I blinked the tears back and felt a moment of disorientation as the man's face swam into focus. Was that...Benjamin? Before I could be sure, he turned and walked briskly toward the elevators.

I paused, wondering if I should run after him. If the man was Benjamin, my theory that he had been hired by Clancy to follow me was looking increasingly correct. On the other hand, being watched by Benjamin had just kept me from being attacked by Dieter. Maybe this was one time when letting Benjamin keep tabs on me was the safest thing to do.

"Dammit," I hissed under my breath. I stood there indecisively for a moment. I felt a prickle on the back of my neck and realized that Dieter was still lurking in the corridor behind me, watching.

The best thing for me to do was to get back to the dinner and say nothing, I decided. Tomorrow I'd be safely away from Dieter and Benjamin, sailing off into international waters with a boat full of people who might not be exactly good guys, but who at least weren't stalking me or trying to assault me. Taking a deep breath, I turned around and walked back to the table.

22

"So…ten o'clock tomorrow morning?" Kyrill said, looking around the table.

"Absolutely," Spiro said, his voice unslurred despite the vast amount of rakia he had managed to pack away.

"Sounds wonderful," I said, thankful that the meal was finally over. Since returning to the dinner, I had mechanically plowed through about a thousand calories worth of mushy baklava while trying to avoid the urge to rub my wrist, which still ached from Dieter's grip. While I had done my best to keep up my end of the conversation with Alexander and Howard, I had little idea what I'd said, and hoped I hadn't missed anything critical.

I said my goodnights and took the elevator to my room, keeping a paranoid watch around me for Dieter and Benjamin. I desperately needed a glass of water, a bed, and a very strong deadbolt so that I could sleep with both eyes shut.

After fumbling with the key card, I finally made it in, kicking off my shoes and feeling for the light switch as I cleared the doorway. I dimly registered a weird smell in the room, which, given the low standards of housekeeping around here, didn't surprise me too much.

My fingers finally found the switch, and I flicked it upward. As the light came up, I gasped, the jet lag and alcohol burned off in an instant. The room was trashed. One of the bedside lamps was shattered, the base lying discarded on the floor. Yellowed blocks of foam spilled from a pillow that had been virtually ripped in half. The mess was so extreme that it took a moment to register the figure on the bed. His clothes were black and shiny with blood, and his shirt had been ripped, exposing ropy tattoos crawling across his chest and up his neck. His colorless eyes were open, his face frozen forever into a sneer that was somehow even more menacing in death than it had been in life. Dieter. Dead. In my bed.

My first urge was to run, screaming for help, but I quickly stopped myself. I was in a strange country, and I was pretty sure that someone—Benjamin or not—had seen Dieter try to assault me an hour ago. Was I being set up? What should I do?

I quickly weighed my options and, grabbing my shoes, left the room and closed the door behind me. I could hear my breath rasping as I waited for the elevator. I glanced up and saw the red light of a camera. I looked at the floor, trying to compose myself. In the lobby, I made a beeline for the bar, scanning faces as I walked through the room.

My eyes fixed on Kyrill and Yuri. Thank god they were still there. I quickly walked over to the table. "Kyrill," I said, interrupting whatever he was saying.

"Lora," Kyrill said, surprised. "You came down for a drink?"

"No," I said. "I need to talk to you. Now. Alone."

Kyrill shrugged. "You can speak in front of Yuri," he said, moving farther into the booth to give me space. I sat down next to him and lowered my voice to a shaky whisper. "Dieter is in my room."

Kyrill raised an eyebrow.

I let out an involuntary hiccup of hysterical laughter. "He's dead."

"You killed Dieter?" Kyrill looked at me appraisingly before shooting a glance at Yuri, who looked, if anything, bored.

"I didn't kill him. I came into my room, and he was lying on the bed. He's covered in blood."

"Are you sure he's dead?"

I thought back to his glassy stare and felt another surge of horror. "Yes."

"Did you invite him to your room?"

"No, I didn't invite him," I hissed. I held out my wrist. Splotchy bruises were visible even under the dim lights. "He tried to assault me when I went to the bathroom during dinner. I told him if he didn't leave immediately, I would scream and he would have to deal with you."

"And he let you go?"

I nodded.

"And you didn't think to mention this?"

"I knew that if I told you, it would cause a big issue with Spiro and Alexander, and I thought I had handled it."

Kyrill snorted. "Apparently, you were wrong."

"There's another thing," I said, wincing. "When I got away from him, I thought I saw someone watching us."

Kyrill's eyes suddenly sharpened. "That is not good."

"It gets worse," I said, closing my eyes. "Benjamin. I thought I saw Benjamin."

Kyrill slammed a hand down onto the table, causing the tableware to jump. "You promised me you would tell me if you saw him."

"I wasn't sure," I said weakly. "It was just a glimpse, and I was far away. I thought I was just being paranoid."

Kyrill narrowed his eyes, tapping his fingers on the table as he thought.

"Should we call the police?"

He let out a snort that could have been taken as laughter. "A man assaults you, leaving you covered in bruises. An hour later, he's found dead in your room. And you want to call the police. What do you think the police are going to do?"

"I don't know," I said, "CSI stuff. They'll find the hair of the killer, and then they'll arrest them."

"They'll find *your* hair because it's *your* room," Kyrill said. "And someone will see those bruises and realize that you have a motive. This is Bulgaria. They're not going to ask too many questions when an easy answer is available."

I was silent. He was right. I was the obvious suspect. I felt a lump in my throat. I was going to spend the rest of my life in some Bulgarian gulag. I clutched Kyrill's arm, hoping for the first time that he really did have something to do with the criminal underworld. "What do I do?"

Kyrill signed the bill and stood up, tucking a cloth napkin into his pocket. "Well, first we should take a look, don't you think?"

Taking a look was the last thing I wanted to do, but I trailed meekly behind Kyrill as we went back up to the room. The hallway was deserted, and Kyrill leaned forward and listened at the door. Apparently satisfied, he removed the cloth napkin from his pocket and used it to turn the knob. We quickly went inside, closing the door behind us.

The room was just as I'd left it. I stood near the door while Kyrill walked slowly around the bed. "This wasn't planned." He gestured at the overturned lamp. "Whoever it was wasn't expecting him to be here."

He picked up a small black zippered case that was lying on the far nightstand. "Is this yours?"

I shook my head dumbly.

Carefully guarding his hands with the napkin, Kyrill unzipped the bag and reached inside. He let out a hiss of air and pulled out a roll of duct tape, a ball gag, and a pair of handcuffs.

I felt a wave of nausea hit. "Was that...did he bring that here?"

Kyrill shrugged. "I would say you had a very lucky escape. And I would say that a man who travels with these items is certain to leave behind many enemies. Or many corpses."

I bent over, putting my hands on my knees, trying to catch my breath.

"Don't be sick," Kyrill commanded. "It will make things much more difficult."

"I'm fine," I said weakly. I hung there for a few seconds, Yuri hovering over me nervously. I finally felt the nausea pass and took a deep breath. "So who did this?"

"It could have been anyone," Kyrill said. "But I would say that the most likely person is your friend Benjamin. He follows you here. He comes to your room, intending to surprise you. He finds another man is already here. He becomes enraged. I told you, Lora. Men in search of romance can be the most dangerous men."

"I..." I wanted to protest, but even if Kyrill didn't have the motive right, he probably had the right killer. I knew Benjamin was capable of taking on someone Dieter's size. I was pretty sure I'd seen him in the hotel. And if he had told Clancy that Dieter had attacked me, maybe Clancy had told him to make sure I was safe— by whatever means necessary.

I looked over at the black pouch and shuddered.

Kyrill followed my gaze. "Whoever killed him did you a favor," he said. "And I imagine that a favor like that is the kind a man likes to see repaid."

I darted a glance at the body, my gaze lingering on the hard, square hands. I rubbed my bruised arm and tried not to think about what would have happened if someone hadn't gotten to Dieter before I came into my room. "What do we do?"

"Yuri, check the hallway, and when it's clear, take Lora's bags to my room."

I held up a hand. "Wait a minute. I'm not really in the mood..."

Kyrill looked at me flatly. "You're not my type."

"Right," I said, flushing. "Of course."

"But you need an alibi, and what is more natural than that we should sleep together? American women are known all over the world for being very willing to have sex. We will just say that you slept in my room and never came here at all." Kyrill nodded, pleased with his logic.

"Uh..." I started. I fell silent. Now wasn't the time to challenge Kyrill's understanding of American women. "But what are we going to do about Dieter? We'll have to stay here for the investigation. It'll be weeks until we are cleared to go."

"We'll take care of it." He jerked his head at Yuri. "Get her out of here," he said, tossing him a room key. I gave a final glance back at the body and turned and silently followed Yuri out the door. Yesterday I had been convinced Kyrill couldn't be trusted. Today I was trusting him with my life.

23

I was woken up at six the next morning by a loud banging. I looked around the enormous room blankly, unsure of where I was. Then I heard a leonine yawn and looked over at Kyrill, who was stretched out on the bed next to me, shirtless and in pajama bottoms.

The banging came again and I realized it was coming from the door.

"Remember," Kyrill said, "you came straight here after dinner." He took a look at my wrist, which was now covered with purple splotches.

"Good," he said. "When I tell you to, tell them what Dieter did to you."

"But you said that would give me motive…"

"Trust me, Lora. Just a minute!" he called out, swinging himself out of bed and strolling to the door, stretching in a way that made him look just like a bear.

He opened the door and spoke briefly to the person outside. I couldn't hear what they were saying. "She's here," Kyrill said, opening the door.

I snatched the sheet up to cover more of my chest as a small, nervous-looking man and two armed security guards peered in at me.

"Well, that's a relief," the smaller man said, pulling a

handkerchief out of his pocket and blotting his upper lip. "But we'll need all the members of your party to come down to my office right away to discuss this terrible tragedy."

"Of course," Kyrill said. "Give us a few minutes to get ready."

He closed the door, and I jumped out of bed and ran over to him. "What's happening?" I whispered, cognizant of the fact that they could be standing outside the door, listening.

"Get dressed," he said, his voice loud enough to carry to the men outside. "We need to go down to the manager's office. Something has happened to Dieter."

I grabbed my clothes and shut myself in the bathroom, trying not to think about what was going to happen next. A dead man had been found in my room. Best-case scenario: I would end up in Bulgaria for weeks while they did the investigation. Worst-case scenario: I blocked that thought from my head.

Kyrill banged on the bathroom door. "Hurry up. I want to get this over with."

I opened the door, and he grabbed my arm, leading me out of the room. "Don't speak unless I tell you to," he said, his voice grim.

One of the security guards was waiting for us in the hallway, and he took us down to the ground floor and led us to a door marked Manager. He opened the door, revealing Spiro, Alexander, and Howard. Spiro gave Kyrill a suspicious look as we walked in.

"Thank you for coming," the hotel manager said. "As I mentioned to you, I'm afraid I have some bad news about another member of your party...Mr. Dieter Kappler?"

"Where is he?" Spiro asked, his eyebrows lowered.

"I'm afraid we found him this morning, murdered, in this young lady's room." He gestured to me.

All heads swiveled to face me. "I, uh..." I looked at Kyrill for guidance, but it was the hotel manager who came to my rescue.

"One of the hotel maids has confessed to killing him. She swears it was self-defense."

The room was dead silent.

"There were certain...items...found with Mr. Kappler that would indicate that he was preparing to...uh...assault...Ms. Godwin," the hotel manager continued, looking desperately uncomfortable.

"Certain items?" Alexander asked.

"Yes. A roll of duct tape. A ball gag. Handcuffs."

"A rape kit."

"I wasn't aware that there was a name for it, but yes. A rape kit." The hotel manager cleared his throat.

"Fortunately, Ms. Godwin had decided to spend the night elsewhere."

Howard looked at me, his eyebrows raised in surprise, and I felt myself flush.

"She was in my room," Kyrill clarified.

"Working late," I added.

Kyrill shot me a warning look, and I sat back in my chair, trying to look penitent.

"Unfortunately, our maid came in to turn down Ms. Godwin's bed, and Mr. Kappler attacked her."

"Attacked her?!" Spiro said. "That's ridiculous."

Kyrill sat forward in the chair, locking Spiro in his gaze. "I'm afraid it's not. Lora told me he tried to assault her earlier." He nodded at me to continue the story.

"Last night when I went to the restroom at dinner, he was waiting for me," I said.

Howard sat up straight, a look of naked concern on his face. I held my arm out so that everyone could see the bruises. "He grabbed me and slammed me against the wall. He told me that I should make time to see him after dinner. I told him no. He got rough, and I threatened to scream. He finally let me go."

Spiro and Alexander exchanged looks. Despite Spiro's earlier protestations, they didn't appear particularly surprised. "I won't deny that Dieter's relationships with women have been...problematic...from time to time," Spiro said.

I opened my mouth to object to the word "problematic" used to describe a sadistic rapist, and Kyrill squeezed my shoulder to silence me.

"But even if Dieter wasn't completely innocent in this respect, I find it hard to believe that a hotel maid could have killed him." Spiro continued. "He was a trained bodyguard and security expert."

I had to admit that I found that pretty unlikely as well.

"Who is this maid?" Spiro asked. "I demand to speak to her."

The hotel manager wiped his upper lip again. "She's being held by security until the police get here."

"Well, bring her in," Kyrill said impatiently, "We have a

127

schedule to keep to."

"I...uh..." The hotel manager looked like he wanted to object, but one look at Kyrill and Spiro, and he shrugged and picked up the phone.

The girl the security guards brought in a moment later didn't look like she could murder a man like Dieter, but she had clearly come close to being murdered herself. The V of her neck exposed by her polyester gray uniform was purpled where someone had tried to choke her. Her wrists and arms were covered with bruises. I looked her over in sympathy. She was hunched in on herself, her eyes darting nervously around at the assembled people. She had high Slavic cheekbones and light blue eyes that might once have been pretty, but her hair was a mousy dishwater color and her puffy face attested to an evening spent in tears. "This is Donya Slavova," the hotel manager said.

"This is the woman who killed Dieter?" Spiro asked, incredulous. "Look at her." He gestured at the girl in contempt. "I don't believe it."

The girl looked at him blankly, twisting a tissue to shreds in her lap.

"She doesn't speak English," the hotel manager explained.

"Ask her what happened," Kyrill ordered.

The hotel manager spoke softly in Bulgarian, his tones soothing.

The girl looked at us in confusion, but haltingly started to speak.

"It's like I told you," the manager said, translating. "She was doing turndown service. She came to Ms. Godwin's room with the cart. She opened the door and saw your friend. She started to back away, but he told her to come in and close the door."

The girl continued, her face crumpling as she went on.

"He waited until she was bent over the bed, and then he grabbed her around the neck and tried to force himself on her. She hit him with the lamp and tried to run. He was trying to grab her..."

The girl's voice rose in volume, and she mimed putting her hands up in self-defense.

"The cart had some dishes she had cleared from the hallway. She saw a steak knife, and she grabbed it. She stabbed him."

The girl's tear-streaked face hardened as she mimed stabbing down with the knife, over and over again.

I rubbed my bruised arm unconsciously. The girl ducked her head, causing her hair to fall forward, shielding her face from the men. In that moment, she looked straight into my eyes and gave me a sly, conspiratorial half smile. I stared at her in confusion, but before I could say anything, she swung her hair back and her face was again a mask of grief and fear. "Sorry," she said in English, reaching out for Spiro, plucking at his shirt. "Sorry."

The hotel manager put a hand on her shoulder to stop her. "I'm sorry to say this, but given what I've heard here, it seems to me that this is pretty clearly a case of self-defense," he said. "The police will have to be involved, of course. I'm sure they'll want to speak to you all. Especially Ms. Godwin, since she was assaulted by the man previously, and the attack took place in her room."

"Of course we would be happy to help the police," Kyrill said. I looked at him in panic. Was he going to leave me here?

Kyrill touched my knee, warning me to be silent. "But I'm afraid we are on a very tight schedule," he continued. "And Ms. Godwin must leave with us. Perhaps we could leave our information so that the police can contact us if required, although as you say, this seems to be a clear case of self-defense."

The hotel manager looked at Kyrill appraisingly. "Well," he said, "if you were to leave some sort of security deposit, perhaps…" He nodded at the guard and spoke briefly to him in Bulgarian. The guard dutifully took the girl by the elbow and escorted her from the room.

"What an excellent idea," Kyrill said, taking out his wallet. "Let us discuss. But in the meanwhile, I'm sure you won't mind if my friends leave. Lora is needed on board our yacht, and I'm sure these other gentlemen need to pack."

Spiro stood up. "Indeed," he said. "It is a great tragedy about Dieter, of course, but clearly he was a man with secrets." He turned to me. "I would never have brought him along had I known he was capable of something like this. I'm sorry, my dear. I hope you can forgive me."

"You can't hold yourself responsible," I murmured. Out of the corner of my eye, I saw Howard's mouth set in a grim line. Clearly, Howard thought Spiro was at least partly responsible.

"You have my personal condolences on your loss," the hotel manager said, barely bothering to hide his joy over the prospect of Kyrill's "security deposit." "Please enjoy the rest of your trip, and don't forget us next time you're in Bulgaria."

Kyrill looked at me pointedly. "We must be prepared to leave at ten o'clock." He leaned over and whispered in my ear. "I suggest you go directly to the yacht and do not leave until we get there," he said. "Just because the hotel manager won't hold you doesn't mean the police will feel the same way."

I nodded, feeling my heart leap. If this was the nicest hotel in Varna, I didn't want to see the inside of the jail. "I'll leave right now."

I left everything in the hotel room, trusting that Kyrill would find a way to get it on the boat. Had I not been in such a hurry to escape from the hotel, I might have been more worried about what I'd find on the yacht. As it was, given the choice between hookers and ferrets versus dead bodies, I was clearly better off on board. On the other hand, given the way the boat had looked yesterday, dead bodies probably weren't completely out of the question. I quickened my pace.

The hotel lobby was almost empty at this hour, and I scanned the couches anxiously, looking for Benjamin. What did one say to the man who had possibly murdered your would-be rapist? I figured even Miss Manners might struggle with that one. I didn't see him anywhere, but just to be safe, I made sure I asked one of the beefier-looking members of Kyrill's entourage to drive me to the boat.

Climbing on board the boat a few minutes later, I pushed my concerns about the police aside and tried to focus on the job. For the next three days, this boat was the most secure place for me to be. Free of stalkers, free of sadistic security men, free of Bulgarian police. For the first time in my life, I understood the appeal of leaving the world behind and sailing off into the lonely sea.

I took a deep breath, both to center myself and to check for any lingering traces of ferret. There was a distinct odor of…pancakes. I followed my nose to the galley, where Jacques had apparently whipped up a pancake breakfast for Sergei and Captain Vlad. He handed me a plate. "I knew you would be here bright and early. Here. Try them with the boysenberry syrup. I made it from scratch last night."

Several trays of hors d'oeuvres had been laid out to cool, and Sergei and Captain Vlad, trimmed, shaven, and respectable looking, were sitting around the counter tucking into breakfast.

"Good morning," Captain Vlad said, taking a bite of pancake.

"You all look very nice," I said, leaning in and subtly sniffing for vodka. Surely it couldn't be that easy, could it? "Everything okay with the yacht?" I asked, trying to keep the suspicious tone out of my voice. "Any wildlife I should be aware of?"

Captain Vlad had the good grace to look embarrassed. "Yes, well…we probably didn't get off on the right leg," he said. "Kyrill called last night and told me this trip is very important and we must be on our best behavior. He said that we are to follow your instructions as if they are his own."

"Well, that was nice of him," I said. It would have been a lot nicer about twenty hours ago, I thought uncharitably. On the other hand, Kyrill had possibly just saved me from life in a Bulgarian prison, so all things considered, I was going to mark us even.

I took a big bite of pancake, figuring that all the worrying I had done recently would probably have burned off enough calories to compensate. "These pancakes are excellent," I said to Jacques, who was hovering nervously as I ate. "Are we all on track with the food?"

"Of course," Jacques said. "We have all the ingredients we need for the menu. Also foie gras, smoked almonds, caviar, truffles…the basics."

"The basics," I agreed, casting my mind back to the Velveeta slices and bag of Wonderbread that had encompassed my understanding of the basics as a child.

"But we're still missing the champagne," he said, visibly worried.

"It was supposed to be here this morning," I said. "I wanted to get Krug, and it's not distributed here. It had to be brought in from Athens." I looked at my watch.

"Hoy!" came a yell from the gangplank. "Shampansko!"

"And that would be it," I said. I felt a surge of giddy satisfaction. Despite stalkers, ferrets, and dead rapists, I was going to pull this off. I was officially the world's most unstoppable event hostess.

I signed for the champagne and pulled out three bottles. "Put these on ice immediately," I said, handing them to Jacques. "I'll deal with the rest. Sergei," I said, "since you were doing the cooking for the crew, I assume I can trust you to help me manage the service?"

Sergei puffed himself up slightly. "Of course," he said. "You just tell me what I do. I also can help Jacques in kitchen."

Jacques looked down his nose at Sergei as only the French can do. "That will not be necessary."

Sergei's face fell.

"We can discuss it later," I said soothingly. "For right now, do you know how to open a bottle of champagne?"

"Of course," he said. He rummaged around in a drawer and came out with a corkscrew, which he held up triumphantly. Jacques snickered.

I sighed. "No corkscrew, Sergei. It's very easy. Just put the towel over the cork and turn while pulling gently." I demonstrated the motion for him.

"Why do you need a towel?" he asked, curious.

"On occasion, particularly if it has been shaken or mishandled," I said, "the cork can fly out of the bottle. It makes the champagne flat, and this champagne is more than a 150 dollars a bottle, so we don't want that to happen, do we?"

"No," Sergei breathed, taking the bottle reverently.

"It can also be dangerous. A friend of mine once almost put someone's eye out opening a bottle of champagne."

"That must have been very bad."

I smiled and patted his arm. Pinkie had been opening the champagne, and the man the cork had hit had been a particularly obnoxious drunk who had bullied his young girlfriend to the point of public tears. "You'd think so, wouldn't you?" I said. "But it turned out to be a very good thing. Let's just say that in this case, it was a 150 dollars well spent."

I made a quick tour through the boat, pleased that everything seemed to be in good shape. Going up to the top deck, I felt my phone buzz. I took it out of my pocket. My brother, Chris. Thank god. Maybe he had news. I looked at the phone. "No new hacks from the Viper, but Mom seems better today. She says to send pictures," he had texted. "We have to live vicariously through you, remember?"

I gave the phone a dark look. The fact that Clancy's black hat hacker hadn't made a second try on my phone was more evidence that he had hired Benjamin. Why watch the phone when you can watch the girl directly?

In response to Chris's request for photos, I moved to the front

132

of the boat and arranged a spectacular beauty shot of the deck, which was completely ruined as Kyrill stepped on board. I quickly sent the photo and dropped the phone into my pocket. Nothing says déclassé like snapping pictures of someone else's possessions.

I sent Sergei off to bring chilled champagne and joined the men on the deck.

I drew Kyrill aside. "Did everything go okay?" I glanced over his shoulder, half expecting a police car to be waiting to take me back to the hotel.

"It's handled."

"But what's going to happen to that girl? Do you think she really did it? Did you pay her to say that?"

Kyrill looked at me flatly. "I think you should not worry about this any longer," he said. "It's finished. Now you need to focus on our guests."

I looked at him searchingly, but couldn't read anything in his face. "Right. Our guests."

I glanced over at Spiro, Alexander, and Howard, who were clustered at the railing, looking at the view. Surely they wouldn't be in the mood to drink and relax after the death of their colleague.

"Lora!" Spiro said. "Come over, and let us have a toast before we embark."

I picked up a flute from the tray Sergei had brought and mentally shrugged. They clearly didn't seem excessively upset. Spiro raised his flute to me, maybe catching something in my look. "This thing that happened to Dieter was very sad," he said. "But we should not dwell on the past."

I raised my flute to meet his, reflecting that sad wasn't exactly how I felt about Dieter being preemptively killed before he could use his duct tape on me.

"Now we are here, on water," Spiro continued, "and we will have the chance to sail together. I can tell you everything about the ocean, the currents, the boats, the fish…you just ask."

I scrabbled around my brain for something I wanted to know about the ocean and came up with a complete blank. No wonder I hadn't ended up as a marine biologist.

"I'll be sure to do that," I said.

I turned my attention to Alexander, who was dressed for boating in white shorts and a black polo shirt. His bare feet were tucked into boating shoes. I would have thought that all my recent trauma would have put sex far out of my mind, but if anything it seemed to have had the opposite effect. Alexander looked, I admitted to myself, quite delectable. He caught me looking and raised an eyebrow. I turned away, pretending not to notice. *Note to self*, I thought sternly, *stop checking out the guests.*

I handed a glass of champagne to Howard. He was wearing white sneakers and a fanny pack and had his feet braced rather awkwardly on the deck, as if the gentle movement of the boat at dock was enough to make him fall over. His paleness was even more apparent here, accented by a streak of white sunscreen running down his nose. His glasses were smudged and seemed to be slipping in the sunscreen. "Do you spend much time on the water?" I asked him.

"Not too much," he admitted, clutching the railing with his free hand. "I'm mostly a desk guy. They just brought me along because I speak Bulgarian."

"And because we like you," boomed Spiro, thumping him on the back.

Howard smiled weakly. I hoped he wasn't going to get seasick.

"So," I said, "Kyrill, do you want to show everyone around the boat, or shall I?"

Kyrill waved a hand. "Please go ahead."

I took the men across the smooth teak deck and into the air-conditioned salon. Now that it had been cleaned and purged of ferrets, it was truly a beautiful room. Leather chairs gave a modern gentlemen's club feel, while pale artwork in creamy colors brought in a sense of light and space. Crystal accents sparkled in the morning sun. A small formal dining room was tucked into an alcove.

Howard looked around and smiled with a naïve enthusiasm that warmed my heart. Luxury, I sometimes thought, was wasted on the rich. People like Howard and me, who had grown up with vinyl-sided houses and chain-link fences, had the right context to appreciate a room like this. As if to prove my point, Alexander stifled a yawn. Apparently, the heir apparent was a little more accustomed to the good life than his accountant.

"I tell you, my dear," Spiro said, "this is a far cry from my first boat. It was just a fishing boat. I had to row it by myself. Back and forth across the harbor. I was delivering fish, you see..." I let Spiro prattle on, oohing and aahing in the right places and listening to

Alexander's little noises of irritation from behind me. Irritating Alexander was a strangely pleasurable pastime, and though I knew it wasn't very professional of me to keep doing it, I allowed myself a little bit as a reward for eating only two pancakes at breakfast despite the stress of almost being raped, killed, and arrested.

While Kyrill's entire preparation for this trip seemed to have been limited to hiring me, he had seen fit to assign the bedrooms. On either end of the boat were two larger suites. The one in front, furnished in delicate shades of gold and ivory that seemed out of character for such a rough-looking man, was Kyrill's.

Spiro's, in the back of the boat, had been done in shades of blue that evoked the Mediterranean. It was exactly the room I would have chosen for a Greek shipping magnate.

Alexander, Howard and I were spread in the remaining suites. Mine was next to Kyrill's, Alexander's was on the other side of mine, and Howard's was across the hallway by Spiro's. All of them had windows that let in the light and were decorated to the hilt in varying styles.

Howard's grin widened when I opened the door, and I couldn't help but smile back. His room had small touches that evoked the classical sailing age. He ran his fingers lightly over a globe. "I had a globe like this when I was a kid," he said. "I used to spend hours thinking about where I could go that wasn't Philadelphia."

"Is Philadelphia really so terrible?" Spiro asked.

"Yes," Howard and I answered back in unison. I flashed him a quick grin.

My room had a slightly harem-like feel to it, with a low bed stacked with silk cushions. "Nice," commented Alexander, peering in over my shoulder. I smiled as I looked at the opulent cabin then frowned as I realized that the cabin had connecting doors to both Kyrill's and Alexander's rooms. Someone apparently wanted maximum flexibility in the sleeping arrangements. Alexander noticed at the same time. "And convenient," he added, trailing a finger lightly over my arm. I subtly moved myself out of his reach.

"That must be your cabin, Alexander," Howard said, stepping between us as he shot me a conspiring glance. I rolled my eyes behind Alexander's back, causing Howard to stifle a laugh. Alexander gave him a suspicious look, but Howard merely blinked innocently at him from behind sunscreen-smeared glasses. *Good have someone from the neighborhood on board*, I thought.

Alexander's cabin, which had been previously fitted with the aforementioned Lightning McQueen sheets, was a deep sage green with a colonial tropical feel, most explicitly expressed in the presence of several brass monkeys supporting lamps, holding up bedposts, and otherwise making themselves useful. "I call this the monkey suite," I said.

"Perfect for you, Alexander," Spiro chortled, thumping him across the shoulders.

I looked over at Kyrill, who had been trailing at the back of the group as we made the tour. "Shall we let people get settled in?"

"Yes," Kyrill responded. "We can meet upstairs when everyone is ready."

"Great. One more thing, Kyrill," I said as the guests headed to their rooms. "I have a list of proposed wine pairings from the chef, but Captain Vlad told me I wasn't supposed to open the wine racks. Is that true?"

"Yes." Kyrill looked at me. "The men cannot be trusted with wine."

"Obviously," I said. "But it's okay for me to go in, right?"

"I would prefer to choose my own wines for our guests," he said. "I'll pick out a few bottles and put them in the kitchen so that Jacques can do the pairings."

I nodded.

Chores done for the moment, I closed the door behind me, checking both of the connecting doors to make sure they were locked.

I grabbed my phone quickly to check for messages, hoping that someone had managed to sort out something while I'd been dodging the authorities. Pinkie had texted me a photo of a sad kitten. "I meow meow miss you," it said. I sneezed twice then called his number. "You know that I hate cats, right?" I asked. "Seriously. I think the picture you sent just started an allergy attack."

"Of course I know, darling. That's why I sent one. A dog you would just ignore, but I knew that if I sent a cat you would call up to remind me how much you hate cats. And you can't get an allergy attack from a picture of a cat."

I sneezed again.

"I stand corrected," Pinkie said. "And before you ask: No, I haven't managed to speak with Clancy yet. He's apparently locked himself away with his spiritual advisor. But don't worry…I'm on it."

"Believe it or not, that's the least of my worries," I said. "Listen. The security guy who came with Spiro was found murdered last night."

"Murdered!? How?"

"Stabbed to death in my bed."

"You slept with Spiro's security guy?"

"No! The guy was a total psycho. He tried to hit on me earlier and I shut him down, and he went into my room to wait for me." I shuddered, remembering the black bag. "He brought duct tape, Pinkie."

For once in his life, Pinkie was shocked into a brief moment of silence. "So it was self-defense?"

"I didn't kill him, you idiot. A hotel maid confessed. She says she came in and stabbed him when he attacked her."

"So…lucky escape then, right? I hope you left a nice tip for housekeeping."

"Right," I said hesitantly, "but I'm not sure that's really what happened. There's this guy I met in Moscow…"

"Is he rich and handsome?"

"Not rich for sure, but that's not the point. This guy, Benjamin, showed me around Moscow, and he seemed perfectly nice. But then at the end of the day, we almost got mugged, and Benjamin, who looks completely harmless, crushed the mugger with karate moves."

"You got mugged?" Pinkie asked. "What is happening over there?! This was supposed to be a normal job. Muggings and dead bodies and impoverished karate experts? If I had known it was going to be that much fun, I would have come, too."

I plowed on. "So Kyrill's henchman apparently knew Benjamin from before, and he told Kyrill that Benjamin is dangerous. And last night, when I was fending off Spiro's security guy, I'm almost sure I saw Benjamin watching us."

"You think this Benjamin person is stalking you?"

"I don't know what to think," I confessed. "My brother said that if Clancy knew enough to hire the Viper to hack my phone, he isn't the idiot I've always thought he was. And then this guy Benjamin shows up in Russia and then maybe again in Bulgaria…" I trailed off. "What if Clancy hired Benjamin to watch me? And what if Benjamin killed Dieter because he saw him trying to hurt me?"

"You think Clancy hired a hit man?" Pinkie scoffed. "Lora, Clancy panics when they change the brunch options at Maxim's. I don't know how he stumbled across this Viper character, but if there's one thing I'm sure of, it's that he really is the idiot you always thought he was. And think about it—why would a hotel maid take the blame for killing someone if she didn't do it?"

"Maybe Kyrill paid her," I said. "When we talked last night, he told me I would be a suspect. If nobody had confessed, we would have had to stay while they did an investigation."

The line was silent while Pinkie processed this. "Did you ask Kyrill whether he paid off the girl?"

"I tried, but he just told me not to ask questions."

"Hmm." Pinkie was silent. "Well, look…if you're worried about being accused of murder in Bulgaria, and you think this guy Benjamin might be following you, I'd say you want to get that boat moving as quickly as possible. Even if Kyrill did pay off that maid, it was to protect you, right?"

"Right," I agreed reluctantly.

"So don't look a gift bribe in the mouth, Lora. You're safe now. Do what Kyrill asks you to do, and let me deal with things here, okay?"

I thought it through. I really didn't see any other options. "Fine."

"And for the love of heaven, try to have fun," Pinkie said. "It's not a tragedy when bad guys get killed, you know. How is the rich Greek playboy?" he asked. "My team or yours? Or maybe a switch hitter?"

"Definitely mine," I said. "At least he manages to hit every point on my stereotype of a rich playboy. And he seems to be under the impression that I'm a prostitute, or at least a slut. I'm going to have to barricade myself in my room tonight because he is definitely not here for business."

"Fun!" Pinkie said, audibly clapping.

"Pinkie, really," I said. "Nothing's going to happen. It would be so unprofessional."

"Darling," Pinkie said, "plenty of professionals would jump at the chance to play around with a handsome playboy. He is handsome, right?"

"As much as it pains me to say it, gorgeous," I admitted. "And very much aware of it."

Pinkie sighed dramatically. "Well, it's your decision, I suppose, but if you're looking for someone who's not going to get all mushy and stalky on you, he sounds perfect. Just don't do anything I wouldn't do."

"Pinkie, if memory serves, you'd do pretty much anything. And anyone," I added.

"I know," Pinkie said. "I don't want to constrain you."

I laughed, feeling my worries lift. "Ciao, Pinkie."

"Ciao, bella," Pinkie said. "Call me tomorrow so I know how things are going."

I hung up the phone. Talking to Pinkie always cheered me up. I felt a low thrum go through the boat and realized that we had pulled away from the dock. I breathed a sigh of relief. We were finally underway. For at least the next couple of days, I had nothing to worry about except keeping the guests happy. No Clancy. No Benjamin. No Dieter. No police. I hadn't realized how nervous I had been until my fears lifted.

I quickly slipped off my sundress, exposing a La Perla bikini that managed to look far more daring than it actually was. I looked at myself critically in the mirror. I had known many women born with fabulous figures that required minimal maintenance. Unfortunately, I wasn't one of them. I adjusted the bottom of the bikini and silently thanked my personal trainer for listening to me whine through what seemed like an eternity of push-ups, sit-ups, and cardio. In your face, Mother Nature!

My phone gave a soft beep, and I picked it up to look at it. One message, from Chris, responding to the photo of Kyrill and the yacht that I had sent earlier. "Nice boat," he said. "Who's the thug? You working with the WWE these days?"

"The thug is Kyrill," I wrote back. "And now you officially have the one thing even you couldn't find online...a photo of Kyrill Antonov."

Dropping the phone onto the nightstand, I sucked in my stomach, plastered a smile on my face, and went to work.

24

Kyrill was the only person on deck when I got upstairs. Barefoot and in swimming trunks, he was looking out over the railing toward the open water. Without a shirt, he was spectacular: heavily muscled without an ounce of fat. I wondered briefly how Fritzie had managed to survive their relationship without being crushed. Fritzie was built like a drinking straw with a head.

"Kyrill?" I said hesitantly.

When he turned, I took an involuntary step back. His face was set in hard lines of determination, and his fist was clenched tightly. He looked like he wanted to kill someone. I sincerely hoped it wasn't me.

"Uh…is everything okay?" I asked.

The expression vanished so quickly that I wasn't sure I had actually seen it.

"Perfect," he said. "You wanted to speak with me?"

"Yes. I just wanted to check in with you regarding the plan for the day," I said. "Are you scheduling any stops along the way? Istanbul perhaps?"

"No," Kyrill said flatly. "We'll be on the boat the entire time. This isn't a pleasure cruise."

"Is there any time you don't want me around?" I asked. "I mean, so that you can discuss business in private, for example?"

Kyrill nodded. "Every day after lunch, Spiro and I will go to the salon to discuss the terms of our arrangement. I would like for you to entertain Alexander and Howard during that time. It's very important that we not be interrupted. Not by you. Not by them. This business is very sensitive. Very," he repeated, looking at me hard to make sure I understood.

"Of course," I said. "Are you happy with the boat? Is there anything I need to attend to?"

He shrugged. "Everything is fine."

Considering the state of the boat a mere twenty hours ago, I thought "fine" was a little understated. Along the lines of saying that the parting of the Red Sea was "neat." I smiled. "I'm glad you're pleased."

Kyrill turned back to the railing, dismissing me. "Just see to it that our guests are comfortable, and make sure that Alexander and Howard don't interrupt us when we're talking. Men like us are accustomed to getting things done. Alexander and Howard will just get in the way."

"No problem," I said. "I'm sure they'll be more than happy to spend the afternoons by the pool chatting and drinking. If there's nothing else, I'm going to go check on lunch." Kyrill nodded curtly, his back still turned, and I headed for the kitchen.

I had just put my hand on the door to the galley when the shrieking began. "You touch my knives again, and I will cut off your cock!" howled someone in a heavy French accent. Jacques. Dammit. I knew the boysenberry syrup was too good to be true.

I opened the door to see an enraged Jacques waving around a gigantic chef's knife hysterically. Sergei was cowering on the other side of the island, his hands up in an attempt to pacify the psychotic chef.

"Sorry, sorry, sorry…" he kept repeating over and over again.

"What the hell, Jacques?!" I said.

"He touched my knives!" Jacques shrieked.

I shot Sergei a look. "I just wanted to see them," he said sheepishly. "They're really nice ones."

Jacques was not mollified. "You tell him that to touch a chef's knives…it is like touching his cock." His eyes narrowed to slits. "You only do it when invited."

"You are telling me to touch your cock?!" Sergei screeched, suddenly going on the offensive. "You think I'm some kind of queer? Russians are not like Frenchmen. We don't fuck everything

141

that moves. Fucking French probably fuck their fucking horses!" he finished in Russian.

Jacques looked at me inquiringly, knife pointing menacingly toward the irate Sergei.

"Dammit, Sergei," I said. "He doesn't want you to touch his cock. But he REALLY doesn't want you to touch his knives. They are the same to a chef. Things you should never touch." I left out the "when invited" part, figuring that would only cause confusion.

Sergei still looked a bit suspicious but calmed down. "I'm sorry. I just wanted to help. You said that I'm very good in the kitchen. I could help." He looked at me with puppy dog eyes.

I didn't remember the exact circumstances of when I told Sergei that he was good in the kitchen, but seeing how it was a complete fabrication designed to soothe the male ego, it did seem like the kind of thing I would say.

I sighed and turned to Jacques. His nostrils were still flared, but the point of his knife was wavering slightly. "He won't touch your knives again," I said. "He just wants to help. He loves cooking. Really. Maybe you could give him something to chop. With his own knife," I added hurriedly.

Jacques puffed his five-foot-seven frame up regally. "I have studied at the finest cooking schools," he said. "I worked at Kronenhalle. Do you know Kronenhalle?"

"Uh…of course," I lied. "Doesn't everyone?"

"And you want me to waste my time teaching this filthy sailor person, who is going to destroy my ingredients, get in my way, and annoy me?"

"Well, when you put it like that…" I said, "maybe if he washed his hands first?"

He held up an imperious finger to silence me. "Fine. I will give him something to do. Just like my first teacher did for me." He smiled evilly. "We start with carrots," he said. "Ten pounds. Matchsticks."

Sergei practically saluted.

"Hand washing first," I reminded him. "Lunch?" I asked Jacques.

"I will bring it out personally," he said. "It will be a triumph."

25

When I came up with Jacques to announce lunch, everyone was on deck. Alexander had draped himself over one of the lounge chairs and was staring lazily out at the water. He had changed into the type of James Bond-style swimsuit that Pinkie had always sworn looked good on no man. Pinkie was wrong, apparently. Alexander looked spectacular. At that moment Alexander looked up, catching me gawking for the second time that day. A slow smile spread over his face. Game on.

Howard had not attempted a European-style bathing suit, which I figured was a good thing. His soft, almost hairless body was hunched over his phone as he typed furiously with his thumbs. "Are you working, Howard?" I asked.

He looked up apologetically. "I'm sorry. I don't mean to be rude, but do you know what happens to a shipment of Bulgarian cheese when it sits in the sun for three days?"

"Probably nothing good," I hazarded.

"Exactly," he replied. "I speak from experience here. I'd like to make sure I don't have that experience again." I smiled and patted him on the back supportively. Apparently, I wasn't the only one who was still on the clock.

Kyrill and Spiro were in the salon talking in low voices. They broke off as I approached.

"Ah, Lora," Kyrill said. "Is it time for lunch?"

"We can postpone, if you're talking about business."

I heard an enraged hissing noise from Jacques, who was trailing behind me. Apparently, the concept of lunch as something that could wait for business did not show proper respect to his art.

"No, no," Kyrill said. "We were just talking. Nothing serious. Let's have lunch. We can discuss our business afterwards." He waved Jacques, Spiro, Alexander, and Howard into the dining room, lingering behind them to talk to me. "This lunch," he said. "It is important that our guests enjoy it."

"Of course," I said. "Jacques has been working very hard to put together a menu, and he assures me that it will be spectacular."

"The food is not important," Kyrill said.

I glanced over my shoulder to make sure that Jacques hadn't heard him say that. I didn't think I had it in me to bring Jacques down from another temper tantrum right now.

"Having fun, drinking—that is what is important," he said. He looked at me meaningfully.

"You want me to get them drunk?" I asked uncertainly.

"No, no." Kyrill said, holding up is hands in protest. "It sounds so bad when you put it that way. I just want everyone to have a good time. With lots of drinking."

I looked at him. "And after lunch you and Spiro will be working?"

"Exactly!" Kyrill said, baring his teeth in what was supposed to be a reassuring smile. "We will discuss our business. He will be relaxed, happy. Business goes much more smoothly that way."

"Right."

"Just business," he said. "You understand. Drinking will make it much more productive. But it cannot be too obvious that you want them to drink." He held up a finger admonishingly. "I wouldn't want them to feel I was trying to take advantage of them."

"Sure," I said, getting slightly worried.

"Nothing to be worried about," he said, baring his teeth in a silky smile.

Now I was seriously freaked out. Nobody said "nothing to be worried about" unless there was something to be worried about. Clearly Kyrill was trying to use my charms and his recently refurbished liquor cabinet to take advantage of Spiro. Maybe it wasn't heroin smuggling, but it didn't seem exactly legit either.

Okay, I told myself. *Settle down. It's probably the Russian way of doing business, and Spiro is hardly a lightweight.* Anyone who had grown up on the docks in Greece could probably match a Russian drink for drink and keep his head clear enough to manage whatever dodgy business propositions Kyrill was throwing at him.

Lots of my clients liked to encourage their guests to drink; they just managed to do it without coming across like villains out of Victorian novels. Clearly this was within the normal scope of my professional duties. "I'll do my best," I said, smiling brightly.

"Excellent," Kyrill said, rubbing his hands together.

26

In the dining room, Jacques had laid out the first course, blini with caviar. "Perfect, Jacques," I said. He waited, hovering. "It looks spectacular," I added, trying to shoo him back into the kitchen.

Jacques let out a little sniff to let me know that my compliment was not quite up to his standards.

"That will be all, Jacques," I said briskly.

Jacques shot me a lingering look that did not bode well for our relationship during the rest of the trip. I mentally sighed. Why were the best chefs always drama queens?

"Gentlemen," I said once everyone had been seated, "in honor of our Russian host, we have blini and caviar to start. And while they can be paired with champagne, they really are best served with chilled vodka. I will be having vodka," I said, nodding to Sergei to pour me a hefty swig. "Of course, I realize that some of you will be working after lunch, so if you prefer something lighter..." I trailed off challengingly.

Spiro waved Sergei over to his side. "I love this woman," he told Kyrill, taking a glass of vodka. Alexander and Kyrill also took vodka. Howard dithered over the tray.

"I really should stick to water..." he started. "The cheese..."

"Nonsense," Spiro said. "You can't let a woman drink vodka while you drink water. Be a man, for god's sake."

Howard flushed. I handed him a glass of vodka. "Looks like

vodka for you," I said sympathetically. I dutifully raised my glass once everyone had been served. "To the sea," I said, addressing Spiro.

Spiro knocked back the vodka with a smile, and Sergei refilled the glasses all the way around. "To our charming hostess," Spiro said.

The men all drank.

I smiled coyly and gestured for Sergei to refill everyone's glasses.

"To new business," said Kyrill. Three shots in two minutes, and I figured we were off to a good start.

The blini Jacques had made were feather-light, and we lingered over them for a while, sipping our drinks and talking lazily about the news. I watched everyone's glasses closely. Spiro just drank whatever was put in front of him. He was five shots in by the time the blini were finished with little or no effort on my part, and was discussing yachts with Kyrill, who looked bored.

Howard was having trouble using his cutlery after the first three shots, so in the interests of not having to chopper him off the boat for alcohol poisoning, I left him to his own devices.

Alexander's vodka glass, however, sat full in front of him while he sipped water. "To a lovely trip," I said, clinking my vodka glass against his.

He picked up the vodka glass and took the obligatory sip, which didn't decrease the level of vodka in the glass. I narrowed my eyes slightly. If he really did the social part of the business as Spiro had indicated, he was probably used to giving the impression of drinking without actually doing much of it. It was an art that I had been working on for years with very limited success.

"Not a fan of vodka?" I asked, raising my glass. "Or worried about your virtue?"

"I wasn't aware that I had any virtue," he said, taking another sip. "What do you mean?"

"I noticed that there's a connecting door between our cabins," I said. "I wouldn't want you to worry."

"Oh, I wasn't worried," he said. "But it's good to know." He raised his glass slightly to me. "You don't have any worries, do you?"

I took another sip of vodka and watched him do the same. "Not at all," I replied. "I'm sure you're a perfect gentleman."

He rolled the vodka around on his tongue for a moment. "I don't know where you would have gotten such an impression."

"Truth be told, I was just being polite," I said. "But I'm not concerned. I'm quite sure I could handle you." I smiled sweetly as he took a healthy swig. I wondered what it must be like to go through life being so incredibly predictable. I bet it was really relaxing.

Glancing over at the end of the table, I saw Kyrill watching me as Spiro pontificated about engine size and hull displacement. He took in Alexander's intent focus and nodded approvingly. Apparently, Kyrill was perfectly fine with me sacrificing my virtue in the interests of amusing his guests.

"I don't know...I can be rather hard to take," Alexander said.

No kidding, I thought, taking another sip.

"No special woman in the picture back in Greece?" I asked.

Alexander poured himself more vodka. "Plenty of women back in Greece," he said, "but nobody special. I'm afraid I haven't been so lucky in love," he said, and I was surprised to hear a note of wistfulness in his voice. "I once did meet a girl, but she died in a car accident. It was a great tragedy." Alexander took a great gulp of vodka, looking momentarily bereft.

"I'm sorry," I said, touching his arm in sympathy. "I haven't been very lucky either. The last adventure in love I had was purely one-sided."

Alexander raised his eyebrows. "He didn't love you back? That's rather had to believe."

"Quite the opposite," I hastened to clarify. "I arranged a trip for him. Strictly professional, you know, and he got it into his head that we were destined to be together."

"That sounds rather romantic, actually," Alexander said. "Don't women like that kind of thing?"

"Not when they get literally twenty phone calls a day and are inundated with crazy gifts."

"Ah," he said, sipping his drink thoughtfully. "What kind of crazy gifts?"

"Candy, flowers, diamond bracelet, car..." I rattled off. "Oh, and a parrot. That was really the last straw." I shuddered, remembering.

"At least you got a nice bracelet and car out of it," he said. "That would cheer most women up."

"Well obviously I couldn't keep them. I sent them back."

"Why? They were gifts."

"It wouldn't have been right. A woman has to have her principles."

"I don't see why," Alexander said, raising his eyebrows. "Most of the women I know manage quite nicely without them. So back to that connecting door…"

"Howard," I said, pointedly changing the subject. "Is everything okay with your lunch?" Howard looked up from the plate that he was energetically cleaning.

"Great," he said. He smiled a little blearily and took a healthy swig out of his glass. I tried not to notice the fact that he had caviar in his teeth.

"If you'll excuse me, I'll go check on the next course," I said, pushing my chair back.

I made my way unsteadily to the galley. My tolerance for alcohol had been honed by an international collection of boozy businessmen, so I was no lightweight, but multiple shots of vodka on an empty stomach were challenging for even me.

In the kitchen, Jacques was awaiting commendation. "Well?" he asked.

"Perfect," I said. "The blini were spectacular."

Jacques nodded. "Exactly. I am famous for them. And for lunch, we have scallops with truffle oil, a spinach tartlet with pine nuts and currants…"

"Sounds great. What wine will we be having?"

He frowned. "A veltliner. But if you are drinking too much, you will not be able to appreciate the food."

"I think you're grossly underestimating the liver capacity of this table," I replied, grabbing the bottle.

I peered around him to where Sergei was chopping away behind a stack of carrot matchsticks. "How is it going?" I asked.

"Great!" Sergei said. "I'm learning how to do carrots."

"I see. Please go in and clear. We're ready for the next course."

Sergei left the room, and I looked at Jacques. "Are we having something that requires a lot of carrots?"

"No," he said shortly.

"So you're just trying to give him a job that's boring enough that he'll give up and leave you alone?"

Jacques silently lifted the corners of his mouth in a chilly smile.

"Carry on."

27

Jacques really was a master in the kitchen, and under other circumstances I would have enjoyed my meal. Instead, I found myself picking at my food as I verbally fenced with Alexander. Normally I was good at flirtatious banter, but I was unusually tired today. I wondered whether it was dealing with Clancy's stalking, worrying about my mother, almost getting killed by a Russian mugger, or finding a dead rapist in my bed that had worn me out. Hard to say, really. I put down the vodka and took a big gulp of water. Given the week I was having, I should stay ready for action. Or, barring that, at least be able to stand up.

I was also trying to include Howard in the conversation, which was difficult since he was eating with the focus of a man who had been raised by wolves. Or perhaps in a Philadelphia Catholic school. I gathered there were quite a few similarities. I glanced periodically down the table at Kyrill and Spiro. Spiro, I noticed, was doing most of the talking, while Kyrill simply made encouraging noises and kept refilling his glass.

By the end of the meal, I surely hoped that everyone was as drunk as Kyrill had intended, because I was tipsy, dehydrated, nauseated, and in desperate need of a bathroom. It was also four o'clock, which made the concept of dinner seem like complete overkill.

Once desserts had been polished off, Kyrill looked around the table, seemingly unaffected by the alcohol he had consumed. "Lora," he said, "I think Spiro and I should probably go ahead and start looking at the contracts. Perhaps you'd like to take Alexander and Howard out on the deck to enjoy the air? I think you can see the lights of Istanbul about this time."

"Ah, business," Spiro said, expansively. "It is everything for men like us, although I am sad that I will not get to spend the afternoon with you, Lora. Kyrill and I will worry about the work." He took my hand in his and kissed it ostentatiously. "I hope you'll have fun with the boys."

Alexander, who had been in an excellent mood until precisely that moment, ground his teeth audibly. Howard popped a chocolate truffle into his mouth and burped, apparently unconcerned with where he stood on Spiro's boy to man continuum.

Kyrill gripped me by the shoulder, his fingers digging in slightly for emphasis. "Please make sure we are not disturbed."

"Of course," I said, getting to my feet and neatly unhooking my heel from the chair leg that it had somehow entangled itself in. Falling flat on my face would hardly be the graceful exit I was looking for. "Alexander, Howard…would you like to join me on deck?" I asked. "Perhaps we should meet upstairs in a half an hour or so? Just so that everyone has a chance to freshen up. Oh, and Kyrill…will we be having dinner?"

Kyrill surveyed the company, who looked as though dinner was the last thing any of them was thinking about. "If you have Jacques pull together some finger food in the dining area," he said, "we can just eat what and when we like. You just make sure 'the boys' are having fun." He smiled at Alexander and Howard flatly, clearly aware that he was pushing Alexander's buttons.

I tried not to take pleasure in Alexander's sour expression and failed miserably. "I'm going to change clothes," I said sweetly. "Meet you back up on deck in a few?"

"Fine," Alexander said.

Once in my cabin, I wrestled one of the big harem cushions onto the bed so that I could put my feet up for a few minutes. Kicking off my sandals, I locked the door behind me and flung myself on the mattress. I lay there, staring at the ceiling for a few moments, feeling like my tongue was Velcroed to the roof of my mouth. I needed to find a real job. The kind that didn't get you mistaken for a hooker. The kind that didn't require you to drink too much and deal with histrionic chefs and surly Russians and sons with daddy issues.

Sighing deeply, I rolled out of bed and dug through my luggage for a cover-up. All the sit-ups in the world wouldn't give me stomach muscles strong enough to hold in my belly after the lunch we'd had. I pulled out a flimsy silk Etro tunic with a paisley print that I figured would work to camouflage the truffles I had overindulged in. It had been a gift from Pinkie, who had a particular love of paisley and a real talent for buying things at unbelievably steep discounts.

I headed up to the kitchen to tell Jacques that dinner was off, mentally bracing myself for the hysteria I knew would ensue. I was not disappointed.

"But I have been cooking all day!" Jacques shrieked. "We have snails. We have soup. We have lamb. What do you want me to do with this? Shall I just feed it to the fish? Or the crew?" he said, his tone clearly implying that feeding it to the crew was several levels more insulting than feeding it to the fish. "Do you know what it is like to work on something and see it completely unappreciated?!"

"As a matter of fact, I do know what that's like," I said, cutting him off. "You want to be a private chef? Well, let me let you in on a little secret from my decade of working in this field. It isn't about *you*. It's about the *client*. And nobody cares how hard you work. They only care about whether the *client* is happy.

"I have spent my entire afternoon drinking more than I should, running back and forth to the kitchen, and dealing with your drama queen hysterics in order to make our client happy," I hissed. "And despite the fact that I have a raging headache and my feet hurt and I am jet lagged beyond belief, I am about to go back out there to entertain our guests. Why? To make our client happy.

"So if you want to work in this business, why don't you try to make our client happy by putting everything on tiny little plates and calling it finger food?"

Jacques's mouth dropped open. Recovering from his shock, he looked at me through slitted eyes. "One cannot eat lamb with the fingers."

I slitted my eyes right back at him. "Then find some tiny fucking forks."

He threw up his hands, muttered something obscene in French, and rearranged his lips into what I supposed was intended to be a smile. "Fine!"

"Fine," I repeated, smiling back grimly. I grabbed a bottle of wine and an ice bucket from the fridge and stomped up the stairs. *Three days of summer fun on a yacht*, I thought, remembering Pinkie's promise. *Happy, happy.*

28

When I came back on deck, Alexander was nowhere to be seen, and Howard was looking out to sea, his phone on the table beside him. "Did you get the Bulgarian cheese sorted?" I asked.

"Hopefully," he said. "I'm not getting a signal here, so I can't check." He sighed.

"Is cheese rescue usually among your duties?"

Howard pushed his glasses up on his nose. "Not usually," he said. "I'm a numbers guy. Most of the time I have no idea what's in the containers we ship. But in this case they needed someone who spoke Bulgarian, so Spiro asked me to handle it."

"Does Alexander speak Bulgarian?"

"Just enough to pick up girls," Howard said. "And when you're rich and look like Alexander does, that doesn't take much." He gave me a rueful little smile. "I try to take some comfort in the fact that he can't use Excel to save his life."

I laughed and offered him a glass of wine, which he took absently. "It's really something, isn't it," he said, looking out over the endless expanse of blue water. "Do you think you'll ever have a boat like this?"

"I don't need to have a boat like this," I said. "I have friends who have boats like this."

Howard looked abashed, and I took pity on him. "Probably not," I admitted. "Even if I were rich, I doubt I'd buy a boat. At this point I'd just be happy to get my car out of hock. But enough about what we don't have," I said. "Tell me something about yourself. How did you choose Bulgaria?"

"Excuse me?" he said, blinking at me owlishly.

"Alexander said you were in the Peace Corps in Bulgaria," I said. "Why Bulgaria?"

"Oh," Howard said. "You don't get to choose, actually. You just volunteer for the Peace Corps, and they send you somewhere. One of my college friends spent two years in Bali." He laughed. "When we got the letters with the assignments, I could have died with envy."

"But it turned out okay?"

"Yes and no," Howard said. "Bulgaria at that time was so exotic. It was in Europe, but it was like a completely different world.

"I got there right after the economic meltdown. People had watched their entire life savings evaporate in the hyperinflation. The lev—that's the Bulgarian currency—was basically worthless. People would sell you anything they had for some hard currency."

"What did you do?"

Howard shook his head. "Not much," he admitted. "The Peace Corps doesn't pay that well, so it wasn't like I was in a position to help out anyone directly. And it wasn't the most stable place to live. The Mafia was really big here. 'Mutri,' they called them. It means 'thick necks.'" He held his hands around his own rather scrawny neck to illustrate. "A lot of former wrestlers and bodybuilder types set up crooked companies. They sold drugs, women, protection…"

"Don't tell me that you were dealing with the Mafia," I said. Howard hardly looked like the kind of man who would be able to hold his own with the criminal underground.

"You don't think someone from Philadelphia could handle Bulgarian gangsters?" Howard asked, lowering his eyebrows in what was supposed to be a menacing scowl. I coughed gently to smother a laugh.

"Umm…no."

"You're right, I'm afraid," he sighed, pushing his glasses back up on his nose. "Every time we'd help one of the guys we were working with get their company to the point where it was making a bit of money, the mutri would swoop in and start blackmailing them. It was completely hopeless. By the end of my tour there, I was so sick of it that I couldn't wait to get back to a functional country."

"So you went to Greece?" I asked, reflecting that of all the descriptions I'd heard of Greece over the years, the word "functional" had never managed to come up.

Howard smiled. "I know," he said. "It's a relative thing. But I was twenty-two years old and the Peace Corps in Bulgaria isn't exactly a résumé line that has people stacked up trying to hire you. When Spiro's company offered me a job, I jumped at the chance."

"Do you miss anything about Bulgaria?"

Howard shrugged. "I don't miss the mutri," he said. "But I do miss some of the people. Of course, since I started working with Spiro I've been back a lot, so it's really the best of both worlds."

"Do you ever think about going back to Philadelphia?"

"God no," he said, appalled. "You ever think about going back to Delaware?"

"God no," I echoed, clinking my glass to his. We both smiled.

"Do you do this a lot?" Howard asked. "Yachting with friends?"

"Whenever I can," I said. "My regular job is pretty stressful."

"Consulting, you said earlier?"

"Events, mostly. If you ever need to organize a bar mitzvah, I'm a good person to know. At least it's not boring—everything from toast scraping to toilet plunging falls under the job description."

"Hopefully not at the same time," Alexander chimed in, snaking an arm around my waist as he joined us.

"Generally not," I conceded, unobtrusively stepping out of his embrace.

"Note to self: avoid the toast," Alexander deadpanned.

I stifled a smile. Really, for all his stereotypical Eurotrashiness, Alexander did have a certain charm.

"Wine?" I offered.

"Are you trying to get me drunk?" he asked, arching an eyebrow as he took his glass.

"Goodness," I said. "Given the amount of vodka we went through at lunch, I would sincerely hope you're already drunk. Otherwise I guess we'll have to tap into Kyrill's supply of Krug again." We clinked our glasses together in a toast.

"So," Alexander said, sipping his wine, "what corporate secrets was Howard here spilling to you?"

"He was just telling me about his time in the Peace Corps," I said. "It sounded fascinating."

"I'm sure it was," Alexander agreed. "Howard loves to talk about the culture and the history of Bulgaria, but of course most men these days only go there for one thing."

"Yogurt?" I guessed.

Alexander shook his head. "Women. The women in Bulgaria are some of the most beautiful in the world. After the communists fell, everyone was desperate to get out. A man could walk in to any bar with a wad of cash and a foreign passport and walk out with a girl on his arm." He nudged Howard. "Even a man like Howard."

Howard colored violently. "I would never date a girl under those circumstances," he said stiffly.

"Of course not," Alexander said. "But lots of men would. It's the way of the world. And who are we to judge? A girl trades her beauty for security. A man trades his money for affection." He shrugged. "It happens every day. Sometimes it even works out fine for them both."

"I really doubt that happens very often," Howard protested. "Successful relationships need to be based on mutual respect and shared values."

Alexander rolled his eyes. "Sometimes I can't tell whether Howard is an incurable romantic or just incredibly naïve," he told me. "But in either case, the cure is more wine." He took the bottle out of my hand and refilled his glass.

"Are you trying to get me drunk?" Howard asked weakly. "I didn't think I was your type."

"You're not," Alexander said, "but Lora here is just my type, and she's so devoted to her duty of keeping us all entertained that the only way for me to get her undivided attention is to get rid of you. So drink up, or I may have to throw you overboard."

"Ah, well." Howard said, taking a healthy slug of wine. "When you put it that way, 'Nasdrave,' as they say in Bulgaria."

29

After an afternoon spent flirting and drinking and swimming, many women would have been energized. But working in a job where socializing *is* the job turns fun into work. Balancing Alexander against Howard so that both men felt they were having a good time was work. Keeping tabs on the alcohol so that everyone was happy but nobody was sloppy drunk (especially me) was also work. With my stomach muscles completely exhausted from sucking in during our four-hour lunch, even standing up was work.

At eight o'clock, when I made my excuses and left Alexander and Howard to go check on things for the next day, I was completely shredded. Kyrill and Spiro had been closeted away the entire afternoon, which did at least keep Kyrill's hulking presence out of my hair.

Back in my cabin with my feet up and a bottle of water in my hand, I ran through the plan for tomorrow. I would have to talk to Jacques again about the food. Less than twenty-four hours into this trip, talking to Jacques had already become my least favorite thing to do. I made my way up to the galley, where Jacques was fussing with some kind of pastry and Sergei was occupied in the corner with a mountainous supply of apples and a small paring knife.

"How is Sergei working out? Have you broken him yet?" I whispered.

Jacques frowned. "Not yet, no. He finished the carrots without complaint. But I have come up with another assignment. Trickier. Apples. They will be cut into stars for apple pie."

"Stars?" I said. "Is that really necessary? I'm pretty sure I've seen pie made without stars before."

"Of course it is not necessary," he said. "But the purpose is not to make pie. The purpose is to get rid of Sergei."

I called over to Sergei. "How's it going, Sergei?"

Sergei's face was glowing with the simple happiness that apparently only the monotonous chopping of food could bring him.

"Great," he replied. "I'm making stars." He held up a five-pointed sliver of apple to show me.

I smiled back. Sergei was definitely growing on me. "You did wash your hands before you started?" I confirmed.

Sergei's face fell. "I…uh…I will be right back," he said quickly, before fleeing through the galley door.

I sighed. On the positive side, it would probably be easier to avoid the apple pie now, I thought.

"Jacques," I asked, "what's on for tomorrow's lunch?"

"Tomorrow we have a light lunch of ceviche with avocado and spring asparagus."

"Perfect. Is everything else okay?" I asked.

"Well, let's see," Jacques said in an irritated tone, "the client does not appreciate my food, and my kitchen has been colonized by a filthy imbecile."

"I'll take that as a yes."

"Will Kyrill and Spiro be needing anything else tonight?" Jacques asked. "I made some little desserts just in case." He gestured to a tray of mini-éclairs.

"I doubt it," I said, helping myself to two. "But maybe we can leave them out in case they want something once they've finished their discussion." *And in case I get hungry later*, I promised myself. "Are they still in the salon?"

Jacques shrugged. "I haven't seen them come out all day."

I wandered up to the salon and hesitated in front of the door. I could hear low murmurs coming from inside. I guessed they were still there. I leaned closer, wondering if I should interrupt.

"What do you think you're doing?" growled a voice in my ear.

I jumped back, startled. "Captain Vlad," I said, trying to bring my pulse back down out of heart attack range. "I was wondering what had happened to you. Is everything okay with the yacht? Shouldn't you be steering it or something?" I made steering motions with my hands to demonstrate.

Captain Vlad regarded me flatly, apparently not impressed by my imaginary boat captaining. "What are you doing here?" he repeated.

"I was just...uh..." I found myself stammering under his glare. "I was just seeing if Kyrill wanted anything else this evening."

"Mr. Antonov is not to be disturbed. Not for food. Not for coffee. Not for boat on fire. He is making business now, you understand? Business."

"Yes," I said, taking a step back. "Fine. If you see him when he comes out, please tell him that there are some sweets in the galley if they want something."

"I will tell him," the captain said, crossing his arms over his chest and scowling at me. "You can go."

Jeez, I thought, *I can take a hint*. "I'm going," I said, holding up my hands. I walked back toward my cabin, feeling Captain Vlad's eyes boring a hole in my back with every step. Apparently, the do-not-disturb rule was a little stricter with Kyrill than it was with most of my clients.

I shut the door behind myself and locked it, letting out a deep breath. Captain Vlad was flat-out creepy. But if it meant I had more time to sleep, I was happy to leave Kyrill to his own devices for the rest of the evening. In fact, if he wanted to shut himself up in the salon for the rest of the trip, I was all for it. Maybe I could just slide liquor under the door every morning.

I glanced at my handbag and pondered getting out my phone and trying to get in touch with my mother again, but something, probably the wine, kindled a spark of rebellion. My brother and I were worried sick about her, and she refused to even do us the courtesy of telling us what was wrong. She didn't want to talk about it? Fine. I wasn't going to lose any more sleep over it. I had enough on my plate.

I grabbed my toiletry kit and headed for the bathroom. In the last few days, I'd survived stalkers, murderers, and Jacques. In my mind, I deserved a medal. I'd settle for a bath.

30

I was lying in bed, completely relaxed after my bath, when the connecting door to Alexander's cabin slowly eased open. Alexander, dressed in a pair of shorts and nothing else, slipped into my room and came around onto the bed. I opened my mouth to ask him what he was doing in my cabin, but he forestalled my objection, putting a finger over my lips to keep me silent.

I felt my heart race as he slowly stroked one hand down my body, skimming over my silk nightgown. I knew I should stop him, but I said nothing. It had been too long. My self-control was shot. His thumb teased a nipple then slipped lower under the gown as he slowly started up my inner thigh.

"You know you want this," he said, his voice hot against my neck.

"Yes," I panted, biting my lip. My breathing was out of control, and I pushed my hips toward him, encouraging him to move higher.

"You're so ready," he said, stroking me lightly. His other hand pressed me into the bed. "Slowly, slowly," he said.

"Please," I begged, beyond all shame.

The handle of the cabin door rattled as if someone were trying to get in.

"Ignore it," I panted, pulling Alexander's head down over mine.

The handle rattled again, more insistently, and I moaned in

frustration as the dream dissolved. I lay in bed, breathing hard as I tried to recapture what remained of my self-control. When I got back from this job, I needed to find a boyfriend. I was a menace to myself and others in this state.

The rattling at my doorknob had been replaced with knocking. Whoever it was definitely wasn't aiming for stealth. I pulled on a robe and walked to the door. "Hello?" I said softly.

"Lora," a voice boomed back. "Why are you in my room? Ah...I know. You are lonely. Looking for companionship. Am I right? I know women. Let me in, my darling."

Oh god, I thought. Spiro. And drunk as a lord, by the sound of it. I waited for a moment, hoping Kyrill or Alexander would come out and deal with him. He rattled the doorknob again. No such luck.

I opened the door a crack and tried to look sympathetic. Spiro stood in the hallway, one hand on the wall, visibly weaving. "Spiro," I said, "I'm afraid you must have gotten confused. This is my cabin. Your cabin is over there."

Spiro spun around to look where I was pointing and lurched alarmingly. "Right," I said. "Let me give you a hand." If Spiro fell and broke his hip, the job would probably be over. And while part of me would have been really happy about that, the part of me that wanted to pay my rent this month would have been pretty sad.

I stepped into the hallway, draping Spiro's arm over my shoulder as he staggered and almost fell again.

"Not my cabin?" he asked, confused.

"Nope," I said. I half walked him and half carried him down the corridor to his room. "Did you and Kyrill finish your business?" I asked. If this was the way Spiro usually conducted business, I was surprised that he still had one. So much for my theory that Spiro was able to hold his liquor.

"Yes. Very good business. We will all make a lot of money. Lots of money." I quickly patted him down, looking for his key. "Oh, you are a feisty one," he said, looking at me with delight.

"Just looking for your key," I said. "Sorry to disappoint." I pulled it triumphantly out of his pocket. "Here we are. Just stay here against the wall for a minute." I leaned him against the wall and quickly opened the room, keeping an eye on him to make sure he didn't slide to the floor. "This is your cabin," I said. "Home sweet home."

Spiro looked around blearily. "You know," he said, apropos of nothing, "I don't like Russians."

I navigated him backward to the bed until his knees hit it and he sat down. "You'd be surprised at how often I hear that," I said, trying to distract him as I swung his feet up onto the covers. "It's practically the national motto of Estonia, apparently."

"They're so rude," he continued. "Just asking and asking. So many details. Over and over again." He shook his head. "But we need this deal to go through. I expanded too fast," he confided. "We need the cash. And this will make us a lot of money."

Jesus, I thought, struggling to get his shoelaces untied. This guy was completely tanked. My hat was off to Kyrill—I wouldn't even have guessed that it was possible to get a man like Spiro this drunk. I abandoned my efforts to undo the knots. He could just sleep in his deck shoes.

"You probably should sleep on your side," I advised him, doing my best to roll him over.

"Really? Why's that?" he asked, his eyelids fluttering.

"Because otherwise I'd say you have about a 20 percent chance of choking to death on your own vomit tonight," I said matter-of-factly.

"Don't worry," he said, flapping a hand at me. "I've been drinking since I was ten years old. I never get drunk."

"I guess there's a first time for everything," I said. I bent over him. His eyes were closed, and he was snoring away.

Men. I shook my head and let myself out. My cabin was invitingly dark and quiet and devoid of self-delusional drunks. I threw my robe in the general direction of the chair and crawled into bed, stretching luxuriantly.

"I was wondering when you'd come back."

"Jesus!" I yelled, scrambling out of the bed. I hit the light switch.

"Alexander, what in the name of god are you doing here?" I hissed at the man in my bed. "Don't tell me you also got lost on the way to your cabin?"

Alexander looked amused. "Who got lost on the way to their cabin?"

"Your father," I snapped. "He was drunk as a skunk."

Alexander waved a hand dismissively. "Nonsense," he said. "He's never drunk."

"Feel free to go to his room to verify," I snapped.

"I think I'd rather stay in this room," Alexander said. "The door was unlocked. I thought it was an invitation."

I crossed my arms over my chest. "It wasn't," I said. "Please get out of my bed."

"If you insist," Alexander said, casually throwing off the sheets and standing up. He was completely naked and, I had to admit, sneaking a look before firmly fixing what I hoped was an outraged glare on his face, absolutely spectacular. My dream from earlier in the evening reasserted itself with a vengeance.

He advanced toward me, holding my gaze as I walked backward. I felt the wall against my back and stood there, trapped, trying to look severe. I realized that my pretense of disinterest was undermined by the fact that I was almost hyperventilating with lust.

"Lora," he said. "We are both adults here. There's no reason to deny ourselves what we both want."

He pushed my hair back over my shoulder and rubbed a thumb lightly over my collarbone.

I pushed his hand away. "Alexander," I said, trying to keep my voice steady, "this is completely unprofessional. I think you should leave. I doubt Kyrill would really appreciate it if I were to carry on some kind of sordid affair with one of his guests."

"Oh," Alexander said, "I don't think he would mind. He's very focused on business, in case you hadn't noticed. And while you may be *old* friends, the fact that you're here alone in your cabin makes me thing that you're not, shall we say, *close* friends."

He ran a surprisingly hard hand up my rib cage. His smell, a hint of cologne combined with a clean, virile scent, enveloped me. He leaned toward me, pausing his hand over my breast, not touching, as if to ask for permission to proceed. I felt the nipple harden. Stupid betraying body.

Alexander saw it and smiled. "You can hardly deny that you want this," he said, tracing a line down the side of my breast.

"I totally don't want this. Nope," I lied, trying to sound like I meant it. I pushed his hand away halfheartedly. The fact that my knees were shaking so badly with desire that I was barely able to stand up was not helping my case.

"You should go," I tried again, weakly.

His fingers trailed lower, playing with the hem of nightgown. He ran his fingers up the inside of my thigh and paused over my underwear, close enough that I could feel the heat of his hands, but not touching. He slipped the other hand under the back of my thigh and lifted my knee so that he could move closer, pressing his hips into mine.

What was left of my professionalism crumbled under an avalanche of long-denied lust, and I ran my hands eagerly over his chest. I opened my mouth to tell him to stay, when suddenly we were interrupted by a loud knocking at the door.

I let out a silent howl of frustration and looked at the ceiling before mastering myself and shoving Alexander away. Wordlessly, I opened the connecting door and motioned for him to go through it. "Just a minute," I said, trying to sound sleepy.

Alexander looked as though he wanted to argue. "Who is it?" I asked, jabbing my finger at Alexander's cabin frantically.

"It's Kyrill. I need to talk to you."

Alexander raised his hands in surrender and slipped through the connecting door, blowing me a kiss as I closed it behind him. I pulled my robe over my nightgown and tried to look like someone who had not been on the verge of hot carnal relations with a relative stranger a mere sixty seconds ago.

Taking a deep breath, I opened the door enough to stick my head out and managed a chipper smile. "You needed something?" I asked brightly.

Kyrill looked agitated but completely sober as he pushed past me into the room and closed the door behind us. "Have you seen Spiro?" he asked in a low voice.

"As a matter of fact, yes I have," I replied. "He woke me up trying to get into my cabin, which he had apparently confused with his own. I took him to his room and put him to bed."

Kyrill looked at me sharply. "Did he see anyone else? Alexander? Did he say anything?"

I frowned at the onslaught of questions. "I'm pretty sure I was the only one he saw."

"Did he say anything?" Kyrill repeated, looking at me intently.

"Not really. He was so drunk that he could barely stand up." I thought it best not to mention his comments about not liking Russians. I doubted that would be good for anyone's business. Plus, being Russian was probably like being American in that you were pretty used to people not liking you.

Kyrill searched my face.

"Is there a problem?" I asked.

"No problem," he said. "He just had a little too much to drink. I wanted to make sure he hadn't disturbed you."

I debated whether I should point out that disturbing me at two in the morning to ask whether I'd been disturbed was probably not the right approach. "I'm fine," I said. "But I wouldn't be surprised if we don't see much of Spiro in the morning. He's going to have a raging hangover."

Kyrill allowed a small smile to cross his lips. "I'd be surprised," he said. "These old sailors handle their liquor pretty well. Sorry to trouble you." His hand on the door handle, he turned as though debating whether to say something else.

"Lora, make sure to lock the doors before you go to sleep," he said finally. "Not everyone on this boat is a complete gentleman."

"I will," I said sincerely. As far as I could tell, nobody on this boat was a complete gentleman. I closed and locked the door behind him then quickly secured the connecting door to Alexander's room before he could barge in and hijack my libido for the third time in one night. As much as my body would prefer otherwise, now was neither the time nor the place for a fling. Professionalism was my new watchword.

I grabbed a pair of earplugs from my bag, put them in, and closed my eyes. Despite the adventures of the evening, or perhaps because of them, I was out cold before my head hit the pillow.

31

When my alarm went off at seven o'clock, it felt like the end of the world. Under the best of circumstances, I am not stellar at dealing with lack of sleep. When I've had too much sun, too much wine, and a particularly embarrassing incident of throwing myself like a dog in heat at a client, I'm even worse.

I took a long shower, hoping the water would steam some of the wrinkles out of my face, then painstakingly massaged in La Mer, my heavy hitter for mornings when I'm feeling particularly fragile. I went for the liquid eyeliner, which I only use when I need to feel tough and strong. In the unspoken language of cosmetics, liquid eyeliner is a woman's way of saying "Stay back."

I pulled on a one-piece swimsuit with scaly silver insets that looked like snakeskin and pulled a maxidress on over it. With all of the traitorous parts of my anatomy covered, I felt more protected from Alexander, who I was sure would by in high gear today now that he realized that I had all the sexual self-control of a toddler at a sundae bar.

Up in the galley, Jacques had laid out scones and clotted cream, but the only people up at this hour were Captain Vlad, Sergei, and me. I looked at Captain Vlad warily, remembering our discussion from the previous evening. "How are you this morning?" I asked.

"Fine."

"Up late last night?"

"Why do you want to know?" he asked, giving me a suspicious glare.

I sighed. "No reason," I said. "Feel free not to answer if how late you were up is some kind of top secret information. You know, if the fate of the free world depends on my not knowing when you went to bed, I'm willing to sit here in dead silence rather than trying to have any sort of conversation."

"Okay," he said, turning back to his coffee.

I shook my head in disbelief and looked over at Jacques. "Everything okay for lunch?"

"Ceviche," he replied.

I blinked. "Ceviche is what we're having for lunch?" I asked. "I know. You told me yesterday."

"Ceviche is a dish made of raw fish marinated in lime," Jacques continued, raising one finger in scholarly dissertation.

"I know what ceviche is," I said, feeling a headache coming on.

"What do you think is the most important thing to remember about making ceviche?" Jacques asked.

"I really couldn't say," I said, letting my irritation show through, "and yet I feel certain that you're about to tell me."

"Refrigeration," Jacques finished triumphantly.

"Refrigeration. Gotcha," I said, taking another sip of my coffee. Clearly I was going to need more caffeine to get through the rest of this conversation. "I'm sorry, was there a point buried in there somewhere?"

Jacques gestured to a large bowl of ceviche on the counter next to the refrigerator.

"Given the importance of refrigeration in the preparation of this dish, can you possibly guess why this ceviche is currently sitting out on the counter rather than in the refrigerator?"

I raised my eyebrows enquiringly and took a large bite of scone to remind myself of why I shouldn't pitch Jacques overboard. It was really a good thing that he had a gift for cooking, since it was hard to imagine too many other professions where you could be so intensely irritating without being fired.

"Because you think that giving your paying client food poisoning is a great line on your résumé?"

Jacques flung the double doors of the refrigerator open dramatically. "Because," he said, "I cannot put it in a refrigerator when the refrigerator is full of wine."

"Really?" I asked.

"Really," he said triumphantly.

"Or you could have just gone with 'Hey, Lora…is there another place you can keep the wine?'"

"I could have," he admitted.

"You could have."

"But I was going for dramatic effect."

"I saw that." I grabbed a few bottles of wine and headed down to the wine cellar. "I'll take care of it, but in the future, a little less dramatic effect might be a nice change of pace."

I looked around for Kyrill on the way down the stairs, but apparently he wasn't up yet. Shouldering my way into the wine cellar, I put the bottles on the floor and closed the door behind me so that I could navigate in the tight space. I felt almost guilty opening the forbidden wine racks, but since I was putting wine in rather than taking it out, I was sure Kyrill wouldn't mind.

I put the two bottles I had with me in the bottom of the coldest rack. There was plenty of space down here for all the wine that was bunching up Jacques's panties. I'd have to ask Kyrill just to leave the bottles he selected in the cellar so that I could take them up as we needed them. I idly ran my fingers over the labels of some of the wines. *Very nice*, I thought.

Really, I was going to have to reconsider my prejudice against the nouveau riche. A steady diet of this stuff might make me a little more willing to turn a blind eye to open Armani shirts, chunky gold medallions, and excessive chest hair.

As I stood up to close the fridge, I noticed that one of the bottles had been wrongly placed. It was a bottle of Screaming Eagle, one of the finest reds in the world. Pinkie would have a stroke if he saw it here in the refrigerated case. I grabbed the bottle by the neck and pulled it, intending to put in the proper fridge before it was completely destroyed. It stuck, as if glued to the rack. Frowning, I examined the bottle more closely.

The bottle was actually attached to the rack at the midpoint. I pulled up on the neck of it at an angle and the whole thing tilted upward as if it were a lever. I looked up in surprise to see one of the racks pivot silently on oiled hinges, revealing a small glass door. Maybe another section to the wine cellar, I thought. That was probably where he kept the good stuff. Now the price tag on the wine cellar finally made sense. That hundred and twenty-five thousand bucks had apparently been spent to protect his most precious bottles from his larcenous crew. Curious, I walked over to the door and looked through it.

"Oh shit," I breathed. Behind the door was a small room that apparently abutted Howard's cabin. It was brightly lit with fluorescent lights, and I could see almost a dozen cots stacked in the claustrophobic space. Padded restraints were attached to the empty beds. A toilet stood against the back of the room. There wasn't a doubt in my mind that I was looking at a cell.

While my brain dimly registered the details, my attention was drawn to a woman seated on the floor. She was young—not out of her twenties—and despite the fact that she wore no makeup and was dressed in simple jeans and a black T-shirt, she was outstandingly beautiful, with clear golden skin and blonde hair. Her eyes were closed, and her head hung down, cradled in her hands. She was rocking back and forth, every line in her body tense. I waved my hand to catch her attention, but she didn't move. One-way glass, I realized.

"Hello," I said softly. Nothing. Soundproofed as well. I stood there, staring, my heart pounding as I tried to make sense of what I was seeing. A woman in a hidden cell on a yacht. A prisoner. Kyrill wasn't dealing in sofas or even heroin, I realized with a cold feeling of terror. He was dealing in slaves.

My breath caught in my throat. I was alone on a boat with people who were willing to imprison and sell innocent people. What were they going to do to this girl? What were they planning to do to me?

The faint noise of conversation in the hallway snapped me to my senses, and I ran back to the case of white wines, scrabbling for the bottle of Screaming Eagle. I pressed it down desperately, praying that the door would move faster. If anyone knew what I had seen, I was dead.

I turned to face the door, half-convinced that I would see Kyrill standing in it, a gun his hand. The door was still closed. Stifling a sob of relief, I grabbed the bottles I had brought and tried to compose myself. I wanted to run, to get as far away from this boat as I could, but we were miles from land. There was no place to go.

I had to get out of the cellar. I listened intently at the door. There was nothing. Whoever had been speaking had passed. I opened it, intending to slip out and replace the bottles in the kitchen.

"Why are you here?" Gasping, I turned around quickly and saw Kyrill coming down the stairs. He looked at the bottles in my hand and narrowed his eyes suspiciously.

I froze, trying control my breathing. For a brief moment that seemed like an eternity, I just stared at him. "I was just looking for a place to store these bottles," I said, forcing the words out through lips frozen with fear. Kyrill looked at me in silence.

I tried again. "Jacques is mad because there's all this wine in his prep fridge and he's making ceviche, which is made with raw fish, so you have to be especially careful, and it needs more fridge space, and I said I'd put the bottles down here, but then I remembered that you're really very picky about how the wine cellar is organized, so I thought maybe there was a mini-fridge or something in one of the cabins, maybe even in my cabin. I haven't really had time to look yet..."

God! I was babbling. He was going to realize that I knew about the secret room, and then he was going to kill me. I stopped myself short with an effort. "Do you know if there's a mini-fridge down here somewhere?" I finished weakly.

Kyrill shrugged off my torrent of words. "Every cabin has one," he said. He gave me a hard look.

"Great," I squeaked. "I'll just keep the wine in my fridge and come down whenever we need a new bottle." I smiled through my terror and edged past him back toward my cabin.

"Lora," he said.

"Yes?" I replied, holding my breath.

"Today we will relax for a while before we go back to our negotiations. I expect you to do your best to make sure our friends have a good time. The discussions last night with Spiro were very successful. I hope that, together, we can make sure that he is equally well prepared for our discussions this evening. Lots of wine. Good fun, right?"

I cast my mind back to Spiro last night, so drunk that he could barely stand up and prattling on about his failures as a businessman. A shudder came over me as I realized how much we were all in Kyrill's power as long as we were on this yacht. Was Spiro a victim as well? Was that why Kyrill wanted him completely incapacitated?

Realizing that I had been silent for too long, I forced my mouth into the shape of a smile. "That's why I'm here," I said. "To make sure everyone has fun." I felt the sudden urge to giggle and realized that I had to get away from Kyrill so that I could pull myself together before I cracked. "I'm just going to put these in the mini-fridge," I said, holding up the bottles. "In my cabin."

Kyrill grunted in response and headed back upstairs.

Once in my cabin, I locked the door and double checked the connecting locks to make sure they were still latched. "Shit, shit, shit," I muttered under my breath as I fumbled through my bag for my cell phone. My hands were shaking so badly that I dropped it three times before finally getting it out. I looked at it for a moment. Chris had said that Viper did work for organized crime. What if it hadn't been Clancy who had bugged my phone? What if had been Kyrill all along? If he was part of the Russian Mafia, he could have had my apartment searched. He could have bugged my phone.

I thought back to the hotel. I had thought Kyrill had bribed the maid to take the rap for the murder, but what if it hadn't been like that at all? I remembered that curious half smile the woman had given me, and it suddenly clicked into place. She was the same woman I'd seen coming out of Kyrill's building in Moscow. Different hair, no makeup, but that smile—I was almost sure I was right. Kyrill hadn't bribed the woman to take the rap for the murder; he had hired the woman to commit the murder.

I dialed Pinkie's number desperately. The phone beeped, and I held it away from my face to look at it. No coverage. "Dammit!" I whispered frantically. Howard had said his phone wasn't working. Maybe we were in a dead spot. I looked at the screen. I had received two high-priority messages shortly after we had cast off. The first one was a missed call from my brother. He had left a voicemail message, but I couldn't access the network to listen to it.

The second was a text message from my brother containing a rather blurry photo of a dapper, effete-looking man with a pronounced double chin only partially concealed by an ascot. I scrolled down to the message and felt my stomach drop. "I found a photo," Chris had written. "This is Kyrill Antonov. I don't know who you're on the boat with, but it's not him. Tell me what to do."

32

It turns out that it's really very hard to think logically when you're facing even a reasonable possibility of imminent death. You'd think that time would slow down so that you could figure out some way to save yourself, but really, it's more like trying to read a sonnet while someone jumps on your chest. It's hard to get into the rhythm of the thing when you feel like your heart and lungs are about to explode.

Okay, I thought, trying to control my breathing. *Let's think this through. Kyrill, who is not Kyrill, is apparently a white slaver. Or,* I corrected myself mentally, *a human trafficker*. Probably the term "white slaver" was hopelessly outdated and possibly racist. *Whatever*, I thought, mentally shaking myself. The point was that this person, who I would continue to call Kyrill since I had no idea what his real name was, had a boat that was designed to smuggle human beings across international waters. A boat that was now cutting through international waters with me on board.

Right. Now that we'd clearly determined that I was on a boat designed to enable criminal activity, I was forced to acknowledge the actual criminal activity that was going on right this second. Clearly, there was at least one person on the boat who was in the process of being smuggled. Possibly two, if I was also being smuggled without my knowledge. I wondered what I would bring on the black market. Probably not very much if I wasn't sucking in and wearing a lot of mascara. In fact, if I gorged myself on donuts and went out without sunscreen, I would be absolutely unsalable by the time we hit shore. I marked that down as Plan B.

I briefly wondered if I could get the door open to rescue the girl. I pictured the two of us, armed with bottles of champagne, holding off Kyrill and the captain. It had a certain *Thelma & Louise* appeal, but I figured it would probably end with both of us dead. Come to think of it, *Thelma & Louise* also ended that way, which was probably why it wasn't the best movie to model my escape after. No, trying to rescue her was a pretty good way to ensure that I would shortly need rescuing myself. If I got off the boat alive, I would go straight to the police. It was the best chance for her—the best chance for both of us.

Now that I had covered the critical points, I needed to figure out what to do. Ideally, I'd like to be about as far away from Kyrill and this boat as possible. Paris in the springtime was probably almost completely white slaver-free, for example. London might be as well. Heck, even Delaware was starting to look pretty good. But how could I get off the boat?

Jumping overboard and swimming for it would have been appealing except for the fact that my swimming skills were pretty much limited to a lazy breaststroke from the steps of the pool to the swim-up bar. If someone came up on a kayak and anchored it ten yards from our boat, and the sea was completely flat, and assuming that a fish didn't touch me, because that would certainly cause me to freak out and drown—if all of those things happened—I supposed I could make my escape that way, but otherwise I figured my chances of death by drowning were substantially higher than my chances of death by white slavery.

What if I could hijack the boat somehow? I ran through the good guy/bad guy numbers in my head. Jacques, who I had hired on my own, was probably a good guy. I mean, obviously he was a neurotic drama queen, so maybe good guy wasn't the exact term I was looking for, but he probably wasn't actively trying to sell human beings into bondage. One for the good guys.

The captain was clearly a bad guy. That evil mole under his eye should have been a dead giveaway. And the name—Vlad like Vlad the Impaler and Vladimir Putin, both notorious bad guys from Eastern Europe. Who names their kid Vlad unless they're expecting them to turn out to be a complete psychopath?

In Sergei's case, it wasn't so obvious, but common sense dictated that as a part of the crew, he was undoubtedly also a bad guy. That probably explained why he was in the kitchen so much. He wasn't there to make apples into stars; he was there to slice and dice Jacques in case he tried to help himself to some Screaming Eagle from the wine cellar.

That was already two bad guys, and that wasn't even counting Kyrill. Dammit! I knew something was off about this job, but like always, I let Pinkie yammer at me until I was ready to discount my woman's intuition. The only thing less believable than Captain Vlad and Sergei being the professional crew of a yacht was Kyrill himself being an interior decorator. The fact that they were white slavers was probably obvious to everyone who wasn't me.

I wished Pinkie were here so that I could kick him with one of my pointiest Christian Louboutin shoes. And so that he could rescue me. Probably I should let him rescue me before I kicked him, although given how terrified and mad I was, I might be unable to help myself.

I chewed on a fingernail obsessively. What about Spiro and his minions? I knew that Spiro was, in fact, the boss of a Greek shipping company. Armand had told me so at dinner, when he was gloating over Spiro's rough year. It was possible that Spiro wasn't aware of Kyrill's sideline. And Kyrill had murdered Spiro's security guy, probably because he found out what was going on. Maybe the business with Spiro was legit and Kyrill was just taking advantage of this business cruise to do a little white slaving on the side. Multitasking for mobsters. On the other hand, maybe white slavery was the business that Kyrill and Spiro were discussing. I couldn't be sure.

I was even hazier on Alexander's and Howard's possible roles in this crime. Kyrill had made it a point of excluding them from the discussions he was having with Spiro. And I had to admit that I found it hard to believe that Howard, a Peace Corps volunteer and fellow mid-Atlantic escapee, was trafficking in women. Alexander, on the other hand, I wasn't so ready to discount. Clearly, he was a little sleazy. And while I didn't know him well, he didn't seem like much of a humanitarian. What if he wasn't involved, but Spiro was? I had to assume that if push came to shoving me off the boat to protect his family, I'd be fish food.

More fingernail biting, which wasn't doing my manicure any

favors. By my reckoning I was on my own in this situation. I couldn't be sure that anyone was innocent, and if I went to the wrong person for help, I was as good as dead.

If I couldn't trust anyone to help me take over the boat and I couldn't dive off and swim to shore, that left me with the extremely unappealing option of spending the next two days eating, drinking, and chatting with men who were very possibly engaged in selling other human beings into bondage. Of course, in all that chatting if I accidentally said anything to arouse suspicion, I'd be dead, which was going to put a pretty serious damper on my witty repartee.

I felt a chill run over me as I suddenly realized why Kyrill had come to my room last night. He wasn't checking to see whether I was disturbed; he was checking to see if Spiro, in his drunken state, had let anything slip. Kyrill wanted everyone drinking so that he could take advantage of them in his negotiations, but if they were too drunk to watch their tongues, I would be the one who would pay the price. I shuddered.

On the positive side, even if he had been wrong about who Kyrill actually was, Pinkie knew that I was travelling with Spiro and Alexander, and they were definitely who they claimed to be. So at least they had to know that if I vanished, questions would be asked. Pinkie, god bless him, could probably rally half the royalty in Europe to put pressure on Interpol to find me.

My brother, Chris, also had a picture of Kyrill and was probably figuring out what was going on even as I sat here. Maybe he'd find Pinkie, and they'd manage to put together a rescue. I mean, agoraphobic computer hackers and social butterfly grifters were totally the dream team when it came to coordinating a rescue from international criminals, right?

And even if they didn't figure it out, I could also take some comfort in the fact that I wasn't a dazzlingly beautiful twentysomething. Given how much I'd always wanted to be one of those, it felt odd to think that way, but while I liked to think of myself as attractive—and god knew I worked hard enough at it—I didn't figure I was actually gorgeous enough to be a target of white slavers. As far as I could see, the most likely reason for me to be on the boat was to pour the drinks, make small talk, and keep Alexander and Howard away from the salon when Kyrill was talking to Spiro.

On the other hand, if I wasn't being smuggled, it wasn't clear to me why Kyrill had hacked my phone or had someone go through my apartment. But maybe he was just doing due diligence. Maybe he wanted to confirm that I wasn't a spy or a police officer or a member of some crime-solving dynamic duo like Rizzoli and Isles. Certainly nothing on my phone would have given him the impression that I was anything other than a woman who spent too much time in bars and too little time getting bikini waxes.

I chewed my lip. Despite my anxiety and terror, the likeliest conclusion was that I was safe for the time being—unless Kyrill found out that I knew about his secret, in which case I was certainly dead, Pinkie or no.

I sat in my room turning the problem over in my head until I heard a sharp knock at the door. My heart lurched, and all of my rationalizations deserted me. They knew. They were coming to kill me.

I steeled my nerves and opened the door. It was Sergei. "Mr. Antonov sent me downstairs to find you," he said. "You need to go up and entertain the guests."

I searched Sergei's face for any hint of evil. It was as round and guileless as always, but I fancied I could detect a little more hardness in his eyes. Of course, that might just have been from five hours spent making apple stars.

"I'll be right up," I promised. I closed the door behind me and checked the phone again. Still dead. Slipping it into my pocket, I took a deep breath and headed upstairs.

33

I stopped by the kitchen, nominally to tell Jacques about the wine, but really to check for weapons. I didn't like my chances against Kyrill and the crew if they found out that I knew about the girl, but if it came to an all-out battle for my life, I wanted to go down fighting.

"Did you find a place to put the wine?" Jacques demanded. "I cannot work under these conditions."

I stifled a shriek of hysterical laughter. *That makes two of us*, I thought.

"The wine's in my cabin," I said. "Just come find me when we're about ready for lunch, and I'll go down and get a couple of bottles."

"If you leave the door unlocked, I can have Sergei take it out. It's just us on the boat. No need to be worried about thieves," he said, chuckling.

Thieves would actually be a lovely change of pace, I reflected. "Trust me," I said, "Thieves are the least of my worries. But I wouldn't want to expose Sergei to the mess in my room. I'll take care of it."

While Jacques prattled on about the mysteries of ceviche, I tuned him out and looked around for anything that might come in handy later. Knives—maybe good for a quick slash before jumping overboard. On the negative side, you had to get really close to use them, and my goal was to stay as far away from any would-be murderers as possible.

The fire extinguisher looked promising. I'd seen plenty of cartoons where the bad guys were sprayed into submission with fire-retardant foam. In real life, though, that would probably just lead to foam-covered white slavers, which was hardly a lifesaving improvement. If push came to shove, I could always use it as a blunt object to bludgeon someone to death, but given its size, I couldn't exactly tuck it in my back pocket and carry it around with me. My butt wasn't quite big enough to hide that, despite what Pinkie said every time I had seconds on carrot cake.

I scanned the counters. Jacques had laid out a lemon zester. I paused, considering. Zesting someone to death would definitely be painful, but it seemed unlikely that the victim could be enticed to stand still for the process. Maybe it was something I could revisit if I managed to single-handedly subdue the bad guys and needed information. Or if I just wanted revenge for all the Botox I was going to need to erase the worry lines my state of mortal terror was causing.

I felt my heart sink. There wasn't anything here that looked like it would help. I picked up another scone and chewed thoughtfully. At least my impending possible death should give me a pass on watching my weight. Nobody cares if a dead woman has fat thighs.

"Are you listening to me?" Jacques demanded.

"Uh...sorry," I said. "Could you repeat?"

"For tomorrow's lunch. Quiche or Spanish tortilla?" he asked impatiently, tapping a foot.

"Aren't those basically the same thing?"

"Fine!" he snapped. "I'll choose for myself."

Backing away, I tried to mollify him. "I'm sure you'll make the right choice."

I furtively checked the screen of my cell phone again. Still no coverage. With my eyes fixed desperately on the No Service notification, I almost ran into Alexander, who was coming up the back staircase. "Aigh!" I shrieked, jumping backward.

Alexander quickly grabbed my arms as if to steady me. "I startled you," he said unnecessarily. "I'm so sorry." He steered me back against the wall. "My, you're so tense," he said, rubbing his hands up and down my arms. "Just relax."

"I'm fine," I said. I waited a moment. "You can let go of me," I said pointedly.

I had completely forgotten about Alexander and couldn't believe that he was interested in sticking to his ridiculous seduction script on a ship full of human traffickers. Except, I reminded myself, Alexander didn't know that we were on a ship filled with human traffickers. Or he did know, and he was one of them. In either case, he was obviously still intent upon playing this scene out to its logical conclusion. I, on the other hand, was really much, much more concerned with managing to make it to Malta without being drowned, shot, or sold to someone who hadn't quite accepted the Emancipation Proclamation.

Alexander let go of my arms and took a step closer so that only a finger's breadth separated us. He ran a finger lightly under my bikini strap, moving it back into place. "I was hoping to see more of you last night," he said. "You locked the door."

"Yes, well," I said. "I really was quite tired."

"You didn't seem tired to me," he murmured, his fingers lingering where the strap met the cup.

I slapped his hand away. "My apologies for any misunderstanding that might have come up," I said. "I'm really just here to help Kyrill run the yacht and to relax. Whatever might have happened last night won't happen again, I can assure you."

"I can help you relax," Alexander said, his nose almost nuzzling my ear.

"I don't need any help relaxing," I said, smiling tightly and ducking under his arm to grab the stair railing. "So if you'll excuse me…"

"Perhaps later," Alexander said smoothly, trailing his hand over my arm as I made my escape. I glanced back over my shoulder to see if he had taken the hint. He was smiling. He had definitely not taken the hint.

Putting my chin up regally, I headed for the railing, hoping to avoid any more conversation with Kyrill.

Kyrill saw me and came over, his face dark. "Where have you been?" he asked in a low, irritated voice. "It's almost nine o'clock. I need you here to entertain our guests."

"I have been entertaining our guests," I said tersely, masking my fear as irritation. "Alexander has decided that I'm available." I neglected to mention that my own behavior last night probably upgraded "available" to "hot to trot." "I've spent the last few minutes extricating myself from the back stairs."

Kyrill waved a hand dismissively. "I don't care about that," he said. "I need you to keep them in a good mood. Pour champagne. Flatter them. Make witty conversation. This is what you are here for. This is what I am paying you ten thousand dollars for."

"Right," I said. Apparently, we were going to drop the polite fiction that I was doing him a favor and he was covering my expenses. I hoped he didn't decide to drop any other polite fictions. I was pretty sure that the polite fiction that he wasn't a white slaver was the only thing standing between me and an untimely death right now.

I didn't know how I was going to manage witty conversation and flattery when my brain was frantically trying to figure out how to get my body off of this boat and to the police, but given the possible cost of failure, I was going to give it my best shot.

Kyrill seemed to sense my ambivalence. He took me by the arm, his hard fingers pressing into the flesh. "This is important," he said, his eyes burning. "Tomorrow night this trip will be over. I need this time. I need them to be happy. I need them to be relaxed."

"I'll do my best," I said, trying to smile through the waves of terror running down my spine.

"Good," Kyrill said, stretching his lips into a humorless smile. "And Lora…"

"Yes?"

"Should you hear anything or see anything from our guests that strikes you as suspicious, I trust you'll come see me."

"Uh, of course."

"Because if there's one thing I've learned in this business, it's that not everyone is who they seem to be." He gave me a hard, fathomless look before turning his back and walking away.

34

Jacques had moved breakfast to the deck so that everyone could enjoy the view while eating. Spiro, who I was half expecting would have died in his sleep, looked remarkably energetic. Furrily resplendent in a microscopic red Speedo, his was tucking into a piece of starry apple tart with gusto. "Lora!" He smiled widely. "How did you sleep last night?"

"Fine," I said warily. "You?"

"I always sleep like a baby when I'm out on the open sea."

And completely hammered, I mentally added. Apparently, Spiro either had no recollection of coming to my cabin last night or was just too embarrassed to talk about it. Either of those was fine with me. I had more to worry about than Spiro's possible death by liver failure.

"Are the apple tarts okay?" I asked. After seeing Sergei's fingernails, I had no intention of tasting them to find out for myself. Maybe if I were lucky, everyone but me would contract a raging case of botulism.

"Perfect," he said.

I scrutinized him for signs of food poisoning. He looked depressingly healthy. "Are you and Kyrill going to be working today?"

Spiro nodded. "Yes. We still have many details to discuss. We will join you through lunch, but then we will have to go to the salon and look again at the contracts. Kyrill," he said confidentially, "is a very cautious man. Very detail oriented. I can see why he has been so successful in business."

"I guess shipping is a very complicated business," I said, trying close down the conversation. The last thing I wanted was for Spiro to slip up and accidentally tell me something about their business that would require my gory death.

"Shipping is the simplest of all businesses," Spiro said. "It's just moving things from one place to another."

"Ah, well then," I said. "When you put it that way, I'm surprised more people don't get into it."

I looked over at Howard, who was staring at his phone. "Did your phone start working again?" I asked, feeling a surge of hope.

He shook his head despondently. "I can't understand it," he said. "I never have problems with this phone. I really need to check on that cheese."

"I don't have any signal either," I said. "Maybe it's sunspots or something."

"Maybe," Howard agreed, staring in frustration at his blank screen.

"You children are too much in love with your cell phones," Spiro said. "You are on a beautiful yacht, and all you can think about is that there might be something better happening somewhere else in the world. Look around," he said, throwing his arms out expansively. "How many times in life are you truly alone? No cars, no buildings, no neighbors, no ringing phones, no television. Just you and the sea and this boat."

"And that other boat," Alexander said snarkily, happy to burst his father's bubble.

"What other boat?" Kyrill asked, sitting up.

"Over there." Alexander pointed back behind our yacht. Sure enough, there was another boat out there within view, just coming over the horizon. My heart leaped. Rescuers! On second thought, the chance of them being rescuers was slim. Witnesses! Almost as good.

Kyrill dug around in a drawer and came up with a pair of binoculars. He looked grim. "I'm surprised to see someone else out here," he said. He held the binoculars to his eyes. "*Fortune's Fancy*," he read. He shrugged. "Never heard of it. Probably just someone out for a sail."

"You know what might be fun?" I said. "Maybe we should have them over for lunch. I'm sure that Jacques would love to whip up a few more dishes. We can head over their direction, send the tender with an invitation…"

Kyrill looked at me as if I had gone mad. "I'm afraid that will not be possible," he said in a tone that brooked no discussion. "We have a timetable to keep to. We don't have time for entertaining strangers."

I grasped at straws. "Maybe you and Spiro could talk about your business, and Alexander and Howard and I could take the tender over to say hi and hang out for a while." *And I could tell them to call the police so I could make sure your white-slaving ass is locked up forever in some horrible gulag,* I silently added.

"Absolutely not," Kyrill said. He flashed me a look that made it clear that this discussion was over. "We sail on."

I sat and watched the boat on the horizon as the men chatted. What excuse could I give that would let me get over to the other yacht without raising suspicion? Maybe a sudden illness. Or something that we were missing. What if the corkscrew broke? Given Kyrill's insistence on keeping everyone drinking, surely a broken corkscrew would constitute an emergency.

Half an hour after we had noticed it, the boat was definitely larger in our sights. Kyrill frowned every time he caught sight of it. It was gaining on us.

"If you'll excuse me, for a moment," he said. "I need to have a brief word with the captain."

He put down his glass and headed for the stairs to the bridge, leaving the rest of us by the pool.

"Kyrill's not really the most social person, is he?" Alexander drawled.

Spiro shook his head. "I don't blame him," he said. "We're in international waters here. Of course the Horn of Africa is much more dangerous than this, but Libya has plenty of pirates, and it's not too far away."

"Pirates?" I asked. "Like eye patch and parrot pirates?"

"No," Spiro said. "Like AK-47 and grenade launcher pirates. Somalis are the most famous pirates today. They almost brought international shipping around the Horn of Africa to a halt a few years ago. There were a lot of kidnappings, murders, hostage situations." He took another sip of his champagne. "Savages."

"They're not savages," Howard said, pushing his glasses up on his nose. "They're people without any other options who are just trying to survive."

"I'll be sure to tell them that you feel their pain if they turn out to be pirates," Alexander snorted.

"You said 'almost,'" I said to Spiro. "What stopped them?"

"Well, the US military went in a couple of times, which helped, but what really made the difference was when commercial shippers and private yachts started carrying weapons."

"Weapons?" I asked sharply. "Where would they keep these weapons? I mean, in a boat like this, for example." I tried to stifle my urge to reach across and shake the information out of Spiro.

Alexander laughed. "Are you planning a mutiny?"

"Just curious," I said, striving not to sound like this was a life or death kind of curious. "I went through the boat pretty thoroughly before we got on, and I didn't see any weapons."

Spiro shrugged. "You'd have to ask Kyrill or the captain. They really could be anywhere. The only thing that's sure is that they're locked up. Piracy may be a threat, but mutiny is always a possibility as well."

The boat suddenly vibrated beneath our feet. We were speeding up.

"What are the chances that the people on that boat are pirates?" I asked. All things considered, I thought pirates were probably a slightly safer bet than white slavers, but I wasn't sure how much of that belief was based on the fact that Johnny Depp in a pirate costume was absolutely adorable.

"There's a very low chance that they're pirates," Alexander said.

"But it's certainly not impossible," Spiro chimed in.

Kyrill joined us again. "I'd prefer if we're not interrupted," he said, "so I've asked the captain to speed up a bit so that we put some space between us and whoever's on that boat."

We looked back at the other yacht. It didn't appear to be disappearing. If anything, it seemed to be gaining on us slightly. Kyrill looked through the binoculars again.

"They've changed their speed as well," he said.

"Maybe we should break out some weapons, just in case they turn out to be pirates," I said, placing a hand on Kyrill's arm. "You know, always be prepared. Like Boy Scouts. If you tell me where they are, I'll get them." I tried to look like the kind of girl you would trust to hand out weapons in the event of an emergency. "Safety first, right?"

Kyrill looked at me dismissively. "Don't be absurd."

We all watched silently as the boat gradually drew nearer. I could feel tension emanating from Kyrill. I supposed that if I were smuggling human beings across international borders in my yacht, I'd be pretty averse to unexpected visitors as well.

Spiro motioned for the binoculars. "Well," he said, peering at the boat, "if they are following us, they will catch us. Their boat is faster than this one. They should have a top speed of 34 knots."

"How fast can we go?" I asked, hoping it was significantly slower than that.

"We can go 22 knots," Kyrill said. "But the tender is faster than that. Maybe 50 knots."

I perked up. If the tender could go faster than the boat, all I had to do was get on the tender and make a break for it. Of course, I didn't know how to get the tender off the boat. Or how to drive a boat. Or how to navigate, even assuming I knew where we were, which I didn't. With my current luck, I'd end up marooned somewhere drinking my own urine. Still, I marked that down as something meriting further thought.

Captain Vlad came down from the bridge and pulled Kyrill aside, speaking into his ear in a low voice. Kyrill looked at me sharply. "The other ship has contacted us."

Alexander raised his eyebrows. "Well? Are they pirates, or are they just some old married couple bored with each other's company?"

"Neither, apparently," Kyrill said, his irritation coming through loud and clear. "The boat's owner is named Lady Esther Harvey. She says that she needs to speak with Lora Godwin. Urgently. In person. The captain told her that we were busy, but she wouldn't take no for an answer." Given how furious both Kyrill and the captain looked, I was surprised that anyone would have the temerity not to take no for an answer.

I shrugged my shoulders as all eyes turned to me. "I don't know anyone named Lady Esther Harvey," I said honestly.

"Are you sure?" Kyrill asked.

I racked my brains. Thanks to Pinkie, I knew tons of titled types, but that name didn't ring a bell. Maybe that divorcée who was always wearing the transparent dresses—what was her name again? Lady Hervey, I thought. But we weren't friends, and while her first name escaped me, I was reasonably sure that it wasn't Esther. In my experience, people named Esther tended to not be people who would take any excuse to rip all of their clothing off and don body stockings for the paparazzi.

"Pretty sure."

"Well, they're sending their tender with Lady Esther now," Kyrill said. "I guess we'll meet her together."

35

Though Lady Esther's yacht wasn't too far away, the tender seemed to take forever to cross the water. Kyrill tracked their progress with binoculars that he didn't offer to share. I could see that the boat was a wooden motorboat. It looked stately and elegant, but not particularly fast. I would have preferred it if they were driving one of those drug smuggler boats from Miami Vice. Preferably one that contained a cop. And as long as I was wishing, I'd be even happier if that cop looked like Colin Farrell.

As the boat crossed the water, I racked my brain for something I could say that would force Kyrill to let me leave. Maybe I could fake appendicitis. I fingered my stomach absently, vaguely noting that a diet of pastries and champagne wasn't doing my waistline any favors. I wasn't sure exactly where my appendix was, but then again, he was a white slaver, not a black market organ dealer. He probably didn't know where my appendix was either.

"What kind of boat is that tender?" I asked Spiro.

"It's a Hacker Craft," Spiro replied. "Beautiful boats."

"Beautiful," I agreed. "Are they fast?"

"Middling," he said. "You could get it up to 40 knots in a perfectly calm sea. They're not for racing, if that's what you're asking."

I mentally grimaced. Kyrill's tender was faster than Lady Esther's. If I were dying of appendicitis, it wouldn't make sense to send me off with a stranger in a slower boat. I tried desperately to think of a ruse. If I was going to get off of the yacht, it would have to be by stealth.

The boat pulled alongside, and Sergei used ropes to help grapple it in place so that he could extend a ladder down to the passengers. The first to ascend the ladder was a matronly woman of late middle age dressed in white capri pants and a tunic-style sleeveless top that managed to look incredibly expensive while remaining woefully unflattering. Her silver hair was stiff and unbending, even in the brisk wind. She looked less like someone who spent time at home baking cookies than someone who spent time at home ordering her personal chef to bake cookies.

Behind her came a man dressed in naval whites, his tanned skin leathery from years in the sun. He was several years younger than Lady Esther, and his face was completely expressionless. A crew member, I assumed. I turned my attention back to the woman, who was scanning our small party with a look of intense distress.

Kyrill stepped forward to speak to her (or, more likely, given the expression on his face, to order her off the boat immediately), but she ignored him completely as her eyes latched onto me.

"Oh," she said, "You must be Lora Godwin." She stepped forward and took both of my hands in hers.

I looked over at Kyrill and shrugged, as mystified as he was. "I am," I said. "Have we met?"

"I'm Lady Esther," she said. "A friend of Prince Philippe's."

"You're Pinkie's friend?" I repeated in confusion. Pinkie had somehow figured out that I was in danger and had sent this...mom...to save me? Where was Interpol? Jesus, Pinkie must be losing his touch.

"Pinkie. Yes, of course, you kids do call him that. I'm afraid I have some rather bad news for you. It's your mother." Lady Esther's face creased in sympathy as my heart dropped into my shoes.

"My mother?" I said. "What's wrong? I knew she wasn't well, but she wouldn't tell us..." I felt tears spring to my eyes.

Lady Esther looked at me sympathetically. "I don't know about that, my dear, but I'm afraid she's been in a car accident. She's in a coma right now. They don't know if she's going to make it." She squeezed my hands. "My dear, Pinkie asked me to get you to the airport in Thessaloniki as soon as we could manage it. There's a flight waiting there to bring you home."

I wiped at my eyes ineffectually even as I tried to process this information. Was this a ruse on Pinkie's part? A car accident? But if she was sick, maybe she had fainted at the wheel. Why hadn't she told us what was wrong? My confusion and distress must have shown on my face.

"I…" I started.

"We are not finished with our trip," Kyrill said coldly.

Lady Esther's chins tightened, and I could see that she was about to give Kyrill a piece of her mind.

"But of course, family must come first," he finished, sighing. "Lora, pick up what you need for the trip, and we will send the rest after you."

I looked into the eyes of the man I knew was a white slaver and saw nothing but sympathy. This guy must be a master at compartmentalization. He probably rescued kittens in trees when he wasn't kidnapping desperate women and locking them in dank little cells.

"I… Thank you," I finished clumsily, blinking away tears.

"Godspeed," Spiro said, shaking his head. "I hope your mother recovers. There is nothing in this world as precious as family." He dropped a heavy hand onto Alexander's shoulder. For once, Alexander didn't look like he was fighting the instinct to fling it off.

Howard took it upon himself to accompany me to my cabin. "I really hope your mom's okay," he said. "There are some really great hospitals in Wilmington. I'm sure it will all work out fine. Cars these days are so safe. She'll be fine," he repeated, trailing off.

I threw some underwear and clothes into my oversized Louis Vuitton and pulled on a jacket. "Thank you for your concern, Howard," I said. "I hope you're right." I placed a hand on his shoulder. "Take care of yourself." I paused, wondering if I should say anything else.

If he wasn't involved in all of this, didn't he deserve to know that he was on a boat with at least one monster? Or that the shipping business that kept him glued to his phone was quite possibly a cover for a white slavery operation?

I couldn't risk it, I decided. Howard got stressed out over warm Bulgarian cheese. There was no chance he would be able to keep this secret until he got to safety. No, he was better off not knowing. Telling him now would only put his life at risk.

Howard smiled sympathetically and grabbed my bag, looking relieved to have something to do.

I made my way up to the deck, my stomach in turmoil. What if my mother really were dying? I felt short of breath just thinking about it. I would have to tell the police about the girl as soon as we hit land. How much time would I need to spend with the police before I could leave to be with my mother? What if they wouldn't let me go? What if I ended up trapped in Greece giving police statements while my mother died? What would happen to my brother if my mother died? He relied on her for laundry and pot roasts and stern lectures that he sometimes even listened to. This would crush him. I felt panic grip my chest.

I followed Howard up the stairs, fingering my phone in my pocket. Maybe the phone would work on board Lady Esther's boat. I could call Pinkie and my brother. Surely if anyone could get me out of Greece in a hurry, it was Pinkie.

Back up on deck, I saw that Jacques and Sergei had joined the impromptu goodbye party. "Don't worry," Jacques told me reassuringly. "We will be fine. It is only today and tomorrow. You need to focus on your family." He paused. "But do you think for tomorrow's lunch shrimp or salmon?"

"Shrimp," I said, stepping off onto the ladder.

"Really?" Jacques said. "I was thinking maybe salmon with a crème fraiche…"

Kyrill turned to glare at him and he fell silent. "Never mind," he said, holding up his hands and backing away from Kyrill. "I will take care of it."

"Goodbye and good luck," Kyrill said heavily. "I will contact you when we are in port to make arrangements. I'm sure I will see you again."

Unlikely, I thought, as I didn't plan on spending any time in prisons in the near future, and I was going to do everything in my power to make sure that that's where Kyrill spent the rest of his miserable existence.

With waves all around, I headed down the ladder, where the dour crewman was waiting with my bag. I waited until the boat was well underway before turning to Lady Esther, who was still holding my hand and clucking sympathetically.

"My mother," I said. "I couldn't say anything on the boat, but she's okay, right?" I flashed back to what my brother had told me.

"I mean, she's not really in a coma, is she? That was just Pinkie's way of getting me away from them, wasn't it?" I held my breath.

A look of surprise came over Lady Esther's face. "As far as I know, she's fine, dear. How clever of you. How did you know?"

"Oh thank god," I said, tears of relief springing to my eyes. I took a couple of deep breaths. For the first time since I had seen that poor girl, I felt as though I might make it out of this alive.

"Well," I said, "when my brother found out that Kyrill wasn't really Kyrill, I was sure he'd figure out some way to get in touch with Pinkie. Because my brother can't leave the house—not without having panic attacks. And Pinkie's always so good at this kind of thing. I mean, not this kind of thing exactly, of course. This is pretty far outside of anyone's normal experience, I'd think."

"Yes," Lady Esther said thoughtfully. "Prince Philippe is rather good at arranging things. But he didn't tell me what was going on. He just asked me to get you off of the yacht. He was the one who suggested that I tell you that story about your mother. We're not in any danger, are we?" she asked, suddenly looking concerned.

I looked at her steadily, hoping she wasn't the type to panic. "I don't want to alarm you," I said, "but they're white slavers. They're holding a girl captive in a secret compartment in the hull. I saw her. We need to tell the police."

There was a pause while Lady Esther looked at me, eyebrows raised, one perfectly manicured fingernail tapping on her arm thoughtfully. "I see," she finally said. She straightened her back and put her chin up in the best tradition of the English upper classes. "Let's get moving then, shall we?"

36

Our little boat pulled up to Lady Esther's yacht, and I waited impatiently while the vessels were made secure. Lady Esther's boat was smaller than Kyrill's, but even from the tender I could see that it had been finished to the highest standard. Whoever Lady Esther was, she wasn't strapped for cash.

I tapped my fingers on the railing and silently willed the captain to move faster as he methodically plodded through the knotting, double knotting and triple knotting that seemed to be required by basically any boating activity.

It was all I could do not to shove him out of the way and climb onboard over his prone body. Now that I knew my mother wasn't in any immediate danger, I was itching to get the police on board that boat so that Kyrill could be put in jail where he belonged. True, I'd be out $10,000, but we'd find the money somehow. And I'd be a hero. Like Catwoman. Except that Catwoman was actually a criminal, now that I thought about it. Really, I reflected, not too many kick-ass female superheroes these days.

Once we'd finally made it on board, Lady Esther bypassed the salon and bustled me into a small, modern cabin. She gestured me into an armchair and sat on the edge of the bed opposite me. "Now," she said, briskly, "let's get down to business. Do you think that these men will come after you? Were they suspicious at all?"

"I don't think so," I said. "I saw the girl by accident. I was looking around in the wine cellar. There's a secret room behind the racks…a cell, really. I got out before anyone saw me."

"Did the girl see you?" Lady Esther asked. "Because if she did, she might tell them. I assume someone has to be feeding her, right?"

I was impressed by her attention to detail. I had often wondered how the British made their upper classes so unflappable. Pinkie put it down to rampant buggery, but that was his excuse for everything.

"I'm sure she didn't see me," I said. "One-way glass. Soundproofing. She was completely isolated in there." I shuddered, imagining how she must feel.

This seemed to satisfy Lady Esther. "Not to pry, dear, but why were you on that yacht in the first place? Were those people friends of yours? It seems like white slavery would be a rather difficult thing to overlook in someone you know well enough to go on an overnight cruise with."

I shook my head. "It was just a job. The guy was supposed to be Kyrill Antonov, a friend of one of Pinkie's old school chums. They had spoken about me. Pinkie said he checked out. I was just supposed to help supervise the staff and keep everyone in a good mood so that Kyrill and Spiro could focus on business."

I laughed shakily. "I don't know what else was going on," I said, "but I think at least my part of the job was legit. Apparently, even white slavers need event hostesses."

"So they have no reason to come after you?" Lady Esther pressed.

"No," I said. "I'm sure they wouldn't have just let me get on the boat with you if they had any concerns. We're fine. We just need to get to the police as quickly as we can so that they can rescue that poor girl."

"Good," Lady Esther said, sitting back in relief. "Do you have a phone?"

"Yes," I said, pulling it out of my pocket. "It wouldn't work on the boat." I looked at it as the signal strength flickered up to three bars. "Thank god it's working again. They must have been jamming the signal."

"Thank god," echoed Lady Esther. "May I see it, please?"

I handed it to her, and she handed it in turn back to the crewman who had been on the boat earlier. "Take the battery out, and throw this overboard, James," she said.

"Yes, Lady Featherstone," James said, tucking it into his pocket.

I gaped at her. "What are you…" I trailed off as the name James had used sank in. "Lady Featherstone?! Like Clancy Featherstone?!" I shrieked. "The Clancy Featherstone who's been stalking me for months?"

Lady Esther tutted disapprovingly, her blue eyes suddenly icy. "Stalking you? Really. As though a little whore like you is too good for my Clancy. 'Event hostess.'" She flicked a finger at me. "What you are, my dear, is a tramp, and I should have had you gutted like a fish and dumped in the Thames the second Clancy expressed any interest in you."

I stared at her, speechless.

"When I saw you on the dock in Bulgaria I really couldn't believe my luck. I figured I'd have to make up a story about what had happened to you, but really, this will work out so much better. You went out alone with a crew of…white slavers, did you say? And you never came back. It seems very unlikely to me that they will be reporting this to the proper authorities."

I lunged toward the cabin door, only to come face to face with James, who was holding a handgun pointed steadily at my head. "I really wouldn't," said Lady Esther. "James is very handy with a pistol."

Lady Esther looked at me, loathing etched on her face. "How you've made Clancy suffer," she said. "First, you got your hooks into him, and once you got bored with him, you just cast him aside."

I held my hands up and tried to look innocent. Since I was innocent, that should have been easy, but the sweating and panicky breathing probably made me look like a deranged homicidal maniac. "Look," I said, "that is totally not what happened. I just planned his vacation for him. That was it. There was never anything romantic between us."

"And then," Lady Esther continued, ignoring me, "when he tried to express his love, you reject him. What was it? Did you move onto some other poor, naïve boy? Or do you just like watching men suffer? Either way, this ends now."

I scrambled for something to say that would convince Lady Esther that she was making a mistake. "Call Clancy!" I said. "Let me talk to him! I'm sure that he and I can work things out. I mean, perhaps I wasn't fair to him." I once would have said that the last thing I ever wanted to do again was talk to Clancy, but in comparison with being shot and dumped overboard by his mother, I was willing to promote that to the second-to-last thing I wanted to do.

Lady Esther looked at me witheringly. "It's a little late for that, I'm afraid. Here's what's going to happen. We're going to continue our trip, and I'm going to think for a while about what to do with you. If you're very lucky, I might call Clancy and give you to him as a little gift. If you're not very lucky, I will have James shoot you and dump your body overboard." She let out a dramatic sigh.

"I know which option is more appealing to me, obviously, but I do have to consider Clancy's feelings in this matter. Even after your appalling treatment of him, he still fancies himself in love with you." She looked up at the ceiling as if in wonder at the forgiving nature of her poor, besotted son. "Sometimes it's hard to know what's best to do as a mother," she said. "Of course, if you try to escape, that choice will be simplified immensely."

She stood up and walked to the door, turning back with her hand on the knob. "White slavers," she said, shaking her head in astonishment. "You really have the most appalling luck today, my dear."

37

The second Lady Esther had left, I started ransacking the cabin. Even if I had been willing to take a chance on being given to Clancy, I knew that wasn't the way things were going to end up. While I'm sure Clancy would have been overjoyed to have me delivered to his doorstep tied up in a neat little bow, any fool could see how that would play out. Clancy, being the lovesick dolt that he was, would immediately untie me. I, being me, would beat him unconscious with the first blunt object I could find before running to the police to have his mother locked up.

Of course, I could try to convince Lady Esther that I'd had a change of heart about her son, but even if she were that stupid, I doubted that she'd be really enthusiastic about adding an event hostess from Delaware to her family tree. My mother's side of the family had enough deranged rednecks to make even me think twice about the merits of reproduction. It was highly unlikely that someone who slept with a copy of *Burke's Peerage* on her nightstand would want to jump into the shallow end of that particular gene pool.

Dumping me overboard, in contrast, was win-win. Clancy wouldn't harbor a grudge because he'd never know about it. And maybe once my hideously bloated, fish-eaten body washed up somewhere, Clancy could finally free himself of his obsession and find some girl who was downtrodden, mercenary, or batshit crazy enough to spend the rest of her life with him.

Clearly, mommy dearest was going to come down on the side of one to the head and into the deep blue sea, in which case I had to get out of here now.

Unfortunately, the cabin was not offering up a lot of possibilities. I went over to the window, a small porthole that looked out the side of the boat. It was tiny. Perhaps a ten-year-old could have squeezed out through it, but a fully grown woman with a love of éclairs had no chance.

Even if I could fit through the porthole, it didn't mean that I could make it back to Kyrill's boat. I looked out the window. We were close now, but we were moving faster than they were. Given my poor swimming skills, even making it there now would be a challenge. In another three minutes, it would be an impossibility.

Turning my back on the window in frustration, I surveyed the rest of the room. The bookshelf contained a few books, mostly of the self-help variety. *The Man Who Loved Too Much. Stop Stalking in 30 Days. She's Just Not That Into You.* I was starting to realize I probably wasn't the first woman who had been on the receiving end of Clancy's soul mate spiel. I picked one up and hefted it in my hand, evaluating its potential as a weapon. It was disappointingly flimsy. Apparently, giving up stalking didn't require a lot of reading. If only Clancy had been a theoretical physicist rather than a neurotic, inbred ditherer! Then his library might have helped me beat his cow of a mother to death.

That left the closet. I opened the door and flipped through a rack of nautical-looking khakis and polo shirts. Under that were two drawers. I slid the first drawer out, crossing my fingers. White men's briefs. White T-shirts. White socks. I rifled through the drawer carefully. That was it. Clancy had to be the most spectacularly boring crazy person I had ever met.

I crossed my fingers before opening the last drawer. Surely it had to contain something useful? A gun would be best, but I would take anything—a pocket knife, a walking stick, a pair of very sharp collar stays. I pulled open the last drawer, holding my breath.

I exhaled in something between a sob and a chuckle. Sex toys. Of course it was sex toys. Given the week I was having, it would have to be either that or a rabid bat. I shook my head.

I poked around in the drawer despondently. Apparently, I owed Clancy an apology. He clearly wasn't as boring as I had always assumed. I picked up what looked like a tiny green feather duster and examined at it critically. It seemed like the kind of thing that would get unsanitary very quickly. Anal beads, also green, no help, and not something I particularly wanted to touch.

What was it with the green? I remembered that the dress I had been wearing the first time I met Clancy had also been green. If only I had been wearing red, perhaps this whole unfortunate sequence of events could have been avoided.

A heavy neon green dildo about the length of my forearm was pushed toward the back. I picked it up, marveling at its size. I couldn't imagine which orifice this was designed to fit into, but I was pretty sure it was one I didn't possess. It was slightly squishy to the touch. Gel. Good Vibrations was written across the base. I flipped the switch to low, and it started humming. I upped the power to high and it kicked into overdrive, jittering and shaking like a snake having an epileptic seizure.

I flipped it back off and brandished it at an imaginary assailant. Possible. Flipping it around so that I had it by its head, I thwacked the realistically detailed testicles into my other hand menacingly. Better. I set it aside. The squishiness made it less lethal than I would have liked, but I supposed it was stiff enough to slow someone down, particularly if they were the kind of people who were distracted by neon green testicles flying toward their heads.

The last two items in the drawer were equally unhelpful. One was a ball gag, also green, to match the dildo, I supposed. The other was a large tub of something called Chocolate Body Paint. ("Brush included!" the label promised.) I really doubted I would live long enough to be concerned about starvation, so I didn't bother to open that. Being the kind of person who struggles to eat nachos after seeing someone else's hand in the bowl, I really didn't want to ponder the bacterial load of Clancy's chocolate body paint.

That was it. I sat on the edge of the bed to think.

What I needed was a way to get a message to someone. Preferably Interpol. Barring that, Pinkie. If even that weren't possible, I'd settle for the ability to contact Kyrill. I mean, white slavers wouldn't generally be my go-to rescuers, but my earlier calculation still had to be valid. As long as they believed I knew nothing about the girl in the secret room, they had no reason to kill me. Who would pour the champagne? Who would play footsie with Alexander under the table? I could still be a valuable addition to their white slavery organization, and as a literal expert in assessing the value of human resources, Kyrill would certainly be able to see that.

With Lady Esther, on the other hand, I was pretty sure I was done for. I looked out the window, grinding my teeth in frustration. I could still see Kyrill's yacht from my window, but we would be out of sight soon. Whatever I was going to do, I had to do fast.

I flipped back the bedspread to lie down. Maybe more blood to the brain would help me think. And if not, I might as well be comfortable in my last few hours of life. I frowned at the bed. Green sheets. Weird.

I sat up suddenly. Green sheets. Tossing the cover aside, I yanked the flat sheet off the bed. It was a standard queen-size the same poisonous green as an appletini. Certainly it was big enough and bright enough to be seen from Kyrill's boat. I bit my nail, thinking. If they showed up without being warned, Lady Featherstone's henchman would just shoot them. I had to let them know what was happening. While I was all for shooting them eventually, I needed them to rescue me first.

My eye was caught by the chocolate body paint. Perfect. Trying not to think about where the brush had been, I quickly wrote a message on the sheet. "Help. Captive. Guns." I surveyed my handiwork. A little weak on plot, but I figured the relevant information was there.

I tied a book into the corner of the sheet to help weigh it down then, opening the porthole, I stuck my head outside and looked up and down the side of the boat. The shape of the boat meant that the banner wouldn't be directly visible from the deck unless someone peered out over the railing. Good. Carefully, I knotted one end of the green sheet to the catch inside the window then fed the rest of the banner out the porthole. It unfurled against the side of the boat.

I shut the window and sat down to wait, my pulse racing with anticipation. If Kyrill saw the banner and if he decided to get the binoculars and if he was able to read to message and if he was inclined to risk his life to rescue one woman from bondage while risking his freedom to sell another woman *into* bondage, then maybe I had a chance.

My pulse ratcheted down a few notches. When put that way, it really did seem fairly likely that I was going to die today. I picked up the dildo and smacked it against my open palm, reassured by its heft. At least if that bitch came back, I'd make sure she got something to remember me by.

38

Several hours later, I was not dead, and I was not rescued. I was, however, bored and hungry. I wished I had picked up some scones before I left. And as long I was wishing for things that I didn't have, a gun would be nice, too. In retrospect, pretty much anything would have been more helpful than the sundress and Agent Provocateur bikini underwear I had tucked into my bag.

I had looked through all of Clancy's self-help books and had finally settled on *Stop Stalking in 30 Days*, after noting that it was a "bestseller in its genre." I was probably the only person alive who wasn't surprised to hear that there was an anti-stalking genre. When it came to me, at least, stalking appeared to be the new Pilates.

The book was filled with surprisingly hands-on advice. "Burning is really the preferred way to free yourself of memorabilia from the object of your obsession," it advised. "Who hasn't shredded a photo in anger just to spend the next three days with a roll of scotch tape and a pair of tweezers, desperately trying to reassemble the visage of a loved one?" Who indeed? Clancy had marked that passage with an exclamation point, which I took to indicate that there was a taped together and/or burned photograph of me somewhere in his house.

Outside it was dark, and I hadn't seen Kyrill's boat in hours. It was time for me to face the facts. If they had seen the message, they hadn't come for me. It looked like I was going to be reduced to trying to batter my way to freedom with a Good Vibrations dildo. I didn't hold out high hopes for the success of that plan, but I was at least happy that details of my death would probably not make my obituary. Surely my mother would be traumatized enough without having to listen to the priest snigger through a heroic retelling of the great dildo battle at sea.

At that moment, I heard a scratching at the door. The stalking book fell to the floor as I jumped to my feet, brandishing the neon cock menacingly. My heart was pounding. This was it. Eye of the tiger, baby.

I heard the latch turn and watched the handle move slowly downward. Raising the dildo high overhead, I readied myself for the blow. "Lora!" Alexander whispered.

"Thank god!" I said fervently, reflecting that this was probably the only time in history I would be thanking an all-merciful heaven for sending white slavers after me.

Alexander slid inside the room, closed the door behind him, and began peppering me with questions. "What in hell is going on here?" he whispered. "We saw the message but couldn't figure out what was happening. What about your mother? " He paused for breath and did a double take. "And why are you holding a fluorescent green dildo?"

"This woman is the mother of that deranged stalker I told you about," I said. "Apparently, he's not the only nut job in the family. She saw me on the dock in Varna and decided to take advantage of the situation to get rid of me. The whole mother-in-a-coma thing was just a ruse to get me here so that her henchman could shoot me and dump me overboard."

"And the dildo?"

"I was planning on bopping her over the head with it when she came back to shoot me. Oh god, Alexander," I said urgently. "James, that guy she was with on the boat...he's got a gun. We've got to get out of here."

"Too late," Lady Esther's silky voice announced. Behind her stood James, his pistol leveled at Alexander. Lady Esther shook her head in mock sympathy. "Really, my dear," she said. "You must know the only white slavers in the world who are caring enough to rescue their idiot event hostess and stupid enough not to carry guns."

Alexander looked at me sharply. "What is she talking about?"

"I'll explain later."

"I very much doubt you'll get the chance," Lady Esther said.

We all turned to look at James, who was standing stock still, gun trained on Alexander. He seemed to have lost track of his role in this drama.

"Well, get on with it, James," Lady Esther said briskly, taking a step backward so the blood spatter wouldn't ruin her hideous capris.

James looked through the sights at Alexander, a faint smile touching the corners of his mouth. A shot rang out. I stared in horror at Alexander, who was clutching his chest. "Alexander!" I cried, reaching out for him.

Alexander stood there for a second, his hands crossed over his heart and his eyes closed. I waited for him to fall. And waited. He removed his hands from his chest, revealing a complete absence of wounds. "What the hell?" he said.

We all looked back at James just in time to see him slump to the floor, dead. Kyrill stood behind him, a gun in his hand and a dour expression on his face. He stepped on James's hand with one heavy boot then removed the gun from his grasp and pocketed it.

"Rahhhhh!" A strangled shriek came out of Lady Esther. "You monster! I'll have you killed! I'll…" She lunged at Kyrill, fingers outstretched into claws.

Before Kyrill could react, I swung the Good Vibrations dildo as hard as I could at her head. It made a satisfying thunk, and she dropped like a bag of rocks. The dildo, which had turned itself on high upon contact, jittered around the floor in an obscene victory dance. "That's for kidnapping me, you evil witch!"

I kicked her while she was down. It was unlike me but, I thought, completely justified under the circumstances. "And that's for telling me my mother was in a coma!" I stood over her, breathing hard. I pulled back my foot to kick her again. Given the fact that I was wearing sandals, I doubted I was doing too much damage, but it did seem to be improving my mood.

"Lora," Alexander said in a low voice, "what she said before you hit her…"

"What did she say?" Kyrill asked, stepping over James's corpse into the cabin.

I shot Alexander a quelling look. "She said she was going to shoot me and throw me overboard for the sharks. And she totally would have done it. And she called me a whore. And she said I was fat." She hadn't actually called me fat, of course, but I felt fat, and since I had someone to blame for everything that was wrong in my life right now, I thought I should make the most of it.

I scrambled around for the ball gag. "With a mouth like that, I think this is appropriate," I said, fastening it over her mouth and securing the straps. Alexander looked confused but acknowledged my unspoken instruction with a barely perceptible nod.

With Lady Esther unconscious, all eyes turned to the dildo buzzing and wiggling around her prone body. Kyrill looked at me questioningly. "I'll just...uh...turn this off." I reached down to grab it, and it jittered out of my grasp. Scrambling across the floor on my hands and knees, I finally managed to wrestle it into submission and hold it still long enough to find the off button.

Kyrill looked at Lady Esther. "Who is this person, and what did she want with you?" he asked.

I shook my head. "A few months ago I planned a trip for her son," I said. "He got a little over-attached."

"Over-attached?" Kyrill asked.

"I'm right on the verge of slapping a restraining order on him."

"That's pretty attached," Kyrill agreed. "Is that his dildo?"

"Yep."

"I'd go ahead with that restraining order."

"Right," I said, blushing. "Anyway, apparently his mother figured that she could get me out of his life more effectively by getting rid of me." I suddenly started shaking as I realized how close to death I had come.

Kyrill tilted his head to the side, considering. "Should we kill her?" he asked.

Both men looked at me. I had seen enough action movies to know that when you had the bad guy at your mercy, the best thing to do was to kill him. The action movie genre was just littered with the bloodied corpses of softhearted idiots who inexplicably decided to let homicidal maniacs live.

"Probably," I said. Kyrill shrugged and raised the gun again.

"But don't," I said against my better judgment. "I think if we can disable the boat and get away from her, she'll probably make this whole thing disappear." *And if she goes to the police*, I thought, *all the better*. Maybe the old witch could still be of some use to me after all.

"In your place I would certainly want her dead," Kyrill said flatly.

"I do. Just not right now. I'm a little murdered out today."

Kyrill shrugged. "It's your decision." He walked over to the side of the boat. "Spiro!" he called down to the waiting tender. "Can you disable her boat and the tender so that she won't be able to follow us?"

"Of course," Spiro called back up, sounding as if there was nothing he would enjoy more. "Howard," we heard him chide, "try not to drown while I'm gone. And don't touch anything."

Kyrill returned his attention to Lady Esther, wrapping her unconscious hand around James's gun. "Stand back," he advised. He fired shots around the cabin until the hammer fell on an empty chamber.

"What are you doing?!" I yelled, my ears ringing.

"Making sure she doesn't go to the police," Kyrill said. The gunshots had brought Lady Esther around, and she was blinking groggily at Kyrill.

"Listen to me, you miserable old bitch," Kyrill said, leaning over the gagged woman. "If it were up to me, one of those shots would have gone into you. But Lora here is apparently a nice person, and she has decided to let you live. So let me explain your situation. You are covered in gunshot residue after having shot your lover with a gun that is, I am sure, registered to you."

Lady Esther looked outraged, more at the insinuation that she would sleep with a servant than from the aforementioned servant's gory end, I felt sure.

"Your boat has been disabled," he continued. "And I'm going to tie you up and leave you here. You seem like a resourceful woman, so I'm sure it will only take you a few hours to get yourself loose, at which point you'll need to make a decision as to whether you call the police. Now you can, of course, call the police and report that someone you never met sailed right up to your boat, snuck on board, stole your gun, shot your captain with it, made you shoot the gun, and left without stealing anything or doing anything else.

"I, for one, think that the police would find that tale slightly, shall we say, implausible. Whereas a crazy old bitch shooting her lover..." Kyrill lingered over the word "lover." "Jail time aside, can you imagine the scandal? The public humiliation? In your social circle, killing your staff member might be overlooked, but fucking him…"

Lady Esther shrieked through the ball gag at this. Given the situation, I almost admired her ability to maintain her class prejudices. In her place, I thought I'd have more pressing concerns than who a white slaver I'd never seen before thought I was sleeping with.

"And there is something else that you should keep in mind," he said, leaning forward and lowering his voice menacingly. "While Lora here insisted that we not put you to death…"

"Reluctantly suggested," I corrected.

"What?"

"I reluctantly suggested that we not put her to death. I feel like it's a decision I could revisit," I said. "Easily. Like at the drop of a hat." I narrowed my eyes at the ball-gagged peeress in front of me. "I'm revisiting it as we speak."

"Right. So while Lora 'reluctantly suggested' that we not kill you, I should tell you that everyone else in our party would have shot you and dumped you overboard without a second thought. But what's more important for you to realize," he said lowering himself into a crouch so that he could look directly into her eyes, "is that the option of a quick, relatively painless death is now off the table."

Lady Esther looked down her nose at him. I never would have thought that it was possible to look so haughty with a ball gag in your mouth. Even with all of Pinkie's training, I was sure I'd never be able to manage it. One of those to-the-manor-born things, I guessed.

"If I find out that you have spoken one word of my presence or that of my friends to any police officers, I will start here," Kyrill said, grabbing her pinkie finger and twisting it viciously. "I will take a hammer. I will crush every bone in your body. Then I will find your son, and I will do the same to him. You will both be alive for hours. Possibly days."

He stood up and dusted himself off. "Do you understand me?"

All defiance had drained out of Lady Esther's face. She looked like she was about to be sick. She nodded and meekly held her hands out in front of her to be tied. "Hands in back," Kyrill admonished her. "No need to make this too easy."

"Lora, take that sheet down from the window," Kyrill

commanded. "I don't want any casual passerby rushing to the rescue any time soon."

I scuttled over to the window and pulled in the sign, my hands shaking. Kyrill's little speech to Lady Esther had made me seriously question whether being rescued by Kyrill was better than being shot and dumped overboard by Lady Esther's henchman. I looked over at Alexander, my eyes scared. His mouth tightened. Clearly we were going to be having a discussion when we were back on the yacht.

As if on cue, the boat suddenly fell silent, and Spiro popped over in front of the door. "It's done," he said unnecessarily. "The boat will be going nowhere without this." He triumphantly held up a mass of cables that looked like a sick octopus, then flipped it casually over the side.

"Ow!" came Howard's voice. "I'm down here, you know. You almost killed me."

Spiro laughed merrily. Apparently he, like Kyrill, found the prospect of the imminent death of others to be a source of levity. "Shall we go?" he asked. "I think our work here is done."

Kyrill looked hard at Lady Esther, who visibly cringed. "I hope so," he said. "We have business to discuss."

I picked up my bag and glanced back at Lady Esther, who was looking at me with an unnerving combination of hatred and fear. "I don't want to see you or your son ever again," I told her. "Or you'll have to deal with him." I nodded over toward Kyrill. He raised one eyebrow at me but turned and scowled obligingly at Lady Esther, causing her to shrink back in terror.

Chances were I'd be dead tomorrow, but if I survived this job I at least wanted to be sure that Clancy and his psychopathic mother wouldn't be bothering me in the future. If being trapped on a yacht with murderous white slavers was lemons, I was determined to make lemonade. Or better yet, lemon chiffon pie. Putting my chin in the air, I daintily stepped over James's dead body and swept out of the cabin.

39

Jacques and Sergei were up on the deck when we came back, apparently waiting anxiously for our return. "What happened?" Sergei asked, his usually cheerful face dark with concern.

I gave them a quick rundown on how I had been saved from almost certain death by Alexander, Kyrill, and Spiro, but I glossed over the less important details, like where Kyrill had shot James in the back. I worried that I might be endangering Jacques's life by providing too much information. While Jacques was a prima donna who seemed to lack all concept of acceptable professional behavior, anyone who had tasted his scones would have to admit that the world would be a poorer place without him, at least in terms of baked goods.

Kyrill insisted that we toast our victory with a round of vodka shots, in what he assured us was the traditional Russian style. After three shots, the normally stable deck started to feel like a child's swing, and I realized that the effects of stress, lack of food, and exhaustion didn't combine well with vodka.

"Kyrill," I said, interrupting another round of self-congratulations, "I think I'm done for. Would you mind very much if I grabbed a sandwich and headed off to bed?"

Kyrill, who had previously shown about as much humanity as a brick wall, had apparently been softened by our shared ordeal. He looked positively remorseful, which was an emotion I didn't generally associate with white slavers. "Of course," he said, taking me solicitously by the elbow. "I'm sorry. I should have realized that you would be hungry and exhausted. Are you okay?"

"Never better," I lied. "I just need a bit of rest."

"Take the rest of the night off," he said. "Alexander and Howard can entertain themselves, and Spiro and I still have much to discuss."

"Truth be told, I've pretty much had it too," Alexander chimed in. "All that sneaking and rescuing and threatening really takes it out of you." He yawned ostentatiously. "If you don't need me for anything, I think I'll head off to bed as well."

Kyrill nodded. "Fine. We can meet back here in the morning."

"You there…cook," he snapped at Jacques.

Jacques looked as though he wanted to take issue with that designation, but a quick glance at Kyrill's expression dissuaded him.

"Jacques," he supplied.

"Whatever," Kyrill said. "Prepare a tray for Lora, and take it to her room."

Jacques nodded and sulkily slouched off toward the galley.

I made my farewells and headed down to my cabin. Jacques was close on my heels with a tray. "About tomorrow's breakfast," he started.

I held up a hand to silence him. "You know what, Jacques?" I said. "I've spent the last eight hours thinking I was going to end my day dead at the bottom of the ocean. I thought about how much my mom would miss me. I thought about my brother and my friends, some of whom need me just to get through everyday life without falling apart. I thought about how I'd never fall in love or have kids or grow old. You know what I didn't think about?"

"Breakfast?"

"Breakfast."

"I was just going to say that Sergei and I would take care of it," he said, a trifle stiffly.

I shook my head apologetically. "Sorry, Jacques," I said. "This has not been a banner day for me."

"Well," he replied philosophically, "tomorrow will certainly be better, no? At least nobody here is trying to kill you."

I felt my stomach twist. "Right."

After devouring the meal Jacques had brought, I unlocked the connecting door to Alexander's room and settled down to wait. I knew that there was no point in going to sleep before Alexander showed up. Not after what he had heard Lady Esther say. I picked up a copy of *The Economist* from my bag and settled down to inform myself about the hilarious hijinks of the international economy. "Corporate   governance   go   round," I read. Five seconds later I was asleep.

40

I woke up to the knowledge that someone was in my cabin. In my bed, actually. I opened my eyes and looked straight into Alexander's brilliant blue ones, about three centimeters away.

"Ack!" I shrieked, or at least I would have shrieked if Alexander's hand hadn't clamped itself over my mouth. I pushed it away. "Can't you knock?" I hissed at him.

I snuck a look down at him. At least he was wearing clothes this time. Although, given what I remembered of Alexander without clothes, I was going to have to put that down as a mixed blessing.

"Shh," Alexander said sternly. He leaned over and whispered into my ear. "I think we need to talk about today."

I nodded, trying to figure out how much information I could trust Alexander with. As little as possible, I thought. "Yes. You were great today. A perfect hero," I said, skipping over the fact that only Kyrill's timely arrival had kept us both from being killed. "But it's been a rough night, and I really need to sleep. I'm not really feeling all that romantic right now."

"That's not what I'm here for," he said. "What did Lady Esther mean? Who does she think is a white slaver?"

"I have no idea," I said. "I think you must have misheard. I didn't hear her say 'white slavers.'"

"What do you think she said?"

"Maybe 'bright knavers,'" I said, wishing I had a rhyming

213

dictionary.

"What the hell is a 'bright knaver'?'"

"How should I know?" I said. "I don't speak British. It's probably some sort of upper class slang for 'guys.'"

Alexander looked at me silently for a moment. "If you won't tell me what's going on, I'm going to have to talk to Kyrill," he said. "If he's involved in something shady, I need to know."

"You can't do that!" I hissed. I took a deep breath. It had never been my intention to trust Alexander, who clearly wasn't trustworthy even if he wasn't a white slaver. Unfortunately, now it looked like I wouldn't have a choice.

"Come closer," I said. "If anyone hears this, we're both dead."

Alexander raised his eyebrows at this but obligingly snuggled closer in the bed so that we could whisper. I noticed a hard bulge in his pants and mentally shook my head in disbelief.

"Kyrill is a white slaver," I said. "And maybe your father, too." I don't know how I expected Alexander to react to that news. Maybe shock and disbelief. Maybe a heated denial of any possibility that his father could be involved in anything so nefarious. I wasn't expecting mild bemusement.

"Really?" he said. "And whatever would have given her that impression?"

"The wine cellar," I said. "I went in there to put away some of the bottles from the kitchen. Kyrill has forbidden anyone from opening the racks there, but I thought that was because he didn't want the crew stealing his wine. Which would have been good thinking," I continued, "because when I got here, the only thing there was to drink onboard was pornographic cough syrup."

Alexander made a get-on-with-it motion with his finger. "Anyway," I continued, "there was a bottle out of place. Not something most people would have noticed, but something that anyone who knew about wine would have been able to see. I went to move it. But it wasn't a bottle at all; it was a lever. I thought it might lead to another part of the wine cellar, so I pulled it."

Alexander gripped my arm, suddenly intense. "What did you see?"

"Behind one of the racks, there's a door to another room," I said. "It's like a prison. Cots, a toilet. There are restraints on the beds so that you can tie people down. The door is one-way glass so that whoever is standing in the wine cellar can see in, but the people inside can't see out."

"Were there people in the cell?" Alexander asked.

"Yes." I let out a shuddering breath. "There was a woman. Young, beautiful. She was just sitting there, her eyes closed..." I trailed off. "She looked like she was in pain. I didn't know what to do. I wanted to let her out, or at least tell her that I would try to help her, but I didn't know who to trust. I figured the best thing to do would be to pretend like I hadn't seen anything, then to go to the police once I was off the boat."

"Jesus," Alexander said. He rubbed his hands tiredly over his face. "Kyrill has always had a reputation in the international shipping community as a guy to move antiques, art, whatever without too many questions, but I would never have guessed he was into something like this."

"There's one other thing," I said, wincing. "That guy isn't Kyrill Antonov."

Alexander froze. "What do you mean that's not Kyrill Antonov?"

"My brother's a computer guy," I explained.

"Like someone you call when your hard drive fails?"

"Like someone who breaks into the CIA and releases a virus that sends every web query to a plushophilia porn site," I corrected.

"Plushophilia porn?"

"It's where you get turned on by stuffed animals or people in animal costumes..." I trailed off at his look of amazement. "It was on CSI," I said. "I couldn't make this up.

"Anyway, I sent him a picture of Kyrill. Or rather the man who we've been calling Kyrill," I corrected. "I didn't mean to; I was just trying to get a picture of the boat. My brother did a little digging. He says that's not Kyrill."

Alexander looked skeptical. "Nobody's seen a picture of Kyrill in years," he said. "He's afraid of kidnappers."

"I heard that too," I said. "And Pinkie, my friend who vetted Kyrill before I took this job, didn't have a picture either. But if my brother says he's found a picture, you can bet your life on it. If he says this guy's not Kyrill, this guy's not Kyrill."

Alexander looked confused. "I thought you and Kyrill were old friends."

I blushed. "Kyrill Antonov—the real Kyrill—went to school with a friend of Pinkie's named Fritzie. Fritzie told Pinkie that everything was fine, that he had spoken to Kyrill on the phone and that everything was on the up and up. Kyrill was the one who suggested that I represent myself as an old friend."

"Didn't that raise any flags?"

"No," I said. "It didn't. Look. Acting as an event hostess is a little different than acting as an event planner. You *hire* an event planner, but for jobs like this, you *invite* an event hostess. Everyone maintains the polite fiction that I just showed up to help out a friend, and the money people give me is always for expenses or for my ticket or something; it's not directly connected to the job. And as long as I'm telling people I'm a friend, why not an old friend?" I shrugged. "I really didn't see the harm."

Alexander shook his head. "Brilliant."

"No reason to be sarcastic," I said, stung. "It's not like I knew."

Alexander shook his head. "Not you, him. We are dealing with a very sensitive piece of business here. We looked around long and hard before we settled on Kyrill Antonov. We checked out his reputation, his network, his business. The only thing we couldn't check out was what he looked like, because of that whole fear of kidnapping thing."

"I heard it's actually a wattle thing," I confided.

Alexander looked at me blankly.

"It's when you get loose skin under your chin," I said. I pinched under my chin to demonstrate. Jesus. I was apparently developing a wattle, too. If I survived this trip, maybe I could get Pinkie to loan me an ascot.

"Whatever," Alexander said impatiently. "The point is that we've been moving slowly, trying to build trust. Suddenly we get an invitation from the man we think is Kyrill Antonov inviting us to take a trip with him on his boat. And who else should be on the trip but you? He's met you before, so he knows who you are. You tell him that you've been friends with Kyrill for ages."

I felt like I had been sucker punched. "I was just hired to provide more evidence that Kyrill was who he said he was."

Alexander nodded. "This guy has Kyrill's boat. He's got an 'old friend' who my father knows vouching for his identity." He shrugged. "There was no reason to even question that this guy was Kyrill. And now here we are with some complete stranger who has an agenda we don't understand."

He suddenly sucked in his breath. "Wait a minute. You helped him set up Dieter." He grabbed my arm, right over the bruises Dieter had left. I stifled a shriek.

"I did not," I snapped, snatching my arm away. "Dieter was a psychopath who got off on putting women in pain. It took me about three seconds after meeting him to figure that out."

"So you killed him."

"No, but I found him," I admitted. "I went down and told Kyrill. I wanted to report it to the police, but Kyrill told me they'd suspect me. I was scared. There are cameras everywhere these days. What if someone saw him manhandling me in the restaurant that night? A couple of hours later, the guy shows up dead in my room. Even I would have jumped to the obvious conclusion."

"What did you do?"

"Kyrill told me he'd take care of it. I left. In the morning, that maid confessed, and I didn't know whether he'd paid her to take the blame or whether it had happened like she said. But..." I paused.

"But what?"

"But I don't think the maid was really a maid," I said. "I think I saw her in Moscow. Coming out of Kyrill's apartment building. She looked different there, but I'm almost sure it was the same woman."

We lay there for a moment in silence. "Look," I said, "I don't want to get into your business, but how sure are you that father isn't involved with this? I mean...what kind of deal are you here to make? It's not for luxury home goods, I take it. Why aren't you and Howard included in the discussions?" I held up a hand to stop him from answering. "Wait. Just to be clear, if you're going to have to kill me if you tell me, please feel free not to answer."

Alexander rolled his eyes. "Don't be melodramatic. The deal was supposed to be transporting antiquities. A few years ago when your country started declaring war on everyone with a beard and a turban, a lot of ancient artifacts started coming on the market. When people are desperate and there's no effective police, they care a lot less about their national history than they do about making sure their families have enough to eat.

"We originally brought over some old Buddhas that a friend of my father's had found in a market in Peshawar. If they had remained there, they would have been smashed by the Taliban, so even though it was technically illegal, it felt like the right thing to do. That deal led to a few more, and now we've got a network of people who help us get things like that of countries where they're not safe. We bring them into Bulgaria and have them certified by 'experts' who provide them with provenance and export certificates. When all the paperwork is done, we sell them to private collectors all over the world."

I exhaled. That didn't really sound so evil. Maybe it even sounded a little bit noble. Could you still be a good guy if you smuggled antiquities? Wasn't that what Indiana Jones did, more or less?

"Why Bulgaria?" I asked. "What's so special about Bulgaria?"

Alexander shrugged. "Bulgaria has two unique advantages. First of all, it has an absolutely corrupt government, so if you know who to bribe, it's easy to get around the law. Second, it's part of the EU. The EU certification of antiquities is the gold standard for resale value. Anything that you can get into Bulgaria is effectively free to move in Western Europe. Unfortunately, it's less free to move into Russia, where a lot of potential buyers live."

"You're telling me that the Russians are trying to make sure export regulations are respected?" I said. "No offense, but the Russians I know don't exactly seem to care about export regulations. Or building code regulations. Or parking regulations. I mean, really, they're not the most law-abiding people I've ever met."

Alexander made a sour expression. "The Russians don't care about export regulations or a transparent international market in antiquities. They just care about making things difficult enough to generate a little profit for themselves. They send in 'experts' to reevaluate the pieces. It's just a shakedown, but we can't afford to make too much of a stink about it, obviously.

"We know that Kyrill can handle the Russian border," he said. "He's been moving all kinds of stuff in and out of that country for years. And he has a lot of potential buyers. We figured if we put our supply network together with his contacts, we'd be able to double or even triple our business."

"I guess if you're looking to sell illegal goods to rich people who have no scruples…"

"It's good to have access to the Russian market," Alexander finished. He took my chin in his hand and turned my face so that I was looking into his eyes. "Look," he said. "I realize I'm not a saint in this story, but you need to trust me. What we do—it may be technically illegal, but it's a victimless crime. And anyone who says that priceless artifacts belong in the countries they're found in has never been to some of those places. I'd rather see those things in the hands of collectors who can care for them than let them be destroyed by religious fanatics or be sold off by crooked curators."

I shook my head. "I'm not going to argue the point. But if that's what's going on, what are your father and Kyrill talking about every night? Why aren't you and Howard part of the meetings?"

"That's no mystery, unfortunately," Alexander said. "Howard's a spreadsheet guy. He just moves numbers around. He doesn't know whether it's cheese or some priceless Sumerian artifact. And as for me..." he paused, his mouth twisting bitterly. "My father has never thought I was tough enough to cut deals with our partners. I'm good enough to go out with them, to drink with them, to get them in the door, but he always has to be the one doing the negotiation."

I could see a glimmer of hurt in Alexander's eyes. It made him more human, somehow. "I guess I'm a little old to still be seeking Daddy's approval," he said, shaking his head in embarrassment.

"Probably," I admitted.

"The question now is what we should do about this girl you found," Alexander said. "I think we're going to have to confront Kyrill. To take control of the ship."

I held up a hand to cut off that line of thought. "Hold it right there. Isn't maybe the smart thing to do here just to keep our heads down and take this to the police when we dock? I mean, there's no reason you would have to be involved at all. We could just call in an anonymous tip. Something like 'Hey...pull on the bottle of Screaming Eagle in Kyrill's wine cellar, and check out this girl who is completely being white slaved into your country. And while you're at it, make Kyrill tell you his real name, because it's not Kyrill.' Wouldn't that be safer than trying some suicidal boat takeover?"

Alexander set his jaw. "I've seen people like this operate. If this boat docks, that girl is as good as gone. This is a yacht, not some fishing boat. Most of the police aren't going to touch it with a ten-foot pole. The ones that will are going to get the bureaucratic runaround because their commanding officers know that messing with rich people based on an anonymous tip is a great way to get fired.

"And if anyone manages to get clearance to come on this boat, Kyrill—or whoever this guy is—is going to know about it about before those guys even leave their HQ. That girl will be gone before they ever step on deck. And whatever evidence they might have found will be gone as well. If you don't want that girl to die, we need to act now."

I bit my lip. I didn't want the girl to die. I also didn't want myself to die. I was having some difficulty reconciling these two positions.

Alexander shook his head decisively. "No," he said. "We have to get my father, and we have to put Kyrill out of commission. It's the only way. We can take control, turn the boat around, and head for Greece, where we have connections who can make sure that he's prosecuted."

"No way," I said. "Were you not paying attention to what happened on Lady Esther's boat? He killed a man in cold blood. He's armed. I don't think he's going to just put his hands in the air and surrender himself to us so that we can have him arrested."

"I'm sure you're right," Alexander said. "But we have the element of surprise in our favor."

"No offense, but I'm no stranger to the element of surprise, and I'm pretty sure it's ineffective against firearms."

Alexander smiled crookedly, reaching into his pocket and pulling out the hard bulge I had felt earlier. He wasn't just happy to see me. It wasn't a banana either. "He's not the only one who's armed," he said. "My father wasn't kidding about the pirates."

I still wasn't happy, but given that the most deadly weapon I had managed to come up with was a lemon zester, I was willing to admit that we were making progress.

"I need to go see my father tonight. For all his flaws, he's a tough bastard in a fight."

"You're going to have to wait," I said. "He's talking business with Kyrill. Even if Captain Vlad let you near the door, which he won't, they'd know something was up if you barged in there with some burning need to talk to your father."

Alexander nodded. "You're right. We'll need to wait for them to finish."

"If tonight is anything like last night, he's not going to be in any state to discuss this when he's done talking to Kyrill."

"What do you mean?"

"I mean that your father was completely hammered last night. I already told you this."

"Look," Alexander said, "just because he was trying to knock on your door doesn't mean that he was drunk. I've seen him drink longshoremen under the table. He doesn't get drunk. Ever. He probably just figured you might let him in. He's a complete womanizer. "

I looked at him pointedly. "Pot, meet kettle. But this wasn't just the fact that he was at my door. He couldn't find his room. He couldn't stand up. He was talking about bad investments that he'd made last year, and for a guy like your father to admit to any kind of business mistake, he'd have to be blitzed. Trust me," I concluded, "he was drunk."

A thoughtful look crossed Alexander's face. "Maybe something else was going on."

"Like what?"

"Never mind. I'll know more when I see him tonight."

Alexander looked at his watch. "If they keep to the same schedule, I've got about five hours to kill."

"We both have about five hours to kill. I want to be there when you talk to your father."

"Don't be silly," Alexander said. "You're completely exhausted. You're going to be of no use to anyone unless you get some sleep."

I looked at him incredulously. "You just told me that we're going to try to take over the boat tomorrow. We're probably all going to be slaughtered by Kyrill, possibly with a hammer over the course of several days, and dumped overboard. Do you honestly expect me to be able to sleep?"

"I think I know something that might help," he said, running a hand lightly over my stomach.

"How can you think of sex at a time like this?" I asked. "We could all be dead tomorrow."

Alexander shifted his position so that he was over me, looking down into my face. "Exactly." He ran a finger down the center of my chest before lazily moving it over to circle the nipple. "I think we were about here, weren't we?" I caught my breath.

"If this is our last night," he said, "do you really want to spend it sleeping?"

He slid his hand lower, pushing up the hem of my nightgown

and exposing my black lace underwear. Slowly, teasingly, he stroked the inside of my thigh.

My brain knew that this was absolutely the wrong thing to do. There was too much at stake here to risk further complications. We should be planning, strategizing.

Alexander's fingers moved higher, slipping beneath the waistband of my underwear. My rational brain shut off completely as I shifted my hips to allow him access.

Alexander smiled and sat back on his heels. Slowly, not breaking eye contact, he unbuckled his belt and slid it out of the loops. I reached up to pull him back down on top of me, but he pulled back, clicking his tongue chidingly.

"Such a hurry," he said. "We've got time. You just need to be still and let me take care of everything. Let me help you." He looped the belt around my wrists then secured them to part of the wrought iron headboard. "Better," he said. "Now let's just take it slow." I bit my lip. I felt like I was on fire.

"Please," I said, panting. Six months of celibacy had zapped all shame out of me. I could be dead tomorrow. And it wasn't like I needed to be professional for the sake of white slavers. I wasn't exactly hoping for a job recommendation out of this.

Alexander slid off his pants then leaned over my body, running his hands up the outside of my thighs before quickly skimming off my underwear. Bending over my hips, he lightly kissed me below the navel then slipped his tongue lower. I moaned like an animal in heat. "Right there. No, left. No, back. BACK!"

"Quiet," he said, flicking a tongue over me teasingly. "I'd hate to have to stop."

I leaned over and bit the pillow. I honestly thought I might have a heart attack from frustration if he stopped. Of course, given the way my heart was hammering now, I might also have one if he didn't go faster.

"Please," I said again, stretching my body toward him in complete surrender.

Despite my twisting and whispered entreaties, he took his time, bringing me to the edge of insanity with his tongue, then his fingers. Finally, when I thought I was going to lose my mind, he plunged into me, hard. I gasped in shock as he filled me, wrapping my legs around him, to pull him in closer.

Alexander began to move in rhythm, then without missing a

beat, guided my legs over his shoulders, allowing him to go even deeper. I felt the orgasm building inside me and rose up to meet every thrust. Finally, I froze, my mouth open in a silent scream of ecstasy. Above me, Alexander stiffened then let out a harsh, rasping breath as he came.

We lay there for a moment next to each other, looking up at the ceiling in silence. Every part of my body was tingling. Finally, I dragged myself back to consciousness.

"Um," I said, suddenly awkward. "Would you mind?" I nodded at my hands still fastened to the headboard.

He quickly undid the knot, turning his head to smile at me lazily. "Any regrets?" he asked, tracing my jaw with his fingers.

"Not right this second," I said. "But I think I'll regret it very much if we're both killed tomorrow because we were having sex when we should have been figuring out how to take this boat without being slaughtered."

Alexander got to his feet and pulled on his pants. "I'll try to make sure that doesn't happen," he said. "Meet me tomorrow morning at eight o'clock at the back of the boat near the tender so that I can tell you the plan." He leaned over and kissed my cheek. "Don't worry," he said. "We'll figure it out."

Alexander slipped out the door, and I heard the lock turn on his side. I lay back down, feeling exhaustion creep over me. I thought about Dieter, licking his lips as he crushed my hand in his. I thought about the girl in the cell. I thought about my mother, and wished I had her strength to face life, head on, without fear or excuses. I thought about Kyrill, shooting James on Lady Esther's boat. I wondered how I'd ever get to sleep. Seconds later, I was out cold.

41

I woke up with a gasp, my heart pounding with fear even before I could remember what I was supposed to be afraid of. Then I remembered. Alexander and Spiro were going to try to take the boat today. We were probably all going to be killed. On the whole, I thought that I was happier not remembering.

I took a quick shower and looked through my closet for something appropriate for a commando-style raid. My clothes were mostly selected by Pinkie and were, he assured me, the ultimate reflection of wealth and good taste. Apparently, wealthy people with good taste didn't need to plan for possible gunplay. Nothing with Kevlar. Nothing even with pockets. Why didn't they make women's clothing with pockets? I finally went with a short dress and a swimsuit, both of which looked woefully non-bulletproof.

Checking myself out in the mirror, I hissed as I looked closely at my neck. Red marks, presumably from Alexander. I burrowed through my bag until I found a little scarf, which I tied around my neck. Like a Girl Scout, I was always prepared.

I took special care with my makeup, layering on creams and powders with grim determination. I might be killed today, but at least I would go out with supple skin and long, feathery eyelashes.

I fussed around with my lip gloss for a while then checked my watch. Almost eight o'clock. Time to meet Alexander and see what harebrained plot he and Spiro had managed to concoct last night.

Maybe all I would have to do was wait in my room until everything was over. That was the kind of plan I could get behind.

I listened at the door and, hearing nothing, quietly opened it and eased out into the passage. Slipping out onto the back deck, I found Alexander waiting for me. He looked serious and determined, and I felt my heart skip slightly as I remembered the night before. Truth be told, it was less my heart than other, less-mentionable portions of my anatomy.

Alexander, however, was all business today. "You were right about my father."

"Your father's a white slaver?"

"No," Alexander said. "When he got to his room last night, he seemed completely drunk."

"Told you."

"But he wasn't," Alexander continued. "I think he was drugged."

"Why on earth would anyone drug your father?"

"There's only one reason I can think of, and that's to try to get him to talk about our contacts. My father's a cagey guy...he keeps everything in his head so that there's no paper trail. If someone wanted to find out who we were dealing with, they'd have to get it out of him. I'm pretty sure he could hold out for a long time if they were questioning him directly, but if they've had him alone for hours, under drugs, I don't know what he would have told them."

I shook my head. "This doesn't make any sense. What you're proposing is a business deal that benefits both of you, right? Wouldn't it be smarter just to do the deal?"

"Doing the deal would be the right move for Kyrill," Alexander said, his mouth set in a grim line, "but this isn't Kyrill. I've been thinking it over since last night. I think Kyrill—the person that we know as Kyrill—is part of the Russian Mafia. I think they've decided to take over our operation. They used Kyrill Antonov as a cover to get us on the boat, and now they're interrogating my father about his network so they know who to come after next. I very much doubt that any of us are expected to leave this boat alive," he finished.

I looked at him, my eyes wide with shock. "The Russian Mafia?" I repeated. "That's bad, right?"

"That threat that you heard Kyrill make to Lady Esther?" Alexander said.

"The one where he told her that he would beat her to death with a hammer over several days?" I asked, sick just thinking about it.

"That's a common punishment used by the Russian Mafia. It serves two purposes. It kills the person who betrayed you, and it serves as a deterrent for anyone thinking about betraying you in the future."

"I guess betrayal isn't a common problem in the Russian Mafia," I said, feeling green.

"No," Alexander said seriously. "It's not."

Alexander saw my concern and took me by the arm. "Come on. We need to talk to my father." He quickly glanced into the hallway then opened the door to his father's cabin, drawing me inside behind him.

"Father," Alexander said. "I brought Lora. We need to talk about what we're going to do about this situation."

Spiro stood up from the chair he'd been sitting in. His face was dark and serious, a far cry from his usual cheerful self. "Good to see that you are okay, Lora. I'm sorry that this person brought you into this mess."

"Probably not as sorry as I am," I said, miserable.

"Tell me again what it is that you think you saw," he said, taking my hand between his.

I described the room behind the wine cellar for him. "And the girl," Spiro asked. "You're sure she was being held prisoner?"

I thought back to the grim room and her expression. "I'm sure."

Spiro sighed. "You're right, Alexander. We have no choice but to take the boat."

Spiro walked over to his bag and rummaged through it, pulling out a wicked-looking automatic pistol and a few cartridges.

"Jesus," I said. "Do you guys always travel armed?"

"International waters are not safe, my girl," Spiro said. "A smart man makes sure he is prepared for any contingency."

Considering the contingency in which we found ourselves, I found that logic hard to argue with.

I shook my head. "I've got a better idea," I said. "I've been thinking about it. If we get into a fight with these guys, someone's going to get killed. What if, instead, we wait until everyone is asleep and rescue the girl. We can get on the tender and make a run for it." I turned to Spiro. "Kyrill said the tender was faster than the boat, right? We could head for land and alert the police. With the girl with us to testify, they can't ignore it. Especially once I get my friend Pinkie to call a few of his friends. There's nobody better connected than Pinkie."

"That's a good plan," said Spiro, "except for two things. First of all, someone is always on watch at night. I don't know if you've noticed, but the men take turns watching the deck. We can't get the girl off of the boat without being seen. That brings me to the second problem: a boat like this is going to have weapons on board."

"You have weapons," I pointed out reasonably. "Shouldn't they cancel each other out?"

Spiro shook his head. "We have handguns. A boat this size will have enough weapons to hold off pirates. That means machine guns. And I'd be very surprised if they didn't have a few rocket-propelled grenade launchers on board. That's really the best way of dealing with pirates. Blow them up before they get to your boat." He smiled as if recalling a fond memory of exploding pirates.

"But they can't use a rocket-propelled grenade on us without destroying the boat, right?" I asked.

"Right," Alexander said, "but the second we get on the tender, they can blow it out of the water. It may be able to outrun this yacht, but it can't outrun a rocket-propelled grenade."

Spiro nodded. "The only way we're going to be safe is if we take control of the boat."

"So what do we do?" I asked. "Do we try to find their guns so that we can arm everyone? We've got more people than they have, right? The three of us, then Howard, and I guess we could tell Jacques as well. If we all have guns we can easily take them, right?"

"I don't think so," Alexander said. "Look, it's one thing to have a gun, and it's another thing entirely to be able to use a gun effectively in a situation like this. If Kyrill and his crew are with the Russian Mafia, they will know how to shoot. They won't hesitate to kill anyone they see as a threat. Someone like Howard, on the other hand, is more likely to accidentally shoot himself in the foot—or worse, one of us—than he is to actually take out a bad guy."

"Hey," I said. "I'm not an expert, but I don't think I'm going to hesitate when it comes to shooting someone. I'm pretty sure I could shoot someone right now. I'm actually almost positive that I could shoot Jacques, and he's not even a white slaver. So can I have a gun? I really think I would feel better."

"I'm sure you would," Alexander said, "but as soon as Kyrill realizes that we're on to him, he's going to try to arm himself. And the fastest way for him to get a gun is to take one away from you."

"It's not that easy to shoot someone," Spiro said. "Trust me on this. Things could get bloody very quickly. No," he continued. "I think the best thing for you to do is to try to deal with the captain."

"What do you mean 'deal with the captain'?"

"We need to get the odds more in our favor," Alexander said. "If my father and I are both armed, we can easily control two men. With three men, there's a greater chance that someone will get away. And if one person gets away and gets a machine gun, we're all dead. We need to get the captain out of the picture."

"And how do we do that?" I asked, a sinking feeling coming over me.

"First, I need you to think," Spiro said. "Most boats this size have at least one room that bolts on the outside. It's designed to serve as a brig in cases of mutiny. Do you know if there's a room like that here?"

I thought back to when we had prepped the boat. "There is," I said, suddenly remembering. "Sergei's room has a bolt on the outside of the door."

Alexander smiled at me. "Good. Now all we need to do is find a way to get the captain down into that room so that we can lock him in. That's going to be your job."

I was aghast. "How do you expect me to do that?"

Spiro shrugged. "Use your womanly wiles."

"Womanly wiles?" I racked my brain for what those might constitute. The fact that I could coordinate shoes and handbags? My ability to put a toilet seat lid down?

"Tell him you are looking for romance," Alexander clarified.

I shook my head. "I've met this guy," I said. "Even if I were looking for romance, he's not. He's not going to fall for it." I remembered the suspicious way he had warned me away from the door when Kyrill and Spiro had been doing whatever they were doing. I doubted that batting my eyelashes at him was going to get him to drop everything and rush into Sergei's cabin with me.

Spiro shook his head. "I think you underestimate yourself. But it doesn't matter what you tell him. Tell him you need to talk to him in private. Tell him you found something you need to show him. Tell him there's a leak in the boat. Just get him down into that room and throw the bolt on the door. He needs to be locked in before we start the second part of the plan."

"What's the second part of the plan?"

"We will go up to breakfast as usual," Spiro said. "Alexander and I will make sure that Kyrill and that waiter are both there. Once we have them both where we can see them, we pull out the guns, and we find out what the hell is going on here."

I thought it through. "It seems like a very weak plan," I fretted. "I was expecting something a little more involved. Code words, signals—you know, an actual plan."

Alexander shook his head. "It's not weak; it's simple. That's why it will work. You've seen Kyrill up at breakfast. He's wearing shorts or a swimsuit. He's not carrying a gun. We just need to make sure the captain is out of the way. And timing is important. The minute the captain is contained, we need to move. If Kyrill notices that the captain has vanished, he might get suspicious."

"How do we get Sergei on deck?" I asked.

"We'll have to manufacture a reason to call him up. Maybe we can ask him to bring some peanuts or something," Alexander said.

"What about Jacques and Howard?"

Alexander shrugged. "You're going to have to tell Jacques something to keep him out of the way. There's no reason for him to be involved. We can fill him in once we've got control of the yacht."

"As for Howard," Spiro rumbled, "I will tell him to stay in this cabin. He would just be in the way."

I wondered why Howard got to stay in his cabin while I had to come up with my own plan to capture and incarcerate Captain Vlad. Probably because he lacked womanly wiles. At this point, I was kind of wishing I lacked womanly wiles as well.

Seeing my indecision, Alexander put his hands on either side of my face and looked into my eyes. "Lora," he said, "that girl is counting on us to rescue her. If we don't get her off this boat, she'll never see her family or friends again. She'll live the rest of her life doing whatever she's told until she's too old to be of use anymore, at which point she'll be killed and dumped somewhere. Can you really live with that on your conscience?"

I blew out a breath of air. "No," I admitted grudgingly.

Sometimes I hated my conscience.

"That's my girl," Alexander said, kissing my forehead. "When you've got the captain taken care of, come up to the deck. Wink at me so that we know it's done. We won't get a second chance."

"Good luck, my child," Spiro said, tucking his gun into the pocket of his baggy linen trousers.

I nodded, my mouth too dry to respond. Taking a deep breath, I slipped out the door to find the captain.

42

I looked in on the galley on the way up to the bridge, ensuring that Sergei was engaged in annoying Jacques as usual. It wouldn't do to get the captain down into his cabin only to be confronted by Sergei in his pajamas. I tried not to picture the horror of Sergei in his pajamas. I needed to focus.

Hovering outside the galley door, I could hear Jacques yelling. "Not like that, you oaf! I said minced, not diced!"

"But isn't very tiny dice just like mince?" Sergei asked.

I shook my head and continued on. Clearly that was a conversation that was going to keep everyone occupied for the foreseeable future.

I paused outside the door to the bridge and took a deep breath, arranging my face into what I hoped was an expression of outrage. In my experience, it's better to go in aggressive and pushy than polite and apologetic. I knocked peremptorily. "Yes?" came the captain's voice through the door.

"It's Lora," I said. "Open this door immediately. I have found something very disturbing, and I need your help."

There was a brief silence on the other side of the door. "What have you found?" he asked without opening the door.

"I can't discuss it through the door. You need to see it."

More silence from Captain Vlad. *Dammit*, I thought, *this is not going to work. He's suspicious.*

"Please," I said, allowing a note of desperation to creep into my tone. "I don't know what to do. You're the captain. The boat is under your command, right? This is something I can't handle alone." If pushiness didn't work, I was prepared to try flattering his manly ego.

I heard the door unlock, and Captain Vlad's evil mole and crafty eyes made their appearance. "What?" he snapped.

I leaned forward to whisper. "I've found something in Sergei's room. I need you to look at it and tell me what I should do. I don't want to let Kyrill know it's there until you see it."

Captain Vlad crossed his arms. "What is it?" he asked, making it clear that was not going to play the rat to my pied piper of mysteriously undefined problems.

I took a deep breath, racking my brain for something that I might need Captain Vlad to see. "It's a woman," I said, finally. "I was just down there looking for Sergei and just as I came around the corner, I saw a woman go into his quarters."

Captain Vlad suddenly looked very, very concerned. "She didn't see me," I said. "If we hurry, she should still be in there. I don't want to disturb Kyrill with this. You know how he is about keeping his business private. I told him I'd make sure the trip ran smoothly. Please, just come with me now."

Captain Vlad nodded shortly, his mouth tense. "Fine."

We stole silently down to Sergei's room. The door was closed. Captain Vlad looked at me fiercely. "Are you sure?" he asked.

"I'm sure." I gestured toward the door. "Check it out for yourself."

Captain Vlad shot me another glance and put his hand on the doorknob. I braced myself.

Opening the door slowly, he looked inside without entering. "There is nobody there."

"Really?" I asked, trying to nudge him into the cabin. "Maybe you should go in and look more closely."

He looked at me with irritation. "I don't have to go in and look more closely. I can see entire cabin from here. There is no woman in this cabin."

Argh! I had never met anyone less cooperative in my life. Time to try Plan B: womanly wiles.

I pushed past him into the cabin. "There is a woman in this cabin," I said, dropping my voice to a sultry whisper. "Right here."

Captain Vlad looked at me blankly. Clearly subtlety was not going to work.

I bent down and in one smooth motion, pulled my dress up and over my head, flinging it to the side in what I hoped looked like an act of passion. "I've wanted to do this since the moment I laid eyes on you."

"Do what?"

I grabbed him by the belt and dragged him into the cabin. He was still between me and the door.

Stepping close, I maneuvered him around so that his back was to the cot.

"Why don't you just lie down and let me show you," I said, trying to keep my voice low and sexy and most of all not hysterical.

The captain suddenly clued into the fact that I was offering him sex.

"Oh," he said, looking at me, surprised.

"Oh," I repeated, nodding.

"I can't," he said. "I have to be on the bridge. I'm the captain."

"I'll be fast," I promised, fumbling with his belt.

Trying not to look down at what I was sure were his grimy underpants, I undid the belt and the zipper and yanked his pants down to his knees while he stared at me, torn between his duty as captain and a scenario straight out of a bad porn movie.

The second his pants were down, I lunged for the door. Realizing what was happening at the last second, he lunged for me but fell flat on his face as his legs tangled in his pants. "You bitch!" he yelled.

"Told you I'd be fast!" I said, evading his grasping hands and slamming the bolt home. I stood on the other side of the door, lightheaded with fear and relief.

"I'll kill you!" I heard him yell.

I leaned against the wall, my heart pounding. I was shaking all over. Captain Vlad was still yelling, mostly in Russian. The soundproofing on the cabins was good, but if someone came down the stairs, they would hear him. I had to get up to the main deck so that we could finish this.

I quickly moved back into the hallway, pausing outside Howard's door. Presumably Spiro had told Howard what was going on and to stay in his cabin. I knew Spiro didn't think Howard would be able to help us with the actual takeover, but maybe he could be our plan B.

Detouring quickly, I rapped on his door. No response.

"It's me. Lora," I said. Howard opened the door, peering out at me nervously. He was still in his pajamas, which had little racing cars on them. "Lora, what are you doing here?" he asked, concern in his eyes. "Spiro told me what was happening. Has something gone wrong?"

"No," I said. "But I was thinking that we should have a Plan B, just in case there are any problems."

Howard looked frightened. "Do you think we're going to have problems?" His breathing quickened as he started to panic.

"No," I said, laying a hand on his arm to calm him down. "It's going to be fine. But it's always good to have a Plan B, right?"

"Right," Howard said, looking unconvinced.

"Right," I said again. "Do you know where the tender is?"

"The tender?"

"The speedboat," I said impatiently. "It's on the back of the yacht."

Howard nodded.

"Figure out how to get it loose," I said. "Don't put it in the water, but make sure you can get it moving in a hurry if we need it. Do you think you can do that?"

"I don't know," Howard said uncertainly. "I'm not that great with boats."

"There's probably a manual or something," I said. "I'm sure a smart guy like you can figure it out."

I looked at Howard searchingly, not at all sure that he could figure it out. His lower lip was quivering. I tried to look confident. "I'm sure the plan will work," I said, "but if we have any problems, I'd rather take our chances in a fast boat in open water than trapped here with the Russian Mafia, wouldn't you?"

Howard paled at the word "Mafia," but nodded, suddenly resolute. "I'll do it," he said. "You can count on me."

"I know I can, Howard. After all, we're practically neighbors, right?" I gave him a brave smile.

Howard smiled back weakly.

"I've got to go up so we can finish this," I said, taking a deep breath. "I'll find you once we've got everything under control."

I left him standing in his doorway and tried to compose myself as I made my way up to the galley. I wished I had time to go put on another dress. Facing murderous white slavers and deadly weapons was tough enough without having to keep my stomach sucked in.

I smoothed my hands over my thighs before opening the door to the galley, where Jacques was continuing to berate Sergei about his dicing/mincing. "Gentlemen," I said, cutting him off, "Kyrill is talking to all three of our guests out on the deck and has told me that he wants the strictest privacy." I smiled in what I hoped was a reassuring manner. "You know how serious businessmen can be about confidentiality."

Jacques shrugged. "I am working. I don't have time to be listening at keyholes."

"I know," I said, "but this is apparently something super-secret, and he wants to make sure only Spiro and Alexander are there."

Jacques threw his hands up in irritation. "I do not care about his super secrets. I am an artist. An artist who is trying to work. But fine! Where does he want me to go? To my cabin?"

Eek, I thought. *He can't go to his cabin because he'll hear Captain Vlad calling down the wrath of heaven on slutty Western women.* I knew I should have put more time into planning and less time into sex with Alexander.

"Uh…Captain Vlad is doing some repair work in that level. Why don't you go into the wine cellar and do an inventory? You can take a look to see if there are any bottles you could recommend to Kyrill for the rest of the meals. But under no circumstances are you to touch any of the bottles," I said quickly.

"Why not?" Jacques sneered. "Because now Kyrill thinks I am a thief as well as a spy?"

"Not at all. Just because Kyrill has them organized in a very specific way. And also because some of the racks have alarms where if you touch the bottles, a siren starts going off. And they might also trigger the room to fill with sleeping gas," I said. Dammit! Clearly I was the world's worst liar. Jacques was going to see right through me.

Jacques looked at me. "Oh," he said. "I've heard of racks like that. Only the ones I heard of had tear gas."

I tried not to look like that was the craziest thing I had ever heard. "Right," I said. "Maybe it was tear gas. The point is that you should not touch the bottles."

"Should I help?" Sergei asked.

Jacques shot him a poisonous look. "I don't need help, you

idiot."

I looked at Sergei and was suddenly struck with inspiration. I knew the best way to get him on deck without arousing Kyrill's suspicion. "Later. First please get out a bottle of champagne. I think Kyrill would like to make a toast. I'll call you when we're ready."

Surely Kyrill would be happy to indulge me with a toast to yesterday's heroic rescuers. Sergei could bring out the bottle, and Spiro and Alexander would have them both there, completely at their mercy. I congratulated myself on my brilliance. I had single-handedly neutralized the captain, come up with a brilliant Plan B, and taken care of the Sergei situation. Clearly, I was a natural at all this boat takeover stuff. Maybe I could get a job as a pirate.

43

When I came up on board, Spiro, Kyrill, and Alexander were standing on the deck talking. I slowly circled around so that Alexander could see me wink deliberately.

"Lora," Alexander said. "There you are. After your ordeal yesterday, I was afraid you might want to spend the day in bed. It's not every day that you get kidnapped and held hostage and almost killed."

Kyrill frowned. Clearly being kidnapped and almost killed didn't strike him as sufficient reason to shirk my hostessing duties. "Yes," he said. "We've been waiting for you to join us."

"Yes, well..." I said. "After all the excitement last night, I was completely worn out this morning." I caught Alexander's self-satisfied smirk out of the corner of my eye and kicked myself over my word choice.

"I'm sure," Kyrill said. "We will be arriving in Malta this evening. Spiro and I will need to spend the day working, unfortunately, but you, Alexander, and Howard can relax." He looked around critically. "Where is Howard?"

"I'm afraid he was a bit under the weather this morning," Spiro said, shaking his head. "So much time in front of the computer has made him weak. He catches every little thing that goes around. I told him to stay in bed until he felt better. That way Lora and Alexander can have fun without him sneezing all over them."

237

Kyrill shrugged. "As long as he's better by this evening," he said. "I have a surprise for you. A little something to celebrate our newfound partnership. And he's a critical part of your business, right? So he also needs to be on deck to celebrate."

I cut in smoothly, seeing my chance. "Speaking of celebration," I said, "I propose that we have a toast. To my rescuers."

Kyrill looked pleased. "What a wonderful idea. We can have a drink or two before Spiro and I get down to business."

I pressed the call button, summoning Sergei. As I waited for him to come, I slowly maneuvered myself so that I was standing to the side of the deck, well out of what I assumed would be the line of fire. Every muscle in my body was tense, and was all I could do not to run, screaming back to my cabin.

Alexander and Spiro were standing with their backs against the railing. I could see the gun tucked into the back of Alexander's waistband. He casually worked his hand around and gripped the butt of the pistol. His face was calm and focused, and I felt a surge of confidence.

Sergei finally made his appearance, a towel over his arm and a bottle of champagne clutched in his hand. I took a deep breath.

"Champagne?" Sergei asked, unwrapping the top of the bottle.

"I don't think so," said Alexander, pulling the handgun out of his pants. "Sit down," he ordered Sergei.

Spiro had his gun trained on Kyrill. "You too," he said, his voice cold. "On the deck. Not too close to each other."

Sergei's jaw dropped. He sank silently to the deck, still clinging to the bottle. Kyrill's face darkened with rage. "What is the meaning of this?" he asked, his voice full of ice. "We're here to make a deal that benefits us both. What can you possibly hope to gain from this?"

Spiro made a tutting noise like an irate librarian. "No," he said, steel running through his voice. "I am here to make a deal with Kyrill Antonov. Not to make a deal with you, whoever you are."

A muscle twitched in Kyrill's jaw. *Gotcha*, I thought. "I am Kyrill Antonov."

"No you're not," I said. "I sent a picture of you to my brother. He says you're not Kyrill. The real Kyrill has double chins and is apparently very charming once you get to know him. You don't qualify on either count."

Kyrill scoffed. "Your brother has no idea what I look like.

Moscow can be a very dangerous place for people like me. Rich people are kidnapped all the time, which is why I keep a low profile. If your brother thinks he's found a photograph of me, he's wrong. I pay a lot of money to make sure there aren't any of them to be found."

He looked directly at Spiro. "What does she know about anything?" he asked. "She's a professional hostess. One step up from a hooker. You want to know how to fold a napkin or give someone a blow job, give her a call. Why would you listen to what she says?"

I looked daggers at Kyrill. "Because I have no reason to lie," I said, "and because my brother is one of the best hackers in the world. He had no trouble finding a picture of the real Kyrill Antonov. Maybe you should hire someone competent to do your cover story next time, you ass."

Spiro nodded. "To be fair, though, the cover story was not too bad. I checked you out very thoroughly before we decided to do business. I would never normally move so quickly on a deal like this. But a man of your reputation..." he sighed. "Business being as it's been, I couldn't afford to hesitate. And once I was on board, why would I be suspicious? The boat, of course, is Kyrill's. How many boats like this are there in the world? And Lora—just the kind of person someone like Kyrill would know, and someone I knew already. The perfect touch."

"So, Kyrill, or whatever your name is," Alexander said. "That leaves us with the question of who you are. To spare us the time you would undoubtedly spend telling more ridiculous lies, let me tell you what else I know. I know that while you've supposedly been talking 'business' with my father, you've really been drugging him and pumping him for information."

Kyrill's eyes narrowed.

"That's right," Alexander continued. "Lora ran into my father in the hallway, and she told me he was too drunk to stand, babbling about business. I knew that something was wrong. I've seen my father drink bottles of vodka with no effect. He's never drunk. So I stayed up last night to wait for him to come back.

"He was barely able to stand up, but he wouldn't stop talking. But when I asked him what you had talked about, he couldn't remember. He just kept repeating that business was good and that we were all going to make a lot of money. What did you give him?

Some kind of hypnotic, I'm guessing. You just pump him for information until you can't get anything else, then tell him what you want him to remember, right?"

Kyrill was silent. I scanned his face for some kind of tell. There was nothing. I bet he cleaned up at the poker table.

"Anyone who came in contact with him would just assume he was wasted," Alexander continued. "Except, of course, for someone like me who knew his drinking habits, but I guess you figured if you kept me drunk and distracted by Lora, I'd be easy enough to manage."

I felt myself go red. Alexander was right. I hadn't just been used as a cover; I'd been used as a distraction. My ending up in bed with Alexander had all been part of Kyrill's plan. Now I felt like a slut as well as a sucker, which almost made me hope that Kyrill would give Alexander an excuse to shoot.

"So tell me," Alexander said, adjusting his aim so that the gun was pointed directly at Kyrill's head. "Who are you, and what information were you trying to get from my father?"

Kyrill looked at him. "I think you know the answer to that question. I was trying to get the names of every contact, every safe house, and every middleman you use when you're selling women into slavery."

Before the meaning of his words sank in to my brain, Alexander, quick as a snake, had grabbed me by the arm and dragged me over beside him. "You told me you were smuggling antiquities!" I cried, struggling to pull free of his grasp. I felt like I'd been kicked in the stomach. I had trusted Alexander. I had *slept* with Alexander. I suddenly felt sick.

"Stand still!" Alexander commanded, moving the gun to my head.

I froze. I had managed to go my entire life without having a gun pointed at my head, and now it had been twice in less than twenty-four hours. This was not a habit I wanted to get into.

"Shoot them if they move," Alexander told his father, gesturing toward Sergei and Kyrill. He brutally twisted my arm behind my back, forcing me to my knees. Fishing around in his pockets, he came up with a zip tie. "I found these down in the engine room last night after we had our fun," he said. "I thought they might come in handy." He zipped my wrists together behind my back, pulling until the tie cut into my wrists.

"To be fair," he said, pushing me to the side and reclaiming his gun, "we do smuggle antiques. But business has been down recently, so we've had to diversify. People are a surprisingly recession-proof commodity."

"You lied to me!"

Alexander looked at me like I was an idiot. "Well, you would hardly have helped us dispose of the captain if I'd told you the truth, now would you?" he asked. "I sell human beings, Lora. Lying goes with the territory. Don't be so naïve, for god's sake."

"You unbelievable bastard," I snarled. "How could you do something like this?" I was terrified, but even more than that, I was furious, both at Alexander for selling human beings and at myself for being a fool.

"Enough," Alexander snapped. He pulled the scarf from my neck and tied it around my mouth, gagging me. "Honestly, this is why I never get attached to women. You just never know when to shut up. There," he said, finishing. "If you move or speak again, I'll shoot you right in the head. Do you understand?"

I nodded, feeling my earlier anger drain away in a new rush of fear. Whether Alexander shot me now for moving or in five minutes for just being in the wrong place at the wrong time, the outcome was completely certain. My throat suddenly felt thick, and I blinked away tears.

Alexander turned his attention and gun back to Kyrill. "So where were we?" he asked. "Oh yes. You were about to tell me who the fuck you are. Stop jittering, you idiot," he snarled at Sergei, who was bouncing his knees up and down like a three-year-old who had to go to the toilet.

In contrast to Sergei, Kyrill looked completely calm. "Why don't you just call me Kyrill," he suggested, "because my name is not really important. What is important are the people I work for. If you harm a hair on my head, they will hunt you down like animals. They will find you. They will make sure you suffer for what you've done. They will make you beg for death."

Alexander let the air out of his lungs slowly through gritted teeth.

"I figured as much," he said, "but I don't really see a lot of alternatives here. At least this way we get a head start." He shot a glance at his father.

Spiro nodded grimly. "And we'll need to kill Lora and the

waiter," Spiro said, all traces of the jovial grandfather wiped from his face. "No witnesses."

"So then," Alexander said, his eyes boring into Kyrill's. "I guess this is goodbye."

Kyrill's mouth curled into a hard, triumphant smile. I looked at him in disbelief. I was willing to concede that Russian mobsters were tough, but I wouldn't have thought they would literally laugh in the face of death. Personally, I was planning on going out blubbering like a two-year-old.

"There's one more thing you need to know," Kyrill said.

Spiro sighed impatiently. "What is that?"

A low, feminine voice cut in. "If you don't put down the gun immediately, I'm going to blow your head off."

44

I turned in shock to see the prisoner from the wine cellar pointing a gun at Spiro's head. Suddenly I wondered how I could ever have mistaken her for a victim. She looked calm, cool, and completely lethal.

"Tatiana! My love!" Alexander gasped. "I thought you were dead!" He took a step forward as if to run to her but was brought up short by the gun she aimed at his heart.

"Of course you did, you miserable excuse for a human being," Tatiana said. "That's just what you were supposed to think. I couldn't bear to spend another second with you, pretending to be your fiancée, when all I could think about was putting a bullet in your head." I remembered my dinner conversation with Alexander. His love, tragically lost in an accident. Or not, apparently.

"But we were together for a year," he said, bewildered.

"A year," she agreed. "A year I spent going through your papers, bugging your phones, figuring out where the girls were coming from, where you were sending them, and how they were being transported. A year I spent gagging every time we kissed."

Alexander looked like he had been gutted. "We were engaged. I loved you. You told me you loved me."

"I lied," she said, curling her lips in a mocking smile. "Don't be so naïve."

I secretly cheered Tatiana, whoever she was. *Take that, you bastard!*

Spiro turned on his son. "You let this Mafia bitch into our home!" he yelled. "You told her our secrets! You imbecile!"

Apparently, the tenuous family harmony that Alexander and Spiro had managed to cobble together so they could enslave and sell other people had come to an end.

Tatiana turned her attention back to Spiro. "Drop the gun, or I shoot, old man," she said. "I never liked you, not even when you were calling me daughter."

"You stupid whore," Spiro grated. "Can't you count? We have two guns. You have one. *You* drop *your* gun!" he commanded, turning to face her.

I looked over at Kyrill and Sergei. Kyrill's face was like stone, his eyes fixed on Tatiana. Sergei was wringing his hands nervously in his lap. He caught my eye and moved slightly so that I could see what he was doing. He wasn't wringing his hands – he was twisting the cork in the champagne bottle, which was aimed squarely at Alexander.

Tatiana stood resolutely, her gun trained on Spiro. I held my breath. If she dropped the gun, we were all dead. With a sudden pop, the champagne cork flew out, pegging Alexander directly in the eye. He shrieked and clutched his face at the same time as I shot my leg out in a vicious kick to the back of his ankle. Alexander went down hard, the gun skittering across the hardwood as he hit the deck.

Kyrill immediately grabbed the gun and trained it on Spiro. "You've already shown that you can count," he said coldly. "Now put your weapon down. It's over."

Spiro ground his teeth but put the gun down on the deck, where Sergei quickly picked it up and tucked it into the waistband of his pants. Though he still looked like the dim-witted chef's apprentice, his movements were now quick and efficient. He quickly ransacked Alexander's pockets, emerging with a handful of zip ties. Kyrill and Tatiana held their guns steady while Sergei secured father and son at the wrists and ankles.

I sighed in relief. I still had no idea what was going on, but at least I didn't appear to be in imminent danger of being shot. Sergei approached and stood over me, a speculative look on his face. My eyes widened as he pulled a large kitchen knife out of his pocket and brandished it in my direction. He looked over at Kyrill.

"Should I take care of Lora?"

Kyrill shot me a menacing glare. "Yes," he said, his tone brutal. "She can't talk."

I watched Sergei approach me slowly with the knife, a sadistic smile on his face. I couldn't believe that he was going to kill and dismember me with the same knife skills I had let Jacques teach him. I'd probably end up in star-shaped pieces at the bottom of the ocean.

Sergei pulled me to my feet and raised the knife. Shrieking through the gag, I kicked him as hard as I could in the groin and bolted for the kitchen. Sergei went down, moaning, his hands cupping his balls. I rushed past him through the galley doors. The doorstop! Frantically, I kicked the doorstop down. It wouldn't hold forever, but maybe it would give me a chance to get to Howard on the tender.

I raced through the galley, wishing I could stop to try to cut myself free. Running with my hands tied behind my back put me off balance, and I knew that if I stumbled, it would all be over. I tore through the hallway, praying that Howard had figured out how to free the smaller boat. As I came out onto the rear deck, I saw with relief that Howard had the speedboat unlocked and was standing in the middle of it, still in his pajamas, armed with a knife he must have taken from the kitchen. Howard took in my gag and bound hands and his eyes widened in horror.

"Arrrr," I shrieked through the gag, throwing myself into the boat. I landed awkwardly on the bottom. "Arrr!" I shrieked again, gesturing downward with my head.

Howard pressed a button, and the boat began to descend. He quickly undid the knot to the gag. "What's happening?!" he asked, panic in his voice.

"Spiro and Alexander are white slavers, and now Kyrill and some woman are holding them hostage, and I think they're part of the Russian Mafia, and they're coming to kill us. God, Howard," I panted, "won't this thing go any faster? They'll be here in a second!"

Howard looked at me in shock. "What?"

"We need to get out of here, now!" I yelled.

"But Spiro and Alexander?"

"They're bad guys," I said. "Those shipments that you're managing on your spreadsheets? They're people, Howard.

People!"

We heard a shout of alarm as Kyrill and Sergei realized where we were, and I looked up to see them pounding down the deck, guns pointed directly at us. "Stop!" Kyrill yelled.

"What do we do?" I asked, panicked. "It's not going fast enough!"

Howard raised the kitchen knife and turned to face Kyrill and Sergei. "What are you doing?" I yelled at him. "You've only got a knife! They've got guns!"

"No," Howard corrected. "I've got a knife and a hostage." He dragged me in front of him and held the knife to my throat, looking toward Kyrill and Sergei. "I'll kill her!" Howard called out, his normally soft voice suddenly hard.

Sergei and Kyrill stopped, guns trained on us.

"Why do you think I would care?" Kyrill asked.

Exactly, I thought. Howard hadn't struck me as a half-wit, but apparently he had missed a critical plot line. On the other hand, if my choice was between a quick death by a knife-wielding Philadelphian or a slow death by hammer-wielding Russian mobster, I was going to have to root for the home team.

"Because it means a lot of paperwork," Howard called back. "Russian police shoot innocent American event hostess in international waters. You'll be running traffic in Siberia for the next five years."

"Police?" I gaped.

"Yes, police," Howard said disgustedly. "My phone hasn't been working this entire trip, but while we were on Lady Esther's boat, it connected. I didn't even realize it until I got up this morning and saw that I had messages waiting. Lots of them. It seems someone has been rounding up our network and arresting our primary contacts. I'm guessing I have you to thank for that, Kyrill, or whatever the hell your name is."

Kyrill smiled. "You can call me Kyrill," he said. "And as of an hour ago, your network is completely down. I was hoping to have another afternoon with Spiro to fill in a few last pieces, but between the people we've picked up and the case Tatiana built when she was posing as Alexander's fiancée, we have more than enough. You won't be running girls out of Eastern Europe ever again."

"I can't believe you're part of this!" I said to Howard. "You're from Philadelphia!" The words sounded stupid even as they came out of my mouth. As if a person from Philadelphia couldn't be a white slaver. Philadelphia was actually a pretty rough town. It was probably loaded with white slavers. "I mean," I tried again, "you were in the Peace Corps. You were so upset about how the girls in Bulgaria were being taken advantage of. How could you do this?"

"Everybody gets to be young and stupid once," he said. "I joined the Peace Corps to make a difference. But then I realized that these girls were no better than whores. They weren't interested in a guy like me, a normal guy who liked them. They wanted a guy like Alexander. Rich. Sleazy. Dangerous. So I made sure they ended up with a guy like that. And I was well paid for my efforts."

"You sold innocent women into bondage! Doesn't that mean anything to you?"

"Trust me," Howard said, his eyes still fixed on Kyrill as our boat lowered. "They weren't innocent. And I'm wealthy enough now that I think I'll be able to find a girl who will overlook my past transgressions. Women seem to have great moral flexibility when it comes to rich men."

"Drop it," Kyrill ordered again, moving toward the railing as the smaller boat lowered so that he could keep Howard in his sights.

"I don't think so," Howard said. "But if you're willing to kill Lora, take the shot. She's just an event hostess, after all. No great loss to the universe. We're going to go now. By the time you get this behemoth pointed in the right direction, we'll be long gone. But don't worry about her. I'll let her go once I'm clear."

"Like hell you will, you lying sack of shit!" I yelled. "Kyrill— whatever your name is—shoot him!"

Kyrill's face above us was torn. I could see him angling for a clear shot, but knew that with Howard behind me and both boats bobbing on the waves, he wouldn't be able to hit him without hitting me.

Howard maneuvered me forward slightly so that he could reach the starter then fumbled as a loud, blaring noise started coming from his pocket. It was his telephone, playing "Ride of the Valkyries" at maximum volume. "What the fuck?"

Kyrill grabbed his pocket as his phone chimed in playing the same tune, at even higher volume. Then the boat's loudspeaker system blared to life, and suddenly the air was filled with the sound of Wagnerian valkyries, shrieking and pulsing and wailing to a crescendo that was so loud that I could feel my teeth vibrating. The music pounded across the water, deafening us.

"What the hell is going on?" Kyrill yelled, looking around frantically. Howard, taking advantage of his opponent's distraction, lunged around me to hit the start button for the engine. Before I could react, I heard a loud crack over the roar of the music, and I felt, more than heard, Howard shriek as a bullet tore into his shoulder.

Hands still bound behind me, I scuttled for the knife, kicking it into the far end of the boat. I followed it, shifting my weight so that I could kick Howard if he tried to get it. "They shot me," he said weakly, blinking up at me in confusion.

"Good!" I snapped back.

He collapsed back against the deck, moaning pathetically.

Seeing that Howard was in no shape to come after me, I spared a glance around. Kyrill, Sergei, and Tatiana were standing on the boat, looking confused. They apparently hadn't been the ones who had fired the shot. As the music slowly started to fade, we heard the distinctive sound of a helicopter.

Police! I thought. I squinted my eyes and looked up. In the bright sunlight, I could see that this was not anyone's standard-issue police helicopter. Teal with golden arabesque designs, it looked like something that would land on Barbie's helicopter pad.

"Attention, bad guys," a voice blared out over the helicopter's loud speakers. "This is Prince Philippe von Hofstedtler, and you are officially under arrest." Pinkie. Thank god. A short scuffle over the loudspeaker ensued, followed by a petulant, "Fine, then. See if I ever give you a lift again."

A flat voice in a heavy Russian accent came over the loudspeaker. "This is Agent Teofilov," it said. "Everybody drop your weapons, and get on your knees."

I looked on the deck to see Kyrill, Tatiana, and Sergei drop to their knees calmly, their hands on their heads. I dropped to my knees as well. Howard shrieked as he put his hands up. He looked pale and shaky, which made my vengeance-loving heart happy. He also looked like he was about to throw up. I sidled slightly farther away. Being thrown up on would really be the perfect ending to this day.

"Enjoy prison in Russia," I whispered, my lips curling in an evil smile. He tightened his lips and said nothing. That was fine by me. I had heard enough lies for a while.

45

Back on the boat, Kyrill and Tatiana were debriefing their colleagues, two dangerous-looking men dressed in body armor and toting high -powered rifles, and a woman who looked no less lethal, but a lot more familiar. The maid from the hotel. Her face was still bruised from her encounter with Dieter, but her mouth was set in a triumphant smile.

I stepped into the salon, feeling tired and shaky and wishing I was wearing more than a bikini. For once, though, I didn't bother to suck in. Given how high my pulse had been for the last hour, I figured I had probably burned off all the scones I had snarfed, and then some.

Kyrill looked up when I came in. "You!" he said, looking at me murderously. "You almost ruined everything."

"I almost ruined everything?!" I screeched. "I found a girl being held hostage on your boat!"

"I told you to stay out of the wine cellar!"

"And you threatened to pulp Lady Esther with a hammer!" I shouted back.

"I was just being nice! In case you weren't paying attention, she kidnapped you so that she could kill you. Do you think she's going to be doing that in the future? No, because she thinks she'll get mashed with a hammer. God," he said, disgusted. "Some people are so ungrateful!"

"My point is," I continued, "how was I supposed to know you were with the police? You guys killed Dieter. And Lady Esther's butler. Killing people and holding them hostage and crushing them with hammers are not things that one normally associates with the good guys."

Kyrill harrumphed. "Obviously you've never spent much time with Russian good guys."

"Oh…" I said, "And let's not forget that you also told Sergei to kill me. That was really the final straw. I'm sure you can see how I got confused."

"I never did that!"

"You never did what? I was here, remember?"

"I never told Sergei to kill you," he said. "The rest of it, yes, okay, I can see how that might have been confusing."

"Hah," I said. "Let me refresh your memory. Sergei walked toward me. He pulled out a knife and asked if he should 'take care of me,' and you said, and I quote, 'Yes. She can't talk.' How else was I supposed to interpret that?"

"You were gagged," Kyrill said reasonably. "You couldn't talk. I told him to take care of it." He mimed cutting the gag off and spread his hands. "Jesus. Isn't English your native language?"

"Do yourself a favor, and stick to Russian," I snapped. "Your grasp of idiom sucks." I flung myself on the sofa and looked around the room in irritation. Howard was cuffed next to Spiro and Alexander. His wound had been disinfected and bandaged. They had also given him something for the pain. I had argued vehemently in favor of allowing him to stay infected and in pain, but cooler heads had prevailed.

Pinkie, dressed in a black military-style jumpsuit fetchingly coordinated with a camouflage silk ascot, helped himself and me to a glass of champagne and joined me on the sofa. "How are you?" he asked, stroking my arm gently. I fought back a lump in my throat at his concern. It was times like this that I realized how much Pinkie and I really meant to each other. "Because you look like complete shit," he continued. "I mean, two words: waterproof mascara. It's a boat, for god's sake.

"And you," Pinkie said, directing his ire at Kyrill. "How dare you put my friend at risk for your stupid Russian police shenanigans?! I'll never forgive you!"

Kyrill had the good grace to look slightly abashed. "I am sorry," he said. "We've been looking into Spiro's company for some time now, working with the Bulgarian police. We were building a case against them using Kyrill Antonov, who had...er...volunteered...to help the police in return for certain...considerations. But four days ago, Bulgarian police stumbled across a warehouse filled with girls in a drug bust in Bulgaria. We got there in time to keep it contained, but we knew that when the girls didn't show up at the next checkpoint, Spiro and Alexander would shut down the network. The whole case would have dissolved overnight."

"Fine," Pinkie said. "So you needed to keep them from finding out about the girls. Why didn't you just pick them up and question them at the station like normal policemen? This seems needlessly complicated and expensive and ridiculous, even for Russians, and that's saying a lot."

Kyrill shook his head. "We thought about it. But Spiro kept track of the whole thing in his head—no paper records—and we didn't think he'd be easy to break. He got his start on the docks as a mob enforcer. They train those guys to put up with a lot of pain.

"Don't get me wrong," he said. "We would have taken him to Russia. He would have talked. But by the time we sorted through his lies and figured out the real contacts, word would have been out, and everyone involved would have vanished. We had three days to get the information out of him, and we took it."

"So you are what?" I asked. "Some kind of interrogator?"

Tatiana, who had been listening over on the side, chimed in. "He is trained in covert interrogation," she said.

"What the hell is covert interrogation?"

"It is interrogation when you don't know that you are being interrogated," she said, smiling like the Cheshire Cat.

Seeing my confusion, Kyrill hastened to explain. "First," he said, "you need to create an atmosphere where the person can relax. For this we used the real Kyrill's yacht. It is luxurious, beautiful. Some of our men have been on the boat for a while now getting it ready, installing the holding cell and the signal jammers."

"Did you know that they also installed a ferret and several prostitutes?" I asked tartly.

Kyrill's lips twisted. "Russian police officer salaries are not so great," he said. "Sometimes the men take some...perks, I think you call it."

"Perks," I repeated. "Of course, what was I thinking?" I'd have to remember that the next time a ferret peed on my rug.

"The real Kyrill would have been a great partner for Spiro's business," Kyrill continued. "Contacts, the ability to get things over the border…it was a perfect match. And Spiro's financial situation meant that he needed to get this done fast. But he's been around a long time," he continued, "and you don't get to where he is by trusting other people. We needed someone Spiro knew to vouch for Kyrill. Someone who would clearly have no involvement with the police. Kyrill had the idea of using you, actually. One of his friends from boarding school had apparently made him sit through a description of every man you had had dinner with in the past few months. When Kyrill heard Spiro's name, he made the connection, and we set it up."

The fact that Clancy Featherstone had been the whole reason I'd ended up in this mess didn't come as a surprise to me. "Plus, of course, you needed someone to clean up the mess your perk-loving crew had created while they had been on the boat," I noted. "And someone to distract Alexander." My stomach still felt sour when I thought of how I'd been used.

Kyrill shrugged, clearly not overly concerned with my scruples. "The drug we used on Spiro is designed to work with alcohol. The subject has a few drinks. You slip the drug into one of them. Like Alexander guessed, it's a hypnotic. They talk freely for about five hours. Then you plant the suggestion you want them to remember."

"That they were going to make a lot of money."

"Right. We mainly needed Alexander and Howard to stay out of the way so that they would not pay too much attention to Spiro. Spiro himself wouldn't have any sense that anything was wrong, but anyone who knew him and saw him after the interrogation might suspect."

I shook my head. "I can't believe you put me at risk this way. For the love of god, I could have been killed. I almost *was* killed," I corrected. "Twice! Three times, if you count Lady Esther's boat. And I don't know what Dieter had planned, but I'm pretty sure I wouldn't have liked it."

Kyrill looked at me seriously. "You have to understand," he said, "that we had forty-eight hours to get this together. Would we have done things differently if we'd had the time? Yes, of course.

But peoples' lives were at stake here—not just yours. We took the information we got from him, and we closed the network down. And because we got to it first, we have a chance to find some of the girls who have been sold. We've already located a dozen and reunited them with their families. I'm hoping that by the end of the week we'll have even more."

"So how was this all supposed to end?" I asked. "I assume that the plan wasn't for me to go crying to the bad guys and for all of us to be held at gunpoint. Because if that was the plan, let me be the first to tell you that it was a crappy one."

"The plan," Kyrill said sternly, "was for Maria to bug everyone's bags so that we could monitor what was happening on the boat and control the situation." He nodded at the hotel maid.

I looked over at Maria. "I'm guessing that didn't work out."

She shook her head. "I was in your room when Dieter keyed in. He saw the bug. He tried to kill me." She trailed her finger lightly over one of the bruises on her face. "I told the truth. I killed him in self-defense."

Tatiana reached over and gave Maria's shoulder a squeeze. "You see? All those judo courses at the academy paid off."

"And the Bulgarian police just let you go?" I asked.

"It took a few calls," she said. "Fortunately, Dieter had a bit of a file with the police."

"A file?"

"He's hurt a lot of women. Rapes. Assaults."

"Then why wasn't he in jail?" I asked, outraged. "I could have been one of those women!"

"The complaints were always dropped," she said, shrugging. "Money, threats…however he does it, he's been getting away with it for a long time."

I tightened my jaw. "Well, I'm glad that he's dead, then."

"You're welcome," she replied.

"Anyway, once Dieter had been killed, Maria had to run," Kyrill said. "She didn't have time to plant the bugs."

"And you went ahead with this whole plan anyway?"

"They were just a backup," Kyrill explained. "There was no reason to think they'd be necessary."

"Wait a minute. Why didn't you just bug the boat?" I asked. "I mean, clearly you installed a really fancy wine cellar designed to hold your backup and prove that you were able to smuggle people.

Didn't it occur to anyone that installing some listening devices would have been a good idea?

Kyrill flushed. "Russian contractors sometimes don't have the best attention to detail."

"Meaning..."

"They forgot."

I held up my hands. "If it were any other country, I'd know you were lying. But given what I know about Russia..."

"Anyway," Kyrill continued, "the plan was to arrest Alexander, Spiro, and Howard once we arrived in Maltese waters. The smuggling ring stretches all over Europe, and we've been working with police forces in the EU. We were planning on getting you to organize drinks at the pool, where we could be certain they wouldn't be armed."

"No kidding," I said. "Those Greek swimsuits leave very little room for guns. Or testicles, for that matter," I amended, recalling Spiro's little red number. "And Tatiana?" I asked. "What was she supposed to do? Just sit there in a glass box looking tragic and making me think you were going to auction her off to some depraved sheikh?"

"You weren't supposed to see me at all," Tatiana said. "Kyrill showed Spiro the cell the night before we left. Any doubts Spiro might have had about Kyrill's willingness to traffic in slaves vanished the second he saw it. You don't build a secret cell in a yacht to move coffee tables.

"It was my idea to use that same cell as my command center. Poetic justice, I think you call it in English. I was coordinating with our teams on the ground and monitoring Kyrill, providing him intelligence that would allow him to get Spiro talking." She tapped her ear. "Two-way radio," she said smugly.

I suddenly felt like an idiot. Only I could mistake a professional police officer providing intel to a colleague for a tragic victim of human trafficking. "You just looked really stressed," I said weakly.

"Of course I was stressed," she said. "I spent a year of my life getting close to Alexander so that we could break this ring. When we started, we had nothing. It was my work that put this case together. I was the one who confirmed that they were trafficking in women. I was the one who planted the idea of partnership with Kyrill in Alexander's head. I wanted to make sure nothing went wrong. I wanted him to see my face when we took him down."

I bit my lip. "I know this is a little bit off topic," I said, "but did you actually sleep with him to make the case? Is that even legal? Did your bosses ask you to do that, or was it your idea? I mean, it just seems really cold-blooded."

Tatiana snorted. "Correct me if I'm wrong, but you slept with him, too. What was your excuse?"

I flushed while Pinkie clapped his hands gleefully. "Really?" he asked. "Was he good? I bet he was. The bad ones are always great in the sack." I shot him a warning look. "Look on the bright side," he said. "At least you don't have to worry about him stalking you. He'll be in prison for the rest of his life."

Alexander, who had been slumped in the corner listening, shook his head, his eyes locked on Tatiana. "You bitch," he said. "I loved you. I treated you like a goddess, and this is how you repay me."

Tatiana turned her ice-blue eyes on Alexander. "You treated me like a goddess," she said, "but you treated hundreds of other women like cattle. This has nothing to do with me. This is karma, coming to get you. Prison in Russia..." She mulled over the words thoughtfully. "Poor people in Russia see a lot of loss in their life. I'm sure a lot of the people you're going to be sharing a cell with have seen their sisters, daughters, cousins, or friends do some pretty desperate things to try to give their families a break. I bet a lot of them will want to make sure you fully appreciate their point of view."

She turned back to me. "When I had what I needed from Alexander and his father, I returned to Russia, telling Alexander that I needed to visit my grandmother. Faking a death is very easy in Moscow," she continued. "Lots of people die there. They get drunk and fall into rivers. They get mugged."

"They get lung cancer from the air pollution," I supplied helpfully.

"They get into car accidents," she continued, ignoring my interruption. "We faked a couple of news clippings about a fatal car accident and staged a funeral service with a tasteful little urn and a bunch of mourners who spoke only Russian. Way cheaper and easier than it would have been in a western country."

"I'll keep that in mind in case I ever need to fake a death on a budget."

"And that's it. I went back to help build the case, and we were just getting ready to move when we got word about the discovery of the girls. The rest you know."

"Not quite," Kyrill chimed in. "I'd like to hear how Prince Philippe…"

"Pinkie," said Pinkie, waving away the formality.

"Pinkie," corrected Kyrill, "managed to show up at the last minute with the Russian police in tow."

"For that," Pinkie said, "I need to credit Lora's brother."

I smiled crookedly. "The music was a dead giveaway."

"Yes, well, when Chris figured out that Kyrill wasn't Kyrill, he called in about every favor he had from the hacker community to figure out who you were with. He was tracking you through your cell phone, so he wasn't too worried—until the signal disappeared while you were visiting one Lady Esther Featherstone."

Tatiana and the two Russians from the helicopter looked up in interest, having not heard this part of the story.

"Uh yes," I said, looking at Kyrill. I wasn't sure how much information he wanted me to divulge on that particular topic. "It fell overboard."

Spiro, sulking in the corner, jumped into the conversation. "This man, Kyrill, he killed Lady Esther's servant. He is a killer. Ask her." He looked triumphantly at the Russians, apparently expecting some sort of promise of an internal investigation.

Agent Teofilov regarded him for a moment then yawned ostentatiously.

Spiro glowered but quieted down, apparently realizing that police misconduct was slightly less of a concern in Russia than it might be in, say, Connecticut.

"So Chris gave me a call, and I rang up a friend of mine with a helicopter: Princess Ayesha, by the way," he said, turning to me. "I think we'll probably want to get her a fruit basket or something. Anyway, I got the helicopter, and Chris told me that he'd identified the fake Kyrill here as a Russian undercover police officer."

Kyrill turned red. "That is top secret information! How did he know that?"

"Internet porn," Pinkie said primly. "The next time you decide to sleep with someone at the office, you might want to check two things. First, check for cameras, and—hint!—if you're screwing someone right in front of their monitor, there's a camera there."

Kyrill turned even redder.

"And second," Pinkie continued unflappably, "I'd make sure you didn't do right in front of the office signage." Pinkie tapped a few buttons on his phone and held it out for me to see. The small screen showed what I had to assume was Kyrill's naked ass being gripped energetically by a pair of legs ending in knockoff Louboutins. There was quite a lot of panting and moaning. Directly overhead was the seal and motto of the Russian police.

"By serving the law, we serve the nation," Pinkie translated.

I held the phone out to Tatiana, who looked at it with interest as the woman began to shriek out a torrent of what even I could tell was very dirty Russian. "Is that Elena?" she asked.

"I don't want to talk about it," Kyrill said.

She handed to phone to Sergei, who took a look and handed it over to Agent Teofilov, who studied it intently. The shrieking rose in intensity, and a loud slapping noise picked up speed. At this point, Kyrill looked like he would have been happier if he had been shot.

"Anywho," Pinkie continued, retrieving his phone, "once he figured out who you were, I just rang up the real Kyrill. He called the police to let them know that their guy's cover had been blown and that you were missing, and we all headed out to stage a heroic rescue. Of course, I insisted that we start out at Lady Esther's yacht, since that was where your phone had you last."

"How...ah...was Lady Esther?"

"Very subdued, now that you mention it," Pinkie said. "She had some rope burns around her wrists, and it looked like she had been smacked around a bit. And, of course, her boat was broken, and her captain appeared to have vanished. In fact, it all looked a bit suspicious to us, so we tied her up again—securely this time—and left her there. I figured that if you weren't on this boat, we'd head back there and talk a little bit more earnestly about your whereabouts."

"You left Clancy's mom tied up on a broken boat?" I asked weakly.

"Well, I always thought she was a complete harpy," Pinkie said, "and knowing of Clancy's, shall we say, fondness for you, I was afraid she might have done something drastic. I guess I owe her an apology."

"I don't think an apology will be necessary," I said, "but I guess we should send someone over there to untie her." I paused, remembering my time with Lady Esther. "I mean, tomorrow should be fine. No need to rush. It's been a long day. We should probably call my brother to let him know that I'm okay, though."

"That won't be necessary." Chris's voice suddenly came out of Pinkie's phone. "I've been monitoring Kyrill's radio since we got into range so that I could help stage the landing. And for the record, I will not be telling Mom any of this. Especially not the part where you slept with a white slaver and kicked a Russian police officer in the nuts. I suppose I should sacrifice a fatted calf or something to thank the powers that be that they didn't remember to wire the cabins. I would have hated to overhear that."

I shuddered at the thought. "Maybe you could just order some more Lone Star home delivery. It's practically the same thing, right?"

"You're paying?"

"Absolutely."

"Wait a minute," I said. "How's Mom doing? I've been worried sick."

"Mom..." My brother sighed.

"What is it?" I asked. "It's cancer, isn't it? God, I knew it." I felt tears prick my eyes.

"Again with the cancer, Lora," my brother said. "It's not cancer. It's menopause. She's completely fine. She was just having some sort of midlife 'I'm not a sex symbol anymore' kind of midlife crisis."

I thought of my mother, who as far as I knew had never been a sex symbol, unless you were into not-so-naughty librarians. "She was crying on the phone because of menopause?" I asked, uncomprehending. "Our mother? Are you sure there's not more to it? Menopause and encephalitis, maybe? I just don't get it. Why would she cry over that?"

"She said that the hormones make you nuts."

"Menopause," I said wonderingly. "I almost got killed because I was trying to save our mother from menopause."

Chris cleared his throat. "Well, it's the thought that counts."

"I think I'm going to throttle her the next time I see her."

Chris snorted.

"Enough about menopause," Pinkie said. "More about Kyrill's sex life." He pressed play on the Kyrill sex tape. "Did you see this part?" he asked, holding out the phone to Tatiana. "It's my

259

favorite. The noise he makes when he comes…"

Kyrill snatched the phone away and hit the power button.

"Wait a minute," I said. "There's one more thing I don't understand. Why did you bug my phone and search my apartment?"

Kyrill looked at me blankly. "Why did I do what?"

"Bug my phone," I said. "Someone's been tracking my phone for the last two months. Chris found the software. And someone went through my apartment and moved my passport. Why?"

Kyrill shook his head. "It wasn't us."

"Then who was it?" I asked.

Kyrill raised his eyebrows. "Didn't you just almost get killed by the mother of your stalker?"

"Yes," I said, "but the guy who bugged my phone—the Viper—was supposed to work for serious people. Governments. Criminals. Google, apparently. Are you sure one of your guys didn't do it? Maybe the guy who was supposed to bug the boat got confused?"

"Trust me," Kyrill said. "It wasn't us."

"I guess it was Clancy after all," my brother said.

"But you said…"

"I said it would be odd," Chris said, "but when you think about it, Clancy stumbling across some world-class hacker is the least odd part of this entire situation. Has it occurred to you that you might have a supernatural power to negate the laws of probability?"

I thought back over the last few days. "It hadn't occurred to me, but it would explain a lot," I mused.

"So, anyway, Lora," Kyrill said awkwardly. "We will pay your expenses, as agreed, and will drop you off in Malta to catch your flight home. The Russian government appreciates your help with this matter."

I nodded wordlessly, too exhausted to think about anything. Pinkie, thankfully, was never too exhausted to look out for his own interests. "Speaking of expenses, to facilitate the treatment of what I'm sure will be an exceptional number of psychiatrist appointments for post-traumatic stress disorder, I'm sure the Russian government would also like to triple—no—quadruple what it was planning to pay her. Good psychiatrists don't come cheap, you know, especially ones that are really good at keeping things like this confidential."

"Quadruple?" Kyrill asked uncertainly.

"Heck," Pinkie said, "Let's just call it 50K, and Lora and I will sort out the split, okay?"

Kyrill looked at Agent Teofilov questioningly. "Is that in the budget?"

Agent Teofilov shrugged. "The wonderful thing about the Russian system is how helpful all of our wealthier citizens have become since we started looking into their books. I'm sure the real Kyrill will be only too happy to pay."

46

"You're sure you're going to be okay alone?" Pinkie asked, fussing over me in my hotel room in Malta. "I mean, if you need me I'll just tell Bertu that I can't meet him."

"Really?" I asked, stifling a smile. "You'd give up your last night with the sultry and exotic Bertu to spend it commiserating with me over dinner?"

Pinkie looked undecided. "When you put it that way," he said, "maybe not."

"Relax, Pinkie," I said. "Go out and have fun. I'm sure I can entertain myself for an evening." The truth was that after the trip on the boat followed by two days in the Valletta police station being debriefed, I was more than ready for some time alone.

I walked around the harbor for a couple of hours, taking in the late afternoon sun. The beaches were filled with tourists from all over Europe sunning themselves with abandon. Nobody here appeared to be remotely concerned with stalkers or white slavers or even skin cancer.

Making my way back in from the harbor to the shade and comparative quiet of the old town, I ended up outside Saint John's Co-Cathedral. The receptionist at our hotel had told me that if I only saw one thing here, this cathedral was the thing to see. I looked at the hours. I had about fifteen minutes until they closed.

Ducking into the dark interior, I walked around the church

aimlessly, silently taking in the opulence hidden behind the cathedral's plain sandstone façade. Like most people, I focused on the floor, which was paved with inlaid marble tombs that featured paeans to their owners' piety and prowess in war as well as admonishments to the living to make the most of the time they had.

My eye was caught by a particularly jolly-looking skeleton waving a flag from atop a clock. A banner below him contained an inscription in Latin.

"His hour has come, and yours will come," said a voice over my left shoulder.

I looked up into a pair of distractingly green eyes. "I was wondering when you'd show up," I said. "Nice entrance, by the way. Totally not creepy at all."

The man standing before me was tall and fit, with dark auburn hair pulled back into a neat queue. He wore an unstructured jacket and a pair of linen pants. He looked, I thought, like a conductor or an artist. If it hadn't been for his eyes, I wouldn't have recognized him at all.

"Is it still Benjamin?"

"You must have me confused with someone else. My name is Constantine." He dug around in his pocket, finally producing a card. Adjunct professor of Maltese history at the University of Valetta. Cute.

"Must be tricky juggling all that history."

"Not as tricky as you might think," he said. "Never let it be said that a liberal arts education is completely useless. Although some of the credit must go to Wikipedia. You wouldn't believe how useful that is in my line of work."

"And what line of work would that be, exactly?" I asked. "Kyrill told me that he knew you from some previous 'projects' you had worked on together? Little interservice rivalry, I think he said?" I looked at him questioningly. "Why didn't you tell me when I was with you in Moscow? You let me get on a boat with a bunch of murderers!"

Benjamin looked hurt. "Well, I did at least try to keep tabs on you."

"I knew it!" I said. "I saw you when I was trying to get away from Dieter."

Benjamin's jaw tightened. "I wanted to step in," he said. "But you weren't supposed to know we were watching you. But you should know that if he'd tried anything, I would have murdered him myself."

"Yeah, well…Maria beat you to it." The meaning of what he had just said suddenly registered. "Wait a minute. 'We' were watching me? You weren't there to watch Kyrill?"

Benjamin winced. "I…uh…"

I suddenly realized who the Viper must have been working for. "You were the one who tapped my phone!"

"Maybe this isn't the best time…"

"And you went through my apartment!" I stepped forward, furious, and gave him a hard shove. "What the hell is wrong with you people? I'm an innocent person with nothing to hide, and my own government is spying on me? For what!?"

"Spying is such an ugly word," Benjamin said. "I prefer to think of it as taking an interest in your life."

I looked at him in rage. "Call it what you like. My question is why were you taking an interest in *my* life? I've been scared out of my mind because I thought I was being stalked, but actually it was just the government I pay taxes to taking an interest in my life?! Last time I checked, there were plenty of more dangerous lives out there to take an interest in. Why me?"

"Because you keep coming up in our files," Benjamin said, throwing his hands up. "The world is a dangerous place these days, and the people you spend time with aren't all the useless half-wits they pretend to be, you know. Five years ago you were a girl from Delaware who waited tables for a living, and lately it seems like every time we pull up a file on an Arab sheikh or a Russian oligarch or a Chinese billionaire, there you are. You're practically the Kevin Bacon of dodgy international types."

I looked at him skeptically. "Really. And did you figure out why that is?"

He gave me a winning smile. "Well, I told my boss it was because you were charming and fun and good company, and apparently some people find that kind of person worth paying to have around."

"And did he believe that?"

"I didn't try too hard to convince him, actually," he admitted.

"Why not?"

"Because," he said, stepping forward and looking into my eyes, "as long as there's a shred of doubt in his mind, I'll have to keep taking an interest in your life. And that," he said, "is a part of my job I can really enjoy."

I felt something spark between us and took a step back to give myself space. "So what you're telling me is that you are, in fact, a stalker, but I shouldn't worry about it because you're a government-assigned stalker? Wow, that's totally reassuring. Because being stalked by someone with satellites and access to black hat hackers is so much less scary than being stalked by some poor deranged fop with mommy issues."

"Well," he said, "there's another option. We could always use someone like you on our team. Maybe we can come to some sort of arrangement."

"Me? Work for the government? I don't think so."

"Think it over," he said. "It pays better than waitressing, and it's not without its perks."

I shook my head. "No. And no more monitoring my cell phone or breaking into my apartment."

"Fine," he said. "But given what you just went through, are you sure that's a wise choice? I mean, when you're trapped on a boat with a bunch of white slavers, the government's not the worst friend to have in your pocket."

"I'll tell you what. On the off chance I find myself trapped on a boat with white slavers again, I'll give you a call. All right?"

"Fine," he said, his eyes crinkling as he smiled. He glanced at his watch. "Just about closing time."

"Will I see you again?" I asked. As the words crossed my lips, I realized to my surprise that despite everything, I really wanted him to say yes.

He stepped closer so that our bodies were almost touching. "Definitely." He leaned over me, looking at me questioningly. I closed my eyes in anticipation, and he kissed me once, gently, on the forehead. When more was not forthcoming, I opened my eyes to find myself alone in the ancient building.

"Really?" I said to the empty church. "I hate it when people do that, by the way."

An elderly docent shuffled around the corner. "We're closing now, my dear," he said, "so I'm afraid you'll have to go." He looked around in befuddlement. "Were you speaking with someone here a moment ago?"

"Nope," I said. "Must have been your imagination."

"Must have," he agreed.

EPILOGUE

Pinkie and I lay on the deck of Kyrill's yacht. Pinkie, an unreformed sun worshipper, was round and tan in a pink Speedo. I was slathered in sunscreen and huddled under an umbrella, a cold glass of champagne by my side.

"I can't believe they gave us the boat for a week," I said, marveling at the historic forts of Valletta. "This really is the life."

In gratitude for our help, "Kyrill" the police officer had forced Kyrill—the real Kyrill—to pay for Jacques and a functional crew for the week so that we could take a well-deserved break. I really had to find a Russian oligarch to blackmail. Why should the Russian police have all the fun?

Pinkie nodded, taking a delicate bite of a crepe stuffed with caviar. "I know," he said. "This was the life I was born to live. A yacht, a chef, a spectacular sunset, and a beautiful woman by my side." He rolled over and glared at me. "If you were a beautiful man, this would really be perfect, but I guess I can't complain." He sighed dramatically and drained his glass.

"Hey…" I said, suddenly remembering. "Did you ever manage to talk to Clancy Featherstone?" After I'd confirmed that my real stalker was Uncle Sam, I hadn't given much thought to Clancy, but it suddenly occurred to me that I hadn't gotten a blocked call notification in days.

"I did," Pinkie said, "and you have nothing to worry about."

"Because his mother's afraid she'll get pulped by the Russian Mafia if he calls again?"

"Because Clancy has fallen in love with a sixty-five-year-old Buddhist nun."

I blinked. "Ah. How's that working out?"

"No idea," Pinkie said. "He's given away all his material possessions so that he can follow her on the path to enlightenment, so unless you're willing to trek to Nepal to ask him in person, I guess you're going to be left wondering."

I smiled. "His mother must be furious."

"Livid," Pinkie agreed, grinning wickedly.

"Maybe it'll be a new beginning for poor Clancy."

"More likely it'll mean that some poor nun gets charged with murder," Pinkie said. "Even nuns have their limits. But speaking of new beginnings, that reminds me. Mr. Schumacher called. He's meeting a potential business partner in Switzerland, and he wanted to know..."

"No," I said.

"Germans," Pinkie said. "They're totally harmless."

"That is the most historically inaccurate comment I've ever heard."

"He's not even a real German," Pinkie hedged. "He's just a German-speaking Swiss person, which is like the safest kind of German-speaking person. The chances that you will be kidnapped or killed are really very low, I think."

"No," I said again. "I need a break."

"I thought you might say that," Pinkie said, "and that's why I brought this." He flourished an envelope in my direction.

"What is that?" I asked warily.

"Open it."

I opened it and scanned it briefly. "A bill from my mechanic? What makes you think... Oh," I said, catching a glance at the total.

"Oh, indeed," Pinkie said. "So I'll tell Mr. Schumacher that Zurich is a go, shall I?"

I took a long sip of champagne and settled back against the chaise lounge. Today I was enjoying the sunset from a yacht, and tomorrow I could be eating schnitzels in Zurich. It wasn't the kind of life people chose, but I had to admit that it suited me.

"Absolutely."

MORE PINKIE AND LORA

Find out what happens next in *Champagne Gold*, book 2 of the Pinkie and Lora series.

When Lora arrives in Switzerland to help an old friend host an authentically Swiss dinner for the world's pickiest travel agent, she figures that the worst thing she'll have to navigate is her unholy love of chocolate...and maybe a cow or two. Pinkie, meanwhile, has his own agenda—recovering a stolen family heirloom from the well-manicured paws of his larcenous cousin Maurice. But when the police connect a brutal murder to Pinkie's godfather, Lora and Pinkie must work together to untangle a decades-old mystery of Nazi gold, family secrets, and blackmail—before the killer strikes again.

VISIT NISSAALEXANDROV.COM
for updates, excerpts, and much, much more

-and-

Join the conversation at
www.facebook.com/nissaalexandrovbooks.

ACKNOWLEDGMENTS
᳘᳘᳘

A book starts as a labor of love and ends up as flat out labor. Many thanks to the following people who lightened that load:

To Judi Foldi, my first fan, who basically nagged me into writing this book.

To Phoebe Baker, my first editor, who did the first hard slog through the manuscript. For free. Honestly, if that's not friendship, I don't know what is.

To my brother, Chris Van Trump, who served as beta reader for everything except the sex scenes. Because, you know, gross.

To Martha Bushko, who was my best friend in high school before going to New York and becoming an editor. Martha's introduction to my agent was incredibly generous, and will serve forever as my proof to my husband that the hours I spend on Facebook are career-relevant networking. Even those hours I spend watching "Dogs who can't manage stairs" videos.

To Jim McCarthy, the agent in question, whose excessive use of exclamation points gave me the confidence to call myself an author.

To Jason Whited for his detailed, humorous, and insanely erudite editing skills.

To Simon Avery, for his inspired covers.

To Ernie Dempsey, for his advice and southern charm.

To every indie author out there who's shared their tips and traumas, hoping to make the path a little easier for the rest of us.

To our friends, whose love of champagne (and insane generosity when it comes to sharing that champagne) inspired these books.

ABOUT THE AUTHOR
ᡃᡗᠺᡗᡅ

After a childhood spent in the Wonder Bread suburbs of Delaware, Nissa Alexandrov fled the country in search of a more global perspective. She has lived in Beijing, Bulgaria, Moscow, and Zurich and visited everywhere from Albania to Zimbabwe. *Champagne Float* is her first book.